PRAISE FOR *BLOOD WILL TELL*

"Blood will tell," the anguished victim of a decades-long hate insists; and in Jean Lorrah's intricate, surprising novel blood does tell—but what it has to say will astonish you. Just when you think you see where she's going, she'll show you something genuinely unexpected, genuinely original, that gives the struggles her heroine endures a depth of romantic poignance seldom encountered in the literature.

This is a fascinating take on the theory of the vampire whose abstract interest alone might be enough to make a satisfying novel, but Lorrah won't settle for "enough," she uses her conception to spike the angst levels of this book to new heights. *Blood Will Tell* has meat for contemplation to beguile an angst junkie long after the last page has been turned.

Delightfully original in concept, deeply romantic in execution—three cheers (and a Bloody Mary toast) for *Blood Will Tell*!

SUSAN R. MATTHEWS, Author, *The Devil and Deep Space* and *Angel of Destruction*

In Blood Will Tell, Jean Lorrah creates an intriguing blend of police procedural, science fiction, and romance with a heroine as strong and appealing as Clarice Starling in Silence of the Lambs. Comparable to the vampire mysteries of P. N. Elrod and Tanya Huff, this novel is a must-read for the discriminating fan.

MARGARET L. CARTER, Author, *The Vampire in Literature: A Critical Bibliography*

. . . Blood Will Tell is the best read I've had in several months. . . . When I finished it, I wandered around my house from stack to stack of books disconsolately looking for another book that good. There wasn't one. I wish every book on the stands was this satisfying, this exciting and profound.

I love this book. It's right.

JACQUELINE LICHTENBERG, Author, *Those of My Blood, House of Zeor*

JEAN LORRAH

BenBella Books
Dallas, Texas

First BenBella Books Edition April 2003

BenBella Books
P.O. Box 601389, Dallas, TX 75360 (214) 750-3600
www.benbellabooks.com

Printed in the United States of America

10 9 8 7 6 5 4 3 2 1

Library of Congress Cataloging-in-Publication Data

Lorrah, Jean.
  Blood will tell / by Jean Lorrah.— 1st BenBella Books ed.
    p. cm.
  ISBN 1-932100-03-2 (alk. paper)
  1. Vampires—Fiction. I. Title.
PS3562.O767B56 2003
813'.54—dc21

                                                                CIP
                                                        2002154553

Cover illustration copyright © 2002 by Marianne Plumridge
Cover design by Melody Cadungog
Interior designed and composed by John Reinhardt Book Design

Distributed by Independent Publishers Group
To order call (800) 888-4741
www.ipgbook.com

To Winston, for the inspiration,
and Roberta, for the setting.
To the Murray, Kentucky, Police Department,
especially the help of
Larry Killebrew
and
Ronald Wisehart.

And, with thanks for their contributions,
Jacqueline, Judi, Katie, K. L., Lois, Margaret, and Susan

Foreword

WELCOME TO A NEW ADVENTURE. Although I have had sixteen novels published before this one, this is only my second attempt at a contemporary work of fiction. The first is the children's book, *Nessie and the Living Stone*, in collaboration with Lois Wickstrom. As you read, please feel free to guess what is really happening in the fictional city of Murphy, Kentucky. If I've done what I intended, each time you think you know, the ground will shift under you once again.

In researching this book, I had the cooperation of the police in Murray, Kentucky. There I discovered that police procedures in small cities in America's heartland are not the big-city tactics seen in books, films and television. They simply don't have the crime scene units and forensics specialists I had in my first draft. I came away from my experience with the local police with deep admiration for their professionalism under difficult circumstances.

My fictional Murphy, Kentucky, police department is not run exactly the way the Murray police department is—that was necessary for my plot. However, good cops working hard for low pay, without high-tech equipment, yet doing an amazingly fine job despite budget restraints, *is* an accurate picture of Murray's police. I hope I have conveyed the essence if not the actuality.

Geographically, my fictional community of Murphy sits right on Murray's site. Its people have the ingrained sense of fair play that governs the real West Kentucky community. Some of the chain stores are even the same. However, no one in this book is based on any real person, nor do the crimes committed, to my knowledge, resemble any real crimes committed in my home town. I hope the residents of Murray will take all the favorable aspects of Murphy as a tribute, and all its unfavorable ones as fiction.

I believe in interaction between writers and readers, and invite comments on my work. Send them to jean@simegen.com.

To keep in touch with readers, I attend two or three conventions and conferences every year, and occasionally teach writing workshops. I also keep my website, www.jeanlorrah.com, updated with all my latest news.

I'm happy to provide information on my projects, or answer the kinds of questions that require just a few words. Unfortunately, there are a few things I cannot do, much as I might like to. I can't read your manuscripts, become your writing tutor, or collaborate with you. I can't be pen pals—there just isn't time to write both letters and books. However, you can sign up for the Lifeforce-l Newsletter at my website, and get a once-a-month report by e-mail about both my writing activity and that of Jacqueline Lichtenberg.

I am grateful to Kathryn Struck of Awe-Struck E-books (www.awe-struck.net), who was willing to publish *Blood Will Tell*. That got it into the public eye. There it won the Lord Ruthven Assembly Award as the best vampire novel of 2001 (not just best e-book—it was up against more than 150 vampire novels published in all forms in 2001), and that led to its being picked up for trade publication by BenBella Books.

I am also grateful for the encouragement my readers have given me over the years, and sincerely hope those of you familiar with my work will enjoy this new adventure. If you've never read anything else I've written, welcome! I hope you'll find something new and exciting in *Blood Will Tell*. To old friends, welcome back! I hope you also find something new here, along with whatever has brought you back for more.

JEAN LORRAH
Murray, Kentucky

ONE

A Corpse
on the Campus

HAVING COME OF AGE in the AIDS decade of the 1990's, Brandy Mather reached the millennium and the age of twenty-eight as a virgin. She was not unique among girls grown up in West Kentucky. In high school she learned several ways to bring a human male to climax without intercourse. In college, she came very close to marrying the first man she met who knew how to reciprocate.

In college she also discovered criminal psychology, which led her first to the Police Academy, then back to her home town of Murphy, Kentucky. Brandy was the first female police officer to move from traffic patrol into the crime division. There were no further divisions; even though Murphy was the county seat of Callahan County, and boasted a regional university numbering 8000 students, the city was not large enough to require separate juvenile, vice, or homicide squads. It was all in a cop's day's work.

Brandy had just been promoted to plainclothes work—mostly because the department felt it wise to have a woman handle the increasing reports of spouse and child abuse as well as rape. That late summer the case occurred that was to change her life. It was a Friday, and Brandy looked forward to having the weekend off.

It had been one of those long, frustrating weeks when leads didn't pan out, stakeouts merely wasted hours, and the local citizenry chose to shoplift, throw eggs at each other's cars and houses, shoot out store windows in the middle of the night, and slash tires. Ex-husbands threatened former wives, visitors forged checks, and the police spent endless hours tracking delinquent husbands to serve flagrant non-support warrants. No satisfying saving of lives or solving of challenging cases. The paperwork thus generated only served to increase stress levels.

By 7:38 P.M. Brandy had finished her final report. "Go home and hug your kids," she told her colleague, Churchill Jones, with whom she shared the tiny detectives' office with its single computer. "Write the rest up in the morning. If you try to do it now you'll be here till midnight." Church was a perfectionist about his written work.

"You okay?" he asked. "Maybe you should see your mom tonight."

Brandy winced. Close to his own parents, Church couldn't fathom the gap between Brandy and her mother, only grown wider since her father's death. Thank God her mom was dating again, Brandy no longer her sole emotional support.

"I'll be all right," she responded. "The VCR's been taping movies all week. I'm going to be a couch potato."

"Not all weekend," Church told her in a tone that brooked no denial. "You're coming to Sunday dinner—noon sharp. I'm barbecuing."

"Okay. I'll bring mint chip ice cream." It was his kids' favorite.

So Brandy was alone when the call from Jackson Purchase State University came in: a dead body in Callahan Hall.

"After this crazy week," she commented fliply, "what's another corpse?"

What it was, was a mystery. The body was in the office of Professor Everett Land, but the curious students and faculty who had gathered said it was not the professor. Campus security had made sure that no one trampled through the room nor moved the body. It sat in the chair behind the desk, eyes closed, hands folded over sunken belly, as if the man had just slept away.

Not a bad theory, for the man was extremely old. Face and hands were bony, flesh shrunken, nose and knuckles protruding. Wispy white hair clung to the skull. The eyes were sunk deep in their sockets.

There was no sign of struggle or pain; the man appeared to have died peacefully, a beatific smile on his face.

But who was he?

The office was one of only three in the Classics Department, one of those subjects, like philosophy, that no one would dream of majoring in. When Brandy had attended JPSU a decade ago there had been talk of phasing out such departments in the regional universities. Who in West Kentucky needed Virgil or Sophocles?

The custodian, Mary Samuels, remembered that Land's office had been unlocked—and that was unusual, as the lights had been off. Dr. Land was normally either in with the lights on, or out with the door locked, when she came to clean.

Samuels was a good witness. "I turn on the lights," she explained, "an' there's this ol' man. But he's . . . you know . . . not moving. I mean at all. I got a creepy feeling, tried to wake him up. When I touched him I knowed he was dead." She wiped her hand on her smock at the memory.

There were no evening classes on Friday. Very few people were in the building. Next door the Philosophy Department was dark and locked. Across the hall in the History Department, Professor Jane Mason had a meeting with a student working on a Master's Thesis. They had brought a bucket of chicken, and were just settling down to work when the commotion in Classics caught their attention. Another history professor, Miller Kramden, didn't know anything had happened until a student poked her head in to say someone had died.

As word spread, more people arrived to check out the rumor. The body could not be moved until the coroner had examined it and Brandy had taken photos and prints. She let people look from the doorway, hoping someone could identify the corpse. No one could.

Meanwhile, she tried telephoning Professor Land at home. She got an answering machine.

Budget constraints required Murphy detectives to work alone, so Brandy enlisted the help of Campus Security Chief Howard McBride, a retired cop with many more years of experience than she had, to investigate the crime scene. While they were working, Dr. Troy Sanford, the coroner, arrived. "Can't be sure till the autopsy," he said, "but there's no signs of foul play. Looks like natural causes."

"But who is he?" Brandy asked in frustration as she searched the pockets and bagged the contents: pipe, tobacco, butane lighter, 73¢ in change, pocket knife, handkerchief—linty, as if carried unused for quite some time—and chalk in a plastic holder. She gave the man's wallet to McBride to fingerprint.

There was $62.00 in bills, a faculty I.D., and a driver's license. The laminated plastic documents showed a man in his forties, with thick curly brown hair and blue eyes. Brandy read the name on the faculty I.D.: Everett Land, Ph.D., Professor, Classics Department.

"Oh, damn," said Brandy. A crime *had* been committed, even if it was only some obscene practical joke. Someone had planted Land's wallet on the corpse. The money in the wallet made it petty theft. There was a MasterCard, too, a group medical insurance card, social security card, and an automatic teller card.

There were no family photos.

Doc Sanford estimated the death as occurring between 5:30 and 7:00 p.m.. "He could have walked in here alive."

"But someone went over the desk pretty carefully," said McBride. "No fingerprints there or on the bookshelves. A few on the filing cabinet and the doorknob, but they'll probably turn out to be the custodian's."

"You're suggesting someone wiped the prints away?" Brandy asked.

"Looks that way—very thorough job, too. There's not even a print under here," he showed her as he pulled the last piece of clear fingerprint tape from the bottom edge of the main desk drawer. It was one of those flat, shallow drawers without a handle, opened by sliding it out with a hand on the bottom of the drawer. "Probably not a student," McBride said. "When we've had break-ins by kids looking for exams or gradebooks, even when they think to wipe away prints they *always* forget that spot. This is a pro."

So someone had searched the desk, "But what was he looking for?" Tired and half giddy from no supper and only microwave soup for lunch, Brandy did not like the direction this event was taking. That was how crimes went in America's Heartland: either simple and straightforward and solved within hours, or totally confused, committed by people with warped imaginations and half-baked ideas of witchcraft and Satanism.

Hardly had the thought crossed her mind than she heard the gossip start. Students, faculty, and staff began to speculate, "Who is it?" "Somebody musta stole the corpse and put ol' man Land's I.D. on it. Show what a mean old bastard he is." "No—it's the Satanists! That *is* Professor Land. They put a death curse on him!"

The headache that had been incipient all day grasped Brandy's skull with fingers of steel. She bagged the wallet and told McBride and Sanford, "Until we find out who this guy is, and locate Dr. Land, it'll be early Halloween!"

She turned to the gathered faculty and students. "You are not witnesses unless you were here earlier, between the time the secretary left—?"

As she hoped, one of the students supplied, "4:30."

"If you were here between 4:30 and the time Security arrived, please try to recall anything that would tell us who brought this body in, and how. Or if you saw the man walk in alive. Did anyone notice when Dr. Land left today?"

There was only head-shaking. The earlier Land had left, the wider the window of opportunity for sneaking the corpse into his office. Brandy remembered her own days as a student assistant in Sociology: even though it was a much larger department than Classics, there were times when absolutely no one was in the suite.

A call to the department secretary produced an answer, of sorts: Land had still been in his office when Ms. Sandoval left for the day.

Criminal intent or a really stupid prank? Brandy had to proceed as if it were the former. The coroner removed the body, leaving her to witnesses with little to contribute until a man Brandy hadn't seen before entered the suite.

Brandy was at the secretary's desk, just finishing taking notes from the history professor who had been working with her grad student. They had noticed nothing.

The new arrival asked, "Are you from the police?"

"I'm Detective Mather," Brandy told him. "We're investigating a body found in Dr. Land's office."

"Rett?"

"No. But whoever put the body there planted Dr. Land's I.D. on it. That means *some* kind of crime was committed, at least a theft. Do you know anything about it?"

"I guess not, then. I'm Dan Martin, from Computer Science." He pronounced his last name "Martine." "I set up Rett's computer, showed him how to access the Internet."

"Did you see him today?"

He pondered. "All the faculty in this building see each other sometimes, in the elevators or the halls. I don't recall seeing Rett today. I just saw them carrying the body bag past my door. Someone said it was Dr. Land, so I came to see what had happened. Listen, I'm sorry for bothering you." He started to leave, then turned back. "But maybe I can help. You said somebody put the body in Rett's office. Do you know how?"

"Possibly he arrived alive, and died in the office."

"What does Rett say?"

"He's not here or at home. Any idea where he might be?"

Martin shook his head. "I don't know him that well—academic rather than social friendship, if you know what I mean. But if the body was moved after it was dead, it didn't have to come through the office lobby."

This was interesting. "Oh?" Brandy asked.

"There were some computers stolen a few years ago," Martin explained. "Thieves broke a ground-floor window to get in. The ceilings are false, with heating and cooling ducts and the sprinkler system above them."

The university was notorious for lack of security; funds barely covered maintenance. Broken windows set off no alarms. Offices and laboratories, where equipment and vital data were kept, were all on upper floors or on inner walls with no windows. Most, like Land's, required not only a key to the office itself, but a different key to the suite door.

But now that Martin mentioned it—"I remember," said Brandy. "They went over the ceilings into some offices and stole several PC's. I was a student at the time."

"It was before I arrived," said Martin, "but they still talk about it. Wouldn't be worth a thief's while today; most of the equipment is badly outdated."

"That must be frustrating," said Brandy, "trying to teach computer science on outmoded equipment."

"Oh, we've got some new technology for the upper-level students. Anyway, the ceilings are just a thought, if the coroner says the body was moved."

Brandy found herself smiling at Martin. She liked him . . . and didn't know why. He certainly wasn't her type.

She didn't care much for intellectual men, although she got along well enough with the university faculty on professional matters. Murphy was three hundred miles from the police laboratories at Frankfort. It was easier to ask a local expert than someone that far away, and JPSU had the largest variety of experts in Western Kentucky.

Brandy didn't generally think of herself as preferring a particular type of man; she had dated blonds, brunettes, and redheads over the years. However, they had always been large and strong and all-American. This man was lean and wiry and faintly exotic.

Like many of the JPSU faculty, he didn't sound like a West Kentuckian, but his accent was Midwest American, nothing foreign about it. His hair and eyes were midnight black, his skin a fine, even gold, but his voice, deep and just a touch gravelly, was both memorable and sexy.

He was nothing like any man she had ever taken an interest in before.

And what was she doing taking an interest in the middle of an investigation? What in the *world* had sent her mind wandering in that direction? Brandy realized she had been smiling at him like a fool for several seconds, and broke the gaze to pick up her pen.

But she had nothing to write. Professor Mason had gone back to her office, and the custodian was waiting to lock up. "I guess I'm finished here for tonight," Brandy said. "Let's check your theory before I seal Dr. Land's office."

Back in the office, where the tape on the chair did not look anything like the shape of a body, they saw no sign that the large ceiling tiles had been moved. But Martin spotted something else. "Rett's backup disks are gone."

"His what?"

Martin gestured to an empty spot on the neat desk. "There should be a box of zip disks right there with all his backup files." He looked over at the bookcases, but there were no boxes of disks there, either. "No one that I train relies on a hard disk as his only copy!" he commented.

"Maybe he took them home. But I'll add it to the report, and we'll see what the autopsy says," Brandy said, locking the door. Then she ran the yellow tape across the door frame, to warn anyone from disturbing the scene.

"Where are you going now?" asked Martin.

"Back to the station. I have to write up a report."

"Now?" he asked in surprise.

Brandy looked at her watch. "It's only 8:50. I'll still get home in time to start a lazy weekend."

Martin walked with her through the corridor, and punched the "Down" elevator button. Then, rather sheepishly, he said, "Look . . . this may sound foolish, but I guess we're all curious about real police work, as opposed to what we see on television. Could I come with you, see what you do—then maybe buy you a pizza?"

"I warn you," said Brandy, "it's not very exciting!"

"That's all right."

"Okay—I'll meet you at the station."

"Uh . . . could I hitch a ride? I walked to campus today," he said as they rode down in the elevator.

"Sure. Just remember, if you have anything weird in mind, I carry a gun."

He chuckled, a small, quiet sound. "Anything I had in mind would not require a gun—or handcuffs, either, in case you were concerned."

On the ground floor they stopped for Martin to turn off the monitor on his computer. "It's still running," Brandy noticed as the power light stayed on.

"Faxes may come in over the weekend," he explained.

Then he locked his office, a claustrophobic one without windows. There was no one else in the Computer Science suite, either, so he also locked the outer door, and they walked out to the parking lot.

The night was almost as bright as day, the full moon riding large over the rooftops. It would be early fall in New England and along the Great Lakes, sweater weather, football weather. In Western Kentucky it was still late summer, hot by day, warm at night.

They talked easily, like old friends, but Brandy could not have said what about. At the station Brandy wrote up her report as quickly as possible, growling as her tired fingers hit the wrong keys.

Martin came up behind her, so silently she didn't know he was there until his soft voice asked, "How long have you been on duty?"

Through a yawn, she replied, "Over twelve hours now." She didn't mention how badly she needed the overtime.

Warm fingers touched the back of her neck, massaged gently. "Relax." The deep voice was hypnotic, the hands magic. He rubbed from her hairline downward, the pain and tension seeming to follow his fingers down out of her head.

Brandy felt like a contented cat, ready to purr under Martin's petting. The cares of the endless week drifted away, and she leaned into his touch, entranced.

When Martin stopped, Brandy wondered if she had been literally in a trance, for she was suddenly wide awake, refreshed, and serene. "If you could bottle that," she told Martin, "you'd be a millionaire!"

"I don't want to be a millionaire," he replied. "I'd have to worry about people liking me only for my money."

It was easy, once her headache was relieved, for Brandy to finish her report. She signed out at last, and they drove over to Pizza Hut. There they discovered that they both liked pepperoni pizza.

Brandy was by now ravenously hungry. They had ordered a medium pizza . . . and only as she halted her reach for the last piece did she realize to her embarrassment that she had consumed four slices to Martin's one.

"Go on," he said when he saw her hesitation. "I had dinner earlier. You obviously didn't."

The place was crowded with college kids, and there must have been a dozen cheery "Hi, Dr. Martin!"'s from students going in and out. But then, the new semester had just begun. Brandy recalled that students tended to like all their professors till about midterm.

She took in stride the stares she received, remembering how odd it was to realize that one's teachers had a life outside the classroom. Probably, she thought, his students wouldn't think much of Martin's taste in women. Brandy was in her plain-neat-suit work clothes, her hair scraped efficiently back into a twist, her makeup minimal.

Now that she thought of it, she was pretty much at her worst. Martin's interest seemed genuine. He asked about her work, family, education . . . and as they sat nursing the final drops of Pepsi in red plastic glasses she realized, "You know all about me — but I know nothing about you!"

"I grew up in Iowa," he said, "until I was twelve. Then we moved to Nebraska. I did undergraduate work in Computer Science at M.I.T., then got my doctorate at the University of Central Florida. I taught for a while at Florida State, then came here. I guess I like Kentucky because I'm still a farm boy at heart."

"You had a farm in Iowa?"

"Till my dad died. Mom couldn't scrape together enough money to run the farm and pay taxes at the same time, so she sold the farm and we moved in with her uncle in Nebraska. One of those big old houses in the middle of wheat fields, not another building as far as you can see."

"We drove across route 80 out to California one summer," said Brandy. "I remember thinking Nebraska was the emptiest place I'd ever seen. That was before we saw the Mojave Desert!"

"Yeah. I like it a little more populated, like here, or Indiana, or Iowa or Ohio."

"Ohio? I grew up in Ohio in the middle of a big city!" said Brandy.

"I meant the farmlands in the southern part of the state. I guess I'll never be completely happy as a city boy. I'm up for tenure this year. If I get it, I'm going to buy a place in the county. Not a farm; there's no future in small farms today, and I really love teaching. But I want some land, some woods, maybe a pond. A place where I can have a garden. And a nice, big, comfortable old house."

Brandy smiled. "I know what you mean. When Dad moved us from Cleveland to Murphy, it seemed like the back of beyond. I thought everyone was a redneck, the kids a bunch of yokels. But I've lived here more than half my life now, and y'know, Murphy's about the best compromise you're gonna find. Big enough to be civilized, small enough to be friendly. There are drugs, but not gangs, and we're not big enough for major dealers. We've got bootleggers, but nobody cares except during election campaigns. If it weren't for the chop shops and family fights, and the drunk drivers, there wouldn't be much for police to do."

"Except investigate mysterious corpses," he said.

"I'm glad I took that call," said Brandy. "This case could take genuine detective work. I went into police work to solve crimes. Except for the ongoing drug operations, not a lot of real detective work is required on my job."

"No unsolved murders?" Martin asked.

"You read the papers. It's always the husband, the wife, the boyfriend, the girlfriend. No work to solve it. Hey!" she realized, "you've turned the conversation back to me again! I want to know more about you. You said your father died when you were twelve. Your mother?"

"Died in a car wreck when I was in college."

"Brothers and sisters?"

"One brother, died in the Gulf War."

Brandy did a quick calculation. "He must have been much older than you."

"No—he went in the army at nineteen."

"Rough. You're pretty much alone, then, except for that uncle."

"He was Mom's uncle, and he's dead now, too. I guess I've still got some cousins, but I never stayed close to them. What about you?"

"My little brother died when I was ten. Hit by a car. I don't think my mother has forgiven me to this day."

"Forgiven you?"

"I wasn't watching him. I wasn't told to watch him that day—it was right after school, no different from any other day. Les was playing ball. I was skipping rope with some other girls. I didn't know what had happened until I heard the boys screaming."

"It wasn't your fault," Martin said.

"I know. I knew then, although Mom almost convinced me I was wrong. But Dad stuck by me, and eventually we got over it."

She blinked. "You did it again! What have I known you for—two hours? And you've got my whole life story! I didn't tell my *best friend* about Les till we'd known each other for months."

"I'm just a good listener," he said. That was when Brandy noticed that he didn't smile the way other men did when they uttered such pleasantries. Had she seen him smile at all? She wasn't sure.

"Well, good listener, I'm afraid it's time to go home," said Brandy as a new rush of customers entered the restaurant. She was amazed to see that it was 11:23. The 9:00 P.M. movie must have just let out.

Ten minutes later Brandy found herself pulling up outside her own apartment building, Dan Martin still in the car. She didn't *feel* tired, though, and the night was bright with the full moon. "Wow. I must be so tired I spaced out," she said. "I didn't even ask where you live."

"That's okay. I'll walk home. But I'll see you to your front door first."

Brandy laughed. "I'm perfectly safe. I'm a *cop*, for goodness' sake!"

"And I'm a gentleman," he replied, getting out and coming around to open her car door. No man had done that since a couple of extremely shy boys in high school!

Deciding she did enough roaring as a police officer, Brandy let him hand her out of the car and walk her up the stairs. At her door, he said, "I want to see you again."

"I'd like that," she replied, and fought down a strong urge to invite him in. This was not the swinging 70's, when safe sex meant not banging your head on the headboard!

She had wanted men before, but never so strongly . . . and never, ever, on a first acquaintance. She had always resisted, successfully.

Dan Martin took her in his arms, and Brandy discovered how comfortable it was to be held by someone only a few inches taller than she was. Their lips met without either getting a crick in the neck. It was as if they had kissed a thousand times before, knew each other's texture and rhythm.

She opened her mouth to his, found warmth and gentle teasing. He nibbled at her lips, then stroked his tongue under her chin and down her throat. It felt both weird and wonderful. She tilted her head, let him caress her neck.

Although they were standing, she practically lay in his arms. How strong he was, never a quiver of his muscles under her weight. She felt secure, protected, and eager. Finally, she knew what she had preserved her virginity for!

But even as Brandy sought to find Martin's mouth again with hers, he let her go. "I'm sorry!" he gasped, breaking the spell. "Please—forgive me."

"There's nothing to forgive," Brandy said, caught between confusion at his sudden change and the lingering desire he had evoked in her. "Why don't you come in?"

"Not tonight," he said, too hastily. "Please—go inside, Brandy. You're too intoxicating by half."

It was not until the next morning that she realized she could not remember telling him her nickname. She had introduced herself as "Officer Mather." He would have seen "Brenda Mather" on the nameplate on her desk. But she hadn't misheard that remark about intoxication.

Brandy woke to her cat kneading her shoulder at 10:00 A.M. on Saturday morning. When she recalled last night's strange events, she knew she would have to find some pretext to look up Dan Martin again.

Unless he contacted her first.

But the weekend passed with no word from Martin. The phone did ring, twice. First it was her mother. Brandy insisted she was too tired to go out to dinner that evening. An hour later, once she got over her disappointment that it was not Dan Martin, the second call made her glad she had refused her mother's invitation.

"Hi, Kid!" It was her friend Carrie Wyman.

"Carrie! Hi. What's going on?"

"I have an empty Saturday night on my hands. I know it's short notice—"

"Come on over!" Brandy told her. "I've got movies and popcorn and nothing else to do!"

Sated on popcorn and the dramatic excesses of Francis Ford Coppola's *Dracula*, the two women turned off the TV to talk. "Why do we still believe in love that will last through time?" Carrie asked.

"I don't *believe* in it," Brandy replied. "It's just nice to fantasize about. What I really want to believe possible is to have my work and still marry a nice man and have a family."

"Dream on!" Carrie said sarcastically. She was only Brandy's age, but last year her husband had walked out on her in favor of a nineteen-year-old. Once she knew that he had been unfaithful, Carrie let him have the divorce. It would be hard for Carrie to trust another man any time soon.

Like Brandy, Carrie was a hard-working, underpaid career woman, the city's last remaining senior social worker. Budget cutbacks had downsized Murphy's social services just when they were most desperately needed, and most of the experienced staff had been replaced with low-paid assistants. Carrie believed in her work, and had added to it a weekly radio show in which she tried to encourage families to find solutions before abuse, drug use, or alcoholism sent them into her overcrowded programs. She was also setting up self-help groups through local churches.

Both Brandy and Carrie had such grueling schedules that it was rare for them to have an evening like this one. But they were old friends from college days. It didn't matter if they didn't see each other for a month; when they got together it was like being with the sister neither one had.

Brandy found herself telling Carrie about Dan Martin.

"You like him," said Carrie with a knowing smile.

"I hardly know him," Brandy protested.

"But you'd like to."

"Maybe. He hasn't called."

"Your phone's unlisted," Carrie reminded her.

"Arrgh! You have no right to be so pretty and so smart!" Brandy growled, tossing a pillow at her friend.

Carrie looked like a young Elizabeth Taylor, or Vivien Leigh as Scarlett O'Hara: huge blue eyes, magnolia blossom skin, and the kind of slender figure designers loved to drape fashions on. Carrie even looked great in the outsized teeshirt and bunny slippers she wore tonight. Furthermore, she had been endowed with thick, wavy brown hair and long black eyelashes. If she weren't so damn nice, it would be easy to hate her!

Observing Carrie's marriage from the outside, Brandy had been able to see what Carrie couldn't: George Wyman had fallen in love with the cute, pretty, bubbly outside, and never seen the serious, dedicated woman within. As Carrie had taken on more responsibility in her work, he had become less supportive . . . and eventually had found himself another cute, pretty, bubbly girl. Brandy could only hope that this one was genuinely shallow; if so, she might be able to keep his interest.

Carrie had intended to stay the night, but at 11:38 P.M. her beeper sounded. She phoned her service, and turned apologetically to Brandy. "It's an abuse case—I've been trying to get this woman to take her kids and run before someone got seriously hurt. Her husband got drunk and hit her three-year-old. Thank goodness it's only a broken wrist. But I've got to go to the hospital and keep her from going back to that louse, at least tonight."

"You need help?" Brandy asked.

"No. She's fragile, Brandy. She believes that beast is her only support and protection. Until she believes otherwise, police intervention will only scare her back to him." Pulling on jeans and searching for her loafers, she added, "This is a breakthrough. Really. A strong woman like you can't believe how battered women think. She's finally asking for the help she needs."

"I understand," said Brandy. "Too bad we couldn't talk all night the way we used to do in the dorm. But a night's sleep will probably do me good. Call me."

"You know I will," said Carrie. "You're *my* lifeline, Brandy. Thanks for being there. And hey—good luck with the new man. Maybe he'll turn out to be the one in a million who's not intrinsically a bastard!"

On Sunday, Brandy went as promised to Church's house at noon. Churchill Jones and his wife Coreen had the kind of life Brandy had always thought of as normal . . . and not hers. Their house was comfortably cluttered. In the back they had built a deck that they planned to screen in. The gas grill was fired up, foil-wrapped potatoes baking, a plate of hot dogs and fish fillets waiting to be cooked. The family had been out to the lake yesterday, where they had caught the fish. The two children, Tiffany and Jeff, were playing with their dog, a golden retriever named Sandy.

If anything, the Jones family was too ideal. It occasionally crossed Brandy's mind that they played it so stereotypically middle class because they were black. She didn't know whether they were pursuing the American dream right down to the latest kitchen appliances, or whether they felt a need to show neighbors who even in the 1990's had resented an African-American family moving onto their street that they were an asset, not a liability.

Actually, race relations were usually calm in Murphy, with errors usually on the side of ignorant good intentions. For example, Brandy had known perfectly well when she was in high school that there would always be a black cheerleader. Although the cheerleaders were chosen by vote of the student body and there were nowhere near enough black students to elect one of their own, the teachers dropped the lowest winning white candidate in favor of the black student with the highest number of votes. Brandy had been in college when what "everyone knew" and believed to be "only fair" became a temporary scandal. Interestingly, the next year there was, as usual, one black cheerleader, no further comment, and so it had gone ever since.

The determined attempts of white Murphians not to offend, to be "fair," might be clumsy, but Brandy found them preferable to the open hostility she had grown up with in Cleveland, the detente that had her going to school and her parents working side by side with ethnic minorities, but never making friends. Churchill Jones was the first close friend she had ever had who was black.

Church was enough older than Brandy for her to respect his experience, but young enough not to be a father figure. Her only problem was, he frequently read her better than she read herself.

Today Church was full of questions about the body in Callahan Hall. He quickly noticed that she had left something out. Unlike Carrie, who would wait encouragingly until someone was ready to talk, Church pounced and questioned. When he pressed, Brandy explained, "There was one more witness, who turned out not to be one. One of the professors had a theory about how the body got there. Everybody thinks they're a detective."

Church studied her. "So why did he impress you? Was he a nuisance?"

"Who said he impressed me?"

"Uh-huh," her friend said wisely.

"Okay, he took me out for pizza," she confessed. "Somebody saw us, right?"

"Not anyone who felt the need to tell me. So why are you paranoid?"

"You always say I'm paranoid when you're the one who's suspicious. Anyway, I'll probably never see him again."

"Do you want to?"

"I don't know," she equivocated. "He's a computer nerd, hardly my type. But not bad looking."

"Even with tape on his glasses and a pocket protector?" he teased.

"No glasses, and no pocket protector either. And he's a real old-fashioned gentleman. We'll see."

On Monday when Brandy got back from lunch, the coroner's report on the body in Professor Land's office was waiting on her desk.

No evidence of foul play. Lividity indicated that the body had remained where it died. Death was from multiple systemic failure due to extreme age. Doc Sanford had appended a note: "The mystery is not how the man died, but where he got the strength to walk into that office."

She added that to the fingerprint results: no prints on the wallet, except for some unknowns on the MasterCard. Why had someone done such a thorough job of wiping prints?

Furthermore, no one had yet located Professor Everett Land. Even if the man had gone out of town for the weekend, surely he would have missed his wallet! The very case that had had Brandy hoping for some real detective work was rapidly turning into another frustration.

Church came in while Brandy was studying the contradictory evidence, and picked up the top folder in his "In" basket. "Hell!" he exclaimed.

"What now?" asked Brandy.

"Judge Callahan ordered the Mortrees let go. All that work for nothing!"

Two weeks ago the Murphy police had participated in a raid on a local farm growing marijuana—probably Kentucky's largest cash crop, if it were possible to get accurate statistics.

State, county, and local law enforcement had cooperated in the confiscation of more than five hundred plants. They had arrested the owner of the property, one Jerrod Mortree, his two shiftless brothers, and an uncle. The police had hoped to bargain with the accused men for names of distributors—but all four men had now been released.

It was not the fault of the police who had raided the farm; everything had gone by the book. They had been certain that this time there would be no legal loophole.

"I knew it," said Church. "Any time it's the Mortrees, there's no chance of an indictment. That family's been sharecroppers on Callahan land for generations, always handy to do the Callahan dirty jobs while ol' Massa keeps 'em out of trouble with the law!"

Brandy knew Church suspected, but couldn't prove, that Judge L. J. Callahan was in on the local drug trade. Every case that came before him ended in a dismissal or an acquittal when the accused was one of the county's good ol' boys. Only independent operators like Dr. McLaren, who traded in prescription medications, were ever convicted.

If only they could find out exactly where Judge Callahan fit in. A corrupt judge, both detectives agreed, but that didn't explain whom he was working for. It was no secret he planned to run for governor in the next election—if he were simply a pawn of some drug lord, he would be discouraged from leaving his very convenient current post.

No, there had to be more to L. J. Callahan. He was power-hungry—there were even rumors that the governorship would be the first step in a campaign for the Presidency. If so, he was gamemaster, not a piece on the board. But . . . what was his game and who were the other players?

To Church's annoyance, there was no way of connecting what had gone wrong this time to Judge Callahan, although of course it was possible that he had paid someone to destroy the evidence. It was "an accident." It "could have happened to anybody." "Sure," Church growled, "anybody who couldn't read evidence tags!"

The 500 plants confiscated from the Mortrees had been stored with evidence from other cases. When they burned the pot from the closed cases . . . somehow the 500 from the open case in Callahan County were destroyed along with the rest.

If this sort of thing happened only once, or once in a great while, it would be frustrating enough. But every time they arrested one of Judge Callahan's cronies they lost the case, in court or beforehand.

But the Callahan family was so old and powerful, the very county was named for them. Church never dared make his suspicions official. All he could do was stay vigilant until he found something that would stick.

Brandy understood her colleague's frustration as she took the thick folder out of his hands, and filed the latest Mortree case as closed.

The phone rang. "Detective Mather," Brandy answered.

"Brandy, this is Dr. Sanford. About your John Doe at the college? You're not gonna believe this. I took dental x-rays, of course, but I didn't expect a quick answer because nobody seemed to know that old man. But I've got an answer already, from Dr. Mulcahey. It's one of his regular patients: Professor Everett Land."

TWO

Murder in Callahan County

BRANDY REPORTED DR. SANFORD'S CALL to the chief, then turned to her office mate. "This is really weird, Church."

Churchill Jones only nodded, but Brandy saw the envy that it was her case, not his. "Isn't there some disease that causes premature aging?" he asked.

"Yeah—but that's something children get," Brandy remembered. "And it doesn't happen in a few hours! Everett Land appeared normal in his Friday classes."

"Find out if he lied about his age," suggested Church.

From the Personnel Office in the University Administration Building, Brandy was directed to the Dean's Office of the College of Humanities, in Callahan Hall.

Land's Curriculum Vita included transcripts from graduate school, tear sheets of publications, and recommendations describing him as an avid scholar and a caring teacher. His sixteen-year record at JPSU was exemplary: he had published a book and been granted tenure, served as department representative to the faculty senate, supervised master's theses, continued to do scholarship, and three years ago a sabbatical had resulted in a second book. Meanwhile he had helped organize a program for JPSU students in Italy, teaching in the program twice himself.

Brandy sifted through the papers. "What about a birth certificate?" she asked.

"That will be filed at the Kentucky Teacher's Retirement System office in Frankfort," the secretary who had provided the folder told her.

Brandy groaned inwardly. She would have to go to the computer for Land's other records. She regularly used the police computer to pull up criminal records, but when it came to employment, credit records, property ownership, investments, or other sources of clues, she was hopeless.

Brandy was coming out of the dean's office when Dan Martin emerged from the computer lab down the hall. A student followed, a striking red-haired girl who said worshipfully, "I never thought I'd understand java script, but you made it so *clear*, Dr. Martin!"

"You do those homework exercises," he told her, "and if everything works tomorrow, you'll know you've got it."

"I'll be in the lab tonight," the girl said, but Martin had turned away from her, his eyes meeting Brandy's. The student persisted, "Will you be in your office this evening, Dr. Martin? In case I need help?"

Martin returned his attention to his student long enough to say, "Bill Harris is running the lab tonight. If you're still having trouble tomorrow, stop in during my office hours." And he left the girl there, calling, "Brandy!" as he strode down the hall.

The unexpected meeting produced a feeling Brandy thought she had left ten years in the past: an adolescent leap of the heart, so that it seemed for a moment as if she would fly away . . . or get sick.

"What are you doing here?" Martin was asking. "Is there news about Rett's death?"

Brandy quickly regained her professional equilibrium. "How did you know the body was Everett Land's, when I just found out this morning?"

"When you left the Administration Building, the news started spreading. The students were buzzing about it in my last class. It's true, isn't it?"

"Yes, it's true," said Brandy. "I'm checking Dr. Land's records. He has no next of kin, and only the minimum life insurance the university provides, with the Red Cross as the beneficiary." Brandy took refuge in professional mode. "You said you were colleagues but not close friends?"

"That's right," said Martin. "I don't know anything about his personal life."

"Who were his friends?"

"I don't know. The closest contact I had with Rett was when I set up his computer. Purely a professional relationship. I'm sorry I can't be of more help."

"But you can," said Brandy. "After I interview everyone who knew Dr. Land—"

"Everyone who knew him!" exclaimed Martin. "That's thousands of students over the years."

"No, we're looking for people who knew him *well*."

"Why are you still investigating? Was he murdered?"

"If he was," said Brandy, "it was not by any means I know. But the cause of death makes no sense—old age in a man in his forties? Until we solve that mystery, we can't rule out murder. It could be poison," she suggested, "or radiation. The coroner's sending tissue samples to the state lab. Meanwhile, we see if Land had any enemies."

"Every teacher has enemies," Martin observed. "Jealous colleagues, dissatisfied students—they all gripe and growl, but there are always an unbalanced few. Students generally attack with hate letters, or 2:00 A.M. phone calls, though. Or charges of harassment these days. Only one in a million tries to gun down the teacher."

"But it does happen," said Brandy. "If this is murder, it's certainly more subtle than using a gun!"

Martin shuddered. "Is there a poison that causes a person to die of old age in a few hours?"

"Not that I know of, but I can't rule out the possibility that someone's invented one. What genetic experiments are going on on campus?"

"None. Purchase is a regional university, not a research institution—at least not at that level."

"Well, I'm not a medical expert, either," said Brandy. "Land could have had some disease we've never heard of. If I start to think I know what happened I could ignore clues that don't fit the theory.

"Dan," she continued, "you're a computer expert. I need to access Dr. Land's medical insurance files to locate doctors who may have treated him, tax files, previous employment and education records, friends or family—"

"Start with Rett's own computer," said Martin. "His e-mail directory will tell you who he corresponds with, and the programs on his hard disk will tell you the things he's—he was—interested in. His correspondence file will give you his snailmail contacts. As campus postmaster, I can access outgoing or incoming mail still in the mainframe."

Land's office was as Brandy had left it, but when they turned on Land's computer they found that the hard drive was not functioning. "It's been formatted," said Martin.

Brandy thought that that would destroy the data—but Martin said, "Not necessarily," and went to his office for a boot disk and a program that would unformat the fixed disk. "If whoever formatted it either didn't know to replace the data with zeroes, or didn't have time, we'll get it back."

The utility program worked; soon Land's hard drive was back in working order.

Because Martin had set up Land's computer, he was familiar with the utilities. He quickly searched out every data file the man had stored. To Brandy's disappointment, nothing was of obvious value.

"You do know one thing," said Martin.

"I do?" asked Brandy, staring at a directory of .EXM files, which turned out to be examinations.

"You know that what killed Rett wasn't radiation. Or if it was, it didn't happen in this room or anywhere nearby. Radiation would have wrecked his computer too thoroughly for us to restore the data."

Brandy smiled. "I don't seriously suspect radiation. We just can't rule out any possibility at this stage."

Land's correspondence files yielded letters in a number of languages, dealing with travel arrangements, scholarly conferences, and publications. To Brandy's surprise, Dan was able not only to outdo her limping Spanish, but to translate French and German as well. Neither of them could cope with Italian, Greek, or Hebrew, though, so they simply printed those letters out to be translated later.

"Professor Land would have been our source for Greek or Hebrew," said Brandy. "I can send the Hebrew to a rabbi in Paducah, but I'm not sure who can help with the Greek."

"Let me use Rett's PC," said Martin. "I'll e-mail the files to a friend at Columbia."

None of Land's outgoing e-mail was left in the mainframe, but they printed out letters other people had sent him. One concerned the business of some state academic assessment committee, and another was an enthusiastic response from a professor at Yale to a proposed section of papers for a national conference. The last piece said simply "Queen to Queen's Bishop 3."

"Chess?" asked Brandy.

"That's odd," said Martin. "If Rett was enough of a chess enthusiast to play by mail, why didn't he join the university Chess Club? I never even knew he played."

"We should send his correspondents the bad news," said Brandy. "Possibly Land's closest friends were at other institutions—after all, how many people do you find in Murphy, Kentucky, who speak six different languages?"

"Seven, at least," Martin said abstractedly. At Brandy's curious look he said, "He had to know Latin, but he wouldn't correspond in it. But you're right—we may find people on the internet who knew him better than anyone on campus. Create a form letter. We'll send it to all his e-mail correspondents, and fax it to everyone else."

"Good idea," said Brandy. "Thanks."

She could type perfectly well, so once Martin called up the word processing program for her, Brandy soon had the message composed. "Put in your e-mail address," Martin told her. "Most people will answer you by tomorrow."

"I don't have an e-mail address," said Brandy. "I'll put in the department fax number."

"Okay," said Martin, "but add my e-mail address, too. I'll send it from my account. Most people will e-mail rather than fax because it's easiest to hit 'Reply.' I'll pass any messages on to you . . . unless there's something you don't want me to see."

"I can't imagine what," said Brandy. They sent the e-mail messages, then printed out a copy of the letter for Brandy to fax from the police station.

"I don't know what to look for next," said Brandy.

"In that case, I can't help any more now," said Martin. "I have another class in thirty-five minutes. What you should do is back up the hard drive, then take the computer to your department expert."

"*What* department expert?"

"Don't you have a . . . I guess you'd call it a forensic computer expert?"

"In Frankfort. If we can't find out what we need, I guess we just have to pack up the computer and send it." Brandy eyed the large but delicate machine doubtfully.

Martin chuckled again, that deep, soft sound he had made last night. It sent a thrill through Brandy, even though he was laughing at her ignorance. "You remove the hard disk and send that, back it up and send them the backup, or shoot them the contents via modem. But let me look first, okay? If it's not tampering with evidence?"

"That would be a huge help," said Brandy, knowing the chief would not bother Frankfort unless he was sure that the Land case was murder. "Now," she said, "can you help me access Land's state records?"

"Not from this computer. I can do it from my own with a couple of marginally legal hacker's tricks. But *your* computer has a perfectly legal police network program, and you have a police I.D. If you like, I can come down to the station after my last class and show you."

"You have no idea how much that would help," Brandy admitted.

But she wasn't at the station at the agreed-upon time. Back downtown Brandy found notice of a parole hearing next week for one Rory Sanford, whom she had arrested a couple of years ago. She entered it on her desk and pocket calendars, and sat down to see what files she could clear off her desk.

"Lunch time!" announced Church. "Let's go over to Sturgeon's."

Sturgeon's was a favorite eating place of Murphy's police: in the morning it was a bakery, with the best doughnuts and pastries in town. At noon it became the place to get huge hamburgers and fries, heart attack heaven.

Brandy decided she could afford the calories. Tomorrow she'd try to eat at a place with a salad bar.

Sturgeon's was plain but clean, tucked into a strip mall between a supermarket and a furniture store. Its customers provided whatever atmosphere it boasted.

It was overlap time: the pastry case was down to the last lonely glazed barnyards and cake doughnuts, the apple fritters having sold out early. A few of the morning crowd still sat talking, crumbs of shattered white glaze revealing their recent indulgence. But the smell of hot grease was in the air, the sizzle of hamburgers sputtering on the grill.

The room was crowded with tables, the square formica kind designed to seat four, which the customers moved about and joined together as they needed them. Men in jeans and cowboy boots occupied two tables, while women in the denim or polyester of housewives grouped at another. The sexes pretty much segregated themselves in the morning; at lunch time more mixed groups arrived.

At the front, near the window, six men in business suits lingered over coffee. Every few minutes a roar of laughter erupted from their table.

Brandy doubted that whatever they had gathered to discuss was a laughing matter; it was simply impossible to get good ol' boys to the point without the ritual of racist, sexist, and political jokes—the secret code of the white male power base. She knew all six of these men: the loan manager of the Bank of Murphy, the owner of the Century 21 real estate office, an investment counselor, two attorneys, and Judge L. J. Callahan.

Brandy wondered what they were plotting; the presence of the lawyers and the judge suggested potential connections with her work.

When the group broke up, the rest of the men left, but Judge Callahan began making the rounds of the rapidly filling tables. He was a big, imposing man—Brandy's mother admiringly compared him to Clint Eastwood—and politician through and through. He knew everyone's name, shook everyone's hand, and gave a big, insincere smile to one and all.

Callahan was somewhere close to sixty years old, but he had aged well. His hair was thick and iron gray, as were his eyes, which held no trace of warmth. He had a deep suntan, but few lines in his face. Brandy suspected he either had a tanning bed or wore makeup so he would always look good if caught by a camera. His suit was conservative but beautifully made, and he had the physique to show it: broad of shoulder, narrow of waist, flat of belly. His hands were big, strong, but uncalloused—only professional manicures could keep them so neat and perfect. His trademark Stetson hat hung nearby—this might not be cowboy country, but both the local rodeo tradition and the fact that Murphy lay between Nashville and Branson made such headgear common. Without a doubt Callahan knew the hat supported his John Wayne/Clint Eastwood/Harrison Ford image.

Callahan knew the law—Brandy had to give him that. He controlled his courtroom brilliantly, and his cases were rarely overturned on appeal.

Although he had not officially announced his candidacy for governor, Callahan's constant politicking had to mean something. He certainly didn't have to work to remain judge; the last two elections he had run unopposed.

Most people were flattered by Callahan's attention. He managed to time his arrival at Brandy and Church's table just as Brandy's juicy hamburger dripped grease down her hands, threatening to soak the cuffs of her blouse. While she struggled with inadequate paper napkins, Callahan turned to Church. "Officer Jones. I saw Tiffany's name on the honor roll. Congratulations."

"Thank you, Judge," Church said in non-committal tones. "We're very proud of her." He knew better than to allow his suspicion to show.

"And Ms. Mather." There it was, as the man turned his attention to her. He could have called her "officer," as he did Church, or "detective," but no, he had to emphasize that "Ms." to show how politically correct he was. Didn't he realize that men who called attention to their use of the term only displayed their discomfort?

"Good afternoon, Judge Callahan," Brandy said politely.

"Church," said Callahan, "why don't you get us all some more coffee?"

Her colleague raised an eyebrow to Brandy, who shrugged. She couldn't imagine what the judge had to say to her that he didn't want Church to hear.

"Rory Sanford's up for parole," Callahan began as he sat across from her. They were alone in a crowd, the buzz of voices too loud for normal conversation to be overheard.

"I got a notice of the hearing," Brandy said in a noncommital tone.

"Well, I don't sit on the parole board, but if I did I certainly wouldn't want *that* man out early."

"Because he's a Sanford?" Brandy asked. The feud between the Callahans and the Sanfords was legendary. Doc Sanford was coroner because his regular practice was limited to those not afraid of the Callahan contingent. When he had turned seventy, the hospital board had revoked his surgical privileges, limiting his practice even further.

Brandy liked Doc Sanford a lot, and he was a damn fine forensic pathologist. She wasn't sure how he stayed in that office, except that Judge Callahan probably considered him harmless there. Rory Sanford was Troy Sanford's grandson.

"No, Ma'am," Judge Callahan responded to Brandy's remark with perfect civility. "I want Rory Sanford to serve out his term 'cause he owes a debt to innocent people. That money was to help our schools. I wish the law allowed me to sentence him to hard labor until he told where he stashed it, so it could go back to the people he stole it from!"

In the abstract, Brandy agreed. However, she suspected that Rory Sanford had no more idea where the money he supposedly embezzled had gone than she did. And Callahan appeared to have forgotten the question of Sanford's plea. Rory Sanford had been treasurer of the school system's booster fund when more than a thousand dollars had turned up missing. So had receipts and other records. Sanford had agreed to plead guilty to one count of misfeasance, claiming he felt responsible for not keeping better records.

Neither the money nor the missing records had ever been recovered, and as Brandy remembered it there had been no absolute proof that the fund had received as much money as was supposed to be missing. Sanford should never have gone for the plea, but it had been one of those spells when the court docket was immensely overcrowded, and everyone was pressured to plead. When Sanford appeared in court, however, Judge Callahan had insisted on taking his plea on one count as a plea on *all* counts, and Sanford's court-appointed lawyer had had no luck arguing otherwise.

"Well," said Brandy, "I don't have anything new to add. I haven't seen Rory Sanford since his hearing."

Callahan gave her his politician's smile, wide enough to reveal gold crowns on his molars. "Good. Good. The board won't listen to them bleedin' heart social workers and psycho therapists." He separated the words, turning "psycho" into a modifier. Brandy gave a reflexive smile at the lame joke, then wished she had not dignified it with a response.

"Saw your mamma at church yesterday," Callahan went on. Suddenly he had Brandy's attention. Her mother had not gone to church until she took up with Harry Davis, owner of a local radio station. Was it really getting that serious?

"Whatever makes her happy," said Brandy. *And keeps her out of my hair.*

"She seems happy with Mr. Davis. But you, Brandy—how come your mother has more of a social life than you do?"

That's none of your business, Brandy wanted to retort, but held it to, "Because I'm working and she's retired."

"You should get out more. You're a very lovely woman." He turned on his best political smile.

What the hell? Brandy could not think of a polite response before Callahan filled the awkward silence himself. "There's a ball at the university on Saturday night for scholarship contributors. Would you like to go with me?"

"You're asking me out on a date?" Brandy blurted in astonishment. *Church, get back here and rescue me!*

The smile almost showed warmth, although it didn't reach Callahan's eyes. "You can put it that way, yes."

You bastard—you sexually harassing bastard! Church is right about you! But what Brandy said was, "Much as I might enjoy going to a ball, I don't think it would be . . . appropriate . . . for us to go out together, Judge Callahan."

"L. J.," he corrected. "Why not?"

Don't play ignorant! You didn't get to be a judge by acting stupid. "Because as a police officer, I must frequently give testimony in your courtroom. I don't think it would be wise to undermine my credibility as a witness . . . or yours as an unbiased judge."

"Oh, I don't think—"

"You think only too clearly, Your Honor. Whatever you're up to, stop before you get us both into trouble," Brandy said, keeping her tone of voice and facial expression neutral. "You haven't crossed the boundary into sexual harassment yet. Please don't cross it, and I will not need to report your indiscretion."

The iron-gray eyes showed feeling now: incredulity. Granted, the man was attractive, but he was also old enough to be her father. Did he actually believe wealth and power made him irresistible?

Before Callahan could respond, Church returned with fresh coffee. As he set the styrofoam cups down, the judge said, as if continuing a pleasant conversation, "Your mother says you'll be taking the sergeant's exam in the spring."

"I'm afraid she's mistaken," Brandy took it up with equal smoothness, ignoring the sick feeling in her gut. "She's trying to persuade me, but I don't feel ready. You know how mothers are."

"Proud of their daughters, as they should be," replied Callahan. "Well, Brandy, when you are ready, let me know. I can help you understand the legal part. You think real hard about taking the exam. I'll bet you could slide right through it." He drained the cup of coffee, stood, and took his leave, picking up his hat and pausing only for a couple of quick handshakes at other tables.

Brandy waited until Callahan was out the door before she said softly, "Damn him!"

"What's the matter?" asked Church.

"First, he's ganging up with my mother against me. Second, what was that—a bribe?"

"What're you talking about?"

"Church, *you* should take the sergeant's exam, not me. You've got more experience, and you *like* to study. But Callahan tells me I'll 'slide right through' the exam . . . right after he makes sure I'm not going to testify in favor of Rory Sanford getting out of prison."

She took a mouthful of coffee—and scorched the roof of her mouth. Swallowing painfully, she realized that the way the judge had gulped his down meant she had upset him more than he had shown. Oh, terrific. All her careful avoidance of the man's bad side, blown in five minutes.

"God, Brandy," Church was saying, "any mention of your mother sets you off. Are you gonna think *I'm* in on the conspiracy if I say she's right? You're qualified. Go for it. Let's both go for it. I will if you will, okay?"

"Oh, Jeez. Now I do feel paranoid," said Brandy. "You know what just flashed through my mind? A conspiracy to set us against each other for promotion!"

Church laughed. "Everything's a conspiracy. Come on, Brandy—let's get back downtown."

There was a message for Brandy: Carrie Wyman had called. She dialed her number. "Sorry I missed you for lunch," said Carrie.

"You actually took a *lunch hour*?" Carrie was usually lucky to wolf down a sandwich between clients.

"Cancellation. I wanted to grump over the fact that my abuse case went home."

"She'll be back," said Brandy.

"Yeah, but who will get hurt the next time, and how badly? Oops! Gotta go. Here comes my next appointment!"

At 3:20 there was a call: domestic violence.

"So what else is new?" Church asked through a yawn, stretching his way into his jacket. "Come on—this may take a woman's touch."

Two uniformed officers were already on the scene, pounding on the door of a dilapidated yellow frame house. From inside a male voice shouted obscenities, against a background of female weeping.

"Open up! Police!"

The male voice shouted, "See what you done! God dammit, woman, yer nothin' but trouble!"

"Ricky, please! No!" the female voice pleaded—and suddenly erupted into wordless screams. A child's voice shrieked in pain.

One of the officers, Jimmy Paschall, shouted, "This is the police! We're coming in!"

The screams became moans of "No! No-oh! No-oh-oh!"

Paschall smashed the glass with his gun butt.

Shots. Three fast ones, a pause accompanied by an inarticulate yell, and two more.

The male voice shouted, "Look what you made me do!" just as the uniformed officers ran into the house, the detectives on their heels, all with guns drawn.

A woman lay in front of the couch, half covering a little girl no more than three. The child wore a cast on her left wrist, and the red welt on her left cheek showed that she had been hit before being shot in the head. The woman also bore wounds in the back of her head and neck.

A boy, perhaps ten, lay in the kitchen doorway, a butcher knife clutched in his hand. He had apparently been cut down coming to rescue his mother and sister. Blood welled from a wound in his chest, and another in his neck. He had the remnants of a black eye, several days old.

In the sudden silence, the boy's labored breathing grated loudly.

The man who had created the carnage faced the police—"Drop the gun!" Church ordered.

Faster than thought, the man put the barrel of his .35 into his mouth and pulled the trigger.

Jimmy Paschall gave a yelp as if of pain.

The other cop, Charlie Rand, said, "Call an ambulance—hurry!" and knelt beside the boy who still clung to life.

Brandy looked at Church. His dark skin had turned a greenish hue. He moved to the woman and little girl, seeking signs of life.

That left Brandy to check the murderer. He was dead, empty eyes staring at the ceiling. She could not close them; the coroner would have to examine untouched bodies.

Just another murder/suicide. Open and shut case . . . with four cops as witnesses.

Behind Brandy, Rand muttered to the fallen boy, "Just hold on, Son. The medics'll be here in a minute." But before the wail of the ambulance sounded in the distance, the labored breathing shuddered to a stop. Brandy heard the beefy cop whisper, "Take him home, Jesus. Welcome him, Lord, with his mamma and his sister. And please—help me to understand why You take young kids like this."

Brandy's father had moved their family from Ohio to Kentucky when she was twelve. The fundamentalists here had driven her nearly crazy trying to drag her into their churches. Over the years she had perceived them as deluded or hypocritical, or perhaps just plain stupid—but she had also gotten to know many of them as friends.

Charlie Rand had his beliefs to comfort him in the midst of senseless slaughter. Brandy had nothing.

Neither had Churchill Jones. His eyes met hers, and she knew that he, too, had overheard Rand's spontaneous prayer. Church was a lapsed Baptist, while Brandy was a never-was-anything. Police work did little to inspire belief in a benevolent force guiding the universe.

Neighbors gathered outside the house. It didn't take long to piece together the story. The husband, Matt Perkins, was laid off when the Western Electric plant closed three years ago. He found a few jobs, but never kept them long. Like almost everyone in this dry county he drank, but under the stress of unemployment he got drunk on a regular basis. Then he beat his wife and kids—and the next day he would be all apologies and promises to lay off the booze.

And so it happened again, a family stressed beyond their capacity to cope, a woman beaten trying to protect her children, and a man brimming over with violence he had no other outlet for. Brandy remembered Carrie's case, the woman who had returned to her husband after he beat their three-year-old girl, broke her wrist—

"Oh, my God," Brandy whispered, realizing that this was the same family. A rope tightened about her skull.

There was no need to send anything from the Perkins house to the crime lab. Doc Sanford made out the death certificates, and the case was closed. All they had to do was notify the closest relatives: the parents of the husband and wife, grandparents of the two dead children.

But Brandy would have to break it to Carrie.

At the station they faced the wrath of Chief Harvey Benton. "Four citizens dead—*after* my officers arrive! What kind of police protection do you call that?"

No one had an answer. Benton demanded, "Well? How'd it happen? You never broke up a family fight before?"

"The house was locked," Church recited flatly. "When Mrs. Perkins screamed, Paschall broke the door. By the time we got in, Perkins had shot his wife, his son, and his daughter. Then he turned the gun on himself."

"Jesus!" exclaimed the chief. "No wonder people call us Murphy's Law!"

"I tried," Jimmy Paschall choked out.

"It happened too quickly," Brandy came to his aid. "Paschall *did* try, sir. Perkins clearly wanted to die—he had no hesitation."

"That's right," Rand backed up his colleague. "No one coulda stopped him, Sir."

Benton studied the four of them. "All right. Reports on my desk by noon tomorrow. People can't think civilians in this town can shoot one another while the police look on! Dismissed!" he added, the order left over from his military experience.

But how could Brandy dismiss that scene from her memory? Half an hour later Carrie confirmed that the Perkins family was, indeed, the one she had been working with. "Oh, God, why did I let her go home?"

"You couldn't stop her," Brandy reminded her. "Listen, you want to get together tonight? Talking might help."

"It probably would," said Carrie, "but I've got to work. Two visits out in the county and then a rape counseling group." Brandy could hear unshed tears in her friend's voice. "I have to keep my cool and get through it. I'll call you later in the week, okay?"

As she hung up, the dispatcher called, "Hey, Mather—visitor!" Brandy found Dan Martin in the waiting area, hat in hand. She had forgotten their appointment.

"They told me you were out on a call earlier," he said. "Half an hour ago they said you were wrapping it up, so I took the chance and came back. You look exhausted."

"Rough case," Brandy agreed. "Murder/suicide."

He nodded. "If you don't want to work tonight, I certainly understand. Let me take you to dinner."

"I'm not hungry," Brandy said truthfully, even though it was 6:11. "This was an appetite destroyer. If you really don't mind, I'd rather work on the Land case than go home and think about what happened today."

The mysterious case of Everett Land was a pleasure because of what it did *not* include: violence toward women or children, grieving friends and relatives, or anything related to the neverending, time-consuming, and ineffectual war against drugs.

The letters in Greek had come back from Dan's friend at Columbia, along with a message: "The longest document, not included here, is in an ancient dialect I'm still trying to identify. It's a manuscript Dr. Land must have been studying. I'll send you the translation as soon as I work it out." The letters which had been translated concerned plans for a trip to Greece the following summer.

Dan Martin knew tricks with a computer that Brandy had never seen before. Soon they had Everett Land's Kentucky Teacher's Retirement records, his insurance records, and his tax returns since he had moved to Kentucky.

The returns provided their first clue: even the first year he worked at JPSU, Land had considerable interest from savings. They followed the money to bank records, where there was no surprise that he had bought CD's when interest rates were high—everyone who had $500 to spare had done so. What was amazing was that in the early 1980's Everett Land had had over fifty thousand dollars. During the years of high interest, he doubled it.

But where had he gotten the original money?

All the computer could tell them was that $53,726.64 had been transferred to the Murphy Savings Bank—a small fortune in 1984. His checking account told them he had spent some of his nest egg on a new car, and later on the down payment for a house, but he had also socked away a good quarter of his paycheck every month.

"Not a risk-taker," said Brandy. "No stocks, not even bonds. I wonder why he didn't have an IRA—or a tax-sheltered annuity? Most university faculty do."

"I'm afraid it's too late to ask him," said Dan.

"Can you trace that money back any further?" Brandy asked. "This is a weird financial picture—as if he wanted that money easily accessible, if, say, he had to cut and run. I wonder if he got it legally?"

Dan traced another bank transfer, this time from the bank where Land had kept his savings during graduate school in California. But the mysterious lump sum had come there as over $36,000 from yet another bank, and increased during its stay. There were weekly small deposits, probably from a part-time job, but the withdrawals outran them, and he used some of the interest from his CD's.

"Shall we try to access his grad school records?" Dan asked.

"Later," Brandy replied. "First let's follow the money to the end of that trail."

Her instinct was right: Land's nest egg had not come to Berkeley from Chapel Hill, home of his supposed alma mater, the University of North Carolina. The money had been transferred from Oxford, Mississippi. The Oxford account had been opened with $27,800.00. No transfer from another bank. And during the four years when it should have been depleted steadily, if Land had been a full-time college student in another state, the money had grown to the amount transferred to Berkeley.

Brandy was ready to quit when the numbers began to blur before her eyes. Then she had a hunch. "Just two more items. Land's tax returns for the years this account was open in Oxford, and his records from Chapel Hill."

The university's records showed Land as a full-time student . . . but the IRS showed him working as a realtor in Oxford, Mississippi! "He went home on weekends and vacations and sold houses?" Dan suggested.

"And made enough in his spare time to sock away nine thousand dollars in four years? Dan, we're onto something here. Get his undergraduate records."

Land had been a B to B- student for two years, then an A student when he hit his stride in his junior and senior years. "So he was there," said Dan.

"Was he?" asked Brandy. "Call up his other university records. The financial stuff. Did he have a scholarship, a student loan? What about housing?"

And there they drew a blank. Except for four years of courses and grades, there was no evidence that Everett Land had ever attended Chapel Hill.

"What would he have needed to get into graduate school?" Brandy asked.

"His transcript, the GRE, some letters of recommendation," Dan replied. "I suppose the letters could be faked, but there's always the chance that someone at Berkeley knows the person whose name you've forged."

"Well, we can check those records tomorrow if Berkeley still has them. IRS computer records go back a few more years. Let's see what Land did before he became a real estate agent and forger of college records."

There they encountered a blank wall: Everett Land filed his very first tax return the year he went to work in Oxford. The same year he was supposedly a freshman at Chapel Hill. "So he *was* older than he claimed," said Brandy. "No kid straight out of high school would get that real estate job."

"Brandy, we don't know the whole story," said Dan. "He could have had family connections—"

"He had that lump sum of money. Maybe he stole it."

"More probably it was an inheritance."

"But he faked his undergraduate records—yet he obviously knew what he was doing at Berkeley, or he wouldn't have gotten his doctorate. He had to have a bachelor's degree from *somewhere*. We're looking at an identity change, Dan. Who was this person before he was Everett C. Land?"

THREE

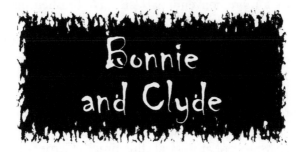

Bonnie and Clyde

BRANDY EVENTUALLY FOUND HERSELF unable to follow what was happening on the computer. It was 10:08 P.M., and she had to be up early.

"I'll take you home," said Dan.

Her car—

Church would pick her up in the morning if she called at breakfast time. "Thanks," she said wearily.

Dan put on his hat. Not a cap advertising some team or local business, but a narrow-brimmed summer cotton hat. It gave him a sophisticated look at odds with the atmosphere of Murphy, Kentucky. You could always tell the university faculty, no matter how many years they lived here.

"You know," Dan said as they went out to his car,"when I said I wanted to see you again, I didn't mean just to help with computer stuff. How about dinner tomorrow night?"

"I'd like that," said Brandy,"but I'm a police officer. If I get caught up in a case like today—"

"I understand," he told her."I'll call first."

As before, he walked her to her door, and kissed her. There was that same wonderful excitement she had felt the first time. "Thanks for your help," she said, reluctant to part even though she had no energy even to talk, let alone do anything more strenuous.

What would it be like to sleep in his strong arms?

"I'm glad to help," Dan said. "Let me know what else you find out about Rett. And I didn't mean I wouldn't help with more computer searches. It is fascinating."

"Okay," she replied, lingering in his embrace.

His warm chuckle vibrated in his chest. "Go to bed, Brandy. Tomorrow night we'll try a more conventional date." He brushed her lips again, then turned her to the door.

Her answering machine was blinking. Carrie had left a message, "If it's before eleven P.M., call me when you get home." As it was only 10:23, she dialed Carrie's number.

"You gonna be able to sleep?" Carrie asked.

It took Brandy a moment to remember. Then she said, "Yeah, I'm okay. I've been working on another case."

"You mean you were at *work* all this time?" Carrie asked. "Honey, you'll burn yourself out. Do you want to talk about the Perkins case?"

Another time, Brandy would have confessed to her best friend how she had frozen on the scene—but that was after the shooting, when the horrified helplessness descended.

Moments when people, especially children, lay suddenly, unexpectedly dead, brought back that day when she was ten years old and had seen her brother lying still and pale in the street, blood running from beneath him like red paint.

"I . . . handled it," Brandy said, realizing the last thing she wanted was to relive the scene she had managed to forget for a few hours.

"They were my clients," said Carrie. "I've been rereading my notes, wondering if there was something I could have done to prevent what happened today."

For once it was Carrie who needed to talk. "Listen—why don't you grab what you need for tomorrow and come over here for the night? You can give me a lift to the station in the morning. I left my car there."

Both women were tired, and both had to be alert in the morning, so Brandy didn't suggest the few beers they might have drowned their sorrows in on another night.

She let Carrie talk. She had been sent twice in the past three months to check on the welfare of the Perkins children.

"I could see fear in their eyes," she told Brandy, "but until Matt Perkins broke the girl's wrist they made excuses. Lily had a black eye one time, and the night she got up the courage to leave him she told me Matt raped her every time he got angry. God, why won't these women press charges?"

"Because they think they need a man to take care of them, even a vicious brute of a man. They don't think they can make it on their own."

Brandy had seen it as often as Carrie had. Even when the wives pressed charges, they were dropped before the husband came to trial.

Carrie sighed."It's enough to make me appreciate George. He cheated on me, but at least he never abused me."

"Not physically," said Brandy. She knew how badly Carrie's ex-husband had hurt her friend.

"Yeah." Carrie raised her cup of herb tea in a toast. "Here's to taking care of ourselves!"

"With a little help from our friends," Brandy amended.

Carrie took a sip of the steaming brew. "You know," she said, "I expected to find you more upset than I am. Usually senseless deaths hit you especially hard."

"I had a little help from another friend," Brandy confessed.

"Church?"

"A new friend. Dan Martin."

"So that's working out," said Carrie. "Is he nice?"

"Very. He came down to the station to help me on the computer. He didn't know he was helping me get over the Perkins fiasco."

"Oh. Another business relationship. Maybe that's all women should try to have with men."

"We're going out to dinner tomorrow," said Brandy. "I'm not sure why. We don't have much in common."

"But you like him," said Carrie.

"Yes, I like him. He's smart, and so polite he's almost old-fashioned."

"Older?" Carrie asked.

"Mid-thirties. You realize it won't be that long before you and I reach thirty?"

"I already feel as old as the hills," said Carrie. "Do you think this could be the one?"

"Carrie, I hardly know him!" Brandy protested. "Besides, it's always the same: at first they're intrigued that I'm a cop. Then they find out about the long hours, eventually somebody takes a shot at me, and pretty soon here comes the ultimatum: the man or the badge."

Carrie studied her friend. "You're a strange one, Brandy Mather. With that badge you accepted responsibility for the whole populace of Murphy—but when it comes to the commitment everybody else takes so casually, all you can do is put obstacles in its path."

The next morning, Brandy told Church what she and Dan Martin had turned up. "Professor Land apparently faked his way into graduate school, taking on a whole new identity. I want to find out who he was *before* that."

"That money," said Church. "Almost thirty thousand—a lot back then. You think he's connected to a robbery, sneaked off with the loot and let accomplices go to jail?"

"Or embezzled from wherever he worked before becoming Everett Land. Maybe it was ransom money, or a payoff. He could be the brains behind some big heist. This guy spoke seven languages, Church. It could be an international thing. Maybe he had the brains to plan it, but then couldn't take a life of crime. So he skipped out, changed his name, and ended up here in the middle of nowhere."

"You think somebody connected with that money finally caught up with him?"

"Could be. Could be *anything*. I love this case, Church. The more complicated it gets, the better!"

But Police Chief Harvey Benton didn't love the case. When Brandy made her report, including requests for help from the Oxford, Mississippi, police department, he told her, "This case is closed, Detective Mather. *Closed*. The man died of natural causes. Now get your butt out of here and do some *real* police work!"

Stunned, Brandy returned to her desk. Everyone in the department received such a dressing down occasionally—but only when they had failed badly, as with the Perkins situation yesterday. She had never before been scolded like a naughty child for going beyond the call of duty.

The only neglected item on her desk was the Perkins paperwork. She toyed with the idea of ignoring it and going back into the computer as Dan had shown her, looking for criminal evidence on Everett Land. Maybe later.

"10-17 at the Bank of Murphy!" That was the silent alarm, indicating a robbery in progress.

The bank, which had just opened for the day, was right around the corner. The police arrived to see a man come running out carrying a flour sack, undoubtedly stuffed with money. He raised a rifle at a uniformed officer. The shot went wild, but police and civilians hit the sidewalk as the man ran for a double-parked pickup.

Brandy caught only a glimpse of the red-haired woman in the truck, but from the hair, the man's flour sack and day-glo orange hunting cap, and the silvered sunglasses both wore, she recognized Chase and Jenny Anderson, wanted in three states for bank robbery, murder, assault, grand theft auto, and assorted lesser offenses. They hit banks in small cities like Murphy, where clerks were not protected behind bullet-proof glass. First thing on a payday, they staged a surprise attack, emptying the tills, then fleeing in a stolen vehicle that would later be found abandoned.

The Andersons robbed a bank only once every three to five weeks, never on an exact schedule, reclaiming the element of surprise whenever they struck anew. They had pulled off five successful robberies in the past six months in Illinois, Kentucky, and Tennessee. The Murphy police were determined not to let them make it six.

The truck was a blue four-wheel drive Ford pickup. Anderson jumped into the driver's seat and careened around the court square to head out of town toward the lake.

That was not the shortest way out of Kentucky, but it afforded a tangle of back roads. Brandy and Church dashed for the unmarked car, and pulled out behind a pair of black-and-whites. In the rearview mirror, Brandy saw a couple of tardy uniforms caught by Chief Benton, and sent into the bank. Everyone wanted to chase the robbers; no one wanted to interview witnesses.

They radioed the state police, but the Andersons knew as well as they did that the nearest post was thirty miles from Murphy in the opposite direction. The sheriff's patrol was already on the way.

The line of vehicles barreled out of Murphy, headed toward the Land Between the Lakes. If the Andersons wanted to escape south into Tennessee, there was only one bridge. The state or county could get a patrol car there before the Andersons arrived.

Realizing that, the fugitives would probably swing north—if their intent was to get out of the state.

But there was nothing to keep them from losing themselves amid the dozens of roads between Murphy and the lake. The Andersons had hunted and fished this area all their lives. They knew the back roads so well that in every previous robbery they had eluded pursuit and disappeared.

"All cars!" the radio erupted."We got a citizen's band report. Blue Ford pickup nearly hit a couple of kids while illegally passing a stopped school bus!"

"That's them!" Brandy exclaimed, and hit the gas.

Church flipped on the CB radio. Most of the police cars no longer had them, but the radios were cheap and their use free, so they were still more common than cellular phones.

The CB was full of voices this morning. "You damned idiot!" someone yelled. "Eastbound 94, you got a asshole in a blue pick'emup burnin' rubber. Watch out—he'll try t'blow ya off the road!"

"Well, we know where he is," said Brandy, hitting the siren to clear the morning traffic on the two-lane road.

The police dispatcher's voice closed off the CB chatter to announce, "The bank guard's dead. Anderson shot him first thing through the door. Get those bastards!"

A new voice on the CB shouted angrily, "Hey—mo-ron! You got yer ears on? Think you own the damn road?"

"Oh, God," said Brandy. "One of these cowboys gets mad enough, they might try to stop him. The Andersons have already killed four people."

Church untangled the CB mike from the police equipment. "Breaker one-nine. Breaker one-nine. This is the police. Report whereabouts of blue 1987 Ford pickup driving recklessly east on 94. Suspects are armed and dangerous. Do *not* attempt to apprehend! Report location. Repeat, do *not* attempt to stop the truck!"

When Church let go of the switch, the reports walked all over one another as good citizens tried to help. "—turned off on 1713," came through the garble.

Then, a different voice, "They just passed us, driving like—" A cracking noise, followed by "Oh, my God! They're shooting at us!"

"Stop your car! Let them go!" Church ordered into the mike as Brandy swung their car onto 1713. Then, when there was no immediate reply, "Are you hurt?"

"No," the voice replied, shaken. "They kept going."

"They must have their CB on," said Brandy, speeding up on the nearly deserted road. They were the first car on the chase now, having just come up on the 1713 turnoff when they got the message. Those ahead of them had to come back to the turn, but in the rearview mirror Brandy could see the blue light of at least one black-and-white behind them.

The road wound, then bounced over low hills. They waved as they passed a green Chevy with a CB antenna, pulled over to the side—their informants.

"Where does this go?" asked Church.

"Take your choice," said Brandy. "Most of the roads on either side will lead back to 94. Straight ahead, we'll come to a split in about three miles, right to the university biological station, left to Red Hill Landing."

"So unless they take a turn somewhere along here, they'll dead-end at the lake."

"I think they're trying to get far enough ahead so we won't see them turn," Brandy told him, gunning the car again. "They may be trying to reach a hideout, or a hidden vehicle. Maybe even a boat."

The truck was now in sight, the police car slowly gaining—but as Church picked up the bullhorn to tell them to pull over, Jenny Anderson leaned out the passenger's window with a shotgun.

Brandy swerved, heard the shot, but nothing hit the car. Church pulled his gun, but did not fire, speaking calmly into the bullhorn. "Cease firing and pull over." He was the coolest cop under fire Brandy had ever known.

As Brandy fought to stay on the narrow road, Jenny Anderson discharged the second barrel. A *thrrruunnnch!* of shot hit the roof and top of the windshield, but the safety glass did its job. A couple of cracks extended downward from the crazing, but Brandy could still see to drive.

Church fired at the fleeing truck. Mrs. Anderson drew back inside, but there was no other perceptible effect. The truck sped on as fast as ever.

"Dammit, they know they can't escape!" said Brandy.

"They're desperate," replied Church. "I'll try to get the tires."

On his third shot, one of the pickup's back tires blew, and the vehicle swerved into the ditch.

Brandy screeched their car to a halt, and she and Church remained inside as the black-and-white drew up.

"Give yourselves up," Church ordered through the bullhorn. "Throw out your guns."

The driver's side truck door opened. Anderson dropped into the ditch and began firing.

"Shit!" whispered Church as he and Brandy ducked below the dash. The windshield was rendered opaque, then gave and fell in on them. Brandy grabbed the rifle out of its case and knocked the remaining glass out of the frame.

Anderson's next shots were accompanied by sounds of glass and metal shattering as he peppered the front of the car. The radiator spat steam and boiling water.

Two other cars with lights and sirens rolled up and stopped. The suspects should have known it was hopeless, but both husband and wife continued shooting.

"Goddamn Bonnie and Clyde!" said Church. "They *want* us to kill them!"

"Probably," Brandy agreed. Rifle lined up through the steering wheel, she entered her private world, sighted carefully, entered the zone—and fired.

Chase Anderson screamed.

Jenny Anderson scrambled back through the truck and out on her husband's side, crying, "Chase! Oh, my God! Chase!"

The police converged, guns at the ready.

Chase Anderson sat in the ditch, nursing a bloody hand. His rifle lay next to him, and his wife finally surrendered her shotgun.

"Great shooting, Brandy," said Church.

A state patrol officer asked, "You *meant* to hit his hand?"

"I had a rifle with a sight," Brandy explained. "There was no reason to kill him."

"And no reason not to," commented Melissa Blalock. In her late thirties, she was the oldest woman on the Murphy police force, a plain, no-nonsense, hard-working cop. She looked at Brandy for confirmation of her feelings about the trash now being read their rights. "Brandy— you're hurt!"

"Let me see!" Church said, turning her toward him.

Only then did Brandy feel the burning sting of the cut on her forehead, the trickle of blood down her face. "It's a glass cut," Church said, reaching back into the car for the first aid kit. "Thank God it missed your eye."

But the cut took three stitches. By the time Brandy was back at the station, it was early afternoon. Chief Benton gave her the rest of the day off. "I'm sorry I yelled at you this morning," he added. "Good work today, Mather." From Benton, it was high praise.

The cut didn't really hurt, and the blow hadn't been hard enough to give her a headache, so Brandy decided to clean up her house . . . just in case Dan Martin finally came in this evening. She was vacuuming when the phone rang.

"Oh. Hi, Mom."

"Brenda, why did I have to hear on the radio that you were in a shootout this morning?"

"Just part of my job, Mom."

"Churchill told me you were injured."

"I wasn't shot."

"I didn't say shot. I said injured. And badly enough to be sent home. I'm coming over."

"No! I mean—I'm just on my way to get some groceries. How about I pick you up, and we can both get some?" If her mother came over, she'd stay all day.

Melody Mather fussed about the bandage on her daughter's forehead. "You shouldn't be out running around. You should be in bed. Doesn't it hurt?"

"No, Mom, I'm fine." *Although I'll probably have a headache by the time this shopping trip is over.*

At Kroger's they separated, to meet at checkout. Brandy got apples, peaches, lettuce, carrots, a couple of potatoes, bread, milk, cereal, and cat food. She hesitated over frozen dinners, a staple of her existence. Did she want to stock her small freezer with those when . . . she just might want to do some actual cooking? She tossed four into her basket and went over to the meat counter.

Men liked steak and a baked potato. It was months since she'd cooked a meal for a man, other than helping Coreen when she went over to Church's house. Something she couldn't mention to her mother, who would wonder why her daughter didn't come to her house on Sundays instead.

It was too long since she'd had time for shopping; she needed everything. Toilet paper, tissues, dishwashing and laundry detergent, scouring powder, paper towels, tampons —

On the shelf beside the tampons were condoms.

Brandy already had some, carried one in her purse, like any modern woman. But those had grown old without ever being used. Defiantly, she plucked a new package off the shelf . . . and buried it under the tampons and paper towels.

Melody Mather was in line when Brandy joined the queue, a cautious three aisles away. The package of condoms scanned correctly. No one had to run to get a price check; no one announced over a loudspeaker that she was trying to purchase a package of Trojans. They went into one of the plastic sacks, and were forgotten.

"My goodness—you've bought out the store!" said Brandy's mother.

"I haven't had time to do a thorough job in weeks," she replied, although it wasn't entirely true. She just hadn't had the energy to do more than run in and throw bread, milk, cat food, and frozen dinners into her cart.

"I don't know why you want to be a policewoman," said her mother. "It's dangerous, it takes up all your time, and it doesn't pay."

"We agree that you don't understand, Mom," Brandy reminded her. "It's what I want to do, and I'm happy."

"You have a teaching certificate."

"I don't want to teach. I want to catch murderers and drug dealers. Doesn't it mean anything to you that just this morning I helped to catch a man who has killed two bank guards, a teller, and a bank customer?"

"It means if he gets loose you could be his next target!" her mother retorted. "I love you, Brenda. I've already lost my son and my husband. Can't you understand that I don't want to lose my daughter, too?"

I understand that it bothers you that you can't control me anymore, Brandy thought, but she knew better than to open that argument. "I love you, too, Mom." She started the car and began to work her way out of the parking lot.

"Oh, Honey," said her mother as if she had just thought of it, "do you still have my food processor?"

"Of course I do." What did she think—that Brandy had sold it? She had borrowed it to shred carrots for a cake for the Humane Society bake sale, and had been intending to get the bulky thing off her counter ever since. Why hadn't she put it in the car on her way out today?

"I need to make coleslaw for the Women's Circle potluck. Why don't we just stop and pick it up?"

Which was, of course, why her mother hadn't mentioned it when she called: now there was no way to keep her out of the apartment. At least the place was clean. As there was no choice, Brandy said, "Sure, Mom," as cheerfully as she could manage.

Melody Mather helped to carry in Brandy's groceries, while Brandy toted the awkward food processor down to the car. *Now she'll snoop to see that I'm living right.* But she had washed three days' worth of dishes, scrubbed the bathroom, and made up the bed before her mother called. For once the surprise raid did not find Brandy's home in chaos.

By the time she wedged the food processor into the trunk, surrounded by grocery bags so it wouldn't bounce around and break, Brandy came back to her apartment to find half her groceries put away and her mother trying to shoo Sylvester, her black-and-white cat, off the counter.

"My goodness, Sweetheart, no wonder you bought out the store. You didn't have a thing to eat in the house!" She opened a can of cat food and put it down on the floor. Sylvester glared balefully at her, but finally gave in and jumped down to get the tuna treat.

It was useless for Brandy to protest that there had been a frozen dinner, a couple of eggs, and two or three cans of soup in the house. And dry food for Sylvester. To her mother's way of thinking, that was nothing.

"Do you want the steaks in the freezer or the refrigerator, Dear?"

If they were for herself, one would go in the freezer, and one in the refrigerator. "And you wonder where I get my talent as a detective, Mom?" Brandy took the meat from her mother's hands and defiantly put it in the meat keeper.

Melody Mather wasn't fazed. She put the potatoes and carrots into the vegetable bin, then turned to the last two sacks, handing Brandy one containing cleanser, toilet paper, shower soap, and laundry detergent. "You know where these things go."

By the time Brandy had put those in her utility closet, the last sack had been emptied, and everything put away except two items. The tampons and condoms sat side by side on the kitchen counter. Melody Mather's patented interrogation method.

All through Brandy's childhood, whenever her mother found something she thought her daughter shouldn't have, such as the $73.00 Brandy had laboriously saved up in a shoebox one and two dollars at a time, or the copy of *Playgirl* magazine she had once hidden under her mattress, she laid the item out in some conspicuous place and never said a word, just hovered and watched Brandy's reaction. Eventually Brandy was compelled to talk.

It wasn't even all bad. The money was for a bike she wanted. Once her mother accepted that Brandy hadn't stolen the money, and wasn't involved in drugs or anything else illegal, they had actually had a productive talk in which her mother explained why she didn't want Brandy riding a bicycle on Cleveland's dangerous streets.

The *Playgirl* incident, however, had been embarrassing and acrimonious. She had been fifteen and full of civics-class notions of freedom of speech and the press, as well as the right to privacy. Unable to answer her arguments, her mother had fallen back on the right of a parent to decide what her child could read, and finally on the old accusations that her daughter was so irresponsible that she had let her own brother get killed.

That was the first time Brandy had come out at the end of an argument believing her mother wrong, herself right, and her punishment unfair. She had never totally respected her mother since.

But there had been many more arguments, often precipitated by this same technique of evidence displayed until Brandy could take it no longer.

No, thought Brandy, *I will not be embarrassed, and I will not discuss these personal items with you, Mom. Let your technique backfire for once.* So she said, "Thanks for helping me put things away, Mom. Come on— let's get your groceries home before they get too hot in the trunk."

The doorbell rang. Who could that be at 4:30 P.M.?

It was Dan Martin. "Are you all right?" he asked, his eyes going immediately to the bandage on Brandy's forehead.

"I'm fine. Just a little cut, all in a day's work."

He still looked concerned."May I come in?"

"Sure," said Brandy, opening the door wider, smiling at his hesitation. Most West Kentucky men would have barged right in. Martin took off his hat and sunglasses as he entered, laying them on the table by the door, beside Brandy's purse, badge, and gun.

When he saw her mother, Martin paused. "I'm sorry. I didn't know you had company. I called the station. I don't have your home number."

Brandy could see her mother adding up Martin's concern, Brandy's clean apartment, the two steaks and two potatoes—

"This is Dr. Danton Martin, from JPSU. He's helping me with a case. Dan, meet my mother, Melody Mather."

"I'm pleased to meet you, Mrs. Mather," he said formally, showing his Yankee origins again. No man born in Murphy could have resisted the opportunity to flatter both women by saying something like, *I see where Brandy gets her good looks.* Dan Martin said, "I'm sure Brandy's told you about the mysterious death of one of our professors."

"Brenda never tells me about her work."

"You say you don't want to know," Brandy pointed out.

"I'd really like to know about cases in which no one is shooting at you, Dear."

"I don't think Brandy is free to reveal the details until the case is solved," said Martin.

"Oh, wait," said Brandy's mother. "Is this the case where a Satanic curse was put on one of the teachers, and he shriveled up and died?"

"Oh, Lord," said Brandy. "Where did you hear that?"

"At choir practice. I hope it wasn't supposed to be a secret, Honey, because everyone's talking about it. A lot of the faculty and students come to our church, you know," she added to Martin.

Our church now, Brandy noticed. *You hypocrite. You never set foot in church till you started going out with Harry Davis.*

"I'm sure they do," Martin replied neutrally. "Brandy, I am sorry to interrupt your time with your mother. If you still feel up to going out, shall I pick you up at six?"

"Yes, that will—"

"Hiss! *Yeeoowwwwrrrgh!*"

Sylvester stood on the kitchen counter, back arched, fur on end, yowling at Dan Martin.

"He doesn't like men," Brandy explained. "He was tortured by some low-life and left to die. I wouldn't let the vet put him to sleep."

"It's all right, Fella," Martin said to Sylvester. "You know I'm not the one who hurt you, don't you?"

Brandy was about to tell him that Sylvester wouldn't even make up to Church, when the cat calmed, backed up a couple of steps, and sat down. He lifted a paw and licked it contemplatively, never taking his eyes off Martin.

Martin's voice was hypnotic. "That's good. I won't hurt you. Good boy."

To Brandy's utter amazement, Sylvester stood and walked cautiously toward Martin, who put out a hand. Again the cat skittishly backed off, but when Martin made no further motion he came up and sniffed the hand, then rubbed his face against it, marking Martin as his property.

"Well I'll be damned," said Melody Mather. "I never thought I'd see that animal get on with a man. Brenda, hang on to this one if you insist on keeping that beast."

Martin ignored the unanswerable comment. "I grew up on a farm," he explained. "I like animals, and I think they can tell." He scratched the cat under the chin, and Sylvester began to purr. Then he turned to Brandy. "I'll see you later. Nice to meet you, Ma'am," he added politely to her mother, actually tipping the hat that he put back on at the front door, and was gone.

Brandy turned to look at her cat in puzzlement. Sylvester was in his Egyptian cat pose, sitting tall with his tail looped over his feet. Immediately behind him, she realized, stood the items her mother had left on display.

Brandy drove her mother home, helped to carry her things in, and was shooed out. A date with a university professor her mother approved of—she was constantly after Brandy to find someone with a secure future, marry, have children, and stop risking her life.

But Brandy loved police work, and cops had a worse record for successful relationships than movie stars. Brandy's own failure rate was 100%—every serious relationship since she had joined the Murphy Police had ended within months. Inevitably, some event would demonstrate the danger of her profession, and the man would give her an ultimatum.

Brandy did not respond well to threats.

But Dan Martin did not threaten. When he arrived promptly at 6:00 P.M., she had potatoes baking and wine chilling. He handed her the evening paper from the doorstep, and said, "I thought I was taking you out."

"I'd . . . like to get to know you better," Brandy explained. "And you might as well get to know something about me. I'm not a gourmet cook. All I know about wine is that red goes with beef. If that's good enough for you, we'll get along."

"That's fine. May I help?"

"Everything's under control," Brandy replied. "How do you like your steak?"

"Very rare."

Brandy blinked. "I thought you grew up in Iowa and Nebraska. Farmers generally like it well done."

"We didn't have steak when I was a kid. We had meatloaf or pork chops. When I was introduced to prime cuts I was also introduced to the proper way to prepare them."

She noted the shift to passive voice, and assumed that it was a woman who had introduced him.

"Yes," said Martin.

"Yes what?"

"Yes, it was a woman. Brandy, can't you stop playing Sherlock Holmes for a few hours?"

"*You*, Sir, are the one who just pulled the Holmes trick of following my train of thought and replying to the end of it." Then she added thoughtfully, "I don't know how to turn my curiosity off, Dan. It's not just police training. I've always thought that way."

"You're a dangerous woman to become involved with."

"Are we involved?" she asked bluntly.

He came around the counter, into the kitchen proper. He smelled clean, fresh from the shower, and his hair was still slightly damp. His presence filled her small kitchen. "I've made it no secret that I find you attractive."

"Yeah, well, I haven't had much success hiding my feelings, either," said Brandy. "Are you sure you want to risk getting involved with a cop?"

"I wasn't planning to commit any crimes," he replied, and reached to take her in his arms.

It took every ounce of Brandy's willpower to shrug him off and retreat to the corner by the microwave. He let her go, leaning back against the counter. "What's wrong?"

"You've seen it already," she told him. "I can't plan on my free time being free. Two or three cancellations without notice are enough for most men."

"The same would be true if you were a doctor, Brandy. Or a social worker or a firefighter. Uncertainty comes with the territory. I should think anyone would understand."

"Not all," she replied, "but yes, there have been men in my life who could accept it. Until something like today happens . . . or worse."

Brandy had replaced the white hospital bandage with a flesh-colored one, but it was still obvious. Had she left the wound uncovered it would have looked worse still, red and puffy, the stitches black and ugly— completely normal, she knew from a dozen previous experiences, but shocking to someone unaccustomed to women in the line of fire.

And what if she had been hit by a bullet instead of flying glass? The one and only time she had been shot, it had ended another promising relationship. Her mother had threatened everything short of having her declared insane when she had refused to quit the force.

Martin studied her with unreadable black eyes. Finally he asked, "What do you want me to say, Brandy? That it doesn't bother me that you were in danger today? How can I care about you and not be concerned? You may become very important to me—I don't know you well enough yet to be sure. But I *want* to know you better."

"I want to know you better, too."

Again there was a long pause. Brandy wondered why she had put him in this position. Did she want to drive him away before she even had a chance to know him?

Martin asked, "Are you afraid I'll try to change you?"

"Men always do."

"If I like you as you are, why would I want you to change? Besides, people never actually change. They may play a role for a time, but they can't keep it up. What kind of life would you have if you had to spend it being something you're not?"

"You have a knack for saying exactly what I want to hear," said Brandy.

"It happens to be the truth. But I don't know yet what you are, as you don't know what I am. Shall we give ourselves time to find out?"

Brandy let out a breath she didn't know she'd been holding. "Yes," she replied.

Brandy's apartment was small. She served dinner in the living room, and afterward Martin insisted on helping her clear the dishes away. Then they sat on the couch and talked—she could never remember talking so much with a man she was romantically interested in.

Sylvester came in and walked over both of them, meowing until Brandy got up to feed him. Martin picked up the newspaper. As Brandy was filling Sylvester's dish, he said, "There's a story about the robbery today, and the chase."

"How accurate is it?" Brandy asked skeptically.

"You'll have to judge. I wasn't there." Reading further, he asked, "You shot one of the suspects?"

"Mm-hmm. I've been lucky. I've never had to kill anyone."

He closed the paper and looked up at her with a puzzled frown. "Are you saying you *intended* to hit his hand? I thought you were trained to aim at the largest target."

"I had a rifle and a steady prop, and Anderson wasn't more than twenty yards away."

"Brandy. . . ."

She grinned. "You really don't know that about me, do you?"

"Know what?"

Brandy went to the bookcase for two framed items. One was a gold medal on a red-white-and-blue ribbon. The other was a front-page newspaper article with the headline, MURPHY WOMAN GOES FOR THE GOLD.

Martin read the article, then looked up at her, astonishment on his face. "I've never met anyone who even *participated* in the Olympics before."

"It was when I was in college," she explained. "The JPSU rifle team wins the nationals most years. That year I was the best on the team."

"The best in the world," he said in awe. "What was it like?"

"It's so long ago now," she said honestly. "It was strange, frightening, triumphant—and it all went by in such a blur it was over before I knew it."

Martin stood, and carefully replaced the items on the bookcase. "This can't be the only medal you've won."

"Mom has the others," Brandy told him. "There's not room h—" She stopped. "I don't want to sound like I'm bragging. It's just a tiny apartment." And she waited for him to digest the fact that she was the local Annie Oakley, and make the appropriate—or inappropriate—remark.

But instead of some smartass crack about how no man would ever dare to offend *her*, he said, "How wonderful it must be to know that you're the best at something—anything. The very best."

"Well," said Brandy, "when it's a sport there's always someone waiting to take the title."

"You lost it to someone else four years later?"

"Four years later I wasn't eligible, because I was a cop, a pro, by then. I've been in police competitions since the Olympics, which is fine. What's not so fine is having the nuts come after you, as if you were one of the gunslingers in the Old West. I'm not a quick-draw artist. I'm a crack shot with a rifle, that's all."

"That's enough, I should think. I'm sorry if I reopened old wounds."

"No, it's okay," she told him. "Most of the crackpots showed up when I first became a cop, when people still remembered the Olympic medal. It's old news now."

"Not to me. I'm impressed."

She suspected that there wasn't a whole lot in life that impressed him.

The phone rang. "Let the machine pick up," said Brandy.

But she had the kind of machine that allowed her to screen calls. "Brandy, it's Church. Call me when you get in, Kid. It's not news to help you sleep, but I don't want you to hear it on TV."

With an apologetic look at Martin, Brandy snatched up the phone. "I'm here, Church. What's happened?"

"A shooting," he replied. "Damnedest thing. Rand and Paschall took the Andersons to the jail in Paducah—only they never showed up. Their car was just found, run into a ditch on the Kirtney Road. All four occupants are dead, shot in the head."

FOUR

Cop Killer

WHEN COPS WERE MURDERED, no police department would rest until the killer was caught. At the next morning's briefing, Brandy studied photos of the crime scene in disbelief.

The preliminary report confirmed the pictures: no sign of a struggle. The prisoners in back and the policemen in the front seat smiled serenely, appearing pleasantly asleep except for the wounds in their foreheads. Chase Anderson's uninjured left hand was still manacled to his wife's right. The officers' guns were in their holsters.

Each victim had a single entry wound in the forehead; the exit wounds had blown off the backs of their heads.

"The car is being examined this morning," Chief Benton reported. "We assume that the victims were out cold from carbon monoxide or some other agent before they were shot."

"What were they doing on the Kirtney Road?" asked Phillips. "That's no way to go to Paducah."

"We don't know," replied Benton. "We don't know much of anything yet, except that four people were shot at close range without putting up a struggle."

Brandy stared again at the photos. "This is gonna sound strange," she said, "but they're all in exactly the same position, wearing exactly the same expression, as Professor Land was when he died last week."

"Jesus, Mather, will you give it up?" asked the chief. "That case is closed. *This* case is open and ugly as an exit wound. You can find out why they were on the wrong road."

Brandy gritted her teeth. The least important aspect of the investigation—or the least likely to afford results.

Except . . . she got some. Prisoner transport was the result of state legislation which set new requirements for county jails, but provided no funds to help counties comply with them. The old and poorly designed jail in Murphy had first been reduced to a forty-eight-hour holding facility, and then to a twelve-hour one. When prisoners couldn't be bailed out at once, it could require two transports per day. There had been griping about inconvenience, the expense of paying other communities to keep Callahan County prisoners . . . but no one had thought of the potential for ambush.

County sheriff's deputies usually transported prisoners, but yesterday one county car had blown a water pump, just when a late summer grass fire had half the county mounties aiding the Fire and Rescue Squad. When the sheriff asked Chief Benton to have his own people do the transport, there had been no dearth of volunteers for the overtime.

The State Police and the County Sheriff were part of the investigation. Because of the fire, most of the county cars had been far from Murphy, but a few maintained patrol. Both a state trooper and a county mountie had heard a distant, broken radio report of a tractor-trailer accident on the Purchase Parkway, with a toxic spill. In each case the officer, not having heard it clearly, had called for confirmation and been told by his dispatcher that it must not be in their territory. Now it turned out there had been no such accident anywhere on the Purchase Parkway.

A trick to get Rand and Paschall to take a different road? Why that back road? When she got back to the office, she showed Church what she had discovered. "They should've taken 641 on to Draffenville, and I-24 to Paducah."

"Unless they received other orders," said Church, studying the map. "They'd have started up 641. The false report others heard faintly must have been clear to them. It was on the police frequency, but it wasn't picked up in Murphy. What about a weak signal, very close to them?"

"The state and county cars were north and west of Murphy. The fake report must have come from a transmitter somewhere north of town. There are people with police scanners out there. Let's find out what they heard."

By the simple expedient of broadcasting a message asking who had heard the fake accident report, they had five responses in ten minutes, including one from Judge L. J. Callahan, whose home was in that area. Everyone had pretty much the same thing to say: the report had warned of toxic fumes, telling everyone to stay off both the Purchase Parkway and 641 near the Parkway entrance.

"So that's it," said Brandy as they took the last identical report. "Rand and Paschall must have been traveling north on 641, heard that report, and decided to go around the obstruction via Mayfield."

"And 1899 over to the Kirtney Road to intersect with 121 would be a shortcut," said Church. "A complicated ambush. Whoever set it up had to know where Car 108 was, and where the other city cars were, to make sure only Rand and Paschall would receive the message."

"The scanners that picked up the fake message were near north 641. If we can find the transmitter—"

But that they found no sign of. A search for witnesses, for tire tracks, for any clue to the perpetrators' identity, proved fruitless.

The forensic report on Car 108 showed why Rand and Paschall hadn't reported their change in route. The radio had been sabotaged: it received just fine, but transmission was squelched down to the lowest range. The officers probably did report, but were not heard.

Thus Brandy, given what had appeared to be the least productive assignment in the case, had the most productive day. Possibly the killer or killers simply followed Car 108 out of Murphy, broadcast the fake message at the point where it was logical for Rand and Paschall to take the shortcut to the Mayfield road, then ambushed them.

But "how" the car was diverted to the deserted road did not explain "why" its occupants stopped and made no effort to escape, or to fight off their assailants.

Dr. Sanford found no indication of carbon monoxide or other poison. The police car yielded evidence only of tampering with the radio, and, it turned out, the air-conditioner. Most of the refrigerant had been bled out. The air would have appeared to work, but after a few miles it would have stopped cooling. The victims must have opened the windows, allowing the killers access.

Without the shotgun shells there was no identifying the murder weapon. The murderer could have picked them up, or the weapon could have been equipped with the "brass-catchers" used by hunters who saved their cartridges for reloading.

When there was no further progress, Judge Callahan showed up at the station. Chief Benton gathered everyone on duty to hear what he had to say.

"I'm a witness in this case, so I can't preside when it comes to trial. *If* it comes to trial. That can't happen until we find the killers. Let me offer any help I can."

"Why?" Brandy asked suspiciously, then immediately wondered if it was wise to call attention to herself.

"Call it a guilty conscience," Callahan replied. "I run that scanner all the time. I heard the accident report . . . but I never listened for follow-up. If I'd've paid attention, if I'd called the police to ask why we weren't warning people to avoid north 641, the investigation would've begun earlier. It might have made a difference."

"I don't think so," said Chief Benton. "The false police reports would have stopped as soon as the victims turned off the highway. We appreciate your help, Judge, but whoever planned this crime was a pro."

"They're probably long gone," said Church. "Where you could help us, Judge Callahan, is in finding out who thought it was so important to get rid of the Andersons that it was worth killing two police officers along with them."

"That's right," added Brandy. "Somebody didn't want the Andersons to go to trial—perhaps somebody they might have given up in a plea bargain?"

Callahan gave her a hard look. "Interesting theory, Detective. I thought the Andersons were freelancers."

"So did we," said Benton. "But think about it, Your Honor. Their victims' families were frustrated about the police not catching them, but once they were caught, they'd have no reason to take the law into their own hands."

"That leaves associates who didn't want them talking," Brandy said triumphantly.

Callahan nodded. "You've got the Andersons' records, of course. I'll call some of my colleagues in Tennessee and Illinois, see if they can shed light on the subject."

But Brandy didn't expect Callahan to be any help, and he wasn't. Church had long suspected, from the pattern of his decisions, that the judge was on the payroll of organized crime, and since his invitation to the ball she found it harder to dismiss her partner's suspicions. The judge's visit only added to them: he now knew exactly what leads the police were following.

The Car 108 trail went cold. The crime lab verified what their own team had found: no chemicals in any of the bodies, and no sign of tampering with the car except for the radio and air-conditioner. They were at a dead end.

And two cops were dead.

Rand and Paschall were not likely the intended victims, as no one knew until hours before the murders that they would get the transport assignment. Nevertheless, the department traced everyone Rand and Paschall had arrested, and anyone else who might have wanted revenge for a loved one's death or incarceration.

There were *too many* possibilities. The perpetrators might not even have cared who was in that police car. Church had seen such power plays up north, cop killings to demonstrate the power of crimelords, frighten the police, and cause citizens to lose faith in them.

But Chief Benton said, "If we accept that theory, then all we can do is wait for another strike. That's not acceptable. Two of our own are dead — and we're not going to rest until we find the killers."

Doc Sanford came to talk to Brandy. "Remember that death you investigated on the university campus?" he asked.

"You saw it too. That same expression on their faces."

"There's something else the same."

"What?" asked Brandy.

"No rigor," Sanford replied. "In both cases the bodies were found within four hours, before rigor mortis usually sets in. But it never occurred in Professor Land, or either of the Andersons. It did occur in both police officers."

"Can you explain that?" asked Brandy.

"No. When I begun work on the Andersons, we thought they mighta been rendered unconscious by carbon monoxide. Delay of onset of rigor is consistent — but the red coloration of tissues was absent. Blood will tell. Toxicology confirmed that carbon monoxide wasn't the cause."

"So why didn't these four bodies exhibit rigor mortis?" Brandy wanted to know.

"That's what's so damn peculiar. Dr. Sendis autopsied the police officers, and observed the onset of rigor right on schedule. Neither of us can explain the discrepancy."

Brandy thought back to forensic pathology class. "Rigor mortis is caused by some enzyme . . ." she recalled.

"By the *depletion* of ATP," Dr. Sanford corrected, "the chemical necessary for muscle contraction. It dissipates after death, causing stiffening which remains until the muscles begin to decompose."

"Are you saying the bodies of Professor Land and the Andersons suffered premature decomposition?" asked Brandy.

"No, I ain't saying that. It could be a theory, but I wouldn't know how to test it, 'less we knew the time of death of a new body, and suspected that it had suffered . . . whatever made these people meet death without resistance. If we froze tissue samples every half-hour, we could study the rate of decomposition."

"Well," said Brandy, "I hope you won't get the chance to perform the experiment."

"There's one more funny thing," said Dr. Sanford. "Y'know, an autopsy don't routinely include the extremities."

"But Chase Anderson had that gunshot wound to his hand. You're very thorough, Doc. What did you find?"

"It makes no sense, but you can look for yourself. The man was shot in the late morning. The slug went through the hand, fracturing two metacarpals. The hand was set and bandaged just hours before his death. But when I examined his hand last night, that wound looked several days old. The bones were beginning to knit."

"How is that possible?"

"I don't know," replied Sanford, "unless the orthopedic team ain't told us they got one of them speed-healing gadgets they use on *Star Trek*."

"Have you told this to anyone else?" asked Brandy.

"It's in my report," the coroner replied. "I'm just pointing it out 'cause you worked on that other case. I still got blood samples from Professor Land. I'll culture them, and the ones from the Andersons, for any odd microorganisms. There's gotta be a connection. I been a doctor too long to accept 'coincidence' when I get the same weird symptom three times in a week."

Brandy and Dr. Sanford were not the only ones to link the deaths of Everett Land with the Car 108 murders. Local newspaper and television reporters speculated about the rash of deaths in Murphy, Kentucky. While serious journalists had too much integrity to suggest curses and Satanism, plenty of other people didn't. As details of the parked car and the lack of resistance got around, there was soon gossip that someone had put a spell on them.

Carrie Wyman managed to find time for a quick lunch with Brandy. Her clients were abuzz with the rumors, some terrified that someone was trying to put a spell on them.

When one of her neighbors asked Brandy if the police were looking for a witches' coven, Brandy gritted her teeth and replied politely, "If a coven of witches had such power, they wouldn't have to lure their victims to a back road and shoot them. They could just let them take the highway to Paducah, and put the driver to sleep on that high entry ramp to the Parkway. The car would run off the ramp, everyone would be killed, and it would look like an accident."

The woman was clearly impressed with Brandy's logic—so much so that she discussed the conversation, or her version of it, with her friends. Before the police memorial service on Friday, Chief Benton came to the detectives' office. "Mather!" he demanded, "what is this shit about you telling people we're blaming auto accidents on witchcraft?"

Brandy had completely forgotten the conversation, only recalling as Benton continued, "I've had two calls this morning from relatives of victims of one-car accidents, wanting me to reopen the cases. Claiming 'one of our female detectives' said witches made the drivers fall asleep!"

"All I said was that if witches had such powers they wouldn't have to use guns."

"Oh, Jeez. Don't you know better than to feed these yahoos' imaginations? I got enough aggravation!" He moved into the hall to include everyone in the squad room in his tirade. "Meanwhile, we got nothin'! Two cops dead, and no suspects!"

Benton's face was so red that Brandy actually feared he might suffer a stroke. He was in uniform for the upcoming memorial service . . . and had obviously gained a few pounds since he'd last worn it. Despite the dressing down, Brandy felt sympathy: it was a service, not a funeral, and he was the one who had to explain to the grieving families why the bodies could not yet be released.

But it was the frustration of the case, leading only to dead ends, that was most on Benton's mind. "We don't even know if the murderer was after Rand and Paschall, and incidentally killed the Andersons, or after the Andersons, and," he choked over the idea, "incidentally killed the officers." He slumped, as depressed as the rest of them. "Get yer damn asses to work. See if we can protect the public, even if we can't protect our own."

They were short two police cars now. 108 was impounded as evidence, and it was doubtful anyone would willingly ride in it again. Its whereabouts on the day of the murder had been traced, from its designation at 1:50 P.M. as the transport vehicle to pickup by Rand and Paschall at 6:14 P.M.. It had stood unattended in the parking lot from the time that Paschall had gassed it up at about 2:30. Although people had been in and out of the lot all afternoon, no one had seen a thing.

By Friday afternoon everyone was exhausted, and the memorial service only increased the emotional burden. When they got back to the station, Chief Benton had a new announcement: the unlimited overtime order was rescinded on the Car 108 case. Budget restrictions again.

Still, there was some relief: their lives could return to what passed for normal. Brandy would have Saturday off, but this week she had Sunday duty.

By the time the memorial service was over Brandy was wrung out. She wanted to find the murderers, but she was too wired to think straight. She felt sweaty and her hair was squashed from wearing her hat in the heat. She poked fitfully at annoying strands straggling down her neck, trying to stick them back in the twist she had started with.

What she really needed was a good night's sleep, something she had missed for three nights running. Perhaps in the morning she would be able to look at this frustrating case with fresh eyes.

As she cleared her desk, Dan Martin entered the office. Oh, terrific — the folks up front were now treating him as her significant other, no longer calling her to reception.

He had left two messages on her answering machine during the week, but she had gotten home late every night since their evening together had been interrupted . . . was it only on Tuesday? . . . and hadn't wanted to make plans. She had even felt a slight annoyance that sometime during the evening he had spent at her apartment he had copied her home number from the phone.

Dan was the last person she wanted to see tonight.

Until he was in the room, and his peculiar magnetism began to operate.

"You've had a rough week, Brandy," he said. "You look exhausted."

"Gee, thanks," she told him. "You don't look so hot yourself."

His low chuckle made the moment intimate. "Let me take you home," he said, adding quietly, "make you some dinner, rub your feet."

"I'll fall asleep," she warned.

"That's exactly what you need. Come on."

Bemused, she let him drive her home in her car. Once there, he shoved her gently toward the hall. "Go get out of that hot uniform. It's giving me high blood pressure just to look at you."

Instead of the long soak her tired body wanted, she showered to try to perk herself up a bit, looked in the mirror, and decided "clean" was the best she could manage. Combing the tangles out of her wet hair, she exchanged her bathrobe for jeans and a loose shirt. When she joined Dan in the kitchen, he was setting two places, Sylvester observing and commenting from a seat on the counter.

"Something smells wonderful," Brandy observed as she scratched her cat under the chin. "What in the world did you find to cook?"

He had concocted a casserole out of instant rice, cheese, and frozen broccoli with some bacon strips on top, and a salad from what little crisp part was left of the lettuce, along with leftover carrots. Now he pulled her "lite" French dressing from the refrigerator door, eyed it doubtfully, and put it back, going instead to the spice rack. As Brandy watched, he located vinegar, olive oil, and a cruet, and concocted his own salad dressing. "It would be better with fresh herbs," he said, "but this is still better than that artificial stuff."

Another good smell made itself known, and from the oven Dan produced a pan of buttermilk biscuits. He must have found those on the refrigerator door. As they looked and smelled perfectly fine, Brandy didn't ask if he had checked the expiration date.

The food was amazingly good . . . or maybe it was the company. It revived Brandy, and she realized she wasn't going to be able to relax easily. Dan was spinning stories of his students—amusing stories when she could focus on them, but her mind couldn't let go of the Car 108 case. It didn't take Dan long to realize that she was not giving him appropriate responses.

When they finished eating, he said, "Go lie down on the couch while I do the dishes."

"Men aren't supposed to act like that," Brandy observed.

"Oh? How are men supposed to act?"

"Nice, when they want something. I've known men who can cook before, too, but the only men I know who do dishes are married or gay."

"What—you've never met a straight man who lives alone?"

Brandy wanted to answer, "Of course I have!" but had to stop and think. Single men in Western Kentucky tended to live at home, maybe staying in the college dorm or an apartment with some other guys till they tired of the frathouse lifestyle. Then it was back to Mom's home cooking and laundry until they got a wife to take care of them.

So she said, "I didn't say *met*. How would I know the lifestyle of every man I've ever met? I said men I *know*, well enough to have been in their home or had them in mine. And I was wrong. All men wash dishes when there are no clean ones available; they don't usually do what you're doing, wash up one meal's worth and leave the kitchen clean. The men I know who do that are married, gay, or *divorced*."

So quietly she almost didn't hear him over the sound of water filling the kitchen sink, Dan added, "Or widowed."

"Oh," Brandy said, caught flat-footed. "Oh, I'm sorry."

He looked up, blinked, and said quickly, "I didn't mean me. I haven't been married . . . in this life."

Brandy's instincts picked up something in the way he said that. She couldn't quite tell if he was lying . . . yet it didn't make sense to lie about something like that. All that mattered if their relationship were to go anywhere was that he wasn't married *now*.

"I'm not," he answered her thought again. "And yes, I hope our relationship goes somewhere."

"After this week?" Brandy asked. "Most men would have given up on me by now."

"Because you've had to cope with an emergency? Police officers don't get murdered every day, at least in this part of the world." He rolled his sleeves up and began washing dishes with the skill of long practice. When Brandy reached for the dish towel he said, "You're supposed to be resting. Besides, it's more sanitary to let them dry in the rack."

Somebody had domesticated this man. That wistful note of sadness in his voice when he had said, "Or widowed," had to mean something . . . perhaps a tragic love affair? But she could not ask, not yet. When she got to know him better . . . *if* she got to know him better.

When he had finished the dishes and dried his hands, Dan turned to Brandy. "Shall I carry you to the couch?"

"I have to warn you," she replied, "I know karate."

"And you also carry a gun. I love dangerous women." He took her hand and led her into the living room area. Brandy did not resist when he sat at one end of the couch and drew her comfortably against him. "The offer of a foot rub is still open."

"Sorry," she replied. "I don't do feet."

"You've got it backwards."

"No, I haven't. I don't accept what I don't want to return."

"Okay," he agreed easily, "I'll rub your head." He put a throw pillow on his lap and drew Brandy down, gently rubbing the tenseness out of her scalp. It was only too easy to succumb to the delicious sensations.

At some point Brandy experienced the guilty thought that she had forgotten all about the Car 108 case.

Then she was asleep.

Brandy opened her eyes to the sight of a woman, half lying, half sitting, hands folded in her lap, face wearing a serene smile. It took her a moment to recognize her reflection in the mirror that faced her bed.

It was morning. She was in her own bed, still in the jeans and blue shirt from last night. Dan must have put her to bed, but she didn't remember. He had not removed the decorative pillows, but just laid her against them, covering her with the blanket that had been folded at the foot of the bed. She did not normally waken to the sight of herself in the mirror.

But as she lay gathering her wits, Brandy suddenly realized why that reflection was so familiar. Her image lost its serenity as she recognized the position and the facial expression, identical to those of Professor Everett Land, and the four victims of Car 108.

FIVE

Day Off

SYLVESTER, WHO HAD BEEN ASLEEP at the foot of the bed, scolded Brandy for disturbing him. Funny he hadn't wakened her, she thought until she looked at the clock: 6:18 A.M.

It couldn't have been much after 9:00 P.M. when she had fallen asleep. She shook off the disturbing image in the mirror. It didn't mean anything . . . unless her subconscious was trying to send her a message. Something to do with the frustrating Car 108 case, obviously. But what?

On the kitchen counter was a note:

> Call me when you wake up. Perhaps we can go somewhere tomorrow where you can't be reached on your day off. D.

And that gave her the connection. She fed Sylvester, ate some cereal, dressed, and coerced her unset hair into a French braid. The stitches in her forehead would be removed Monday. If they had been anywhere but on her face she would have left them uncovered, but they were just too Bride of Frankensteinish, so she covered them with another flesh-tone band-aid. Finally, at 8:00 A.M., she allowed herself to dial Dan Martin's number.

He didn't sound as if she woke him. After the usual pleasantries, he asked, "What would you like to do today?"

"Dan, what happened to Everett Land's computer?"

"What?"

"Dr. Land's computer. After the police decided it wasn't evidence in a crime. Where is it now?"

"I have it," he replied.

"*You* have it?"

"It belongs to the university, so it came back to my department to be assigned to somebody else."

"Have you done that yet?"

"No. Brandy, what is this about?"

"Were there any more messages? What about Land's correspondents? Anything connected to his identity change? Any remote connection to Chase or Jenny Anderson?"

"Brandy, are you saying you want to spend your day off—my day off, too, I might add—with Rett's computer?"

"Aren't *you* curious? How can you stand to leave him appearing out of nowhere in Oxford, Mississippi? Please—help me with the computer this morning and then we'll go out to the lake this afternoon, for swimming and a picnic."

There was a moment's silence. Then he said, "A trip to the lake will reveal one of my weaknesses."

"What—you've *got* weaknesses? How refreshing. Want me to meet you at your office?"

"Yes, since I have to walk. I left my car at the police station last night. See you in about half an hour."

Dan met Brandy at the door to Callahan Hall. Today he wore jeans and a loose shirt, baseball cap and sunglasses.

He took her into his office, saying, "We don't need to set up Rett's computer just to read his mail, or responses that came to my ID. I haven't deleted anything from his hard disk, though, so if there's something on that—"

"Not today," she said, "but please warn me before you delete anything, just in case."

"For now that computer's a spare. The university shunted Rett's students into other courses and sections. He won't be replaced until next semester. His computer will only be needed if someone else's breaks down."

"Okay. Let's see what's in the mail."

Dan turned on his monitor and with a few keystrokes entered the mail facility. There were several replies to the messages Brandy had sent last week, all saying they were sorry to hear about Land's death but offering no clues to the man's mysterious past.

There was another cryptic chess move: "Pawn to King's Knight four."

"Is that from the same person as the first one?" Brandy asked.

Dan compared ID's. "No. He must have had two games going. Funny—Rett wasn't in the campus chess club. If he was enough of a chess fanatic to play by mail, why would he ignore local sources of a game?"

"Two possibilities," said Brandy. "One is that these are not chess moves, but code for something else entirely."

"That's a nice mysterious theory. What's the other?"

"A clue to Everett Land's former identity."

"How do you figure that?"

"Something Church once told me, from his work in Chicago's Organized Crime Division. When criminals take on new identities, it's not names or dates or jobs that make it possible to find them. It's hobbies."

"Really?"

"One mob boss who disappeared to the Bahamas was an avid coin collector. They advertised some coin that would fill in a gap in his collection, and followed the purchaser straight to the man. Another time it was someone who liked a very specific kind of pornography. He was so dumb he sent in a change-of-address form to some skin magazine!"

"So dumb or so obsessed," Dan said. "This is absolutely fascinating, Brandy."

"We can trace backwards as well as forwards," said Brandy. "Dr. Land was good enough at chess to play by mail, yet he didn't play locally. Another chess-playing college professor wouldn't stand out much, would he?"

"No. Probably fifteen to twenty-five percent of any university's faculty play."

"What would be the most likely reason for Dr. Land not to join the university chess club?"

"Ordinarily I'd say he didn't feel qualified. But given his play by mail, perhaps he didn't want to call attention to himself. If he had excelled he'd have been pushed into tournaments."

"He wasn't afraid to appear at academic conferences," said Brandy. "Probably something he didn't do in his former life. He earned his Ph.D. after he became Everett Land. If he stopped playing chess when he changed his identity, it could be because he'd be recognized in chess circles. Dan—what if that money he had was won in chess tournaments?"

He was staring at her. "You're amazing."

"I'm speculating," she corrected, "but I have to check it out. Let's go to the library."

The university library was the largest in West Kentucky. The budget constraints of recent years did not affect its older holdings, so it didn't take long for Dan and Brandy to locate *Chess Review* for the 1960's.

There were photos of regional, national, and world champions, including one Marvin Clement of Monsey, New York, Northeast Regional Champion for 1966 and 1967, U.S. Champion for 1968, and semi-finalist in the World Championship for 1969. And after that year he disappeared from the records.

"What an incredibly cautious man," said Dan. "He must have set himself a specific amount, and when he reached it, he changed identities." For the face in the photos was that of the man Jackson Purchase State University had known as Everett C. Land.

"It would be hard to come that close to being world champion, and not go for it," said Brandy. "He appears to be what, late thirties or early forties in these photos?"

"It's the haircut and conservative clothes," said Dan. "If he were wearing a headband and love beads, he'd look twenty-something."

"Mmmm," Brandy equivocated. The photos were neither large nor clear. "Blowing up screened prints will enlarge the dots, not give us details. If he was in his thirties or forties in 1969, he'd have been in his sixties or seventies when he died. Yet he was passing for forty-something *now*." She looked up at Dan. "This is truly weird."

"But not criminal. If the man won his nest egg playing chess, there's no international conspiracy of atomic spies or jewel thieves. You've solved your case."

"It ain't over till it's over," Brandy muttered, feeding dimes into the copy machine to make sure the evidence could not conveniently disappear. But Dan was right: there was still no evidence that either Land or his alter ego, Marvin Clement, had committed a crime.

So *why* had he changed his identity?

And why had he not aged for thirty years, and then grown old and died in a few hours?

Brandy's stomach growled, and she looked at her watch. 11:54am. Remembering her promise to Dan, she put the photocopies into the backpack she had brought instead of a purse for today's outing. "Okay— let's go get your swimming trunks, and stop at Kroger's for picnic stuff. I promise: no more detective work today."

"You really want to go swimming?"

"This could be the last hot weekend of the year."

He gave in. "Okay, but I have to stop at a drugstore for sunscreen. I've got a sun allergy, Brandy. Too many direct rays and I get a rash that would put Job to shame."

"So that's your big secret," she said. "I thought you couldn't swim. Get some SPF 30. I'll rub it on your back."

Brandy drove Dan to his car, and went to purchase food. Then she drove to his apartment for the first time. "Come on in if you like," he said as he opened the door.

He had a small, well-worn backpack open on the couch, obviously about to put into it the towel, swim trunks, and sunscreen laid out on the cushions.

"Haven't you been out to the lake?" asked Brandy. "There aren't any cabanas. We wear our suits under our clothes. If we're too wet when it's time to go home, we can go up to the lodge and change clothes in the restrooms."

"Okay," he said. "I'll just be a minute." That gave Brandy the chance to look around.

Dan lived in one of the newer apartment complexes north of town. Brandy was astonished at how much more spacious his living room was than hers, until she realized that the illusion was created by a mirror-lined wall.

The apartment was a plain beige box, a rectangle divided into four smaller ones. The first was the living room, and beyond that the kitchen, sharing plumbing with the small bath at one end. Behind the kitchen was the bedroom—an economical plan used for at least half the apartments in Murphy, as it neatly fit the entire living quarters for one or two people into a fifteen- by thirty-two-foot area.

Dan had personalized it with plants, soft green drapes, and bright Oriental throw rugs over the wall-to-wall carpeting. His bookshelves were massed with books, one layer standing straight, another stacked atop them. A low shelving unit under the window was laden with videotapes and game cartridges. In front of it stood a television on a rolling cart complete with VCR, Playstation, and other electronic components.

Near the bookshelves, a small desk held a closed laptop computer, more books, a stack of folded printouts with a post-it note saying "CSC 243," and a green gradebook.

Brandy turned from that end of the room, and faced a display on the opposite wall, which had been to her left when she entered. Everything else in the room was new and modern; this piece had the look of great age.

It was a stone crucifix, a good three feet high, mounted against a deep red mat. The figure was broken in some places, worn and weathered in others, but the power of suffering shone in the distorted position of the limbs, the tortured eyes whose detail peered from beneath the shelter of weathered brows.

Although she had no particularly Christian feelings, the emblem made Brandy stop to stare even though it made her uncomfortable. Dan emerged from the kitchen. "I see you've discovered my contraband Christ."

"Contraband?"

"It's from a bombed-out cathedral in what used to be East Germany. When I was in college, I was part of a team excavating the cathedral— we were only supposed to take photographs. Then the professor learned that we were being used to locate forbidden religious objects, which were to be destroyed."

"So you managed to save this one piece, Indiana Jones?" she asked.

"We saved more than one. I suspect the customs officials didn't like their cultural heritage being destroyed any more than we did. We gave away our clothes to the German friends we'd made, and loaded our luggage with what we could carry. We had to leave most of it behind as it was. This was the heaviest object we managed to get out—and as you can see, it was in pieces."

In some places iron bands held pieces of stone together, while in others there were wide gaps.

Dan continued, "Professor Everholt packed part of it in his luggage, and I took the rest. We pieced it together, and it was displayed in the department office until Professor Everholt retired. He left it to me in his will."

"Well, now I know how you came to be fluent in German," said Brandy.

He chuckled. "I've never met anyone whose mind works like yours, Brandy. Everything's a clue to a puzzle."

"Isn't that what life is?" asked Brandy. "A puzzle for us to solve?"

"A whole series of puzzles," he agreed. "Solving one just leads to another one, usually even more confusing."

"More challenging," she amended. "What's life without a challenge?"

The story he had told her, which entailed a truly foolish risk of life and liberty for the sake of a few lifeless objects, made her rethink her assessment of Danton Martin . . . again. And at the lake, when he took off his shirt and jeans, she was forced to rethink again.

The man was beautiful.

Brandy had only seen him fully dressed, and now that she knew about his sun allergy she understood why he always wore long sleeves. In his professor's clothes he looked nice, attractive, even handsome in a conservative way. But when he stripped down to his bathing suit she saw for the first time the power in his compact body.

Broad shoulders, flat belly, narrow hips, neat round buns, and nice long, firm legs. Although the hair on his head was thick and black, he had only a modest amount on his chest, none on his back or shoulders.

Immediately, he opened the tube of sunblock and began slathering it on every exposed square inch, saying, "Sorry—this must be done. It's embarrassing, but at least since they invented this stuff I *can* go out in the sun. It wasn't much fun in college when my choices were not to go to the beach, or to be all covered up in long sleeves and a hat."

"How'd you survive in Florida?" Brandy asked.

"Night classes." He handed her the tube. "You promised to put it on my back." And he stretched out on his towel.

She looked at the label on the tube. It was SPF 30, and guaranteed waterproof. There was a small note that it was used by the U.S. Olympic Team, chosen to protect athletes who exposed their skin to grueling summer sun.

Brandy routinely wore makeup containing sunscreen, a modern woman's weapon against premature aging, but she didn't bother with the rest of her body unless she would be exposed for the entire day. She tanned easily, and this late in the year needed no protection for a couple of hours.

She was perfectly content to baste Dan, though. He was not only gorgeous to look at, he was pleasant to touch, his skin smooth and soft over hard muscles. She lifted his sunglasses to put sunscreen behind his ears and all along his hairline, then let her hands rove down across his broad back. There was something odd —

No blemishes. No pimples, blackheads, scars, or even rough areas marred his perfect skin. Would everyone's skin be this smooth if they kept it hidden from the sun?

But if he always kept his skin covered by clothing or sunscreen . . . "Why aren't you pale?" she asked.

"Mmpf?" He sounded half asleep.

"If you're always covered up, how did your skin get to be such a nice golden color?"

He lifted his head to look at her over one shoulder. "You promised no more detective work today."

She couldn't resist giving him a light slap on one buttock. "Just answer the question."

"Police brutality!" he protested.

"Answer the question or I won't put any sunscreen right on the place nobody can reach by themselves."

"Okay, okay, I give in. I'm a typical American mongrel with ancestors from lots of different places. My coloring might come from Spanish or Italian ancestors, or maybe from the Apache brave who kidnapped and married my great-great-grandmother."

"You're making that up!"

He grinned, an expression she had never seen before. "You'll never know, will you?" he teased. "That's family oral history you won't find in the library or the computer. Now if you'll just finish your job before I start to go up in smoke, we can have lunch." And he put the broad-brimmed straw hat he had brought over his head, hiding even the side of his face as he pillowed it once more on his folded arms.

"Let's swim first," said Brandy, feeling embarrassed as she realized she had been treating Dan like a suspect.

The beach was not sand, but smooth stones. They wore their shoes to the water's edge, kicking them off to enter the lake. Eyes followed them, for the beach was crowded with high school and college kids. Brandy knew they made a striking couple—they could have been models in a magazine ad. No one called out Dan's name today, but that could be simple shock to any of his students discovering what was usually kept concealed beneath his modest clothing.

Brandy swam strongly, stretching her body, letting the hard work raise her heart rate. She hadn't found time for the gym this past week. It felt good to test her limits.

She had always been athletic. Her wind was better than any man's she had ever swum with . . . until Dan Martin. He kept up stroke for stroke, not even laboring for breath when Brandy tired enough to tread water. She grinned at him, panting through her teeth in sheer exhilaration.

When they had caught their breath, she said, "I didn't know you were in such good condition. Most of the men I meet think golf is hard exercise!"

"I knew you were," he replied. "You are beautiful, Brandy." And he kissed her.

They were out farther than any of the other swimmers, so if there were some of Dan's students here today they wouldn't be able to see their professor twine his body with Brandy's.

Distracted from paddling, they went under for the duration of the kiss. As before, it was intoxicating—Brandy almost forgot to breathe when they surfaced. After a moment to reoxygenate, Dan kissed her again.

Brandy's bathing suit was as skimpy as West Kentucky mores permitted—modest by California standards, perhaps, but she was skin to skin with Dan for most of the length of her body. Where they touched, their water-cooled skin became warm again, as did Dan's hands and arms against her back. Only her back. He neither groped downward, nor tried to bring a hand between them to touch her breasts.

She wanted him to, wanted an excuse to mold her hands around the perfect buttocks she had only dared to slap playfully earlier. She wanted to touch this man all over, to make love with him . . . but the perfect courtesy that informed his obvious interest made it impossible for her to initiate such a move.

They resurfaced to breathe. Treading water, they gulped air until Dan said, "I think we'd better swim back before we get in too deep."

"It's not too deep," said Brandy, not meaning the lake.

But Dan was already swimming steadily toward the beach. By the time they returned to their picnic spot, Brandy had cooled off enough to wonder why Dan was so reluctant to follow through on feelings she had no doubt matched hers.

A tragic love affair in his past? Someone he had loved had died, she was sure. Was it any wonder he was reluctant to get involved with a woman who lived in the line of fire?

They didn't stay in the sun for long. Brandy was ready to go home, hoping to continue in privacy what had started in the lake, but Dan said, "You brought me all the way out here. Let's see some of the natural beauty of the area."

So they pulled on their jeans and drove to one of the shady nature trails winding through the Land Between the Lakes. Then they walked, hand in hand once Dan turned to give Brandy unnecessary help over a steep rise and didn't let go.

Brown leaves were falling, but there were no bright colors because there had been no frost. Summer's greens had darkened, and the only spots of color were the yellow of daisies, dandelions, and goldenrod. Thank goodness neither of them suffered from hay fever.

The woods were full of the laughter of people taking advantage of these last warm days. A turn in the path took them into a secluded area, where Dan pulled Brandy to him for another kiss. When they broke apart, she said, "Come on—let's get back to town!"

Crunching of leaves, and a big young dog, trailing a leash, came barreling down the trail past them, barking joyfully. Both Brandy and Dan instinctively made a grab for the leash, but only managed to get in each other's way. The animal slipped between them and galloped on.

"That looks like—" Brandy began, when two children scrambled down the hill, calling, "Sandy! Here, boy!"

From behind them a woman's voice called, "Tiffany! Jeff! Watch where you're going!" Brandy's fellow detective and his family were also enjoying a day away from the city.

Brandy also called out, "Hey—Tiffany, Jeff, slow down! We'll help you catch Sandy!"

But the children paid no heed.

The light filtering through the trees turned yellow with hints of orange as the sun dropped toward the horizon.

"It'll be dark soon," said Brandy. "Those are the Jones kids. Church and Coreen will be worried sick if they get lost."

"We've been circling," said Dan. "The lodge is ahead of us now. The kids will get there before we do."

"A Boy Scout, too!"

"Actually, no. Like Captain Kirk, one thing I have never been is a Boy Scout."

"But you are a Trekkie."

"Do you know anyone involved with computers who isn't?"

Church and Coreen Jones came panting up the rise. "Brandy!" exclaimed Coreen. "Hon, have you seen our kids?"

"They're okay," said Brandy. "This trail leads to the lodge."

"I'm gonna kill that damn dog!" Church said, although Brandy knew it was all bluster.

"He's just being a dog, Church," Coreen soothed. "How often does he get to run like that?"

"I told the kids to hold on to him!" Brandy's colleague grumbled. "If he gets out on the highway—"

Shadows fell through the woods. The two couples moved after the children as quickly as possible, but the trail was steep, the path eroded by summer rains. They were picking their way across a dry stream bed when there was the sharp yelping of a badly frightened dog in the distance.

"Oh, God!" said Coreen, "if Sandy's hit by a car—"

"They're not that far away," said Dan.

His words were cut off by a child's scream, followed by, "Mamma! Daddy!" on a rising note of panic.

"Please, God, protect my babies!" Coreen gasped, and hastened her pace despite the rough terrain.

"We're coming!" Church shouted, scrambling up the bank.

The last orange rays of sunlight dappled the trail, making it hard to see their footing. They could hear the sobbing wail of a frightened child.

The trail made a sharp turn at the top of a steep hill. A rail fence protected hikers, but by the time Brandy and Dan got there Church and Coreen were looking down over the fence, Church obviously about to climb over it.

"What happened?" Brandy asked.

"It's Jeff!" Coreen gasped, pointing.

Both children were below their parents, on a rocky outcropping. Tiffany knelt, crying, beside her younger brother. Jeff lay frighteningly still.

It was easy to guess what had happened. Chasing their dog, the children had gone under the fence to a ledge immediately below. Pieces of hard Kentucky clay showed how the dry earth crumbled, toppling them onto the rocks below.

Tiffany, who showed only some scratches, looked up and sobbed, "I killed him! The monster jumped at me and I fell on Jeff and killed him!"

It was no monster, but a boulder their fall had dislodged, now lying a few feet away from the children. Had it hit Jeff, knocked him out?

For a moment, memories of her little brother lying dead in the street kept Brandy from moving.

Church skinned under the fence and lowered himself to the first ledge, keeping his feet against the wall of earth.

"Let me help," said Dan, as Brandy came out of her trance and held Coreen back from climbing down after them.

"It seems steady," Church said, reaching a hand up to Dan. "Try not to land on the edge."

"Coreen, stay here," Brandy insisted. "I'll go down and help. You stop people coming by, see if anyone has a rope—and send someone to the lodge for help!"

"He's alive!" Church reported, and Brandy felt Coreen go limp with relief.

"Go ahead," said Coreen.

Brandy slid down as Dan had, and wormed her way over the side to the outcropping. Tiffany was still sobbing, but Brandy soon saw that Jeff was breathing.

And, thank goodness, he was coming around. "Don't move," his father warned him. "You'll be all right, Son. We'll get you out of here, okay?"

With relief Brandy saw Jeff's eyes focus on his father as he whispered, "Did you shoot the monster, Daddy?"

"He's awake!" Church reported to Coreen, then, "I'm here, Jeff. No monster can hurt you while Daddy's here."

Crunching leaves announced the return of Sandy, who sniffed at his fallen master and began to whimper.

At the sound of voices above, Brandy saw that Coreen had been joined by two girls in JPSU tee shirts. "My son's been hurt," she was telling them. "Please go to the lodge and get help. Tell them to bring emergency equipment."

"Right away!" said the girls, and ran on up the trail.

Brandy turned back to Jeff, who was trying to sit up. "Don't," she said, remembering her first aid training. "Does your head hurt?"

"No," he replied. "I'm okay," and he tried to push her away, crying out sharply in surprise. "My leg!" he gasped.

He had been lying on his left side. Now, despite Church's efforts to hold him still, he turned so that his left leg came into view. It was jammed into a crack in the rock in a way that could only have happened if that boulder had struck it. With the dim light and the boy's dark skin, Brandy couldn't tell how badly the leg was injured.

"Lie still!" Brandy insisted, as Church wrapped his arms around the child. "Your leg may be broken, Jeff, but that's nothing to be afraid of. Don't move. Dan, take his shoe and sock off in case of swelling."

Coreen's face above was hard to see in the gathering twilight. Night was falling fast. How long would that rescue team take?

A man came along the trail, asking, "What's happened?"

"We've got a boy fallen from the ledge," Brandy replied. "We've sent for help."

The man dug into his backpack, coming up with a flashlight. Dan scrambled up for it, saying, "Thank you! This will help."

He returned to them, shining the light on the injured boy. What it revealed was not reassuring: Jeff's leg was starting to swell, his ankle twisted at an impossible angle. Dan handed the light to Brandy, saying to the little girl, "Tiffany, why don't you let me lift you up to your Mamma?"

"Who're you?" Tiffany asked, staring doubtfully at Dan.

"He's a friend of Brandy's," said her father. "Let him lift you up to Mamma, Honey."

Brandy started to help Dan, but he said, "I've got her," and picked up the little girl with ease, lifting her over his head to her mother's eager arms. The dog, Sandy, scrambled up after her.

Jeff was starting to assimilate what had happened to him. Sweat broke out on his skin as fear took over. Brandy tried to reassure him, "You're going to be fine. The rescue team will lift you out, and then they'll take you to the hospital. The doctors will put your leg in a cast, and the kids at school will write and draw things on it. It's fun."

Church gave her a grateful smile and added his own reassurances, trying to keep the boy's mind off his fear, but the minutes dragged by and no rescue team appeared. Jeff gave a whimper. "It hurts," he said.

The numbness was wearing off. It would only get worse now, until someone was able to sedate the boy. Jeff shivered, his skin clammy. "Dan," Brandy whispered, not wanting Coreen to hear, "he's going into shock."

Dan knew at least enough first aid to strip off his shirt and put it over the boy. Church already had his head and shoulders in his lap, giving as much warmth as he could. Jeff started to cry, his dog prancing above them, yipping and whimpering in sympathy.

Brandy played the flashlight onto the boy's broken leg, and saw the swelling trapping it more firmly between the rocks and cutting off circulation. The foot was misshapen with swelling. They had made the wrong decision between unwedging the leg earlier, when it would have been easier, and waiting for the rescue team. They should have taken the risk of compounding the fracture to free the leg.

The flashlight beam dimmed. The batteries wouldn't last much longer. "Church, Dan," she said softly, "we've got to get his leg out of there before it swells any more."

The man who had provided the flashlight called, "Here's something that will help."

Dan scrambled up to take the object. "It sure will!" he said, bringing a rock-chipping tool into the light. "We'll get you out now, Jeff."

But the moment they started to work, Jeff screamed. "No! No! It hurts!" Then he lost coherence and merely shrieked. Nothing his father could do would comfort him, and Brandy felt the edge of terror in the other detective even as he tried to remain calm for his son's sake.

It was possible to die of the combination of shock and pain. They tried to soothe the boy, but he could not focus on anything except his agony.

When Jeff's shrieks died back to moans, Dan said, "Jeff, are you familiar with the Vulcan nerve pinch?"

The moaning paused fractionally, while the boy gave a suspicious, "Yeah."

Although he spoke to Jeff, Dan's eyes were fixed on Church's, pleading for understanding. "I'll use the nerve pinch to put you to sleep, so your leg won't hurt, okay?"

" . . . okay."

"Dan—" Brandy began in annoyance.

"Shhh! I have to concentrate. This isn't very easy for humans to do, you know."

"Go ahead," said Church, adding, "Jeff, you told me you saw Captain Picard do it once, remember? So some humans can learn to do it."

Brandy didn't try to interfere again, knowing how desperate Church was to ease his son's pain.

Anyone who had watched television since the 1960's was familiar with the way Dan placed his hand on the supposed nerve points where neck met shoulder. "All right—now!" he said, and squeezed.

Jeff's weight sagged and his head lolled as he fell unconscious.

"How did you *do* that?" Brandy asked in astonishment.

"Power of suggestion," Church said, as Dan turned to the job of freeing Jeff's leg. "Thank God it worked."

With the boy unconscious, Brandy and Dan worked around the broken leg, until the light went out entirely.

"Sorry!" called the man who had supplied the flashlight. "Those were my last batteries."

"Where's that rescue team?" Brandy asked. Now she couldn't see a thing.

"I think I can do this," said Dan, removing the rock chips. "I can feel it. He's almost free . . ." There was a sudden, sharp crack, as of splitting rock. " . . . there!"

Brandy felt the tension give, and then the two men were helping her lay the boy flat, carefully supporting his broken leg just as lights coming down the trail heralded the arrival of the rescue team.

With the proper equipment, Jeff was quickly strapped into restraints, then pulled up to where his anxious mother and sister waited. By the time the party reached the lodge, the ambulance from Murphy had arrived.

Explaining to the rangers what had happened was as bad as writing up a police report. Furthermore, in the light of the lodge they noticed that Dan's hands were bleeding. Despite his protests that it was nothing, he was taken off to have the cuts and blisters cleaned and disinfected, delaying his telling his version of the story.

Dan's hands rarely did anything more strenuous than tap a keyboard. They were certainly not used to digging rocks. Brandy found it somehow comforting to discover another vulnerability. When he returned, he told her, "The blisters will heal up in no time."

No time, indeed. Although his fingers and palms were rough and reddened, there were no open wounds. So where had the blood come from? Jeff? Dear God—how bad was the boy's injury?

It was 8:27 P.M. before Dan and Brandy were released to drive back to town. "I notice you didn't tell the rangers about the Vulcan nerve pinch," Brandy observed.

"It only worked because Jeff desperately wanted to believe it. In a sense, he hypnotized himself to escape his pain. I had to go on pretending because in trance he could still hear every word. Church understood."

"Are you sure that's all it was?"

"What—now you think I'm a Vulcan?"

"Not with that sun allergy. Vulcan is a desert planet."

He gave his deep, rich, sexy chuckle. "Now who's the *Star Trek* fan?"

She let him change the subject, because she didn't *want* to question him as if he were the suspect in some crime. Yet the more she found out about him, the more mysteries she uncovered. She didn't want to think about the impressions she had gotten after the flashlight went out, either: that he could see in the dark, and that once no one could see him do it, he had shattered the rock with his bare hands.

That was nonsense. Her mild-mannered college professor was no Superman. He didn't even wear glasses.

Come to think of it, at his age, doing all that reading and work at the computer screen, *why* didn't he wear glasses, other than his ubiquitous sunglasses?

Brandy, she told herself, *you keep this up, and pretty soon you'll have yourself convinced that Dan Martin is secretly Elvis Presley!*

"You've gotten awfully quiet," said Dan as they approached Murphy's city limits. "Tired?"

"Not really. Let's stop at the hospital, see how Jeff is."

The boy was in x-ray, his anxious family waiting for news. "But it's just his leg," said Church. "He'll be okay, thanks to you two. Dan, I can't thank you enough for knowing how to calm him down. I was afraid he'd die of the shock and pain."

"Oh, Church!" exclaimed Coreen. "I didn't know it was that bad!"

"It's over, Honey," he reassured her. "All they have to do is set his leg—lotsa kids break their legs, Babe. You didn't know me when I was a high school football hero. Half the time I went around with some part of me in a cast."

"I'm glad that's all it is," said Dan. "Tell Jeff we'll come visit him."

"Okay," said Coreen. "And thank you. That's so inadequate." She kissed his cheek. "You saved my baby's life. If I can ever do anything for you, just ask."

As they left the hospital, Brandy realized, "I'm hungry."

"It's late," Dan said. "How about we pick up some Chinese food and take it home?"

"Your place or mine?"

"Yours . . . if you'll let me use your shower."

Brandy smiled to herself. So he was finally ready to make his move.

Well, she was ready, and very much willing. "My place it is. But I don't think I have a lace robe to lend you, like in a Cary Grant movie."

"Trapped again!" he said. "I came prepared, with clean clothes in my backpack. Actually," he amended, "I just thought we'd want to change before going out to dinner."

By which he gracefully allows me the right to say no, thought Brandy. Dan Martin was either the nicest, or the smoothest, man she had ever dated.

Yet every time she thought she understood him, she discovered she was wrong. Again.

When they got to Brandy's apartment, he asked, "Do you want to shower first, or shall I?"

"We could shower together," she suggested. "Save both time and water."

"I doubt that would save either," he replied. "We're hungry, remember?"

So she let him shower while she put the food in a warm oven, rummaged in her closet for something seductive . . . and then had to tidy up the closet to get the door closed if she were to have Dan in her bedroom.

Brandy owned nothing blatantly sexy. Nightclothes were too obvious, and her cocktail dress was inappropriate. She settled on a pair of new shorts and a silky blouse, with sandals to replace the Keds she'd worn all day.

Dan emerged in his usual nondescript shirt-and-trousers outfit. Brandy decided it was camouflage, but with his dark good looks and magnetic personality it didn't work.

He had left her bathroom neat as a pin, even remembered to put the toilet seat down. Oh, yes—*somebody* had domesticated this man. She had a sudden horrified thought: what if he found *her* a slob?

Brandy didn't take long to shower, for she *was* hungry, and she had plans for after dinner. They ate at the kitchen counter. Cleanup meant tossing cartons and chopsticks into the trash. They adjourned to the living room couch.

This is it! Brandy thought when Dan kissed her. Things progressed sweetly for a few minutes, followed by passion as he began that strange exploration of her face and throat with lips and tongue. Odd, she had never known that her neck was an erogenous zone. She lay back, twining her fingers in his thick hair, waiting for him to go further.

When all that happened was that his lips returned to hers, Brandy decided he must need a signal. She insinuated a hand between them and began to unbutton his shirt.

Dan's hand caught hers. "Don't," he said softly.

"Why?" she murmured. "We both know what we want."

Gently, he moved so that he held her with an arm about her shoulders, but the intimate contact was gone. "Brandy, we've only known each other for a week."

"So? I know enough about you—"

"No you don't!" he said with sudden vehemence. Then, more calmly, "You've waited this long. Take time to be certain I'm the right person."

Good God. Was she so clumsy that he recognized her virginity? Her face burned with embarrassment as she mumbled, "I thought you were."

"Perhaps I am," he said tenderly, "but in that case why rush? If you and I are as right for one another as I think we are, then we can take all the time we need."

And she realized *he* needed time. She remembered his hints about a tragic love. How far in his past? He said he hadn't been married. Well, he was certainly too smart to lie about something so easily checked. But if he had loved—loved as Brandy had always dreamed of, a Shakespearean love that counted the world well lost—and then lost that love, he might well be reluctant to risk his heart again.

So, "You know where to find me," Brandy said.

He smiled his rare smile. "I know. Just dial 911."

SIX

BRANDY WAS AT THE POLICE STATION by 7:45 A.M. Sunday morning, busy at the computer. She knew how to look for criminal records on Marvin Clement.

He had none.

But he did exist outside the annals of chess. Knowing that he had lived in New York, she was able to find out that he had owned a car, and that there was one fender-bender accident on his record before he disappeared.

Church came in after a while, looking as if he'd been up all night. "How's Jeff?" Brandy asked.

"His knee was crushed," her friend replied, "and there were other fractures and damage to nerves and blood vessels. He'll need more surgery."

"Oh, God, Church, I had no idea it was that bad. What are they going to do?"

"He goes to Memphis tomorrow, to a specialist. Coreen will go with him. Her mom's coming to stay with Tiffany."

"Church—why did you come in today? You're exhausted," said Brandy.

"I'm going to take time off when they actually do the surgery—and it's gonna be expensive, Brandy. The medical benefits will never cover it."

Brandy understood. Police pay was barely enough for her to live comfortably as a single woman; Church moonlighted, and Coreen worked summers at a local toy factory, from which she had just been laid off when the Christmas line was completed. Jeff was looking at a long recovery; Coreen wouldn't be able to take another job until the boy went back to school.

"So what are you working on?" Church asked, peering at the computer screen.

Brandy told him what she had found out about Everett Land, showing him the photocopies from *Chess Review*. "So you've solved the case," he said.

"A closed case," she said with a sigh. "But it's not really solved, Church. We don't know *why* Marvin Clement became Everett C. Land, or what he died of."

"But you *have* solved it," he said. "The man really *was* old. How he passed for thirty years younger may be a mystery, but not what he died of: old age."

"But why change identities? He had no record."

"It was the Cold War. He was hobnobbing with Russian chess players. Who knows what he was mixed up in? He could have been in the Witness Protection Program. The C.I.A. won't tell us just to ease some Kentucky cop's curiosity."

"Okay, okay," said Brandy. "We've got more important cases to work on."

"One," Church agreed.

But the Car 108 case remained stalled.

Saturday night was always busy for the Murphy police; on Sunday morning they might still be processing people picked up during the night, but everyone else was either in church or sleeping off Saturday night. The detectives caught up on paperwork or rode patrol to supplement the single black-and-white touring the empty streets.

The phone in the detectives' office rang. "Detective Jones," Church answered it. "Oh, hello, Mrs. Mather. Yes, Brandy's right here." He handed her the receiver.

"Hi, Mom."

"I called all day yesterday, Brenda. Where were you?"

"Out at the lake. There weren't any messages on the machine."

"I know to hang up before the fourth ring. Honey, when do you get off duty today?"

"4:30."

"Come to supper at six. I won't take any excuses."

"But, Mom—"

"This is important, Brenda. It's good news. You can bring that nice professor if you like."

"No, I don't think so." She didn't want anyone to observe if her mother's "good news" turned out to be something to fight about.

"I thought you liked him, Dear. You were out at the lake with him yesterday."

"Are you having me followed, Mom?"

"Why, no. Mrs. McCuiston called this morning." She gave the name the West Kentucky pronunciation, "McChristian." "You and Professor Martin are heroes. Now why did I have to hear that from someone else, Brenda?"

"Because all we did was try to help. There was nothing heroic, Mom."

A sigh of annoyance. "You only think it's heroic when you get shot at."

"Church's son Jeff is the hero. He's facing orthopedic surgery. He'll have to be very brave."

"You were . . . with Detective Jones and his family?" That part of her speech was tinged with disappointment, but then her native sympathy took over. "Is there anything I can do to help? Babysit the other child? I'll make them some casseroles—Mrs. Jones won't have time to cook if she has to be back and forth to the hospital."

"I'm sure they'll appreciate it, Mom," Brandy said.

"I'll call Mrs. Jones right away. Why didn't you *tell* me Churchill's family was involved? Honestly, Brandy, you never tell me anything." Then her tone changed again. "I'll see you at six this evening, Honey."

Honey, Dear—her mother was buttering her up for something. When Church asked, "What's wrong?" she realized she was frowning at the phone. "Mom. The last time she told me she had good news, she had made an appointment for me to have a job interview at some damn insurance company!"

"She means well."

"I know, I know, I should be grateful I still have my mother and that she cares about me, but frankly, Church, she drives me crazy!"

"She's being a mother. Why do you let it get to you?"

"I don't know," she admitted. "Anyway, by now she's driving Coreen crazy with offers of food and babysitting."

"More power to her. Your mom is really a nice lady, Brandy. If you and she could just forgive each other for that one time when you were both under terrible stress, I think you'd find a whole lot to like."

Around noon on Sunday, the city of Murphy came to life. Churches let out, and there was suddenly not an empty seat in any restaurant. At 1:00 P.M. the stores in the shopping centers opened, as did the movie theater.

Visiting hours at the hospital began at 2:00 P.M.. Brandy let Church go ahead while she stopped in the lobby to buy a mylar balloon. By the time she found Jeff's room, Dan Martin was already there.

"Well, hi," she said. Jeff, Church had explained, knew only that other doctors would have to look at his leg before it could be put in a cast. Meanwhile it was immobilized by traction. Coreen Jones sat in the armchair, looking very tired from last night's ordeal and her worry about tomorrow.

But Jeff had obviously gotten some rest, for he was bright and cheerful. "Oh, hi!" he said excitedly. "Look at the neat game Dan brought me!"

It was one of those golf-tees-in-holes puzzles, where you tried to get them all off the board by jumping one tee over another. Brandy always ended up with at least two left, on opposite sides.

"That's great," she said, placing her balloon amid the others tied to the bed and wishing she had thought to bring the boy something to cope with hours of boredom.

"Thank you," said Jeff politely, clearly more interested in the game. "What's the trick?" he asked as he came out with three tees left, all in corners.

"No trick," said Dan. "Just logic."

Thank you, Mr. Spock, thought Brandy, and caught the sly look Dan gave her.

"My friends Tommy and Kent came to visit," Jeff told Brandy. "They didn't believe me till I showed 'em *this*," he said, pulling the hospital gown down over one shoulder. Where neck and shoulder met, bruises marred the young skin. "The Vulcan nerve pinch," he exclaimed proudly. "Will you teach me how to do it, Dan?"

"I'd like to, Jeff, but it's very difficult and very dangerous. When you're older, if I'm still around I'll try to teach you, but not all humans can learn it."

"I wonder if it would work on that monster that scared Sandy," Jeff pondered.

"Jeff," Coreen said in quiet exasperation, "there was no monster in the woods. The sun was setting, the shadows were strange, and you just *thought* you saw something."

"Wait," said Church. "Jeff, your sister talked about a monster, too. Why don't you tell us exactly what you saw?"

"Church," Coreen protested, "our son is not a suspect in one of your cases!"

"I want to know what happened, Corey. Jeff? What did you see? Another dog, maybe? Did it look like a wolf?"

"No. It looked like Dracula," said Jeff.

"Like a person," prompted Brandy, "not an animal?"

"Yeah. Like a big man all made outa shadows. With big long teeth."

"Church, he's imagining things!" said Coreen. "He's on pain medication."

"That's right," Dan spoke up. "And what we did—what I did—only stimulated his imagination."

"Maybe," said Church, "but Jeff was out cold when Tiffany mentioned the monster. Corey—don't say a word to her about it. When I get home, I'm going to ask her to describe the monster she thought she saw."

Dan said, "Brandy, why don't you and I leave the family to talk?"

"I'll meet you back at the car, Church," Brandy said.

"Rough day?" asked Dan as they rode down in the elevator.

"No, not at all. Sunday's pretty dull. I'm just not looking forward to this evening. Supper with my mom."

"What's wrong with that?"

"She has something she calls good news. Generally, that's something I consider *bad* news."

"Such as?"

"Any of a hundred things. I guess the worst was the scholarship to JPSU, when I wanted to go to UK. Of course Mom was ecstatic that her little girl got stuck at home for four more years."

"And how did it turn out?" he asked.

"Good, damn it," she admitted ruefully. It was true: if she had gone elsewhere she would not have been on the best rifle team in the nation, and probably not the Olympic team. "Thank you, Professor Pangloss," she said sourly.

"I didn't say anything," he pointed out.

"No, but you thought it. Well, if everything is for the best in this best of all possible worlds, I'll extend my mother's supper invitation. I had intended to spare you."

"But I'd be delighted to come," he said.

Dan showed up with flowers for their hostess. When they went into the living room, Brandy was relieved to see Harry Davis there. Her mother was always in a good mood with Harry around. Tonight she was positively bubbling.

Brandy liked Harry, a tall, soft-spoken man with receding gray hair. He owned one of Murphy's two radio stations, and was an outspoken political opponent of Judge L. J. Callahan. At first Brandy had just been happy that someone took up some of her mother's time, keeping her attention off her single career-oriented daughter. Then, as she got to know Harry Davis, she came to wonder what such a nice man saw in Melody Mather.

Harry and Dan began talking computer communications, quickly engrossed in microwave towers, phone lines, fax, satellites—Brandy couldn't follow it all.

The dining room table was set with real linen and Mrs. Mather's best china. *Something* was certainly going on. When her mother brought out a bottle of champagne and four glasses, Brandy knew it was something big.

As Melody Mather handed the bottle to Harry to open, Brandy caught the flash of light from her finger.

Brandy's emotions went into turmoil. Her hands were cold and slightly shaking as she accepted her glass, determined not to spoil her mother's Big Announcement.

"Brenda, sometimes I have to think of myself. I'm a very lucky woman. Harry has asked me to marry him . . . and I've accepted!" Her voice rose in a breathy giggle on the last phrase, and she held out her left hand, showing a ring with a diamond that had to be more than a full carat. Knowing Harry, Brandy was sure the stone was real.

Brandy said what she knew her mother wanted to hear: "Oh, Mom, I'm so happy for you. Harry, congratulations. You take good care of her now."

Harry Davis and Melody Mather looked at one another, their hearty smiles fading. "Honey," said Brandy's mother, "there's more."

"I'm retiring," said Harry. "I've had the station up for sale for over a year now. I've finally found a buyer."

"That's good," said Brandy.

"But I want to retire to Florida," Harry explained. "I have a condo in Ft. Walton Beach. Your mother has agreed to live there with me."

"Brenda, I'm giving you this house," said her mother.

"Mom, I can't—"

"Of course you can. You'd inherit it anyway. This way I don't have to sell it, or try to rent it out. Harry and I are getting married in three weeks, so we can be in Florida before winter sets in."

Brandy's thoughts were in a whirl. It was what she wanted, her mother out of her hair through a happy occasion. Florida was perfect, close enough for visiting, too far away for her mother to expect her for weekends.

But giving Brandy her house—that was odd. She would have expected her mother to try to tie her to her apron strings, not to Murphy, Kentucky.

"Your mother and I both have children," Harry explained. "Our lawyer suggested that Melody give her home to you, and I give mine to my son and his wife. I have land out in the county for my daughter and her kids. We'd rather you had the property now than there be squabbles when one of us dies."

Brandy had lived in this house from the age of twelve until she had gone to the Police Academy. She had fought bitterly with her mother over her refusal to move back in once she had a job and a salary.

And now—

She saw her mother's plot: a safeguard, a retreat in case Harry predeceased her, or in the event of a divorce. She would be able to move in with her daughter, who would of course have plenty of room for her in this big house, and owe her because the house was a gift.

But Harry Davis was a healthy man in his sixties. He didn't smoke, he wasn't overweight, and Brandy had never heard him complain of health problems. She decided not to worry about fifteen or twenty years from now. She would simply be happy for her mother, and for Harry.

During dinner, Harry told how he had found a buyer. "Ed Mifune was looking for an established radio station, and I was looking for a buyer, but we didn't know about each other until Judge Callahan told Ed about me."

"Judge Callahan?" Brandy asked suspiciously.

"Yeah. Who'd believe ol' Callahan doing *me* a favor?" He laughed. "I guess he's happy to see me leave town. But Mifune wants to expand the radio station, and add a TV station. I should've done that, and upgraded the satellite equipment, but I've spent too many years working my way out of debt to want to get mortgaged to the hilt again."

"Not if you're going to take care of my mother," Brandy agreed. She didn't like anyone in her family beholden to Judge Callahan, but what could she do about it? Besides, it wasn't Harry that Callahan would seek to influence, but his successor. The favor to Harry Davis was incidental.

"Harry," she said, "the one thing I do suggest is that you insist on the bank financing Mifune. Get your money out of the station free and clear."

"Don't worry, Brandy," he said. "Mifune's overextended himself before, but he's an honest man. I think he'll succeed, but I'm not about to stake my retirement on it!" He sighed. "I'm a little concerned about your friend Carrie. If Ed goes for the commercial slant, some of the public service programs will have to go."

Carrie's program was her means of assembling self-help groups. Many people didn't read, even the local newspaper. It was too bad Brandy hadn't known about this earlier; Sunday was usually the best day for a long chat with Carrie.

By the time they left her mother's house, Brandy was beginning to accept the change in her life. Melody Mather was happy, and Harry Davis would take good care of her.

The wedding was less than three weeks away, and the newlyweds planned to honeymoon on the way to Florida. Brandy was pretty sure they were honeymooning already, although it was a difficult mental leap to think that of her mother. When the thought crossed her mind as Dan drove her home, she couldn't help wondering if she were transferring because of her own frustrations.

As usual, Dan parked and came around to open Brandy's door for her, then walked her to her front door. "Early day tomorrow?" he asked.

"Yes, I'm sorry to say."

"It's okay. I have an 8:30 class. I won't come in tonight." But as usual, Dan's kiss took Brandy's breath away, making her feel both desired and protected.

Too soon Dan broke off the kiss, bringing his hands to the sides of her face, caressing her cheeks as he looked into her eyes. "Shall I call you?"

"Yes, please," she replied. "I'll have Friday off this week, unless—"

"I understand," he told her. "Let's plan to go out to dinner Friday, maybe see a movie."

"Okay."

"Then good night," he said, giving her another brief kiss and pulling away.

Brandy made herself let him unlock her door in his old-fashioned way, wishing he would follow her in. But he didn't, and as soon as she closed the door she heard his footsteps going down the stairs.

She put her hands to her cheeks, where his had rested only moments ago. Her face was hot, her hands cool, not warm like Dan's. And hers were calloused, his smooth as —

Smooth?

Last night he had torn and blistered his hands digging Jeff Jones loose from the crevice in the rock. A day later he should have scabs, even if the blisters had healed. Instead, she had felt only the preternatural smoothness that characterized his skin.

Brandy, she told herself, *you are a nutcase. This is the nicest, most eligible man you've met in years, maybe ever. He is clearly interested in you. And you're suspicious because the man doesn't have callouses? He's a teacher, for goodness' sake, and does his work on computer keyboards. He probably doesn't even have a pencil bump.*

She remembered how he had let her know, even if teasingly, that he didn't like her questioning him like a suspect. She had to get over that habit.

Give the man a break, she scolded herself.

She got ready for bed, then called Carrie to tell her the news. "I think it's wonderful that your mom's getting married," said Carrie. "Harry's such a nice man."

"Yeah. He even thought about you," and Brandy explained about the sale of the radio station.

"It'll be okay, Brandy. The FCC requires a certain number of hours of public service programming. If Ed Mifune changes the format, deejays or news people might have to go, but my show is likely to stay. Anyway, let's talk about you. How are you and your professor friend getting along?"

∾

The next week passed rapidly, not so much with police work as with everything that had to be fit into the nooks and crannies *between* police work. Church was away for three days for Jeff's surgery, returning depressed because the doctors could not guarantee the boy full use of his leg.

Church's daughter, Tiffany, had independently confirmed Jeff's story of a shadowy man with fangs, frightening both dog and children. "Some moron out to frighten kids caused that accident," he fumed, "and we'll probably never know who it was. But my boy may pay for the rest of his life."

Her mother asked Brandy to be maid of honor at the wedding two weeks from Saturday. It was to be a simple afternoon wedding, followed by a reception at the bride's home. The bride and groom would spend their wedding night at the groom's house, do their final packing Sunday, and leave for Florida Monday morning.

The bride's mother not being available, the planning fell to her daughter. Everybody expected it, Brandy discovered, even Chief Benton, who told her that barring emergencies she could take as much time off as she needed. She understood: every scrap of overtime now went to Church, to help with medical bills. Unfortunately, that left Brandy free to plan the wedding.

Drowning in boring details, Brandy fumed silently. If she were a son instead of a daughter, she wouldn't be burdened with this wedding. As she was a woman, everyone assumed she had some inborn talent for such nonsense.

"It will be over in three weeks," Carrie told her. "You can stay sane that long." And she found time to help.

There were no bridesmaids or ushers to worry about, but when Mrs. McCuiston called to ask when the shower was, Brandy realized that that was her job, too. She enlisted the older woman's help, and thus lost the Sunday afternoon of her last day off before the wedding, which she had hoped to keep free for last-minute details.

There were appointments with lawyers, and a dozen messages on her answering machine whenever she got home. She ordered a wedding cake, arranged for a photographer, found it impossible to get engraved invitations on such short notice, and nearly forgot to order flowers.

This was a "simple" wedding? Brandy decided that if her turn ever came, she would definitely elope.

The only time she managed to reserve for her own purposes was her date with Dan that first Friday—an evening she protected fiercely against encroaching wedding plans. Neither her mother's circle of friends nor Murphy's criminal element managed to spoil the evening. Mother Nature tried, though. Brandy's period started, three days early.

A healthy, fit young woman, she didn't normally suffer cramps or other symptoms. When she developed an interest in Dan, however, she had gone back on the Pill. Murphy's gynecologists must know every time a single career woman found a new love interest. She had had to sit there nodding politely once again through the lecture about how the Pill protected against pregnancy, but not STD's.

Despite her attempts to match the two, the artificially imposed cycle clashed with her natural one this first month. At the end of an exhausting week, she felt like canceling out and going to bed early.

But Dan, with the almost supernatural intuition she was coming to depend upon, drove them to Paducah for an evening away from telephones, nosy students, or friends of Brandy's mother. They ate dinner at Tracey's, saw a movie, and talked comfortably all the way home. Brandy went to bed relaxed and had the best night's sleep since her mother's announcement of her upcoming marriage.

In the midst of all that, an article appeared in the local paper: Everett C. Land had left his life savings to the JPSU Humanities Scholarship fund. That fact alone would not have bothered Brandy; it was the accompanying photograph showing the Dean of the College and Judge L. J. Callahan receiving the check. Callahan was identified as a trustee of the scholarship fund. But Brandy had too much on her mind to give it more than passing attention.

Nature was kind to Melody Mather. A brief cold snap colored the leaves a few days before the wedding, but the weather warmed up so that on the day itself the white church gleamed in brilliant sunshine against a backdrop of bright red, orange, and yellow. Elegant in a cream-colored suit, her mother made Brandy cry, both with happiness for her and with the sense of loss, the passing of a time of her life that, for all its annoyances, would never come again.

The evening was topped off with a harvest moon rising huge and golden, to the admiration of the wedding guests. They were an eclectic group—Brandy's police colleagues, her mother's friends, Harry's friends and employees, and friends of both the bride and groom from church.

Carrie Wyman was there of course, with a video camera borrowed from her new boss. Glowing with excitement, she told Brandy that Ed

Mifune thought her work with drug addicts, alcoholics, and children was perfect for a show on his new TV station. Meanwhile, he had her developing a cable access program.

Watching Carrie, Brandy wondered if her friend might move from overworked and underpaid social worker to talk-show hostess. She was certainly photogenic, her southern belle beauty set off to perfection today by a blue dress that matched her eyes. Carrie preferred pastels with hints of lace and bows—but she managed to carry off that suggestion of Victoria's Secret without diverging into either Frederick's of Hollywood or *Hee Haw*.

Today, of course, Carrie was filming a wedding, not a documentary on addiction or domestic violence. Having fun with her new toy, Carrie made Melody and Harry a lovely present at the same time. Brandy saw her showing off the small lightweight camera to Dan. "State of the art, digital recording," she was explaining as Brandy passed by, refilling glasses. Dan asked something concerning focus and tracking that was beyond Brandy's comprehension—except to reassure her that he was more interested in the camera than the operator.

Brandy had to stay at her mother's house—her house, now—until the last guest had departed, but Dan Martin stuck it out with her, even though a couple of her mother's women friends tried very hard to be the last to leave. Carrie helped to shoo them out, then turned to Brandy. "You did a great job, Hon."

"Thanks," said Brandy. "I'm just glad it's over."

"Do you need help cleaning up?" Carrie asked. "Jack Crenshaw promised to help me edit this tape tonight so the bride and groom can have it before they leave town, but if you need me—"

"We can handle it," said Dan. "Thanks for the offer."

As Dan carried the remains of the wedding cake into the kitchen, Carrie hugged Brandy and said, "That is a really nice guy—and great looking, too. I like him—for you!"

The last guest out the door, Dan helped Brandy scout for everything that had to be refrigerated or otherwise stored away. Brandy had heard the "tsk-tsking" of Mrs. McCuiston and her ilk at the paper plates and plastic champagne glasses—but in ten minutes two people had all that stuffed into garbage bags and set outside for collection. The silverware, platters, and chafing dishes went into the dishwasher, Brandy turned it on, and she and Dan went out onto the back porch while it ran its cycle.

The moon rode above the trees, glorious in a cloudless sky. It had turned from gold to silver, painting the landscape in black and white, no mitigating shades of gray.

The old porch swing still hung where Brandy's father had installed it. How many high school and college dates had she sat with on this swing? How many summer evenings had she and her parents carried their supper out here, or her father barbecued on the grill he had built, now sitting unused at the far end of the porch?

"When are you moving in?" asked Dan.

"Next weekend, probably," she replied, surprising herself. Well, it didn't make sense to stay in the apartment. Renting the house out had crossed her mind, as she certainly didn't need all this room, but the thought of strangers in her home made her uneasy. "I'll be on call even when I'm off duty, though, after all the time I've taken the past two weeks."

"You need some help?" he asked.

"Every strong back will be welcome," Brandy replied. "Church has already volunteered his pickup, so it's just a matter of boxing up my stuff, and finding a time we can all agree on. And deciding which of my furniture to keep, and which of Mom's," she added with a yawn.

"I can't help you with those decisions," Dan said, "but let me know once they're made."

He moved closer, an arm around her shoulders. The last crickets chirped loudly in the back yard. Inside, the dishwasher rumbled as it changed cycles. Dan drew Brandy into his arms, kissed her lips tenderly, almost lazily.

She rested her head on his shoulder. "There was a full moon the night we met," she remembered.

"Yes," was all he replied.

"So we've known each other for a month now."

"Not quite."

Well, this conversation was going nowhere—at least not where Brandy wanted it to go. "You've been very patient with me," she tried.

"Weddings don't happen every day."

"But it's over now," she said, nibbling kisses across his cheek. He hadn't shaved since morning, and a stubble of beard scratched Brandy's face. She liked the sensation, pleased to find another flaw in his annoying perfection.

She kissed him gently, then ran her tongue across his lips, seeking entrance. Stubbornly, his lips remained closed. Brandy drew back, puzzled. "What's wrong?"

"Nothing."

"Dan—"

The dishwasher turned itself off with a loud snap.

Dan got up. "Come on. We'll finish up here and I'll take you home."

"Dan, what did I do?" she asked. "If you're afraid I've got marriage on my mind, forget it. But . . . don't you think it's time we made love?" she said bluntly, horrified the moment the words were out. God, she was ruining it!

His face was in shadow, but the moonlight lit his eyes, hiding his expression behind silver like the mirrored sunglasses hoods used for that very purpose. "Don't shut me out, please," she whispered in panic. "I'm sorry. I don't mean to push you into something you don't want."

"Don't want? Brandy, I *do* want to make love with you . . . but not tonight. It can't be tonight. Not under the full moon."

The words seemed to choke him. He hadn't been himself since they had come out into the moonlight. And he had become reticent from the moment she mentioned the moon.

What if he had met the woman he loved and lost at the full moon? What if it had been shining the first time he made love to her? It could be simply painful memory, or it could be the fear of jinxing what he had with Brandy.

"You don't have to explain."

"Yes, I do," he said tightly. "I have to explain it all to you." He shook his head. "But I don't know how. I just don't know how."

If she had not been physically and emotionally exhausted after the wedding, Brandy would probably not have slept. As it was, despite this new and very important mystery, she returned to her apartment, practically fell into bed, and dropped into oblivion.

She was wakened by the telephone at 8:23am Sunday. It was Church. "Up and at 'em, Kid. We're on call, and they've called us."

"On Sunday morning?" she protested blearily.

"It's another murder, an ugly, nasty, bloody one. In the city park." Hence the call for detectives.

Church picked Brandy up, and they drove to the crime scene.

Murphy's park was in general a safe place. There had certainly been some rapes committed there, of the "victim knew perp" variety, undoubtedly some drug sales, and some citizens were annoyed about its occasional use as a rendezvous point for local gays, but there had never been a murder in the park before.

Church was ahead of Brandy, and therefore saw the victim before she did. He turned, grabbing her arms and turning her away, his face stiff with shock. "Church! What is it?" Then she realized, "*Who* is it?" She tried to see past him, but he held her.

"Brandy, it's your friend," he said softly, trying to prepare her.

Dan! her mind screamed, and she broke from her partner and dashed to look.

It wasn't Dan.

The victim was Carrie Wyman. Her throat had been cut. Dr. Sanford looked up as Brandy and Church approached. "I'm sorry," he said. He knew Carrie, too, of course; everybody who worked with the police did. "I'll have to do an autopsy, but the cause of death is obvious."

Carrie still wore her blue silk dress, the bodice stained with blood. Her throat had been slashed, not once, but a number of times—hacked until the flesh was ragged.

Rigor mortis held her in the position in which she had died: arms folded, head resting on the root of a tree . . . and on her face a smile of utter serenity.

SEVEN

The Smile on a Dead Man's Face

CHURCH TOOK OVER THE INVESTIGATION. Brandy had the terrible job of breaking the news to Carrie's parents. She didn't go as a police officer, but as a friend, free to break down and cry. Her best friend's death meant a void in Brandy's life almost as great as the one in theirs.

When she was back in her car afterward, Brandy started for her apartment . . . and suddenly realized that any time she had felt this bad, her instinct was to call Carrie.

Her mother—

Melody Mather would understand. But Brandy's mother was Melody Davis now, and would hear the dreadful news soon enough. Her daughter had no right to ruin the first morning of her honeymoon.

It was 11:02 A.M. on Sunday. Brandy sat at a stop sign, tears dribbling down her face, until a pickup truck pulled up behind her. The driver blew his horn.

Brandy turned right, and drove aimlessly . . . until she found herself in front of Dan Martin's apartment building.

She should telephone, be as polite as he always was.

But her heart ached, and she needed strong arms around her. Defiantly, she parked in the visitor's spot, walked to Dan's door, and rang the bell. There was no response. Perhaps he was at church, although he had never brought up the subject of religion.

Dan's car was in its parking space, but she knew that he often left it and walked—one of the things that set him apart from typical West Kentuckians. He could have gone for a paper or to work in his office at the university. Damn.

Frustrated, she rang again, pressing for a good ten seconds before she let go. This time there were soft noises from inside, and then Dan's voice: "Just a moment!"

She had wakened him. The stubble on his jaw was even darker than last night, his hair was disheveled, and he wore a bathrobe. When the morning sunlight hit his face, he winced. "Brandy," he said in obvious surprise.

She felt horribly embarrassed, and would have turned to leave except that he took one look at her and asked, "What's wrong? Come in and sit down. I'll make coffee."

Brandy found herself on Dan's couch, a box of tissues on the table at her elbow, and Dan seated beside her to lend support as he said, "Tell me what's happened."

Her years on the street might never have been. The moment she said, "Carrie," her tears started to flow again.

"Carrie?" Dan prompted.

"Carrie's . . . dead. Murdered."

He went pale. "Oh, God." He was tense and silent for a few moments, then asked, "How did it happen?"

"In the park. Someone . . . slashed her throat."

"What was she doing in the park?" Dan began to ask, but as Brandy sobbed at the memory of her best friend's body covered in blood, he stopped himself. "That doesn't matter. You've lost a friend." He took her in his arms, where she sobbed like a child . . . until a new awareness intruded on her grief.

Dan Martin was unfailingly polite—the nicest man she had ever met. His good manners seemed effortless . . . until today. Now he offered comfort because Brandy needed it, but men disliked the open expression of grief. He would hold her for as long as she needed to cry, but the tension in his body told her it was out of duty.

Dan Martin was the last person Brandy wanted to hold her from duty.

Distracted by her thoughts, she blew her nose and said, "You were going to make coffee?"

Clearly he was glad of something to do. He excused himself while the coffee perked, returning in jeans and sweatshirt, his hair combed, and smelling of toothpaste. He didn't take time to shave, though, so was back by the time the coffeepot gave its last huffing sighs. He poured two cups and brought them to the couch.

"I know it's hard on you," Dan said. "Carrie was your friend. Will you be allowed to work on the case?"

"Everyone will work on it," she replied . . . but stopped herself before she mentioned the expression that tied Carrie's death to five others in the past few weeks.

"Do you have any suspects?"

"She was going to meet Jack Crenshaw. We'll also question Carrie's ex-husband, but he was unfaithful, not violent." She took a shaky breath. "There will probably be others. We won't have the forensic reports until tomorrow."

On Monday morning they had a full report. Carrie Wyman had died at approximately midnight. There was no sign of a struggle. Her purse had been found at the scene, everything including money and car keys intact. Her locked car was in the parking lot of the city park. There were no footprints, no fingerprints, no handily dropped matches or handkerchiefs or coins.

And no murder weapon.

Jack Crenshaw, an engineer at the cable company, was one of the last to see Carrie alive. He had helped her edit her videotape. She had left after eleven. Fortunately for him, when he was walking Carrie out to her car they met one of the other engineers. He invited them to drive "down south" to Tennessee for a few drinks. Carrie refused, but Jack went. The men thus alibied each other.

After preliminary reports, the police adjourned to the morgue. Doc Sanford, too, had been friends with Carrie—had known her longer than Brandy had, in fact. Although his eyes were red and puffy, his report was purely professional.

No skin or blood under the victim's fingernails. No fibers or hairs or other foreign objects on her person. She had not been sexually assaulted, nor had she recently had sex. There was a trace of alcohol in her system— wedding champagne—and no drugs except an antihistamine which matched allergy pills found in her purse.

Dr. Sanford was obviously angry, and his assistant cringed at the tension in his voice as he said, "Uncover the body. Let the detectives see what we've found."

The coroner's assistant clumsily removed the covering. Brandy didn't want to look into her best friend's dead face again, so she watched the assistant—and recognized him.

It was Rory Sanford, paroled from Eddyville last week. Brandy hadn't gone through Carrie's appointment book yet, but it was almost certain he would be among her clients.

Rory was around Brandy's age, but had the haggard look of someone who had been through an ordeal. He had never admitted to the crime that ended his teaching career. He had been a middle school math and science teacher before he was charged with embezzling from the booster club fund.

The bookkeeping for the fund was onerous, and there were always inaccuracies. Some contributors wanted to remain anonymous while others gave supplies or equipment rather than money. Rory Sanford had reported the discrepancies, only to be charged with theft! Then he had agreed to the fatal plea of misfeasance, which Judge Callahan had taken as a plea of guilty on all counts. It had gone hard for the young man, because he could not return the money—he claimed he didn't have it because he never took it.

Apparently the only employment he could get now was as an assistant in his grandfather's morgue. Rory looked sick this morning. Little wonder. Brandy had found it hard not to get sick the first few times she had viewed bodies. It was worse when she knew the victim. Rory didn't merely have to view; he had to assist in the autopsy, and clean up afterward.

Dr. Sanford continued, "No sign of a struggle, but the murderer coulda held a gun on her. What's so strange is, she didn't struggle even when he hurt her. She was found in the same position and wearing the same expression as five other corpses I've examined recently.

"Other than that damned smile, there is no connection among three separate incidents." He shook his head. "I've never seen nothin' like it. What does this murderer do—knock his victims out with the Vulcan nerve pinch?"

Brandy started, causing Church to look at her. She covered by asking, "The cause of death was definitely the throat wound?"

"Yeah. She bled to death," said Sanford. "There's only one odd finding," he added.

"What's that?" asked Church.

"Besides the wounds that killed her, there are two puncture wounds in her throat immediately over the jugular."

"As if the murderer stabbed as well as slicing?" Brandy asked.

"No . . . as if there were two weapons. Something like a meat fork with two prongs, maybe, as well as a knife."

"Oh, Jesus," said Captain Benton. "A knife and fork? Some cannibal thing?"

Doc Sanford seemed reluctant, but then steeled himself. "There were traces of saliva in the puncture wounds."

That was too much for Rory Sanford. He rushed from the room, undoubtedly seeking the nearest bathroom.

Brandy was too horrified to ask a coherent question. Church shuddered in disgust, but maintained his composure. "What have we got here? A Jeff Dahmer?"

"Not the same MO," said Dr. Sanford. "Except for the throat wounds the body wasn't mutilated. Nobody bit her—" His voice trailed off as he gave it a second thought. "No human being, anyway. Those puncture wounds look like a snakebite, like they were made by curved fangs," he held up two curved fingers to demonstrate, "but that don't make sense. Only poisonous snakes strike like that, with just their top fangs. There was no venom." He shook his head. "Forget I said that. All I found is that she had two puncture wounds inflicted before the knife wounds, and whatever punctured her had saliva on it."

Disgusting as the idea was, Brandy had to ask, "The killer . . . licked the fork or ice pick or whatever it was?"

"Looks that way," the coroner replied. "Real sick mind. I've got a theory, but you gotta understand it's pure speculation: the killer somehow put the victim out cold—we don't know how yet, but he had to. Then he punctured her throat with something and . . . licked the blood off of it. Maybe he licked or sucked the blood from her throat."

Brandy said, "Doc, you're talking vampires."

"The murderer may think that's what he is," Doc Sanford replied. "With Hallowe'en so close, television's full of horror movies that could have inspired this guy. The victim's blood clotted and the wounds closed up. So he stuck her again, introducing a trace of saliva into the wounds.

But she still wasn't bleeding enough to satisfy him, and obviously she wasn't going to die, so he slit her throat. His anger at having to change his plans would account for the hacking and slashing."

"Crazy as it sounds, I have to ask," Chief Benton put in. "Could those wounds be made with false teeth? You know, theatrical dentures actors wear to play vampires?"

"I know what you mean," said the coroner. "I don't think those things are long or sharp enough to cause these wounds without the incisors leaving an impression. There's no evidence of that, but it fits my alternate theory. After he got his kicks the killer got frightened either that the victim would identify him or that the MO would give him away. He hacked her throat to kill her and to hide the puncture wounds. It did obliterate everything except the two deepest punctures."

"DNA identification from the saliva?" Church asked.

"There's no genetic material in saliva," explained Dr. Sanford. "You get enough of it, there's a possibility of cells from mouth tissues, but not in this little trace. Besides, if we did have a DNA analysis, we don't have anything to test it against."

"You didn't find saliva anywhere but in the puncture wounds?" Brandy asked. "You said he might have . . . drunk some of her blood."

"The blood washed away any evidence on the victim's neck," the coroner explained.

"We've been saying 'he,'" Brandy noted. "Are you sure the murderer was male?"

"Can't tell," Sanford admitted. "Obsessive, fetishistic crimes are usually carried out against the opposite sex, but not always. Dahmer's victims were male. Women almost never commit this kind of murder, but no, officially we can't determine the sex of the killer."

"Or connect him with the killer or killers in the Car 108 case," added Benton.

Church looked down at the dead woman. "All through the attack, without drugs, without a blow to her head, she just lay there smiling."

Brandy forced herself to look at Carrie. The dead woman's expression reminded her of something. All the other smiling corpses, of course, but something else as well, that her mind refused to process.

Carrie's photo went up beside those of the Car 108 victims, and again Chief Benton gathered his officers. "There shouldn't be a connection between a professional hit, like the Car 108 murders obviously were, and a psycho killing like Carrie Wyman's. But look at those pictures. Murder victims don't lie back and smile, people. They're laughing at us, for not making the damn connection!"

"Captain," said Brandy, "if that smile is the link, then the Land case should be reopened."

A series of expressions flitted across the police chief's face. Brandy understood his reluctance; it was hard to believe that only a month ago she had reveled in the mystery of Everett C. Land, welcoming the chance to exercise her deductive powers on a real challenge. But then, a month ago she had fully expected to *solve* the mystery.

Ideas flitted through Brandy's mind, Church's comments about Land hobnobbing with Russians during the Cold War, the possibility that he was in the Witness Protection Program. What if he knew about some new drug? Carrie had worked with drug addicts; any one of them might be in the employ of organized crime—and why wouldn't the CIA, the KGB, and the mob all want the formula for something that would make a person so compliant that he would sit and smile while his brains were blown out, or her throat was cut? Could someone in such a trance be ordered to stop his heart? Could an old man like Everett Land simply be ordered to die?

This could be far more dangerous than heroin.

Finally Chief Benton said, "Put the Land picture up there. Maybe somebody will figure out what the hell's going on in this town!"

Unsolved murders were almost unheard of in Murphy. Paducah was large enough that the occasional street person was killed without much follow-up. Nashville, Louisville, St. Louis—all were large enough for organized crime to bring in hit men.

But Murphy didn't admit to having homeless people, or anyone else that nobody cared about. No one here knew how to contact professional hit men. Murders were crimes of passion—when someone like Matt Perkins killed his whole family, even if he didn't suicide, other people were safe. The volcano had blown and would go back to quiescence.

The citizenry had been reassured, too, that the Car 108 murders would not be repeated. It was assumed that the Andersons were the targets; there was speculation that their activities in Southern Illinois had angered Chicago mobsters—or alternatively that they were the pawns of said mobsters, who had had them executed to keep them from turning state's evidence. It was all speculation, but it kept the people of Murphy from fearing for their own lives.

Now, somebody had slashed a woman's throat in the park where their children played. The city hall switchboard was flooded, and the mayor called a special session of the city council. Chief Benton put an extra patrol on the park, and fought with the mayor about overtime funding.

Leads to Carrie Wyman's friends and acquaintances went nowhere. She hadn't had a steady boyfriend since her divorce, not even a date in the past six weeks. Her ex-husband turned out to have been visiting relatives in Elizabethtown over the weekend. Unfortunately, Carrie had been in daily contact with unbalanced people. She could have been the focus of any number of fantasies, and never known it.

Harry and Melody Davis' honeymoon was interrupted by the police, but they knew nothing about Carrie after they left the wedding reception. Harry recalled no threats to Carrie concerning her radio appearances. The bride and groom were able to leave Monday morning as planned.

Ed Mifune, who had run the radio station for the past two weeks, also had no clues. The police searched through Carrie's notes, played the tapes of her interviews, and came up zip. Brandy remembered something, though: the camcorder Carrie had used at the wedding and reception. It had not been found with her body or in her car, nor was it at her apartment. It had not been returned to the radio station. A potential clue at last: if they found that camcorder, they might find the murderer.

But Murphy, Kentucky, and all the surrounding county were a very large haystack in which to hide one electronic needle. It would have been tempting to enlist public help, but that would have told the murderer to get rid of the incriminating evidence.

By Tuesday evening, the Murphy police were even more frustrated. In 72 hours they had not found a single useful clue. On the heels of their failure to find the killers of their colleagues, it made them feel useless, incompetent, and angry. On the first two, the populace of Murphy agreed.

When she got off work, Brandy called Dan. No answer at his apartment. When she called his office at the university, he told her, "I have to cover the lab tonight."

"I need to talk to you."

"Sure. I'm finished at ten o'clock."

Oh, damn. She was tired, and this discussion would require diplomacy. "Let's make it tomorrow," she said. "What's your schedule? Can you come down to the station?"

"Is 12:30 okay? I'll take you to lunch."

"Yeah, that's fine," she replied. She felt guilty for misleading him into thinking it was a social invitation. What she wanted was more help with the computer, to search for connections—other than the smiles on their faces—between Everett C. Land, Chase and Jenny Anderson, and Carrie Wyman.

Sylvester nudged Brandy, demanding attention. She petted the cat distractedly while she nuked a TV dinner, watched a sitcom, and drifted into mindless stupor.

Brandy was interested in the show when she sat down; soon she drifted between wanting to wake up and follow the plot, and wanting it to be over so she could go to sleep.

Sleep won.

Brandy was in the Land Between the Lakes, hearing the cries of Jeff Jones. Then she and Dan were down on the rocky outcropping, trying to help.

Church was not in the dream; only Jeff, Brandy, and Dan. Brandy held Jeff spoon fashion, his weight heavy on her chest.

Dan touched the boy, pinching his neck where it met his shoulder. He slumped back against Brandy, unconscious. She and Jeff were alone in the night, the full moon casting black shadows across the silver rockface. The boy's back was warm where it touched her, but his arms and legs were already growing cold.

He was dead.

I'm dreaming, Brandy thought, struggling to wake from the nightmare. She forced herself awake, finding herself in her own bed, the room almost as bright as day with the moonlight streaming in the window.

But her breathing was hampered by the weight still on her chest. She was half sitting up, against the piled-up pillows. Jeff lay dead in her arms. She couldn't move, and realized that she, too, was dead.

She could see both their faces in the mirror on the opposite wall, both wearing that same serene smile —

"No!" Brandy gasped, sitting up.

Sylvester, who had been lying on her diaphragm, kicked the breath out of her as he leaped to the back of the couch.

Brandy sat shivering and panting, putting together the shards of reality that had formed her dream. She had fallen asleep on the couch, propped against the cushions at one end, the television playing. She had slept through the news, for *Nightline* was now on. The sounds had kept her from deep sleep, making her dream horribly real.

The temperature was dropping; that's why her arms and legs were cold. In typical cat opportunism, Sylvester had decided to use her as a heating pad, and his warm weight had become the body in her dream.

It made sense, sort of.

But Brandy's mind could not dismiss it as a nonsensical mix of recent events with sensory input, like the toilet dream everybody had, searching and searching through streets or corridors for a bathroom. That always occurred toward morning, on a full bladder. This dream had similarities, but the toilet dream had no significance. Brandy could not help thinking that this dream did.

As she got up and turned the heat on, she tried to analyze what her subconscious was telling her. Why had Jeff been dead in her dream, when she knew he was alive? She remembered Dan's "Vulcan nerve pinch," and the pang that had gone through her when Dr. Sanford had mentioned it in connection with the mysteriously smiling corpses. Hence the association with death in her dream.

Okay. It made sense. She dug flannel pajamas from her bottom drawer, hoping to drive the chill from her bones.

But as she tossed the extra pillows from her bed and prepared to crawl under the covers, she saw her reflection in the mirror. It brought back the dream image of herself and Jeff, both smiling that damned mysterious smile . . . and the real image of herself the morning after Dan had put her to bed, smiling that same smile.

What if the undetectable drug that put people into a cooperative trance were not a drug at all? What if it were some technique involving acupressure points?

Jeff had slumped when Dan touched him. She hadn't seen his face— it had been dark, no moon that night.

But if she had seen it . . . would Jeff's face have worn that same serene smile that was the single clue uniting six mysterious deaths in Murphy, Kentucky?

Dan Martin showed up promptly at 12:30 Wednesday. Brandy deliberately took him into the room where they had set up the bulletin board with the photos of the smiling corpses. As she expected, he was immediately drawn to it.

"My God," he said flatly. Then, "I don't have to ask you why Rett's photo is here." He started to examine the pictures more closely, but winced and turned away when he came to the bloodsmeared image of Carrie Wyman. "What does it mean?" he asked Brandy.

"Dan, will you teach me the Vulcan nerve pinch?"

"There is no such thing."

"Oh, it's not Vulcan," she said. "It's some kind of karate thing, isn't it? Pressure points? What's important is where you learned it."

He appeared puzzled, but not guilty. "Are you suggesting that I had something to do with—?" He swept a hand toward the bulletin board.

"No. You were with me when Rand and Paschall and the Andersons were killed."

"But I have no alibi for Saturday night," he said. "I can't prove that I didn't murder Carrie."

"Did you?"

"No. Do you believe me?"

"Yes."

"Then why are you questioning me?"

He was so calm. She would expect anger from an innocent man . . . but she would also expect it from a guilty one. Dan Martin simply waited patiently for an explanation.

"I think you know how it was done," she told him.

He didn't ask what "it" was. "Are you saying all these people were rendered unconscious in the same way?"

"Yes. Dan, *tell* me! What's going on, some Ninja thing? Kung fu? I don't think you had anything to do with the killings, but you may lead us to whoever did."

He was silent, thinking. Then he said, "I can't help you, Brandy . . . and you have no idea how much I wish I could."

"Why?"

"I'm no happier than you are at five unsolved murders and a death under mysterious circumstances in the community where I live."

"No. I mean why can't you help me?"

He sighed. "Because there's no such thing as the Vulcan nerve pinch! You can knock someone unconscious by putting pressure on the carotid arteries, but I hardly have to tell that to a police detective."

"None of the victims had bruises to indicate such pressure, and besides, they would have struggled."

"Well, then, you know whatever it was, it wasn't what I did to Jeff. He had bruises, remember?"

He was right. "Why, if it wasn't real?"

"Jeff had to *think* it was real, or it wouldn't work. I gave his shoulder a good squeeze to convince him I was digging down to find the nerves. I didn't mean to hurt him. Are you going to charge me with child abuse?"

"No. I'm sorry. I never meant to charge *you* with anything, Dan. I just hoped that you had the clue we need, that you were a secret Ninja or Shaolin priest or whatever the person or persons are who do *that* to people." She waved toward the board in her turn.

"I'm sorry to disappoint you."

She couldn't help asking, "Why aren't you angry with me?"

"For doing your job? You saw a possible connection, and you followed it up." He gave a snort of sardonic laughter. "I wish I had a rational explanation, no matter how far-fetched. Maybe ex-CIA agents gone wild, using the secrets of the Far East to—what? Aside from the expressions on their faces, what is the connection, Brandy? And have you decided Rett Land was murdered after all?"

"Not by any method I know," she replied, "but there is that damned connection you see there in the photos. You are the best person I know to help me find other connections."

"Back to the computer?" he asked.

"Back to the computer," she agreed.

"Lunch first," he told her. They joined Church, and ate at Judy's on the court square, an old home cookin' restaurant famous for its pies. It was too crowded at lunchtime to discuss police work.

Judge Callahan was in one of the booths, looking as powerfully perfect as always: the epitome of the southern politician from his perfectly-barbered iron-gray hair to his perfectly-polished half-boots. As he had never approached Brandy again after that day at Sturgeon's, she was losing the nervous tension that had plagued her when she saw him.

John Metawan, loan manager of the Bank of Murphy, sat across from the judge, his lunch left half eaten. It was clearly not as congenial a meal as she had seen them taking together a month ago, just before the Car 108 murders. From where Brandy, Church, and Dan were seated, Brandy could see only Callahan's back, but the grim look on Metawan's face told her something unpleasant was happening.

Finally Callahan took out his billfold and laid some money on the check. Metawan got up, still looking none too happy, turned and went out the door. He did not go toward the bank, but turned to the right. In that direction were a dress shop, an antique shop, the radio station, a dentist's office, a furniture store, an appliance store, and the police station. Brandy could only hope that Metawan's expression meant he was headed to the dentist, and not to deliver bad financial news.

Meanwhile Judge Callahan did his usual politicking, moving from one booth or table to another, greeting everyone by name. The place was filled with working class people, and the judge's good 'ol boy accent was at its thickest. When he got to Brandy's table, she was surprised when he said jovially, "Well howdy, Dan," extending a hand to shake. "You keepin' them college kids in line?"

Dan shook hands as he replied, "We try, Judge."

Callahan's joviality disappeared as he turned to Church and Brandy. "You folks got a lead on the killin' of that pore lil' gal yet?" The implications were obvious: what were Murphy police doing lollygagging over lunch when there were murders to solve?

"Yessir," Brandy replied defiantly. "In fact, Dr. Martin is helping us to follow up some leads this very day."

A flicker of a frown crossed the politician's face. Then he resumed his friendly air. "Well, I'm certainly glad someone's workin' on it. There's a psycho out there needs to be stopped!"

"Dead in his tracks, Judge," said Church.

"I hope so," said Callahan. "Find him guilty in my court, 'cause I ain't afraid of the death penalty. You lock up dangerous animals like that, and the bleedin' hearts let 'em right out. You know the parole board released Rory Sanford?"

"He's hardly a dangerous animal," said Brandy. "All he did was juggle some books."

"Well, if I have anything to say about it, he'll never be in a position to steal honest people's money again!"

Brandy was quite certain of that. She just wondered if Rory would be able to make anything of his life at all.

After lunch they went to the computer. Dan began trying to find connections between Land, the Andersons, and Carrie Wyman.

"How about Rand and Paschall?" asked Church.

"I thought we decided they were killed to get at the Andersons," said Brandy.

"We don't *know* that," Brandy's colleague pointed out.

Oddly enough, there was a connection between Land, Wyman,

Paschall, and Rand: Judge L. J. Callahan. Carrie's college records showed him as her sponsor for a scholarship. He had recommended Rand for promotion two years ago, and Paschall to the Police Academy two years before that. And in the material Brandy had gathered at Jackson Purchase State University, there was a letter of recommendation from Callahan for Everett C. Land's most recent grant.

"Busy man," Dan commented.

"Full-time politician," said Church. "The man knows *everybody*."

"Unfortunately," Brandy added, "finding Judge Callahan's name on these recommendations is about as suspicious as finding the high school principal's."

"I take it you don't like Judge Callahan," observed Dan.

"I don't trust him," Brandy said. "He's too smooth, too insincere, and he plays both sides of the fence. You heard him, all strict law and order about Doc Sanford's grandson. Callahans don't get on with Sanfords. But just try to get a search warrant if you suspect one of Callahan's cronies! You could have seven eye witnesses and a smoking gun, and he'd say it was insufficient evidence."

"All we've found so far is connections between Callahan and the *victims*," Church pointed out. "Let's see if there's any connection with the criminals."

There they drew a blank. The Andersons had never appeared before Judge Callahan, never been arrested with a warrant he had issued, nothing. Chase and Jenny Anderson had records before their spectacular bank robbing spree: shoplifting, poaching, unlicensed firearms, bootlegging, forged checks. However, they had never been arrested in Callahan County before the robbery in Murphy.

"Let's try employment records," Church suggested. "Social Security records will tell us if they ever worked for the same employer."

Another blank.

Dan had to go back to campus for a meeting. Brandy and Church continued plodding along at the computer, until Chief Benton called everyone into the squad room.

The people of Murphy were fed up with murderers going uncaught. There was talk of forming vigilante groups, and they all knew what that meant. Untrained people arming themselves. Mob psychology, even lynchings, if they thought they had found the murderers. The police had to act quickly to repair their image and head off violence.

Soon every cop in Murphy found his spare time going to help organize neighborhood watch programs. After working her regular shift, Brandy now had Monday, Tuesday, and Thursday evenings taken up with citizen's groups.

If the people of Murphy were this excited now, how would they react if the coroner's report on Carrie Wyman were revealed? They had withheld the information about the puncture wounds and saliva, the missing camcorder, and the strange smile—routine precautions to forestall false confessions, deter copycat killings, and prevent destruction of evidence. It frustrated certain kinds of criminals; some obsessive murderers had been known to reveal themselves by bragging about clues the police had missed. But days passed, and the Murphy police had no such luck.

Sunday rolled around, with an invitation to Church's house. "Bring Dan Martin along," her friend suggested.

Brandy hadn't talked with Dan since the day he had helped them on the computer. Because she hadn't been able to catch him at home, he hadn't been there when she squeezed moving into Saturday morning, with the help of several colleagues. But when Brandy called on Saturday evening Dan was home.

"I'm sorry I missed helping you move. I was at a conference in Lexington, and just got back two hours ago."

He agreed readily to the invitation. "I'm grading midterms. Sunday dinner will be a welcome break." Brandy heard no recrimination in his voice.

Now that she had time to think about him, she wondered how much Dan cared about her. It seemed never to bother him that her work kept them apart. Since Carrie had been murdered, he had withdrawn. She couldn't blame him; that brutal crime demonstrated the harsh reality of Brandy's work. Maybe he realized that he could not live with it.

On the other hand, he always made time when she was available. An attractive single straight male of Dan Martin's age could be out every night if he wanted to. Yet not once in the six weeks or so she had known him had he turned down one of her last-minute invitations.

Her doubts disappeared when Dan appeared on Brandy's doorstep. As soon as she was in his presence, they seemed made for one another.

The day was extremely pleasant. Hallowe'en decorations rivaled Christmas decorations in Murphy, and the Jones house was no exception.

Jeff was finally out of the hospital, his leg in a heavy cast-brace. He was excited about going to a neighbor's Hallowe'en party.

The children were certain to win a prize for costumes: Tiffany was a cave woman carrying a club and wearing a bone in her hair, while her brother's wheelchair was hidden under the body of a dinosaur, his outstretched leg and foot disguised as the neck and head, his real head hidden by a finlike structure on the creature's "spine."

"A whole afternoon of adult conversation!" Coreen exulted when the children had gone. "Church, don't you dare bring up murders or robberies or criminal stuff. Dan, tell us about what you do. I need to get a job now that Jeff can go back to school. Should I take a computer course?"

"You should learn to use them," he said, "but you don't need the courses I teach. What kind of work have you done?"

"I like this man," Coreen said to Brandy. "Notice he assumes I've worked before, that I'm not a parasite." She returned her attention to Dan. "Here I've just done temporary work, but I was a secretary in Chicago. I did learn to use a word processor, an IBM Displaywriter."

"One of the old workhorses!" Dan said. "Well, it gave you the basics of word processing. You'll find it easy to learn the new programs. Do you want to continue as a secretary? Or do you plan to become an executive or a manager, or start your own business?"

"Brandy, where did you *find* this 21st century man?" Coreen demanded. "Actually, I don't know what I want to do, but . . . we've got to get more money coming in. I'll take what I can get, but I think I can do more than type and file and answer the telephone."

Brandy was content to sit back and listen, as was Church. Both were tired after two nights of activity. The weekend before Hallowe'en was filled with egg throwing, loud parties, fights, idiots setting off fireworks or starting bonfires, and just plain pranks.

Unfortunately, some people used Hallowe'en as an excuse for hate crimes. Following up on a report of auto theft, Brandy had found the car being driven by Ricky Chu, a senior at Murphy High who was going to be his class valedictorian . . . if he didn't spend the next few months in jail.

The Chu family were one of very few Asian families in Murphy. Almost stereotypically, they worked exceptionally hard, running Murphy's excellent Chinese restaurant. There would not have been any particular problems over their success at that; it certainly took no business from other establishments in a town full of hungry college students. The problem was the brilliance of the three youngest Chus, Ricky, Sandra, and Jane. The latter two had been born in Murphy, and all three were native-born Americans who dressed and sounded just like all the other kids in town. However, they would always look different . . . and they were not athletes, whose differences Murphians were willing to forget if it got them a winning team.

All three Chu children led their classes academically. One such child the citizens of Murphy might have tolerated. Three of them strained their peculiar sense of "fairness": when there was a Chu in the class, no other children got to be first.

Overt acts of racism were infrequent in Murphy, but as Ricky worked his way through high school, his sister Sandra two grades behind, their social life dwindled. Ricky was the only student in Murphy High that year to make the National Honor Society in eleventh grade, although several seniors did so.

And then last night Ricky had been arrested. Brandy was positive he was telling the truth, that Don Pringle had lent him his car for a date with Don's twin sister Paula. Paula was very pretty, very popular, and considerably brighter than her brother. She and Ricky Chu were in the honor classes together, and the Pringles hired Ricky to tutor Don, to keep him eligible to play basketball.

Whatever Brandy might believe, though, Don Pringle claimed that he had never given Ricky permission to drive his car. Paula claimed that Ricky had stopped by with a book for Don, and told Paula Don had said it was all right for him to take the car. He had taken the keys from the sideboard, she said, and asked her to go for a ride to see the Hallowe'en decorations. She claimed she didn't suspect a thing.

Ricky claimed that Paula had invited him to go out for a date while they were still at school on Friday, and talked her brother into lending them the car then. There were no other witnesses to the conversation. Even though Brandy was positive the Pringle Twins had set Ricky Chu up, they were two to one against him and obviously carefully rehearsed.

Brandy wondered if the plot had been thought up by Don, by Paula, or perhaps by a number of Murphy High students envious of Ricky Chu's success. The boy might be brilliant academically, but he was starving for social acceptance. Thinking he was friends with the Pringle twins, he naively accepted his good fortune.

Now Ricky's life could be marred forever with a record of grand theft auto. His parents were devastated. There was nothing Brandy could do about the situation today, though. Vowing to try again to break the Pringles' story tomorrow, she determined to forget that and the unsolved murders, and enjoy her day off.

Coreen's pot roast recipe had won the Women's Club contest last year. Church opened the bottle of wine Dan had brought; serving four people, it was just enough to give a mellow glow to the dying afternoon.

It was after dark when they prepared to leave. As Coreen got Brandy's coat for her, the older woman said softly, "Don't let that one get away, girl! He's handsome, he's nice, he's employed, and he's liberated. Honey, you don't *find* that combination. Grab him while you can."

Brandy was seriously considering "grabbing" Dan Martin in a much less metaphorical fashion. The more time she spent with him, the more she wanted to evolve their relationship.

On the drive home he commented, "You were pretty quiet today. Tired?"

"It's been a hectic week."

"I won't come in, then."

"No, Dan!" she said, hating the desperate quality in her voice. It made her feel like Cathy in the comic strip. Forcing a calmer tone, she explained, "I mean, I'm not in the mood to go dancing, or argue politics, but it would be nice to spend a quiet evening together if you can spare the time."

She waited again for a response that didn't come. Why didn't he throw back at her that she was the one who could never spare the time? But all he said was, "I'd like that."

There were unpacked boxes in the dining room of what Brandy still had trouble thinking of as "her" house, as well as in the spare bedroom upstairs. Sylvester, who had occasionally stayed with Brandy's mother, had spent yesterday hiding in protest at being moved. Now he was ready to come out and be sociable, so when Dan and Brandy arrived he greeted them with purring and rubbing. Brandy was still amazed at how her man-hating animal accepted Dan.

Brandy put on coffee to brew. Coreen had sent a wedge of her spectacular chocolate cake with them, as they had all been too full for dessert after dinner. Brandy unwrapped it, and started looking for a knife.

She liked this kitchen, with the table where she and her parents had eaten all their meals except on Sundays and special occasions. The refrigerator was adorned with magnets. Once they had held notes to family members, important letters, snapshots, Brandy's drawings or A papers. Now there was nothing but her grocery list. Dan looked at the magnets. "Nice souvenirs from your travels," he noted.

Brandy searched the drawers for a cake knife. Her mother must have taken hers, and Brandy's wasn't unpacked yet. Other than flatware, the only knife she found was a sharp butcher knife. She took it out, telling Dan, "I don't need all those magnets. Can you use some? Help yourself."

He backed away. "Oh, no, I don't dare carry magnets."

Allergy to the sun she had heard of, but to magnets? What was this man, some kind of android? "Why not?" she asked curiously, taking cups and plates out of the cupboard.

"Because I could forget one in my pocket," he explained. "You know what magnets do to computer disks."

Brandy had just picked up the glass pot, full of fresh hot coffee. Tired, strung out, overwhelmed by a week in which her only spare time had been taken up with the exhausting job of moving, she was overcome with giggles at the idiocy that had flashed through her mind. The heavy pot tilted in her hand as she laughed helplessly—hot liquid sloshed over, and she dropped it.

The pot shattered. Hot coffee splashed. Brandy jumped back. Sylvester gave a yowl and disappeared into the dining room. Dan turned, exclaiming, "Brandy! Are you all right?"

Reaction followed reflex. Even though the burning liquid had not struck her, Brandy felt weak. She reached back to steady herself on the counter—and gave a yelp of pain!

Her hand was bleeding: she had sliced a finger on the butcher knife.

"Let me see!" said Dan, grasping her hand. Blood welled up from the cut, but all she needed to do was let some cold water run over it—

Dan said, "It'll be all right," and before she realized what he was doing he lifted her hand . . . and took her finger in his mouth!

For a fraction of a second Brandy hung suspended, before pure fear broke the spell. "Dan!" she gasped, snatching her hand away. "What do you think you're doing?" He stared in confusion, saying nothing as she ranted on, "You idiot—do you want to die?"

He clearly didn't comprehend.

"How do you know what might be in my blood?" she demanded. "How can you take the risk that—?"

Utter horror sent such a pain through her chest that she couldn't go on. What if he could take that risk because it didn't matter to him? If he already carried death in his veins? Was that why—oh, God—was that why he had never made love to her?

EIGHT

Arrest

BRANDY KNEW AT ONCE she wasn't thinking straight. If Dan carried AIDS, or any other disease, he would not risk passing it to her. But . . . what was he thinking?

"I'm sorry," said Dan. "Of course it's not safe to use that technique anymore. But look: the cut wasn't as bad as it appeared."

Brandy did look. Positioned on the inside of her index finger, the cut would annoy her for a few days, but it was not deep or dangerous. She bent her finger, surprised to see that the bleeding had stopped.

Still . . . police were particularly trained about the dangers of body fluids, as they often had to deal with injuries. "You're in no danger from me so far as I know," she said. "But Dan, how could you do that?"

"I didn't think," he replied softly. "I just reacted. And you needn't be afraid, Brandy. I don't have anything you could catch." He didn't give her a chance to ask whether he meant he had been tested or had been celibate . . . that long? Impossible. "Let's clean up that glass."

After cleaning up the mess, Brandy added a note to her list to pick up a new pot for the coffeemaker. Meanwhile, she found a jar of instant coffee, and they had their delayed dessert before Dan left to finish grading midterms.

~

Monday morning Ricky Chu appeared in court. Brandy was there as arresting officer. To her amazement, Judge Callahan announced, "I have talked with the principals in this matter. Don and Paula Pringle have admitted to a practical joke that got out of hand. Richard Chu had permission to use Donald Pringle's car. Paula Pringle was part of the setup.

"I want it a matter of public record that Richard Chu committed no crime. This is not a matter of insufficient evidence; the boy's record is totally clean. Don and Paula Pringle, if you ever do anything like this again, you will be charged with malicious mischief, falsifying evidence, perjury, and anything else I can think of, you heah?"

The Pringle twins looked suitably subdued, their parents suitably furious.

Judge Callahan continued, "Furthermore, I want it on public record that in Callahan County we have fair and equal treatment under the law, regardless of race, creed, religion, or national origin! We will have no false charges in my jurisdiction. Now, this case is dismissed!" And he leaned forward to say to the Pringles, "I suggest that you folks make a sincere apology to the Chu family."

Mr. and Mrs. Chu were all bows and gratitude. Brandy wondered why Judge Callahan had taken a personal interest in the case, until she saw the reporter from the *Murphy Ledger* taking down every word. Campaign strategy. Hence the speechifying about truth, justice, and the American way.

Later that day, Brandy asked Church to swing by Wal-Mart on their lunch break so she could buy a coffee pot.

"Your mom take yours?" her partner asked.

"No, I broke it." That reminded her of the cut on her finger, but when she looked for it, there was not so much as a scratch.

During Hallowe'en week everyone put in extra duty. The days combined happy children parading in costume, drunken adult parties, accidents, bonfires, domestic violence, and three deaths by drug overdose, one of them a thirteen-year-old. All this in addition to the usual stolen vehicles, breaking and entering, and shoplifting.

Three days after Hallowe'en, Brandy was sent to serve a warrant on Ed Mifune for missing his November 1st payment on the radio station. On the one hand, Brandy was greatly relieved that the money was owed to the bank, not to her new stepfather. On the other, she was sad to see the handwriting on the wall.

Soon Ed Mifune would have to shut down or sell out . . . probably to someone in Judge L. J. Callahan's political machine. Brandy was sure that what she had observed in Judy's restaurant that day was the judge pressuring the bank loan manager to tighten the reins on Mifune. There wasn't usually a warrant issued over the first late payment.

On Friday Brandy arrived home after 8:00 P.M., not particularly tired, but with the feeling of something missing from her life. She found a letter from her mother, with snapshots of the honeymoon couple on the beach, at Epcot Center, and in their new condo. To her surprise, it brought tears to Brandy's eyes. She reached for the telephone, and was disappointed that there was no answer.

So she called on Saturday morning, and thoroughly enjoyed talking with her mother.

The first weekend in November was Homecoming at the university. Dan Martin invited Brandy to the football game and a faculty party. They were together all day without a moment's privacy. At the party Brandy found herself surrounded by faculty wives who wanted to talk quilting, children, charity work, crafts, and canning.

Just about the time Brandy decided maybe a relationship with a professor was not a good idea, Dan appeared at her side and drew her away to a group of male and female teachers, spiritedly discussing Kentucky's educational system. Even though Brandy had no children, the public schools were of constant concern to the police.

The conversation came around to drugs, dealers now targeting the middle schools to get kids hooked before high school, where the major anti-drug campaigns took place. Although pot was still Murphy's drug of choice, crack was starting to appear—not a lot yet, but it would not be long before they found crack houses in their own back yards.

Murphy had so far had one incident of a gun in school—merely one student showing it to another—"But there could be worse to come," Brandy warned. "We're no better at understanding our kids than Heath High in Paducah."

"Do you want to put metal detectors in our schools?" asked Dr. Anthony.

"I hope it won't come to that," said Brandy, "but it could happen. There's not much police or school personnel can do about the kind of rage that erupts into senseless shootings—those problems come out of the home. But there are other reasons for guns in schools that we *can* do something about. While we have all our attention focused on math scores, the drug dealers are scoring hits. Once you have drugs in the schools, weapons follow."

"There's not much of a drug problem in Murphy," one of the women protested. "I have two kids in Forbes Middle School, and they've never seen any drug use."

"They're not telling you. They're afraid of your reaction or, more likely, repercussions from fellow students. It's even possible they don't recognize what's going on. I'm sorry to tell you this, Dr. Swenson, but the more ignorant your children remain about drugs, the more easily they can be led astray."

"Oh, my children will have nothing to do with strangers," the woman said confidently.

This was how the dealers won: brilliant, successful people like Darla Swenson, Ph.D., had no idea how they operated. "The pushers are not adult strangers," Brandy said. "They are ten- and twelve-year-olds, your own children's classmates."

There were gasps. Then one of the men, Dr. Bradley, asked, "Why don't we hear about this?"

"They're juveniles, protected under the law. But your children know which kids had all the latest fad clothing, video games and CD players, fancy bikes, their own TV's and VCR's and cell phones—and then suddenly disappeared from school. They probably know who took their place, and what they're selling. Your kids may not use, but they know whose grades have suddenly dropped, who never has their homework, who's constantly late or absent, who falls asleep in class, who doesn't seem to care." She shook her head. "I give this lecture to teachers, to the PTA, every year, but it does no good. Parents believe it can't happen to their kids."

"What can we do?" asked Dr. Swenson.

"Talk to your kids. Snoop. They'll forgive you when they understand that you care. I grew up in Cleveland," she suddenly found herself saying, "where there was a drug problem long before it reached places like Murphy. When I was eleven, I wanted a ten-speed bicycle. My parents said it was too expensive, so I saved my allowance, lunch money, birthday money, anything I could get for odd jobs. I had $73.00 in a shoe box in my closet when my mom found it."

Even as she spoke, Brandy was astonished at her new perspective on the incident. "Mom panicked—just as you ought to if you find one of your kids with a large sum of cash. I thought she was afraid I'd stolen it. I was furious with my mom for snooping. Now I know she was terrified that I was either buying or selling drugs."

"So what happened?" asked Dr. Anthony.

"When I told her how I'd saved the money and what it was for, we ended up really communicating. Mom admitted that she and Dad could afford the bike. They didn't want me to have it because Cleveland's streets weren't safe, and the kind of bike I wanted was a red flag to thieves—the way city mothers have to explain today that their kids can't have athletic shoes or fancy jackets that gangs might kill them for. I left that talk feeling grown up." She smiled. "And when we moved here to Murphy, I got the bike."

"You're telling us to invade our children's privacy," said Dr. Swenson.

"I'm telling you to *talk* to them!" said Brandy. "They've got problems you can't *imagine*! Even a fight can lead to communication." She shook her head. "I don't want to arrest your kids. I don't want to see them dead of an overdose. I don't want some drug-head shooting or knifing or running over *your* child. I've seen all those things as a cop in Murphy." She paused for effect, and added, "I've seen all those things just this fall."

There was dead silence, and Brandy was suddenly embarrassed. "I'm sorry," she said. "It's a party. I shouldn't have gone into police mode."

"No," said Dr. Anthony, "You've given all of us something very important to think about."

Dr. Swenson added, "We think we're apart from all that. We give our children travel, music lessons, computers and library cards . . . but we send them off to school alone. I am going to talk to my children. Thank you, Brandy."

Nevertheless, Brandy worried she had overstepped her bounds, and when Dan took her home and again said goodnight with only a kiss, she feared that he had decided she didn't fit into his life, or fit in with his colleagues.

And yet the next week he took her to dinner and a play at the campus theater. Brandy wished she could invite him to spend some time alone with her, like their day at the lake, but she was still making up for lost work time.

November brought cold rain. There were no more smiling corpses, but unsmiling ones aplenty as the party season progressed. It began with Hallowe'en, continued through Thanksgiving, and climaxed with the madhouse of the Holidays. Most of the deaths were vehicular, often manslaughter or DUI, too many for the traffic division to handle alone. The victims were crushed, beheaded, burned, or twisted in the wreckage. Two of the accidents Brandy investigated had victims who lived, maimed for life.

And once again, as she wrote up report after report, she saw the toll on her community's future: every victim was younger than she was.

It was hard for police, firemen, and medical personnel to get into the holiday spirit, but they tried valiantly. As party plans proceeded, Brandy realized that for the first time in her life she would not be at her mother's table for Thanksgiving dinner.

She did, however, get Christmas off, and was able to claim enough vacation days before and after to drive to Florida. She looked forward to the trip, but it made her question her relationship with Dan Martin.

The holiday season always brought chaos to Brandy's love life. If she was dating someone, the increased social whirl caused him to demand more of her time just when she had less to give. The single women's wisdom that any more-or-less steady relationship broke up just before Christmas went double for female cops.

Brandy and Dan were invited to Church's house for Thanksgiving. Brandy hadn't told Dan yet that she would be away over Christmas. Her mother said Dan would be welcome, but inviting him to spend Christmas with family implied a seriousness to their relationship that Dan did not seem to feel. He fit himself into her free time, but never complained when she had to cancel, sometimes at a moment's notice. So as Thanksgiving approached, Brandy turned over in her mind whether to invite Dan for Christmas.

There was another crack overdose in the middle school, but the boy lived to identify the two kids who were selling. They, however, either would not or could not identify their suppliers, who abandoned the twelve-year-olds to the system. They would disappear into juvenile detention homes for the next six years, emerging with a confirmed hatred for the system, uneducated except for a crash course in crime.

Cocaine, crack, pills, and marijuana were all in the horde the young pushers had for sale. The first three could have come from anywhere, but most of the pot sold in Murphy was grown locally. Analysis showed that it was a West Kentucky product. Brandy questioned the Mortrees again.

"Yer barkin' up the wrong tree," Jerrod Mortree told her. "We got no fuckin' supply! Anyway, we don't sell to no school kids."

"Right!" said his brother. "Hell, it's the teachers come lookin' for the stuff, not the kids."

"Yeah," said Mortree. "You know who come out t'the farm lookin' fer some green? The Sanford kid, Doc's grandson! Ain't that a parole violation?"

"Did you sell him any?" she asked.

"Tol' ya. We got none to sell."

Back at the station, Brandy asked Church, "Should I check out Rory Sanford?"

"On *their* word? Leave it to his parole officer. And his grandfather. You really think Doc wouldn't know if Rory was smoking pot?" the other detective replied.

So they turned their attention to other local growers, hoping to put more of them out of business.

Brandy was sent, along with Dr. Sanford, to present another program to the Forbes Middle School students. Rory Sanford volunteered to join them. "I taught at that school," he said, "and I never knew what was happening. Seeing the bodies of those poor kids, I realize how bad it is. I'm a good teacher. Maybe I can get through to them."

It was the most enthusiasm Brandy had seen Rory exhibit since he had been on parole, and he looked very professional in his business suit instead of the scrubs he wore at the morgue. She hoped for Doc's sake as much as Rory's that the young man was finding himself.

At the assembly there were grins and waves from the students, and shouts of "Mr. Sanford! You comin' back?" But Brandy had the feeling that they were wasting their time, preaching to the choir for those kids too smart ever to touch drugs. The rest . . . they'd be lucky if they could get them to see a difference between the marijuana grown and used so freely in their home state and the cocaine and crack that promised an end to all their troubles.

Murphy was no different from any other American community: despite the increasing use of hard drugs, the chemicals favored by teenagers were still alcohol and nicotine. Kentucky was a tobacco state, so those whose livelihood depended on it ignored or refused to believe in the dangers of their crop. The tobacco industry put up billboards citing how many college tuitions were paid for by tobacco. Even in this audience where the oldest child might be fifteen, kids who thought alcohol or marijuana the path to hell already smoked or chewed tobacco.

But Brandy was here to do a job. There was some interest from the students in the police techniques used to trace drug dealers. She refused to acknowledge the cynical thought that they wanted to learn how to avoid being caught.

When the assembly was over, the students departed for their classes. Rory Sanford said, "You guys go on without me. I'm going to talk to the principal."

"Rory—" his grandfather said in concern.

"Yeah, I know, don't get my hopes up. But if Fred Trenton will support me to the school board there's a chance of getting reinstated."

When the younger man had gone, Dr. Sanford shook his head sadly. "He's settin' himself up. There's no hope in hell that he'll teach in Callahan County again. I wish I could find him some other job, but no one will hire him."

"Why?" asked Brandy.

"You know why. He's a convicted felon. Even if someone *would* give him a chance, they're too afraid of Judge Callahan."

"But why are you trying to find him some other job? He seems efficient enough in the morgue."

"The kids in this school could lay out instruments and clean up after an autopsy—but none of them would want to do it! Rory hates the morgue, and I don't blame him. I get the interesting part. He has nothin' but the dirty work."

Brandy liked Doc Sanford, and knew how he loved his grandson. She also knew he was convinced that Rory had been framed. There was no use talking about it; what was done was done, and Rory was being a man about it. She had seen him working several times since Carrie Wyman's autopsy, and he had obviously gotten used to it, never again reacting to even the most gruesome of wounds.

What Brandy didn't want to say to Doc Sanford was that Rory's best chance once his parole was up was to leave Callahan County and preferably the state of Kentucky. He might make a fresh start someplace far away from Murphy . . . but that also meant away from his grandfather.

A few days later, Dr. Darla Swenson, whom Brandy had met at the Homecoming party, called her. It was early Wednesday morning. "I had that talk with my children," she said. "Now . . . they need to tell you what they told me."

"I'll come over."

The Swensons lived in Oxford Estates, in an elegant home with a good acre of lawn. Inside the house the tension level threatened to explode. The two frightened children were Charlene, age thirteen, and Brian, age eleven.

"We're not supposed to tell," Brian explained. "I mean, lots of kids smoke pot—it's not like crack or something!"

"It's still illegal," said their mother.

Brandy said, "I won't ask about your friends who smoke pot, Brian. Really, I'm not here to get them into trouble."

The boy nodded, blue eyes wide.

His sister, more sophisticated, said, "They want to catch the pushers, stupid."

"Charlene, don't make things more difficult for Brian," said Dr. Swenson. "Why don't you tell what you know first?"

"You know that program you did the other day?"

"Yes," said Brandy.

"Well, the next day there was pot all over school, and the kids were laughing about how dumb the police are."

"So the dealers increased their efforts the day after the assembly. That sounds as if they were scared that the assembly had worked, doesn't it?"

"No!" Brian squeaked. "They were laughing cause—" He stopped, fear again taking over.

Brandy squatted down in front of the boy. "Brian, I'm not going to hurt you or any of your friends, even if they bought some pot. I only want to know who sold it."

"That's why the kids said you were stupid," put in Charlene. "You brought the pusher with you!"

Brandy frowned. "What do you mean?"

"Mr. Sanford!" said Brian. "I saw him. I did—I saw him in the boy's bathroom, giving it to Billy H— to a couple of the boys. That's why they had plenty to sell."

Brandy felt as if a knife had been stuck in her gut. Poor Doc. This couldn't be true . . . it couldn't! But even if his grandson proved innocent, it would put the old man through hell all over again.

Brandy was careful and thorough, reassuring Brian, but still questioning him one way, then another, as to time, what he was doing there, how good a view he had had, etc. No matter which angle she took, the boy's story held. He even produced the hall pass, with the time and the teacher's initials on it, that had allowed him to go to the bathroom.

And of course Rory Sanford had been in the school at the time— ostensibly talking to the principal.

What if, for once in their lives, the Mortree brothers had told the truth?

"Charlene," Brandy asked at last, "can you verify what your brother says?"

"Of course not. What would I be doing in the boy's bathroom?"

"Then what do you know?"

"I told you. It was all over school that the police brought in the dealer."

"Do you know Mr. Sanford?" asked Brandy.

"Sure," said Charlene. "He was my teacher before he went to jail."

"Did you like him?" asked Church.

"I did then," the girl replied. "I didn't believe he stole that money. Now I do."

Brandy was writing up her report when Church arrived back at his desk. She told him what she had found out and asked, "Now what do I do?"

"Get a search warrant for Sanford's apartment."

"Church, you don't think—"

"You can't *afford* to think on this one, Kid. Just do it by the book. I'll back you up—it could be dangerous."

Judge Callahan was in his office, as if waiting just for them. Within half an hour the two detectives were on their way, warrant in hand.

Rory Sanford lived in a shabby but clean apartment complex near the center of town, within walking distance of his job. Brandy remembered Doc Sanford's pride in his grandson's choice of the independence of his own apartment over car payments and his grandfather's charity.

Sanford opened the door. "What's wrong?" he asked. "Granddad woulda called if there was an emergency."

Church held up the warrant. "We have a warrant to search these premises."

Total confusion. "Why?"

"Suspicion of possession of a controlled substance," recited Brandy. Then she couldn't help adding, "Just let us look, Rory. We'll be through in no time."

The apartment was tiny, one room with two doors on the opposite wall, one to the bathroom, one to a closet. The kitchen was one of those all-in-one units in an alcove, and the table doubled for dining and deskwork.

It was easy to search, for Sanford, only out of prison for a month, had few possessions. Neither officer wanted to find anything, but they followed routine. Search dresser drawers, turn over to find anything taped to the bottoms. Check inside and back of the dresser. Nothing.

Brandy went to the closet, Church to the kitchen, searching the refrigerator as Brandy finished the nearly-empty closet and began on kitchen cupboards.

"Aw, no," said Church in a voice of grave disappointment. He tossed an ice cube tray into the sink and turned on the hot water. Brandy glanced to see that the tray had no dividers, just a solid block of ice with what looked like money frozen into it.

It could be only a few dollars, the young man's "mad money" tucked away from a prying landlord or anyone he might let into the apartment.

While the ice melted, Church tried the bathroom. Brandy heard the clunk and slide of the toilet tank lid, and Church's curse before he called, "Brandy, come and witness."

Taped to the inside of the porcelain lid were three plastic freezer bags, well-stuffed with something green.

The tiny bathroom became claustrophobic as Rory Sanford filled the doorway, his face going white as he saw what they had found. "That's not mine!" he exclaimed. "I never use that stuff!"

"Smart pushers never do," Church said grimly.

"Pushers? No!" the young man said, backing into the main room. "Oh, no, no, no . . . not again!" and he slumped onto the couch.

Church said, "See what else you can find."

Brandy returned to the kitchen drawers. The top one held cheap flatware, some utensils, and a pair of potholders. She shoved it closed and went to the second, more unwilling than Church to perform the arrest. Rory Sanford wasn't going anywhere.

The large bottom drawer held dish towels . . . but there was something under them. Lifting the towels, Brandy beheld four items: a small camcorder, a videotape, a long-handled cooking or barbecue fork with two sharp curved tines, and a butcher knife.

Brandy gasped. "Church! Oh, my God, come here!"

"What is it?" Church asked as Brandy carefully held up the recorder with a gloved hand.

Rory Sanford looked up. "That's not mine," he said. "How did that get here?"

Brandy carefully upended the videotape in the drawer, so she could read the label without smudging any prints on it. It was neatly typed: *Wedding Day—Harry Davis and Melody Mather.*

They arrested Rory Sanford for possession of a controlled substance. Murder charges could come later; neither Brandy nor Church was about to risk having the arrest declared invalid, so they stuck to what it said in the warrant, and let him call his attorney.

Sanford was now in police custody. If he *was* the psychopath who had murdered Carrie Wyman at the last full moon, he would have no chance to strike again. Sanford was perfectly cooperative, simply denying every criminal charge in a monotone.

He admitted that he had not been able to get in to see Middle School Principal Alfred Trenton on the day of the assembly. When the secretary turned him away, he claimed that he left the school and walked to his apartment. There he ate lunch, then walked to the morgue. He knew of no one who could alibi him from the time he had left the principal's office until he arrived at the morgue.

He insisted he did not know where the pot or the money had come from, or the camcorder either. Someone was trying to make him look like a thief and a drug pusher.

By the end of an hour of grilling, both Brandy and Church had noticed something very peculiar. They adjourned to the corridor. Rory sat slumped, the weight of the world on his shoulders. "The camcorder means nothing to him," said Church. "He doesn't connect it to murder, only to theft."

"He's only concerned about the drug charges. But Church, there was a knife in that drawer, too, and . . . a fork with the kind of prongs to make puncture wounds. Either this is a frame good enough for the Mona Lisa, or he's blacked out the murder. If he did kill Carrie, I don't think he knows it." Brandy tried to ease the tension in her shoulders. "I need a cup of coffee. How 'bout you?"

They went into the squad room, and Brandy ducked into the ladies' room for a moment. When she returned, headed for the coffee maker, she found Church confronting a livid Dr. Troy Sanford.

"What's this about you arresting my grandson?" the coroner demanded. "Drug pushing? *Murder*? Are you crazy?"

"Doc, we're just doing our jobs," Church said in his most reasonable voice. "And he hasn't been charged with murder yet. When we see what the evidence tells us—"

Just then Dan Martin entered the squad room, and Brandy remembered that they were supposed to go out to dinner. Was it that late? She looked up at the clock: 4:52 P.M..

Dan waved to her and took a chair by the water cooler, indicating that he would wait. Torn between disappointment at having a pleasant evening spoiled again, and the excitement of today's arrest, Brandy was about to go explain to him when Doc Sanford burst out, "You *know* Rory didn't murder Carrie Wyman! Did you ask him about the puncture wounds? We held back that evidence to catch the real killer, remember? You can bet my grandson don't know about saliva traces in puncture wounds!"

The man's words rang off the walls. Dan Martin could not help but hear, and Brandy saw his face twist in revulsion. He rose, clearly shaken.

"Dan, I'm sorry," said Brandy. "We've finally made an arrest in Carrie's murder. I'll be tied up for hours."

"It's all right," he said. "You—go on with your work." He was backing toward the door. "I'll call you," he added unconvincingly, turned, and hurried away.

Well, thought Brandy, *that's the end of that*. Dan had held out against her work longer than most men, but it always got to them in the end. Why did it still hurt?

She went back to where Church was trying to calm Dr. Sanford. "Doc," she said, "we're just questioning Rory at this point. But I have to tell you it looks bad."

"It is bad," Church added. "I'm sorry, Dr. Sanford, but . . . you always say blood will tell. That knife in Rory's kitchen drawer. It was wiped clean of prints, and had been washed, but not thoroughly enough. We found traces of blood . . . Carrie Wyman's blood type."

"It's a frame!" said Dr. Sanford. "Let me talk to Rory. Or you ask him about Carrie's wounds."

"Doc," Brandy said, "Rory was at her autopsy. He does know about the puncture wounds. It was when you reported the saliva in the wounds that . . . he ran out of the room."

Rory Sanford was charged with the murder of Carrie Wyman and sent over to the jail. By that time it was 7:30 P.M., so he didn't have to be transferred until 7:30 the next morning. Church and Brandy sat down to study their preliminary findings before deciding whether to question Sanford further.

Dr. Sanford had calmed down, and used his authority as coroner to accompany his grandson to the jail. The two detectives were glad to see the man take hold of his emotions again. He was usually so sharp and spry that they forgot he was in his seventies.

Church studied the fingerprints they had taken. "Most are Sanford's, of course, with a few strays that could be guests, landlord, anybody who's been in there recently."

"Anything to show we may have the wrong suspect?" Brandy asked.

"Not much. By the time the money was thawed out of the ice cube tray, it was washed clean."

"$1200," said Brandy. That certainly wasn't mad money.

"No prints on the marijuana bags, like they'd been handled by someone wearing gloves. Even if Sanford hadn't opened them yet," Church mused, "you'd still expect his prints on the outside."

"Maybe he was super-cautious," suggested Brandy. "What I find odd is the drawer where we found the video camera and the murder weapons. There were no fingerprints on any of the items, and none on the drawer handle, even on the inside."

"Gloves again, or else a thorough cleaning when the stuff was put away—but the murder was more than three weeks ago," said Church. "Assuming Sanford did it, why would he put the evidence in a drawer and never open it again? He never needed a clean dishtowel? He never looked to see that the stuff was still there? Why didn't he go out to the lake and throw it off the bridge? What if he is telling the truth, and this is a frame?"

But then he added, "Sanford's the coroner's grandson. His grandaddy raised him after his parents died. He grew up around forensic reports. He might know to wipe prints off the inside of the drawer handle."

"To the contrary," said Brandy, "he'd know his prints *should* have been on that handle if he was going about his daily business without knowing items were planted in that drawer. If he were the murderer, he'd get rid of the evidence. He had over three weeks."

"But," said Church, "obsessive murderers keep things associated with their crimes, both souvenirs of the victims and the same murder weapons, to use again. And you're forgetting the kids, Brandy. How likely is a frame to include kids?"

Not very. But, "Rory didn't react to the tape or the camcorder."

"If he's a psychopath, he could have blanked the murder out of his mind," said Church. He pushed his chair back, tilted it dangerously as he spoke. "We need a psychiatric examination. I saw a case in Chicago, serial murderer, all the evidence in the basement of his house, but he didn't remember a thing. Sanford's been under a helluva lot of stress. We don't know everything that happened to him in prison."

He let the chair legs down with a thud, and added, "Consider this: Sanford can't get anywhere in life no matter how he tries. His parents are killed in an auto accident when he's ten years old, leaving his grandparents to raise him. When he's fifteen his beloved grandmother dies. This kid is *living* stressed. But he goes to college, becomes a teacher, has his grandfather proud as punch . . . and he can't take it."

"Why not?" asked Brandy.

"Because all his life he's been told by the community that he's nobody, another worthless, shiftless Sanford. He doesn't deserve even modest success. Consciously, he feels good about himself. Subconsciously, unconsciously, he sabotages himself by embezzling and gets sent to prison. The good kid is stuck in there with all those hardened criminals for a crime he can't remember committing!"

"You think it's a case of multiple personalities?" asked Brandy.

"Possibility," said Church. "If so, Rory is absolutely right that he's been framed. What he doesn't realize is that he did it himself."

Brandy sighed. "He'll have to be examined by a psychiatrist. Just in case your theory should prove true, I wouldn't want him out walking the streets again with the next full moon coming up—" she glanced at the calendar, "—Saturday night."

Once again, Brandy had missed dinner. Although she was ravenous by now, she stopped at the jail, where it was no surprise to find Dr. Sanford. The only comfort she had to offer was that there would be no more questioning tonight.

"Come on, Doc," she said. "I'll bet you haven't eaten either. Let me buy you a hamburger. And you need to get some rest, 'cause if I know you, you'll be here to see Rory off in the morning."

They went to McDonald's. There were few customers at 9:41 P.M. on a Wednesday. Doc Sanford was quiet, looking very much his age tonight, but over a Big Mac he perked up enough to say in a conspiratorial tone, "It's Callahan. I know it is. The drugs are the connection—we all know he's getting drug money, even if the police can't prove it."

"Doc, there've been suspicions about Judge Callahan's drug connections before, but no one's ever proved a thing. As for murder . . . that's really not his style, is it?"

The coroner stared at her. "His father murdered my sister," he said grimly. "They passed it off as suicide, but he killed her no matter which of 'em pulled that trigger. Blood will tell. All Callahans are alike, none of 'em any damn good! I won't let him kill my boy, Brandy."

Brandy could do nothing more than sit and listen to the old man's ramblings. She had never seen him like this before, not even when Rory had been convicted of embezzling. Age was catching up, making him tired, incoherent, obsessed.

"Murdered Cindy Lou," muttered Sanford. "Now he's tryin' t' kill Rory, wipe all us Sanfords off the face of the Earth!"

"Doc," Brandy said gently, "it was Judge Callahan's father who was married to your sister."

The old man frowned, then nodded. "Yeah. But L. J.'s the spittin' image of his daddy. You'da thought he'd a turned out different, wouldn't you? He was like a whole different person when he was a kid. No one accepted him. His daddy hurt his mom, finally killed her. But he grew up into a Callahan anyway, didn't he? Blood will tell, Brandy. You mark my words. Callahan's gonna get his, 'cause in the end, blood will always tell!"

NINE

Confession

WHEN BRANDY GOT HOME, she found a message from Dan on her answering machine. When she returned his call, he told her, "We need to talk, some time and place where we won't be interrupted. There are things I need to tell you . . . soon."

"I'm on duty tomorrow and Friday, but unless some case breaks late I'll have the evenings free."

"Will you be on call?"

"Dan, what's this about? If you want to break up—"

"No!" Then, more calmly, "No, Brandy, but if our relationship is to grow as I hope it will . . . there are things I must explain. It's . . . complicated. And it's important that you don't get called away in the middle."

"You gonna tell me your life story?"

"Yes. But not over the telephone."

"I have Saturday off," she said. "Come for lunch."

There was a pause before he said, "All right, Brandy. I'll see you at noon on Saturday."

The next day Brandy told Church what Doc Sanford had said. "He claims Judge Callahan's father murdered Doc's sister. Have you ever heard about that?"

"No, but sometimes even if you're paranoid there are people out to get you. You remember the Meerschaum case?"

A chop shop operating out of the biggest auto body shop in town. "Yeah, I remember it."

"And the Dennis case?"

"Yeah." An automobile dealership accused of odometer rollbacks on used cars.

"The Honeywell case?"

"That happened while I was in college—but that wasn't your case, either, Church."

"I know, but it has something in common with the others."

"A dean accused of running a student prostitution ring? What's that got to do with automobile scams?"

"Not the cars," Church prompted.

She thought a moment. "The prime suspects were all acquitted. In fact, did any of them ever come to trial?"

"No. They were all frames. A salesman was setting the odometers back to increase his sales, an employee and some buddies were operating the chop shop after hours, and some students were running the so-called dating service, using the dean's computer."

"What you're saying," said Brandy, "is that Murphy seems to have an inordinate number of cases in which somebody is framed."

"Not just somebody. All the suspects were either wealthy or influential, or both. And guess whose political campaigns they now all support?"

"I don't need three," said Brandy.

"Judge L. J. Callahan declared insufficient evidence in every case. That left a sword still hanging over each man's head until, after a time, the true culprits were discovered."

"After a time, or after a bribe?" Brandy wondered. "But Rory Sanford's not rich or influential."

"Callahan hates him just for being a Sanford."

"Why?" asked Brandy. "Callahan's mother was a Sanford. Doc Sanford's sister, the one he claims was murdered."

"A *family* feud. The worst kind." He continued excitedly, "Brandy, help me find other cases like these three. Look for a pattern: Callahan wants a wealthy or influential backer, the person is reluctant; the person is accused of a crime that would ruin him, Judge Callahan comes to the rescue, and suddenly he has a loyal backer!"

When they found two more such cases, Church and Brandy decided it was time to go to Chief Benton.

The police chief scowled as he flipped over the pages. "Is this what you're paid for—to dig up closed cases? What the hell do you think Judge Callahan did—forced honest people to commit crimes so he could blackmail them? Do you know how crazy that sounds?"

"But the evidence—" Church protested.

"The evidence shows that L. J. Callahan has been our local judge for the past fifteen years! Of *course* he's involved in these five cases—hundreds of *other* cases, too! God Almighty, the man has to pay just like his father for the sin of being rich and powerful."

"His father?" Brandy pounced.

"People claimed he murdered his wife. Or rather, the Sanfords claimed it. The woman was caught in adultery and committed suicide. Doc Sanford can't accept the truth. He's the one who keeps that feud alive."

Church refused to be deterred. "Sir, a little investigating can't hurt. We've found five suspicious cases. Suppose—"

"Suspicious? I'm suspicious that you two won't work on *open* cases! We still don't know who killed Rand and Paschall! We'll have no more of this shit. Suspicious," he muttered again, pulling a file from his "In" box and slapping it on his desk as a dismissal. Brandy and Church had turned to go when he suddenly called after them, "Why ain't you suspicious of your professor boyfriend, Detective Mather? He did all that computer work for Judge Callahan last summer. You think maybe he's into white-collar crime?"

The dig came as a blow to Brandy's solar plexus. All *what* computer work? Was Dan in Callahan's clutches? Or was there something even more sinister?

Everything strange about Danton Martin poured back into her mind, from the Vulcan nerve pinch to his sun allergy. As she went about her work, Brandy's mind replayed every moment she had spent with Dan, every conversation. He seemed so open, yet she found herself trying to patch together his background from bits and pieces.

His "contraband Christ." Willed to him by his archaeology professor? It wouldn't have *belonged* to that professor, she now realized, but to the university that funded the expedition. How did it get into private hands?

And sunscreen. Dan had said that when he was in college he had had to cover up or not go to the beach. Exactly when had he been in college?

The university offices were still open when Brandy got off duty, so she stopped by Personnel and requisitioned Dan's records. Graduate transcript and letters of recommendation were there. For his undergraduate work there was only the transcript from an Omaha community college followed by upper-level work at the University of Nebraska.

He had been an undergraduate from twelve to fifteen years ago, when Brandy had been in middle and high school. She clearly remembered one of her classmates, a magnificent redhead with skin like milk, slathering on high-SPF sunscreen and swimming with the rest of the kids.

Dan had said he had had to cover up or not go to the beach. Beach? In Nebraska? A lakeshore, maybe—but how could he not know about sunscreen?

Brandy copied down the names of the high school in Nebraska and the elementary school in Iowa that Dan supposedly attended. Back at the station she ran background on Danton Martin. He had no criminal record—at least not under that name. He owned a car, which she knew. He had one speeding ticket, from eighteen months ago.

Trying to remember how Dan had done it, Brandy got into several wrong menus before she managed to access his bank records. She could find nothing unusual. Dan now had $5769.20 in a savings account, $1340.33 in a checking account, and just under $25,000 in certificates of deposit. When he had arrived in Murphy he had opened the savings and checking accounts with less than $4000 transferred from Tallahassee. His money had grown slowly over the past five years—the one thing in common with Everett Land was that he saved an exceptionally large percentage of his pay.

On the other hand, both were single men without families, and Dan had mentioned a reason for saving: he was up for tenure this year. If he didn't get it, he would have to move on; if he did he planned to buy a house. In either case, that money would become important.

She went on to his school records, sure that the ones from Florida Central were real. Computer records at the University of Nebraska confirmed what was on the transcript.

She found his birth record in Iowa, but for ten years on either side of that date she could find no record of the brother he had told her about.

The elementary school records were not computerized, but Dan's high school and college records were available.

Brandy went home to Sylvester and a frozen dinner. But the next morning she could not resist calling the schools in Iowa and Nebraska, asking them to fax her photos of Danton Edward Martin.

She didn't know what she expected. A little boy with Dan's black eyes huge in a young face? A gawky teenager with a bad haircut and a promise of grace to come? Or, would the photos show some blond, blue-eyed child who had at some point been replaced by the man she knew?

In the end, it was none of the above. All three schools faxed back that they had only computerized records. Dan's hardcopy files were missing. The high school vice-principal included the fact that there was no Danton Martin in the yearbooks, and that he had gone so far as to question two teachers who were on staff at the time he was supposedly enrolled. Neither remembered such a boy. What was going on, he wanted to know. Was it a criminal alias of someone who had gone to their school?

It was clearly the most exciting thing that vice-principal had come upon in ages. Brandy faxed back thanks, and asked for his confidence. She probably made his day.

But he had unmade hers.

She was certain that if she got her hands on the yearbooks for the University of Nebraska for the two years Dan supposedly attended, they would also have no photos, and no references to him. He hadn't gone to college there, probably not anywhere in Nebraska . . . and wherever he had gone, it was earlier than he claimed.

It was the same kind of manufactured identity as Everett C. Land's, and Dan was obviously claiming to be younger than he really was.

The date of birth on Dan Martin's driver's license made him thirty-five. Could he really be forty-five? Fifty? She thought of his smooth, unmarked skin, his black hair with no hint of gray. Did he dye it?

What was Dan Martin?

Brandy prayed "Witness Protection Program" with all her heart. But she knew, deep inside, that that would not explain Danton Edward Martin any more than it did Everett Charles Land.

On Saturday morning, Brandy threw her nervous energy into cleaning. Then she showered, and debated over what to wear to confront the man she . . . was involved with . . . about the web of lies that bound his life.

Too serious for jeans, she decided, but not an occasion to dress up.

She put on her best gabardine slacks with a dark green lambswool sweater and a tweed jacket.

It was cold but sunny, an almost painfully brilliant day. The first snow of the season had fallen in the night, enough to make a pretty coating on trees and lawns without disturbing traffic.

Dan wore his ubiquitous hat and sunglasses as he got out of his car and followed the path she had swept to the front steps. Brandy's first thought was, "We made the same decision about what to wear!" for Dan was in brown wool trousers, a maroon sweater, and a tweed jacket. But for the first time, the compelling magnetism Brandy always felt around him was completely missing.

"Would you like some lunch?" she asked.

"Not now," he replied. "Coffee might help, though."

All she had to do was punch the button. She had also put out a can of soup and a saucepan, a frying pan, and bread, intending to make grilled cheese sandwiches.

As the coffee percolated, Dan picked up the soup can. "Campbell's Tomato," he said. "My mother used this."

"Oh? A farmer's wife in Iowa heated up canned soup?"

He turned abruptly. "That's what I came to talk about, Brandy. I'm not . . . exactly the person I told you."

"I know," she said. "I don't know what name is on your real birth certificate, but it's not Danton Edward Martin."

He nodded slowly. "How much have you found out?"

"Everything about you before you enrolled in the Ph.D. program at Florida Central is faked."

"Not the GRE's," he said. "I took those as Dan Martin. But you're right. When did you discover it?"

"I confirmed my suspicions yesterday."

"Can I convince you that I had already planned to tell you everything?"

"Including why you never react like a normal man?"

"What?"

"Anyone else would be furious."

"What good would that do?" he asked. "I have to tell you, though you won't want to believe it."

"You're whatever Everett Land was," said Brandy.

"That's right."

"Witness Protection Program?"

"No. I changed my own identity."

The coffeemaker heaved its last steaming sigh, and Dan poured them each a cup of coffee. He stared into the dark liquid as if searching for words. Finally he said, "I'm older than the records show."

"How much older?"

"Seventy-four."

"That's not possible," Brandy said flatly.

"And that," he said, "is the *easiest* part to accept." When she didn't respond, he continued, "You are perceptive, intuitive, and strongly attuned to me. You guessed I was married."

"Are you?"

"I was. It was a happy marriage until my wife died."

"Did you kill her?"

He looked up in hurt surprise. "Cancer killed her. I loved Megan— part of me always will. You're the first woman I've cared about since."

Brandy let the ensuing silence drag, an interrogation technique when one had no idea what to ask next. It worked.

"I actually grew up in Newark, New Jersey," Dan continued. "One of the things I abandoned when I changed lives was a hospital certificate with my mother's fingerprints and my footprints. Beth Israel Hospital is still there. I'm sure you can get access to the records."

"Beth Israel Hospital is in New York," said Brandy.

"Mom went into labor on the New York City subway. I don't think you'll need proof after tonight, but if you do, the Jersey address will be in the hospital records."

"After tonight?"

"Thank God sunset comes early in November. I wanted to tell you yesterday or the day before, Brandy. It's hard to believe unless I can show you."

"Show me what?"

"Why I had to change my identity. Why I'll have to do it again in a few years. And why . . . I can help you solve the murders of those police officers."

"What do you know about *that?!*" Brandy demanded.

"Not who did it. But how it was done, why no one resisted. What I don't understand is . . . why Carrie Wyman was murdered, and why in a way to threaten me?"

"What are you talking about?"

"The murderer thought you'd tell me about the puncture wounds, the saliva—but what good is a threat if I don't know what it's supposed to make me do? Or not do?"

"Dan, you're not making sense," Brandy said gently, his sudden irrationality frightening her.

"I'm sorry," he said. "It's hard to come out and say it." He managed a wan smile. "Promise not to throw me out before sunset?"

"I promise," she agreed.

He took a deep breath, and once again addressed his coffee cup. "Remember the night you cut your finger? Did you wonder why it healed so fast?"

"It wasn't serious."

"But it would have been painful for a few days if I hadn't healed it for you. Please—don't argue, Brandy. Let me get through this. That day in the woods, when we rescued Jeff Jones—you asked how I hypnotized him, but not how I got his leg unstuck."

"You tore your hands up breaking the rock."

His eyes met hers. "Did you observe what happened to my hands?"

"They were completely healed the next day."

"Have you also noticed that I can see in the dark?"

"I half suspected it."

He studied her. "I wish I had the proof of my age. I've been weighing the benefits of having it available against making a connection between my old identity and my present one. I should have taken the risk. For now, will you take my word that I was born seventy-four years ago?"

"Dan, how can I believe that? Look at you."

"Yes," he said in sudden excitement, "look at me, Brandy. There *is* something I can show you now."

She looked at him as he asked, at first seeing only the man she knew . . . then . . . there was gray in his hair, bags under his eyes. The firm young skin of his face was replaced by sagging jowls and liver spots.

"Oh, my God," she whispered. "You *are* seventy-four."

"But this is not how I look. Touch me."

Hesitantly, she touched his face—and felt his familiar smooth, youthful complexion, not the aged, blemished skin her eyes perceived.

"More hypnosis," she said.

"Related. But a mirror will show its limitations."

There was a full-length mirror in the entry hall. Brandy led Dan to it.

She backed off, putting him between herself and the mirror, and still could not believe what she saw: the man before her looked like the old man he claimed to be; the mirror showed the young man she knew and—

"I can't fool mirrors or cameras," Dan explained.

It *had* to be a trick . . . but how was it done? When she touched him again, the aged image dissolved. "Bring the old man image back," she said.

"What?" he asked, glancing reflexively at the mirror, then back to Brandy with a self-deprecating shake of the head. "What do you see now?"

"You. Or what I thought was you."

"You can penetrate the illusion," he said, something like awe in his voice. "All right, Brandy—I'll stop trying to make you see anything but the truth. Now it's time to *tell* you."

But Dan would not simply state his "truth." Back in the kitchen, he urged, "Add it up. Put the fact that I'm seventy-four together with mirrors revealing the truth, rapid healing, hypnotic powers, extra strength, sun allergy—?" He looked at her hopefully, the professor waiting for a student to draw the correct conclusion.

In her research she had run across a possibility for some of his odd quirks. "You have porphyria?"

He blinked. "Have you considered trying out for *Jeopardy*? How many people have ever heard of that disease?"

"I looked up causes of sun allergy. Is that it?"

"No," he replied. Then, steeling himself, "I'm a vampire."

"No you're not," she said automatically. "You're out in daylight. You eat—even food with garlic. You show in mirrors. You've got a crucifix hanging on your living room wall, for goodness' sake!"

"Bram Stoker researched the superstitions, not the truth. I'm what started the legends. We are few, but we're human. I'm not a resuscitated corpse. I don't sleep in a coffin or fear religious objects. You've just seen where the superstition about not showing in mirrors comes from."

"You show."

"*I* show, as I really am. If I used influence to look older, to stay in one place for many years, if you looked for 'me' in the mirror, you wouldn't see an old man. You might conclude that I didn't show at all."

"Oh," said Brandy. This was getting too complicated.

Dan started to reach toward her, but pulled back. "If I touch you it's too hard not to influence you," he explained. "You must see the evidence. I'm a vampire, not a psychopath. You can't kill me with a bullet."

"Not even a silver one?"

"That's werewolves. You could kill me with a dum-dum bullet if it destroyed my heart or my brain. Otherwise the damage would heal, rapidly and without scars."

Brandy remembered blood on Dan's hands after they rescued Jeff Jones . . . blood that washed off, leaving partly-healed skin underneath. And the next day there had been no blisters, no scabs, no scars—

She turned his hands palm up on the table. They were, as always, far softer than hers. "You don't have callouses," she said.

"My flesh regenerates perfectly. A disadvantage, actually. Manual labor causes cuts and blisters."

"And the next day they're gone."

He let out a breath. "You're starting to believe me."

"It's not a logical explanation."

"It is to me," he said. "I live with it."

"How did you—?"

"I was born this way. It's an extremely recessive gene. My parents weren't vampires—"

"You're adopted?"

"No. I assume they both carried the gene for vampirism. But it had never happened to them, so they were no help when I started showing the signs at puberty. A craving for blood at the full moon is pretty frightening to an adolescent! But I learned to hide it, and began to research what I really am. It's hard to sort out superstition from fact, but I learned from experience. By now I have a pretty good idea of the truth."

"Which is?"

"I don't have to kill—I never have. You've seen my hypnotic powers."

"Why can't you just make me believe you?"

"I don't want our relationship to be forced. I'm working very hard not to influence you," he explained. "I wanted to tell you all this yesterday or the day before. Tonight the full moon rises at sunset, and I don't know how well I'll be able to control myself."

"Do you turn into a bat?"

"I'm not a shape-shifter, either, although sometimes you make me feel as if I've melted into a puddle."

"Nothing happened at the last two full moons," Brandy pointed out.

"Last time I had to tear myself away before I—"

"—tried to suck my blood?"

"Yes," he said, almost defiantly.

Sylvester, whom Brandy had left on her bed upstairs, came in and hopped onto Dan's lap. He petted the cat while Brandy thought over what she had just learned. The last full moon had been her mother's wedding reception. "When you left me, did you go after Carrie instead?"

There was a long pause, during which Brandy could hear the beating of her own heart. Then, "Yes," he said. "I put the puncture wounds in her throat. But I didn't kill her."

"Oh, God," Brandy whispered helplessly. Could her mild-mannered professor be the psychopath who had murdered her best friend? Cold prickles ran over her skin, but with the same discipline she used when she was shooting, she listened dispassionately.

"I . . . almost took from you—but I couldn't without your permission. The Craving was so strong when I left you that I took the easy way. Carrie knew me. She wasn't afraid."

"You . . . drank her blood."

"I don't deny it," he replied, "but that's all it was. Just an ordinary feeding."

"Ordinary!" Brandy gasped, his casualness penetrating her enforced calm as no ranting could have.

"Ordinary to me," Dan explained. "I feed at every full moon. I never hurt my donors—I don't even frighten them. It's easy when the person knows me—just a little influence to avoid questions. I flagged Carrie down and told her my car had stalled. She offered me a ride."

"And you killed her."

"No!" he insisted. "I influenced her to go to her own house and park in the drive. Brandy, I left her safely asleep in her car. I locked the doors when I left."

"Did you wipe your fingerprints off the car door?"

"I didn't have to. I . . . don't leave fingerprints."

Brandy accepted that statement at face value, for, "No prints but Carrie's were found in or on her car. If you don't leave prints, that implicates you."

"Or . . . another vampire," said Dan. "Carrie should have wakened naturally some time after I left her. She wouldn't have remembered seeing me."

"How did she get to the park?"

"I don't know!" Dan said vehemently. Then, "She could not have wakened before the wounds on her neck had healed. At least two hours. When I heard that you had found puncture wounds, I knew there was another vampire involved."

Dan's story became more pathetic with every new embroidery. He was mad—but calm for the moment. Sunset was her deadline; meanwhile Brandy's safety depended on keeping him talking. "What other vampire?"

"Whoever used his influence to override mine," Dan explained. "He made Carrie wake up and drive to the park . . . or just had her open the door, and he drove. Then he . . . murdered her. He wanted you to find puncture wounds, so he cut her throat."

Brandy shook her head. "The slashes were made to obliterate the puncture wounds."

"No," said Dan. "Just the way my saliva healed the cut on your finger, all sign of the puncture wounds would have disappeared long before morning. Carrie was killed to stop the healing process, leaving the bite marks as evidence. Didn't you run a DNA test on the saliva?"

"There was so little, there were no skin cells in it." The cop in her wanted to scold the woman in her for her relief, and both were angry at her stupidity: she had a confession. There was no need for physical evidence. Except —

Brandy took a glass from the cupboard and wiped it clean, then handed it to Dan with the towel. "Show me," she directed. Obligingly, he gripped and released it. She held it up to the light. No prints.

Again Brandy felt the shiver she had known when the mirror told her something different from what she saw looking at Dan. She now knew why no prints but Carrie's were found in her car.

Dan was suffering from schizophrenic delusion. He probably wasn't fit to stand trial, but she needed to take him into custody before he tried again to act out his fantasies. *Keep him talking while you figure a way out.*

"Why do you think whoever killed Carrie left evidence of a vampire's attack?"

"It's directed at me," he repeated. "I'm the only vampire likely to hear details of a murder investigation. Only you're too good a police officer to discuss your cases, so I didn't know till Dr. Sanford blurted it out. You said Carrie died of knife wounds. She wasn't drained of so much blood that she died first, and then her throat was cut."

"No."

Dan thought a moment. "You think I'm the killer. A man who thinks he's a vampire tries to act it out, and slashes his victim's throat when he can't drink enough blood to kill her."

Now it had hit the fan. Brandy's gun was in the front closet. She had training in unarmed combat, but she also knew Dan's strength.

Sylvester was bumping Dan's chin, trying to soothe away his tension. Why was her cat sympathetic to a psychopathic murderer?

Dan stroked the cat, but his eyes were on Brandy. She saw sadness in them, perhaps fear, but no anger.

And no madness.

"You think I killed Carrie," he repeated. "How can I prove what I am without terrifying you?"

Dan rose to his feet, dumping Sylvester off his lap. "What if the murderer planted vampire clues in Carrie's murder to scare me away from you? I've put you in danger!"

"More danger than being here with you?"

"I won't hurt you. But if there's another vampire who doesn't want the police to know that we exist—" But then he shook his head. "After tonight it won't matter. Either way, he'll know his secret is safe."

"Either way?"

"If after tonight I don't see you anymore, and you don't reveal my secret, he'll assume you don't know. But . . . if we remain together he will know you'll never reveal that vampires exist."

"How would he know that?"

"Because to reveal his secret would be to reveal mine." He sat back down and took her hand. "I love you, Brandy. But you don't know whether I'm a madman, possibly a psychopathic killer. After sunset you will see the truth."

Brandy stared at the man whom only days ago she had thought to be a nice if rather stuffy college professor.

A man who thought he was a vampire.

If she pretended she believed him she would have to point out the holes in his logic—such as that even if a vampire killed Carrie, it was still her job to apprehend him.

Just as she was about to plead too much coffee for an excuse to escape, Dan said, "Please don't go."

Usually it was comforting or humorous when he read her mind. Tonight—

"I'm sorry," he said. "It's hard to resist our rapport. I hope I'll never have to fight it again. I almost couldn't last month—but if you tell me to go away, somehow I'll find the strength. For now . . . get your gun, Brandy, handcuff me if that will ease your fears . . . but please, stay with me until the sun sets."

Daylight was dimming, but as Brandy got up she noted that it was due to snow clouds gathering again. It wasn't sunset yet. Dan's story was utterly bizarre . . . but how could she believe he was a dangerous psychopath?

What it boiled down to was logic vs. emotion.

Oh, thanks again, Mr. Spock! she thought. But it was still true: there was no way she could believe that Dan Martin was a vampire, twice as old as he appeared to be, a being with supernatural powers who wanted to suck her blood. His trick with the mirror was only hypnosis, but it could be dangerous if he could use it to make her hand over her weapon. She had no idea why he didn't leave fingerprints, but it implicated him in Carrie's murder. She should cuff him and march him down to the station.

And yet—Dammit, she spent her life rounding up and questioning every imaginable kind of loony. She knew how they talked and acted. This man, for all his impossible beliefs, struck her as eminently sane.

She wanted desperately to trust him!

When Brandy returned to the kitchen, Dan said, "Call Church. Tell him to call you here at 6:00 P.M., and if he doesn't get an answer to come over with a SWAT team."

"Murphy doesn't have a SWAT team," said Brandy, "and if we did, what good would they be against a vampire?"

"Brandy," Dan said, "you are only in danger if I'm *not* a vampire."

"Maybe. Just remember, if I'm found dead, or not found at all, you will be the first suspect."

"If I were delusional, I would think I could get away with it, wouldn't I?"

Mind games. Brandy checked that her gun was loaded, then put it on the table in front of her, out of Dan's reach. "Now I'm only in danger if you're not an ordinary human," she said.

Dan shook his head sadly. "I'm human, just not ordinary." Then he added, "You'd better frisk me."

"Why?"

"I don't want to be shot for reaching for my handkerchief. I may heal rapidly, but it still hurts."

He did have a handkerchief, a pen, a billfold, a few coins, keys, and a Swiss army knife. That last he placed in the middle of the table, with a shudder. "I never realized before . . . it could be used to slit a throat." Then he looked sadly at Brandy. "It would be easy to use my influence to keep you from feeling apprehensive. But if this is going to work, it must be of your own free will."

"Is that how it was with your wife?" she asked.

A puzzled look came into his eyes for a moment. Then he said, "The answer is, yes and no. Megan knew what I am, and loved me anyway. Brandy . . . I'm not confessing to criminal activity, to an addiction, or to having a dread disease. I'm telling you what I *am*, and hoping that you can accept it."

"So you can drink my blood."

"Yes," he said flatly.

"And turn me into a vampire, too."

"No."

"No?"

"Vampires are born, not made."

"I thought anyone bitten by a vampire becomes one."

"Add it up, Brandy," said Dan. "If that were true, with every vampire creating twelve or thirteen vampires every year, eventually everybody would be a vampire!"

"You have thought this all out, haven't you?"

"I'm not making it up," he said gently.

"More coffee?" Brandy asked, unnerved by his calm certainty.

"Not for me," Dan said. "To keep from influencing you, I prevent you from influencing me. I won't be able to ingest anything more until. . . ."

At the idea of his sinking his teeth into her throat, Brandy rose, tucking her gun into her belt. She put the mugs in the sink and started to clean the coffee pot. But she couldn't turn her back on Dan. He took over, threw out the old filter full of coffee grounds, installed a new one.

Brandy couldn't look at Dan Martin and see a madman.

But if he wasn't insane, then he was a vampire, and that meant *she* was crazy! She'd better take him down to the station, let what happened at sunset happen —

"The sun is setting," said Dan.

Too late. She would have to play it out here. Determinedly, she did not hesitate to touch his hand . . . with her left hand, her right on her gun. The familiarity of walking beside him, his smell, his size, his shape and movement, contrasted with the apprehension in her gut as they went to the living room. Brandy sat on the couch she had moved from her apartment. Dan seated himself carefully on the edge of the coffee table, facing her.

What did he expect to happen now? Did he think his eyes would glow, that his features would become monstrous? That he would grow fangs?

Outside, light snow fell. There was no red or golden sunset, nor could they see the moon rising behind the clouds. Daylight simply grayed toward black.

The furnace gave a click, and warm air stirred the drapes. Moving slowly, unthreateningly, Dan leaned toward Brandy.

She drew her gun, but kept it pointed at the floor.

She let him kiss her, felt him lick her lips in his strange sensuous way, and by habit opened her mouth to him as she had a hundred times before. That was safe enough—but what if he proceeded to lick her neck? Now that she knew his unique caress was part of a vampire fantasy, could she remain calm?

His mouth stayed on hers, tongue caressing, then moving to stroke the roof of her mouth, on either side where the valleys led back toward the soft palate. Brandy let her own tongue follow his, repeating the motions—

His taste was familiar, but the contours of his mouth seemed strange . . . crowded? What was this? Instead of the normal valleys on either side of his hard palate, she felt ridges. Strangely not put off, she explored curiously —

Something moved!

The hard but yielding texture of palate parted to release smooth, unyielding bone or—

As Brandy's tongue withdrew, it was followed by —

"Oh, my God!" Brandy gasped, withdrawing only far enough for her eyes to focus on his mouth.

Teeth.

No, fangs.

Unfolding from the roof of his mouth like a viper's fangs, there emerged long, needle-sharp teeth.

TEN

Proposal

DAN OPENED HIS MOUTH wide to allow the fangs to clear his lower lip. When they were fully extended, reaching a good inch past his incisors, he could not hide them. They curved slightly, just like —

Just like the tines of that fork that had so precisely fit the wounds in Carrie Wyman's neck.

But Brandy couldn't think about that now. Something had happened to Dan's eyes, too: they were red, more reflection than glow. The part of Brandy's mind divorced from her immediate feelings diagnosed dilation, allowing light to reflect off the retina, the look of an animal caught in a car's headlights. Together with the fangs, it gave the man before her a surreal look.

If she had not felt the fangs emerge, Brandy might have thought them a theatrical appliance. But they were unquestionably real . . . and that meant—

Helplessly overcome with relief, Brandy giggled.

"That was not among the reactions I was prepared for," Dan said. The fangs caused him to lisp slightly.

"I'm sorry." Brandy fought incipient hysteria. "This is a bit of a reversal on Beauty and the Beast!"

She heard relief in his familiar deep chuckle. Then he said, "I didn't know how else to prove it isn't a trick." He looked into her eyes, the eerie glow focused on her. "You're not frightened." It was a statement of fact.

"No," she realized. The hard knot of fear in her belly had melted in the face of irrefutable evidence. "You're not crazy," she said. "As long as you're not some psycho killer, whatever else you are we can work through."

"Oh, God, I love you," he growled, started to reach for her, then paused to . . . retract his fangs. They folded back up behind his upper teeth, into either side of his palate. At the same time, his eyes resumed their usual appearance.

When he kissed her, Brandy probed curiously with her tongue. The fangs lay covered but palpable on either side of his palate. Dan broke the kiss in exasperation. "Could we have a little more romance and a little less investigation?"

But she had to ask, "Why didn't I ever notice that swelling before?"

"Once I've . . . fed, they don't come down into striking position until the next full moon. Bran-dee," he protested as she tilted her head, trying to see into his mouth.

"Let me look," she insisted until he gave in. Everything appeared amazingly normal. He had all his teeth, but three lower molars and one upper one were crowned, and she saw a number of fillings. From any angle she tried, there was nothing visibly abnormal. "Doesn't your dentist notice? What about x-rays?"

"Dental x-rays are taken from the sides. If the fangs show at all, it's just a shadow. Are you about finished?"

For answer she tried to give him a proper kiss, but had to interrupt her embrace to put her gun on the coffee table. Her fear was gone, their rapport returned. It wasn't what he called influence—he wasn't experiencing anything except relief at her acceptance. She could read his feelings easily, and something of his knowledge, too . . . one of the things she read, without question, was that Dan had not killed Carrie, nor anyone else.

Brandy pulled Dan onto the couch, then settled beside him. "I'm sorry. I've never known a vampire before. Are you all right now?"

"Much better than all right," he said, giving her a gentle squeeze.

"You haven't, uh—"

"Not until you're ready."

The reminder of what he expected was unsettling. Those fangs penetrating her throat—she supposed she could accept it as she did a flu shot if it was what Dan needed to live. Perhaps his hypnotic powers kept the pain away. "Will you answer some more questions?"

His deep chuckle rumbled in his chest. "I fell in love with a detective. I'll live with it."

"Did you . . . drink my blood the night you put me to sleep in my apartment?"

She sensed his confusion for a moment as he tried to remember. "No. It wasn't near the full moon. The Craving starts two or three nights before, but it's only relentless that one night. But yes, I put you to sleep, and yes, it was the same thing I did to Jeff. There were witnesses that time, so I called it the Vulcan nerve pinch to make you think it was just the power of suggestion."

"But you're planning to drink my blood tonight."

"Only if you want me to," Dan replied.

"You could make me want it."

"I don't think so," he said. "I don't think I can make you do anything against your will, Brandy. In any case, I won't. Any more questions?"

"Hundreds! Let me just get the big ones out of the way."

"All right."

"Health," she said. "You drink a different person's blood every month. Ever been tested for hepatitis? AIDS?"

"Yes, but not because I thought I had either," he told her. "I don't even catch cold. But I had a blood test last year, when they were looking for a marrow donor for that student with cancer."

"You . . . would have donated?"

"Of course! I obviously have a superior immune system. If my blood type had matched hers I've have gladly donated, but it didn't." He paused, and added, "I was both relieved and disappointed. Certain things about my nature, such as rapid healing, would have been revealed . . . but I might have learned something about vampire physiology. Anyway, they did a full-spectrum test on everyone who gave samples, and I got back a clean bill of health. If you want me to, I'll be tested again."

"Blood tests don't show that you're a vampire?"

"They weren't screening for vampires," he explained. "I have no idea whether some sub-factor would indicate it."

"This superior immune system . . . that's how your saliva heals other people?"

"It heals wounds," he said. "It won't cure colds . . . or cancer. But yes, when I licked the gash in your finger, that stopped the bleeding and made it begin to heal."

"It was gone the next day," she acknowledged. But her line of questioning had obviously set Dan to thinking.

"Did you see the autopsy report on Everett Land?" he asked. "Was there anything to indicate that he wasn't an ordinary human being?"

"Oh, God," Brandy remembered. "Land didn't develop rigor mortis. Neither did Chase or Jenny Anderson, but Officers Rand and Paschall did. And the bullet wound to Chase Anderson's hand was healed as much as if days instead of hours had passed!"

Dan stared at her. "Two *more* vampires? I had no idea. How many of us are there around here?"

"You'd know better than I would. But . . . wait a minute. The Andersons had fingerprints."*

Again Brandy felt Dan's bewilderment. "I thought . . . not leaving fingerprints was a sign of vampirism."

"The only thing I know it's a sign of is old age," said Brandy.

"It is? I didn't know that."

"I guess the police don't broadcast it to avoid tempting geriatric criminals. Have you *never* had fingerprints?"

"I did as a child. I only encountered the idea of vampires not having fingerprints in some Victorian text a couple of years ago, and checked it out on myself. Before that, I tried to avoid getting fingerprinted because I didn't want prints on record when I changed identities. Rett didn't leave fingerprints."

"But he was over 65, and so are you," Brandy pointed out. "The Andersons might have been the age they appeared, mid-thirties." She thought a moment. "You didn't frame Rory Sanford, then."

---

*AUTHOR'S NOTE: When I was in England in the summer of 1992, I sat in on a trial at the Old Bailey. An 80-year-old woman had been murdered, and a Scotland Yard detective was testifying. All the fingerprints in the woman's apartment were of the woman's caretaker, who was charged with the murder. When the judge asked why no prints of the victim were found, the detective replied, as if it were something "every schoolboy knows," that people over 65 don't leave fingerprints! I had never seen that piece of information anywhere. In the summer of 1994 I taught at a writer's workshop at the University of Georgia, and took the opportunity to attend other sessions presented by forensics experts for people interested in writing mysteries. I asked, and was told yes, it's true. Ever since, I've been looking for the right place to use this piece of information.

"How do you come to that conclusion?"

"The drawer in which the evidence was concealed was wiped clean of prints. Someone without fingerprints would have left it with Rory's own prints on it."

"Well, it's nice to know there's one crime you don't suspect me of. But still . . . all these vampires. I thought we were extremely rare. Of course we all cover our tracks. I've only discovered one other vampire before— two, if you count Rett, although I hadn't gotten up the nerve to confront him. His death provided confirmation that vampires suddenly age and die when their time is up. I'd like to know how old Rett really was."

"We can try to trace back beyond the two identities we know," said Brandy, "but it gets harder before the 1950's. Dan, could the Andersons have escaped from jail?"

"I'd expect too many safeguards and too many other prisoners for them to influence a jailer to let them go. It wasn't terribly smart, calling attention to themselves with a bank-robbing spree. If they were put in prison— imagine a surveillance camera catching a vampire feeding!"

Brandy added, "The next time Chase Anderson's bandage was changed, the doctor would have found his hand completely healed."

Dan nodded. "I think . . . their recklessness made them dangerous, so another vampire killed them."

"Well, I know that wasn't you, either. You were with me when the Car 108 murders occurred."

He gently squeezed her shoulders, as if to reassure her . . . or himself. Brandy continued thinking out loud. "Dan . . . whoever made certain the evidence of a vampire's bite remained on Carrie's body might not have had you, specifically, in mind."

"Only another vampire could influence Carrie," said Dan. "That's four besides me. Brandy, this is crazy."

"No—one of the vampires may be, though. The one who murdered the Car 108 victims . . . and Carrie."

"The same person?" Dan asked.

"You said Carrie's death was a warning. To you, or to any vampire in the vicinity? Dan, I need more information. You don't live on blood. You have a healthy appetite."

"I need only a few ounces of blood, once a month. It seems to be a vital supplement, not food. I have no idea if I'm lacking some hormone or enzyme that I get from human blood, or if it's something else entirely.

All I know is that without blood I would die. Maybe in my next identity I'll study biochemistry, try to find out how it works."

"This is . . . your second identity? Or were there others?"

"This is my second. I was an engineer before, helped to build dams and other projects after World War II."

"You have hypnotic powers. You can see in the dark. You're immune to diseases. What else?"

"During the hours of darkness I have greater strength than other people."

"How great?"

"I'm not Superman. I *can* lift more than the strongest Olympic weightlifter . . . although the one time I pushed it to the limit I put my back out. My muscles can't support such effort. But by the next day my back healed. In an emergency I wouldn't hesitate to try again."

"This rapid healing—?"

"A blessing and a curse," he explained. "I'm not a biologist, but I think what makes me different from you is not so much the content of my cells, as that it duplicates rapidly and perfectly. Current theory says human cells slowly lose that ability. It would explain vampire longevity—as well as the fact that we don't scar or callous. My body automatically maintains itself in a healthy state, but I can't 'buff up.' My light sensitivity—the reason for sunglasses even in the winter—lets me see in the dark. There's nothing supernatural about it."

"And you don't really have a sun allergy," said Brandy. "You just can't tan, so you burn."

"Gruesomely," he agreed. "It heals overnight, but that doesn't keep it from hurting. I'm lucky, though, to have some natural color in my skin. Northern European types stay very pale. That was one reason I suspected Rett Land."

Because he had appeared so old, Brandy had found no significance in Land's pallor. "You think he died of . . . natural causes?"

"I think so," Dan told her. "I assume our cells, too, lose the ability to reproduce accurately. Just the timing is different: in most people it happens gradually; in vampires it's sudden. But that is just a theory.

"Brandy, I don't have all the answers. Vampire lore is a mass of contradictions and superstitions, not scientific studies. I don't know how long I can expect to live before I wear out, the way Rett did."

"You said you can be killed by destroying your heart or brain," said Brandy. "The Andersons' murderer knew that."

"Beheading also kills us," Dan said, "or burning. Such forms of execution were once used so if criminals were vampires they wouldn't come back from the dead. There's supposed to be another method, draining out all the vampire's blood, but that's pretty hard to do. It's easier to cut the vampire's head off, or burn him at the stake."

Brandy shuddered. "What about the traditional stake through the heart?"

"That would pretty well destroy it," said Dan. "Mr. Pointy is not the safest way to kill a vampire, though."

"Why not?"

"Most people don't know exactly where the heart is, and ribs can deflect the blow. Miss, and you've got one very angry vampire."

"I see," said Brandy. "And you wouldn't lie still for it, either. I already know you don't sleep in a coffin." That reminded her of something else. She took his hand, as warm as her own, and felt at the wrist for a pulse. A reassuring beat thrummed beneath her finger.

"I'm not dead, Brandy. I'm a genetic variant, not a walking corpse."

"It sounds as if being a vampire is a pretty good thing."

"In some ways. Sunburn, hurting yourself because your body doesn't develop defenses—those are minor annoyances. Missing teeth in a young, healthy person were the mark of a vampire in the Middle Ages, because teeth wear out with age. Now we have them repaired, capped, crowned. It's easier than ever to be a vampire today.

"The hard parts are the same as always, though: making friends, loving people, and leaving them behind. Either they die, or you watch them grow old while you don't. Eventually you fake your own death and go away, never to know what happened to them."

"I see," said Brandy again.

But Dan wasn't finished. "The worst part is the Craving. Each month at the full moon I must hunt."

"You've never killed."

"That's right. But . . . I'm capable of it. I . . . lose control, Brandy. You have to know the whole, ugly truth."

His eyes met hers again. "When the Craving is in me, I know what drug addicts suffer when they need a fix. I won't kill my donor—we are in too close rapport. But I fear someone else coming between me and my . . . prey. If anyone tried to stop me, I'm afraid I might kill, like some mindless beast."

Brandy remained silent for a time, trying to digest all he had told her. But there were still questions. "You said . . . you were married."

"Yes."

"Your wife knew what you are."

"Yes."

"Do you have children?"

"No. It was over forty years ago. In those days people didn't rush to fertility clinics when they weren't pregnant in a few months of trying. When Megan finally went to a doctor . . . he found cancer. Today she might have survived. In those days . . . despite surgery and radiation she was dead within a year."

Forty years ago. Far longer than Brandy had been alive. Yet Dan still felt the dull ache of a wound healed, but not without a scar.

"I searched for other vampires after that," Dan continued. "I thought I could avoid such pain by befriending, possibly loving, my own kind. I did find one other vampire, a woman. She told me what I really needed . . . but she could not be that for me, nor I for her."

Brandy could feel him wanting her to ask what that was, but resisted the compulsion, seeking other information first. "How . . . long do you expect to live?"

"I don't know. Possibly centuries."

Brandy slid away from him. "In thirty years I'll be old," she said. "In fifty years, I'll likely be dead."

"No," he said calmly.

"Dan, I don't want an affair."

"I don't either," he replied. "I want to marry you."

"And put yourself through what happened with your first wife? I don't have a fatal disease that I know of, but you'd feel awful watching me age, and I'm vain enough not to want to watch you *not* age. What would we do, change our identities in a few years, to pass me off as your mother?"

"Brandy, you don't have to age that fast."

"You said you couldn't turn me into a vampire."

"I can't. But you and I have something I didn't have with Megan. I had decided it was just another myth. Now I know it's possible."

She saw it coming: if she wouldn't ask, then he would tell her. "Brandy, you are my perfect match."

"What, blood type?" she quipped angrily.

"No. It's a mental, physical, and emotional match. From the moment we met I sensed it. You did, too. Not only do I know your thoughts, but you know mine. And you can influence me. No one I've ever met before can do that."

"You *want* that?"

"When it goes both ways." He turned her to face him, searching her eyes. "I don't want to change you. I *can't* hurt you—it would hurt me equally. Can't you tell that we're made for one another?"

Although she could not deny the feeling, she said, "I suppose with your hypnotic powers you could offer some wild emotional high—but it wouldn't be real. Loving you would eat the heart out of my life, so that when you left me—"

"I won't leave you!"

"You'll have to change identities and move on, leaving me too old to get married and have children, and possibly incapable of loving anyone else."

"I want you to have *my* children."

"Is that possible?"

"Of course it is. It's true any child of mine might be a vampire. I don't know the statistical probabilities. Unless you carry the gene too, I think they're zero, but if it happens our child would be better off than I was. I could at least tell him what I know."

Brandy had never been one to follow her feelings and face the consequences later, so she refused the urge to collapse into his arms like the heroine of some insipid romance. "We could get married," she said, "and go on living here in Murphy for fifteen or twenty years."

"Longer," he said, "either here or elsewhere. I would want to retain my present identity until our children are grown. How many children do you want, Brandy?"

"Two, I think. Do you want more?"

"I'm just glad you want kids, because I've missed that. I'll take one or a dozen, whatever makes you happy. Assume two, and assume for the sake of argument we have them within five years. Another twenty-five years to be sure they're okay. We can make it work with a little makeup and acting."

"Thirty years," said Brandy. "Lots of people never get that long. Dan, I think I would be happy with you . . . but I don't know how badly that happiness would be spoiled by knowing when it would end."

"But we *don't* know," he said.

"Not to the day. But about thirty years from now you'll have to leave me . . . and of course you could decide to leave sooner."

"You don't understand. You will be in a symbiotic relationship with me. The information is scanty, so I don't know if it's a side effect of excellent health or a benefit in itself, but you will live an exceptionally long life."

"How long is exceptionally long?"

"I found a mention of centuries, but not how many. It's the same for me—I don't know if I can expect two hundred years or a thousand. I only know I don't want to spend them without you."

Again she fought his influence. "You're also hungry, and want to drink my blood."

"When I'm with you I don't feel the compulsion. That's how I first realized our potential. The night we met, after I left you, the Craving hit as never before. Your mere presence had assuaged it . . . long after I had stopped searching, I had found my perfect match."

Brandy recalled that night, Dan's sensuous kisses, how she had uncharacteristically melted in the arms of the dark, handsome stranger. "You could have . . . "

"I could have taken from you, yes. When I realized that what I felt was desire, not compulsion, I broke away. The potential between us was too important, and at that point I could not have allowed you to remember anything except a sexual encounter."

"I wanted it," Brandy remembered.

"Your blood called to mine. Denying it was the hardest thing I had ever done, and the next full moon it was even harder. Tonight . . . if you tell me to leave, I will, but I can't unless you mean it with all your heart."

"Dan . . . this is crazy," said Brandy. "You're offering me—"

"Long life, excellent health, my protection for whatever that may be worth to a police officer. But none of that matters unless you love me. I want a normal life, Brandy, family, someone to turn to in good times and bad. That's what I'm offering."

"And you are asking—?"

"The same from you . . . plus less than a pint of blood at each full moon."

"That's all?"

"That's all physically. Emotionally . . . I can guarantee you pleasure. What I need is not just proteins and sugars. Dead blood from the blood bank is useless. I want to share everything, the act, the afterglow, having you remember what we did and anticipate the next time."

"You had that with your wife?"

"Yes, even though Megan and I were not a perfect match. If we had been," she felt his pain, "she might not have died—not become ill in the first place. But Megan is the past, Brandy. You are the future."

Brandy had finally run out of questions. What she had learned was unbelievable . . . yet fit the facts. Dan needed her more than he realized. There were other vampires in the area. Whoever killed Carrie had sent them a message: behave or be exposed. Or killed, like the Andersons.

Those mysterious smiles. The Car 108 murders had been committed by a vampire using influence, the shotgun blasts used to cover the fact that only the Andersons needed to be eliminated in a particular way.

Could one vampire overpower another? Perhaps with the element of surprise. Perhaps some were stronger than others. The Andersons were not very bright; perhaps another vampire outsmarted them. Dan, she knew, was very smart.

But Brandy herself was Dan's alibi for Car 108. Somebody else was killing vampires. Did they know about Dan? How much danger was he in?

As her thoughts churned, two things became eminently clear: Brandy loved Dan, and she wanted to protect him. Both desires would be best served if—

"You'll move in with me right away," she said decisively.

"What?" he asked blankly.

"There's plenty of room. Mom used the spare bedroom as a sewing room. We'll turn that into your office—"

"Brandy!" His eyes glowed with nothing more supernatural than the excitement of a happy man. "Are you saying yes?"

"I love you," she replied.

He drew her into his arms again, and all thought fled except the warm, sweet closeness. As he had often done before, he slid his lips down her throat, licking gently. Brandy arched her head back, trusting him not to hurt her.

"It's more than just not hurting you," he murmured against her neck, then got up and drew her to her feet.

They went upstairs to her bedroom. Without turning the light on, Dan began helping Brandy out of her clothes.

Under her sweater she wore a silk camisole. Dan stripped her that far, knelt to remove her shoes, then picked her up with ease and laid her against the throw pillows. He took off his jacket, kicked off his shoes, and settled comfortably with an arm about her against the chill. Outside, snow fell again, flakes large enough to throw shadows from the street light on the curtains.

Dan was in no hurry, kissing and caressing Brandy until she relaxed. It couldn't be any worse than donating blood, she reassured herself. Her eyes had adjusted to the dimness, but when his fangs extended she felt no fear. She leaned forward to brush her lips against his, ran her tongue down to one razor-sharp fang tip, felt it cut at the merest touch. She brought the tip of her tongue to his, offering.

He gasped, accepting. When he bent his head to her throat, Brandy instinctively arched her head back. A touch of lightning flashed along her nerves.

The experience bore no resemblance to donating blood. Instead of the lassitude she expected, sweet warm strength sang through her. The feeling was akin to assuaging hunger or thirst, but unique, powerful, and good. The pleasure intensified, carrying her to a crescendo of satisfaction.

It wasn't like orgasm, either, but equally fulfilling. She was content on one level, inspired on another. Dan lapped gently at her throat as Brandy ran her fingers through his thick dark hair, feeling an overpowering love for this man who needed her so, who gave her such incredible warmth and closeness.

When Dan's lips returned to hers, Brandy slid her hands under his sweater, feeling his deep chuckle reverberate at her desire. "Oh, yes," he murmured into her ear, and stripped off first his sweater, then the shirt he wore under it. Kneeling beside her, though, he found the will to pause and ask, "Do you have protection?"

Brandy laughed giddily. "You've just had your teeth in my neck. It's a little late for latex, don't you think?"

He smiled his rare warm smile. "I believe in getting married before starting a family."

"I'm on the Pill."

"Good." He kissed her again. There were no foolish questions, no insincere apologies: each knew what the other was feeling, which meant that Brandy couldn't hide her apprehension concerning her technical virginity.

To her annoyance, Dan was pleased—she didn't know why it surprised her to find that in some ways he was a typical male. But she reminded herself that he had grown up in a earlier era—actually, he had done an incredible job of turning himself into a modern enlightened man.

"Hey," he murmured, "pay attention."

"I'm nervous," she admitted; it was useless not to.

"Oh, Brandy," he whispered, "you're not afraid of facing bullets or giving me life. Don't be nervous about loving, Sweetheart." The endearment caught her unawares, stinging her eyes with tears. He kissed them away.

The preliminaries Brandy was quite familiar with, although every man was different in precisely how he touched, what he preferred, where his attention focused. Dan experimented, caressing her breasts, stroking her legs as he divested her of the last of her clothing. She hadn't noticed when he had abandoned his.

She touched him in return, running her hands over his preternaturally smooth skin, feeling the play of muscle beneath. He felt different from any other man she had ever known, smelled different, enticing, intoxicating —

When his touches became more intimate, Brandy let her own hands slide down to cup the perfect buttocks she had admired that day at the lake. She felt more than saw him smile at her boldness, and took it as a sign that he didn't mind her aggression. "I'm yours, Brandy," he whispered, voice gone rough with passion.

Brandy abandoned herself to pure sensation, her tendency to analyze lost. Dan was gentle until he felt her respond, then just as aggressive as she needed, attuned to her every desire. They soared to a peak of pure pleasure, and together, clinging, floated in lovely lassitude.

As the warmth of passion seeped from their bodies, Dan pulled the comforter over them and cuddled Brandy tenderly, his fingers threading through her hair. "I love you," he whispered. "When would you like to get married?"

She snuggled closer. "When we're ready, let's elope. I don't want to go through what I did for Mom's wedding."

"How about Christmas vacation?" Dan suggested.

"I have only six days, and it's unfair to ask to rearrange the Christmas/ New Year's schedules."

"Spring Break, then. Except that I don't want to wait till March."

She laughed. "What's the difference? You're moving in tonight. Are you too old-fashioned to live with me before we're married?"

"I'll try not to be," he said. "I'll look up the exact dates of Spring Break tomorrow. The weekends are included, so we have nine days if you can get that much time off."

"I can get it if I put in now. Where shall we go? Las Vegas?"

"Florida," Dan said firmly.

"Florida! Then Mom will expect—"

"—what she has every right to expect. She's the only family either of us has."

She heard the sadness in his voice. "You had to leave them all behind?"

"I told you the truth, except for dates and places. That's one secret of living a lie: tell as much truth as you can. My parents are dead. My brother died in the Pacific in World War II, not in the Gulf War; my feelings are real, so people believe me no matter which age-appropriate war I say it was. The cousins are in Delaware, not Nebraska, but they certainly wouldn't know me today, nor care." He hugged her. "Don't leave your mother out, Brandy. She won't be there forever."

"Okay," she said. "We'd better wait till next summer."

"Why?" he asked. "What's the point in putting it off?"

"Mom will want to do something fancy. Give her time. That reminds me: you're invited to Florida for Christmas. Mom likes you. She'll be pleased to hear that we're getting married, but she'll want you to get me to quit my job."

"I can't," he said, "much as I hate the risks you take. As you get used to our match, you'll find that we *can't* pressure one another to act against our natures. I'll always be involved in something to do with numbers and structures, and you'll always use your curious, puzzle-solving mind." He nibbled gently on her ear and murmured, "I'll always be a hopeless romantic, and you'll always be pragmatic. We're two halves of a whole."

Brandy kissed him. Then she said, "If I'm the practical one, I suggest that we take a shower together—"

"That sounds like fun," he said.

"Yeah, it always has. I've never done it before. But it's dinner time, and while you may be satisfied—"

"Only temporarily."

"—I have had neither lunch nor dinner today. Let's order in a pizza, and then call Mom."

"An excellent plan," he agreed. "Make it a large pizza. You won't get five-sixths of it this time. I am happy and satisfied and very hungry!"

~

Brandy's mother was thrilled, only lamenting that they would have so little time at Christmas to make plans.

"You get too fancy, Mom, and Dan and I will just stop off in Georgia and get hitched," Brandy threatened. She wanted very much to avoid the church, the bridesmaids, and the reception for five hundred intimate friends.

They talked for almost forty minutes. When they finally hung up, Brandy said to Dan, "Let's go get your toothbrush and pajamas."

"I don't wear pajamas."

"Now why doesn't that surprise me? Anyway, let's get what you need for the weekend, and move the rest later."

"You have to work tomorrow?"

"Church will pick me up at quarter to eight."

"Too bad. I was hoping to keep you up all night."

Moving Dan into her house in the middle of a snowstorm was the last thing Brandy had planned. He packed a suitcase with clothes and toiletries, but his car was soon loaded down with two computers and their multiple attachments, a laser printer, boxes of disks, textbooks, and videotapes.

They were not alone outdoors. The snow fell in large, beautiful flakes, and as they drove slowly on the snow-covered streets they saw people out laughing and slipping and throwing snowballs. Dan took a shortcut through the campus, where the students had deserted the dorms and the library to play in the snow.

"What a perfect evening!" Brandy exclaimed.

"Our first," said Dan. "Besides—you ain't seen nothin' yet!"

"You have some power over the weather?" she asked.

"No—but you've experienced only the tip of the iceberg of some of my other powers."

They dumped most of what Dan had brought in the room that would be his office. Brandy's bedroom closet was crammed, and the dresser was the one from her apartment, brought here full, so she had to move some of her clothes into the guest room to give Dan a share. When she came back, he asked her where to put his empty suitcase.

"Stick it in the kitchen for now. When you've finished moving in, it can go in the basement or the attic."

"Brandy, I didn't realize how big this house is. You're bringing more into this marriage than I am."

"Nonsense," she said. "You earn more than I do, and you have over thirty thou— Oops."

He laughed. "You told me you checked up on me. It's all right. I haven't checked what's in your bank account, but this house is worth more than I have to offer. Is that why you're putting off the wedding?"

"Of course not! I love you, you love me—why shouldn't we live together?"

"Maybe I'm old-fashioned. But I need to get along with your friends, Brandy . . . and I believe Church is one of your closest?"

"Yes."

"Churchill Jones is the last person I want worrying that I'm taking advantage of you. You know how easy it is to find out that Danton Edward Martin doesn't exist outside computer records. Another secret to successfully living a lie is not to raise suspicions."

She realized he was right, but, "He won't want me to rush into anything as important as marriage."

After a pause, Dan nodded. "You're right. He hardly knows me. I'll have to work to impress him. You'd better let drop that you've already investigated me, so he won't. He might follow the clues to those falsified records."

"I'm only beginning to realize how devious you are," Brandy said. "But you've got an advantage with Church: you helped to save his son's life. You didn't . . . engineer that fall to become a hero, did you?"

"Don't even think such a thing," he replied. "That poor kid may have a bad leg for life." Again he studied her. "Brandy, do you think me capable of such a thing?"

"No, I don't," she told him. "It's just . . . so convenient that you were there with your hypnotic powers and your strength to break the rock. As if someone planned it."

A moment's pause, then, "Someone did," said Dan.

"What do you mean?"

"There was one of those high-pitched dog whistles that most people can't hear."

"But you can?"

"Yes. I didn't think anything of it at the time, but it's what got Sandy to run away."

"And once he was close . . . that influence you have over animals—"

"—called him to lure the children to that dangerous drop. And . . . the 'monster' the children say they saw."

"Dracula," Brandy remembered. "A shadowy figure with fangs."

"At sunset," Dan added. "I wanted to say something then, Brandy, but how could I? I forgot about it until I found out about Carrie's puncture wounds. There's a pattern here, another vampire letting me—or other vampires—know he's in the vicinity, but not who he is. I don't know what to expect next."

"Why hurt Church's son?" Brandy asked.

"It could probably have been any child that the vampire could entice away from his parents. Am I being paranoid? Or are these warnings aimed at me?"

"I suppose after tonight whoever it is will think you have me in your power," said Brandy.

"It's you who have me in yours," said Dan, "but it doesn't matter as long as you're out of danger. You're right that it's best I move in." He looked around. "I'll leave the computers in the spare room, and hook them up while you're at work tomorrow. Is there a phone jack?"

"No, but we can have one installed."

"I'll do it," Dan said. And he went downstairs to get the last items they had brought.

Thus Brandy had time to think for a moment away from Dan's influence. Computers and a phone jack . . . a modem . . . fancy, complicated computers—Something had been nagging at the back of Brandy's mind ever since Dan had chosen that equipment as his first contributions to their joint household. Suddenly it leaped to the fore, producing a stab of near-pain to Brandy's gut. Although she didn't say a word, Dan practically leaped up the stairs. "Brandy! What happened?"

She pushed him away. "You made me forget about it! All the time you claimed you weren't influencing me, you were making me forget what Church told me!"

"Forget what?"

"Your damned computers! I never asked you what you were doing installing computers for Judge Lee Joseph Callahan!"

ELEVEN

In the
Light of Day

DAN STARED AT BRANDY. "I couldn't have influenced you not to ask me about that," he said calmly, "because I had no idea you wanted to know."

"Church found it out. When he told me about it . . . I set out to investigate you."

Dan frowned. "I couldn't get a summer teaching position because I'd taught the summer before. Judge Callahan wanted a system installed."

"What kind of equipment did he get?"

"A Pentium III with CDR-W, 16 gigabyte hard drive, and a fax/modem. He's got a DSL line through the cable company. Brandy, the man is a judge, a lawyer, a businessman, a politician. What in the world do you find suspicious about his acquiring the latest technology? Or my helping him learn to use it?"

"What did he learn?" she demanded, trying to remember what Church was looking for. "How to change police records? Is the mob computerized? Did he learn how to locate and hire a hit man?"

"Besides Internet and e-mail access, he was interested in database programs, and constituency information available on ROM disks. It's no secret that Judge Callahan plans to run for governor."

She could feel Dan's utter bafflement at her reaction, his frustration at her lack of trust.

And then she realized what it *meant* that she could feel them. The connection had been growing all evening, unnoticed when the feelings were pleasant, but now—

"I warned you," Dan said softly. "Brandy, this degree of closeness is just as new to me. I *felt* that shock when you thought I had deceived you, like a physical blow."

"It was," she said shakily. Then, "What's your name, Dan? Your real name, on your real birth certificate?"

"Eduardo Tomas Donatelli. We can send for the records."

"There's no need to," she recognized. "You're not lying. I can tell."

"Yes."

"Is it going to get stronger than this? Will we have no privacy at all?"

"I don't know," he replied. "It will be weaker from sunrise to sunset, stronger at night. And it's related to influence, which requires physical closeness."

"You felt my feelings from downstairs."

"A strong shock. The rest has been weakening and strengthening as we've been apart and together."

"I didn't notice."

"You weren't looking for it. I was . . . and reveling in it. I think we'll get used to it. But . . . I doubt we can lie to one another, at least not for any length of time."

"I've never been so close to anyone."

"Neither have I. But I've been searching for it all my life. Let me show you how wonderful it can be."

When he kissed her, the physical contact increased her sense of his feelings. His sexual desire woke, but he didn't want a mere physical exercise. His desire was directed at Brandy, waking hers.

Earlier, Brandy had been content to be passive, but knowing Dan's responses directly she didn't have to worry that he would find her too aggressive. When she accidentally tickled him, she didn't have to wait for his protest, but moved on to more erogenous regions, enjoying his pleasure as much as her own.

If she had known sex could be this much fun she would have indulged in it earlier. But then, with any other man it couldn't have been so involving, so reciprocal, so wickedly, wonderfully delicious.

～

When the clock radio came on at 7:00 A.M., Brandy reached automatically to turn it off. As she tried to turn over and encountered resistance, she remembered that she was not alone. Memories of last night surfaced, and she became aware of how good she felt.

Dan was still asleep, lying on his back with Sylvester curled up on his chest. Neither man nor animal showed any sign of rousing, although the cat cracked one eye and closed it again, playing possum.

The sun was rising. Dan was right: the intense emotional rapport of the night was gone—hence he hadn't wakened when she did. Still, she felt a reassuring sense of his well-being, telling her last night, impossible as it seemed, had been only too real.

It gave her a sweet pang to look at Dan, to remember their intimacy, to look forward to more. There wasn't time this morning, but she smiled as she looked at her new—first—lover, watching him sleep.

Dan was not snoring, nor had she heard him during the night. She wouldn't mind; she recalled her father's snores echoing down the hall, and the terrible silence in the nights after he had died, sometimes broken by her mother's weeping when she thought her daughter safely asleep.

It was unlikely, Brandy realized, that Dan would leave her as her father had her mother. Even if his promises of long life came true for her, it would probably not be as long as his. He had lost one love, but had the courage to find another. As her mother had found Harry.

She didn't want to think of Dan with another woman.

Focus on the positive, she told herself, shivering her way into the bathroom, where her flannel pajamas hung on the linen closet door. She was glad Dan hadn't wakened, for her morning routine took forty-five minutes, and she had already dawdled some of that time away.

She turned on the coffee-maker Dan had set up yesterday, then went into the living room and stuck her exercise tape into the VCR for a hard-driving fifteen minutes. When she went back upstairs for her shower, though, the bed was empty and the bathroom door was closed.

That was not the problem it would have been in either of their apartments: Brandy grabbed her robe and showered in the guest room bath. By the time she was finished, Dan was out of her bathroom, wearing one of those sexy black silk karate coats usually seen only in movies. He greeted her with a chaste kiss tasting of toothpaste, and a "Good morning. I smell coffee."

"Come join me for breakfast," she suggested. "I have to warn you that I only allow five minutes for a bowl of cereal. I mustn't be late for work. I should have thought to set the clock earlier."

"It's all right," he said. "We'll find a routine that works."

Outside, the snow sparkled. Murphy had gotten less than two inches; the storm was probably dumping a foot or more on Eastern Kentucky by now. Dan squinted against the brightness, human and scruffy in the morning light. He needed a shave, and his thick black hair, wet from the shower, curled waywardly. A man of his apparent age in most professions—except possibly rock star—would consider it too long.

Brandy didn't say anything. Dan had promised not to try to change her, and she owed him the same courtesy. Besides, she had fallen in love with him just as he was. She felt a pleasant pang as the phrase "fallen in love" crossed her mind, and Dan looked up with a confirming smile.

Brandy found the spare house key. "Thanks," Dan said. "I'll move some more of my stuff over, and set up the computer. Shall I make dinner?"

"You'll spoil me."

"You can cook the days I work and you don't."

"You're a better cook than I am."

"Then we'll work out a different arrangement. Let's not try to decide everything today, okay?"

"Okay," she agreed tentatively, testing the restraints of domesticity.

They inched a little tighter when Dan came into the bathroom while Brandy was putting on makeup, finding no mark on her throat. She had left the door open so they could talk. The master bath was big enough to allow both of them to use the large mirror, yet the intimacy of his placing a casual kiss on her upturned throat, then shaving while she put on blusher and struggled with her unstyled hair, was somehow greater than yesterday's indulgently shared shower.

Dan put on jeans and a Jackson Purchase State University sweatshirt, which made him look younger than the thirty-five years he claimed. Pulling on a worn leather jacket, he accompanied Brandy downstairs. "Why don't you invite Church in for a cup of coffee?"

"Uh . . . I was going to break our news to him a little more gently," she admitted.

"Brandy, my car's in your driveway, the tire tracks are filled with snow, and Church is a detective."

"Why do you always have to be right?" Brandy asked.

Church hugged Brandy, shook Dan's hand, and said, "I'm really happy for you. When are you getting married?"

"Probably next summer," said Brandy.

Church frowned. "Why so long?" Then he paused, and asked very seriously, "Are we gonna lose you, Brandy?"

"No," Dan and Brandy replied in unison, then looked at one another and smiled.

"Well, I see it's a mutual decision!" said Church. "And I'm very glad to hear it. Dan, I gotta warn you that a cop is not the easiest person in the world to live with. But you do anything to hurt this girl—"

"I won't," Dan said. "It took too long to find her."

Brandy and Church drove through streets more deserted than usual, for even light snow kept many people from going out for donuts or the Sunday paper. At the station, Brandy stared at the bulletin board as she considered her dilemma.

She now knew the source of the mysterious smiles: the "influence" of a vampire. But for all the nonsense about Satanism in this area of the country, nobody, but *nobody* in Murphy would to accept the idea of vampires! Worse, the only way she could prove that vampires were real would be to expose Dan.

And since she had no idea who the murdering vampire was—except that it wasn't Dan Martin—any mention could tip off the real killer. She looked through the office door to where Church was working. He labored at the computer, adding, deleting, and rearranging his report into a masterpiece of rhetoric.

Church could be trusted with her secret, but only with Dan's permission. But even that would be on a need to know basis. It was best if Brandy could find and expose the killer vampire without involving Dan.

She sighed, thinking how naive Dan was to think Brandy was safe if the killer vampire thought her "in his power." As long as she continued to work on this case, they were both in danger. She *could* fool him, she realized: let Dan think he was protecting her while she protected him. The only way either of them could be permanently safe was to find Carrie's murderer.

Her only choice was to investigate on her own, to look for pale people who wore sunglasses in the winter, who seemed younger and stronger than their age suggested, and who perhaps didn't leave fingerprints.

Three of the six murder victims were vampires. The police officers had been murdered to remove witnesses and confuse motives. Only Carrie's murder was inexplicable. Brandy felt no ill effects from Dan's taking as much blood as he needed. She had been left unmarked. If Carrie's throat had been slashed by a vampire, it was not to obliterate bite marks. It was a setup—but by a vampire to rid himself of a rival, or by a vampire hunter? On a hunch, Brandy went to the log called the Crank File.

All calls were considered serious until proven otherwise—even someone who thought he saw an alien park a UFO in his back yard might actually, as had happened last year, have seen a motorcyclist in helmet and leathers hiding his hog in thick bushes. The shining black and silver luggage box peeking through the foliage did look like the edge of a spacecraft. Actually, it was the getaway vehicle from a liquor store robbery in Paducah, and the "crank call" had allowed the Murphy police to apprehend the suspect and reclaim the stolen money.

Brandy found four calls concerning vampires. The most recent, three days ago, said "People are being murdered! Why aren't the police doing anything? Free your mind from the vampire's spell. Beware the full moon!"

The next most recent was two days after Carrie's murder. "The vampire has killed again! Has he taken over the minds of the police? Stop him!" There was a call two days before Carrie's murder: "When the full moon rises on Saturday night, the vampire will strike. How many people does he have to suck the life from before you stop him?"

The earliest one said, "There is a vampire in Murphy. He gets into your mind, into your mind. He'll steal your life! Stop him from killing again!"

And that was it. Brandy searched further, but found nothing. The calls had all been made from a telephone booth on Main Street, between midnight and 2:00 A.M. on weekdays.

That public phone, Brandy couldn't help noticing, was the closest one to the morgue outside the hospital complex. Rory Sanford probably passed it walking to and from his job. The first call had come two days after he got out of prison.

They were obviously calls for help—but what kind of help? Knowing about Dan's "influence," Brandy could almost believe the caller was fighting such hypnotic power. If the killer vampire knew about the calls, what better than to kill someone and plant the evidence on the caller?

Brandy now knew that Rory Sanford had not used that stupid fork to puncture Carrie's neck: Dan had bitten her. The fork was a red herring, planted to fit Doc Sanford's cannibal theory. She could feel the sneering sarcasm, framing his grandson according to the old man's wrong guess!

Rory was innocent of Carrie's murder, then, and probably the drug charges as well. But how could Brandy get him out of jail without implicating Dan?

The first thing to do was ask Rory Sanford if he had placed the calls. Brandy showed the transcripts to Church. "We should have checked this out earlier," he said. "Shit, why didn't we check the Crank File for vampires the moment Doc Sanford turned up those puncture wounds? Good work, Kid. The location's right for Rory Sanford. Let's find out if he made the calls."

But their call to the Paducah jail was put on hold. Finally, instead of the jailer, a man identifying himself as Detective Sergeant Raymond Candless of the Paducah Police came on the line. "We got a mess on our hands," he said. "I can't let you talk to Rory Sanford because he's dead."

"Dead!" exclaimed Brandy.

"Apparent suicide. He tore the edging off his mattress and used it to hang himself. Wasn't found till breakfast time. Listen, don't spread this around. We're tryin' to locate his next of kin—that's his grandfather."

"Yes," said Church, "Dr. Troy Sanford. If he's not at home, try the morgue. He's our coroner. You know how Saturday nights are."

"Okay, thanks. Say, you guys know him. Would you be willing—?" Candless broke off. "No. It's our fault. We'll tell him. But if you're his friends, maybe you can help him cope."

"Oh, God," said Brandy, sitting down heavily. "Oh, poor Doc. Church—"

"There's nothing we can do," her friend said. "He'll have a million questions. Let's hit the streets for a while, then go see Doc later, when we may be some help."

"A million questions we can't answer," said Brandy, staring at the Crank File. "I'm certain Rory Sanford made these calls. You know how this will be taken: as an admission that he killed Carrie!"

"Wait for the full report. Maybe it wasn't suicide. But hell, who could get into that jail cell and murder him? The kid just couldn't take any more."

Soon they were rolling, needing fresh air. It was a glorious day, strong contrast to Brandy's gloomy thoughts. Children were building snowmen.

As if to clear the air of the latest depressing news, Church changed the subject to Brandy's marriage plans. "Is Dan planning to stay at Purchase State?"

"If they'll let him. He got his promotion to Associate Professor last year, so that makes it pretty hard to deny him tenure. He's already been approved at the departmental level, which he says is the hard part. Did you know you have to have a book published to get promotion and tenure?"

"I had no idea," said Church. "Does he have one?"

"Yeah, something about networking in an academic environment. I don't think I'll ever keep up with that computer stuff, but I understand more than I used to."

"Good. You can help me search for more of those blackmail or bribery cases. I know I'm onto something. Maybe I can get enough evidence to convince the chief."

Brandy didn't answer immediately, wondering just how much help she could ask of Dan in an investigation of the judge. She couldn't directly lie to him. How far could she carry an interest in learning to use the computer?

"Earth to Brandy," said Church. "You gonna be off there in cloud-cuckoo-land till the honeymoon's over?"

"Huh? No, I wasn't thinking about that. I was just wondering how much more Dan will be willing to show me. I don't think he'd help us break into Judge Callahan's computer files."

"He can do that?"

"I don't know . . . but if the judge leaves his computer on all the time with the modem hooked up, it might be possible. Dan said he installed a fax/modem for Callahan."

"Good work, Kid," said Church. "But you be careful. That's a helluva nice guy you've found yourself. Don't make him think you're using him."

Brandy smiled to herself, remembering why it would be impossible for Dan to misinterpret her feelings.

They got some coffee, then stopped at the city park, near where Carrie Wyman's body had been found a month ago. Church produced a portfolio, and drew out three more case folders. "I'm going through the closed files, picking out the names of supporters of Judge Callahan."

The first was a child abuse charge against one Darren Lyle. "I don't know him," said Brandy.

"You know his dad," said Church.

"Carson Lyle? Sweet-Pop Popcorn?"

Six years previously, Darren Lyle's wife had accused him of abusing their two small children and filed for divorce and custody. Lyle had been jailed, but the charges had been dismissed in Judge Callahan's court.

The police report showed only charges and denials, no hard evidence. "This isn't much to go on," said Brandy.

"I found out the rest of the story," Church explained. "Melba Lyle, Darren's wife, took the children and ran. He tracked her to a Wyoming motel, and beat her with a tire iron. The motel owner shot Lyle dead when he wouldn't stop. Melba died of head injuries."

"God," Brandy murmured. "Those poor kids."

"They're back here in Murphy with their grandparents. And none of this made the local news."

Brandy frowned. "You'd think Carson Lyle would blame Judge Callahan for his son's death."

"Lyle prefers to blame his daughter-in-law. Judge Callahan made sure the Lyles got custody, and not Melba Lyle's sister, as she had in her will."

"What are the other cases?"

Less heart-wrenching, they were similar to the earlier cases Church had showed Chief Benton: the owner of a real estate agency charged with conflict of interest when she purchased farmland and sold it as an industrial park. Callahan ruled insufficient evidence. An air cargo operator out of the small local airport charged with transporting drugs. Once again Callahan had cleared the man's name and made sure his plane was not confiscated.

"I don't know," said Brandy. "The first two cases show the judge favoring people who can help him politically. But some other judge might rule insufficient evidence because the third case shows the other side of the story."

"What other side?" asked Church.

"Callahan *also* helps people with no political clout. Ace Air Cargo is hardly a major business."

"Brandy, if Callahan is involved in the drug trade . . . ? Maybe he was protecting an employee!"

"Okay," she conceded, "but what about the Chu family? They don't have any political power, but remember how Callahan cleared Ricky Chu's record so publicly? What earthly good could the Chus do him?"

"Good publicity. Grandstanding. Maybe he's planning for the future. Those Chu kids are likely to become influential, bright as they are."

"I suppose that's possible," said Brandy. "I'm just trying to see past unsupported suspicion."

"You're in love," said Church. "I don't think you're in the mood to see bad in anyone today."

Maybe her friend was right. That only made it harder to face Doc Sanford's grief when she and Church stopped to see him that afternoon.

If Troy Sanford had looked his age the night of his grandson's arrest, today he looked twenty years older. He had been drinking, but not much: one beer can sat on the table, and he was drinking a second. His shoulders slumped, his hands shook, but his eyes burned. Sloughing off their condolences, he said, "Rory wasn't suicidal! Somebody murdered him—the same person that killed Carrie Wyman."

"Doc—" Church began gently.

The old man shook off his support. "You think I'm crazy with grief, don't you? Well, that don't change the facts. Don't let Chief Benton say this proves my Rory killed Carrie and close the case. You find out who really killed her. Clear Rory's name!"

"We'll continue the investigation," Brandy promised. "Have you got anyone to stay with you?"

"Mrs. Diugood was over here earlier. I sent her home."

"I know her," said Church. "She lives next door. Doc, she does your housekeeping, doesn't she?"

"Yeah."

"I'll get her back. You shouldn't be alone tonight. She can get your house ready for all the people coming—"

"Coming to stare! Coming to laugh! Coming to lie about Rory selling drugs and murdering people! Don't want no one in my house telling lies about my Rory."

"No one's going to do that," said Brandy. It was almost possible to guarantee such an unfounded promise. Southern custom kept people from speaking ill of the dead.

"Keep the Callahans out," said Dr. Sanford. "Joey Lee, that dirty bastard, and his no good son both! Killed Cindy Lou, now my Rory. Filthy rotten wife-beating bastards!"

Brandy looked sadly at Church. Joseph Lee Callahan had been dead for nearly forty years. The judge, his son, had been widowed for at least ten. But she promised, "No Callahans will come here. We'll see to it, Doc. Now, have you seen a doctor?"

"I *am* a doctor!"

"Yes," Brandy said gently, wishing she had Dan's influence, "but you can't prescribe for yourself, Doc."

"Agh, Dr. Montrose was here, left a prescription for a sedative." He waved vaguely toward the sideboard. "I don't need to be sedated. I need to prove my grandson's not a murderer!"

"I'll go have this filled," Church said, picking up the small square of paper. "Can you handle him?"

"I think so. Doc, let's go into the kitchen. I need a cup of tea, don't you?"

There were already a pie and a loaf of home-baked bread on the kitchen table, Murphy's response to death. In the refrigerator Brandy found lasagna and a quart of home-made chicken soup, along with the rest of the six-pack. Soup was what Doc needed; he probably hadn't eaten all day. She poured out a bowl and set the microwave while she put the teakettle on and searched for cups and teabags. Then she cut a couple of slices of the crusty bread.

Doc Sanford sat quietly at the table, but when Brandy joined him, he pinned her with red-rimmed eyes and said, "L. J. Callahan had Rory killed. You'll have the devil's own time proving it, but he killed my grandson just as sure as his father killed my sister. Blood will tell."

Brandy was grateful that the teakettle whistled just then, and she could busy herself making tea and putting steaming soup before Dr. Sanford.

He picked up the spoon, but did more talking than eating. "Callahans and Sanfords useta be good friends. My daddy was mayor in them days, and ol' L. J., the grandaddy of that bastard we got now, was on the school board and the city council. When he was elected to the legislature he done good for West Kentucky. Got us roads an' bridges, brought electricity and phones in. L. J. was the last good Callahan, and he died young—kilt in the First War.

"His son Joey Lee was a right bastard. Oh, charmin', smooth as silk when he courted Cindy Lou. I was just her kid brother then. No one took no mind that I was the only one didn't like Joey Lee. My daddy lost a bundle in the '29 crash, so he thought it was real good thing when Joey Lee took a interest in Cindy Lou. The only dowry he could give her was a parcel of land bordering on Callahan's property. You know what that land is now?"

He paused, taking a couple spoonfuls of soup while he waited for Brandy to answer. She stalled, hoping he would eat more, but when he stopped and stared at her, she answered, "No, what is it?"

"The airport!" Sanford said triumphantly, and took another spoonful of soup. His body probably craved food, so if he had to keep his mind elsewhere to eat, so be it.

"So the Callahans made a lot of money from it."

"Still do! Judge Callahan rents it to the county. Greedy bastard, just like his father. Spittin' image of ol' Joey Lee. I was there when he come home from college an' proved my sister weren't no whore."

" . . . what?" Brandy asked, confused at the logical quantum jump.

"She never cheated on Joey Lee. He had no reason to kill Carl Mishinski, and Cindy Lou had no reason to take her own life, 'less that bastard drove her to it."

"Who was Carl Mishinski?" asked Brandy.

"Filthy commie," Sanford replied. "Bolshevik, we called 'em in them days. Teacher at the college—Jackson Purchase Normal School, it was then. Raised a big stink teaching evolution t' them young teachers."

Brandy realized he was talking about the 1930's, when people had a mind-set so alien to the one she had grown up with that they might as well be Martians. This was the part of the country where all the fuss had happened. Just down the road in Tennessee the Scopes trial had taken place in the '20's, and to this day some people tried to get required prayer and creationism back into the public schools. Signs bearing the Ten Commandments were to be seen in front yards all over town, and only the order of a Federal Judge had recently prevented state funds from being used to build a Ten Commandments monument in front of the state capitol in Frankfort.

Doc Sanford's story was fascinating. With judicious questioning, she garnered the Sanford side. When Church returned, they got the sedative into Doc and put him to bed.

Leaving the neighbor, Mrs. Diugood, to keep watch, they went back to the station for the rest of their duty shift. Sunday was still a quiet day, and the news of Rory Sanford's suicide made the duty officers quieter still. Bill Phillips, a Murphy native, commented, "I like Doc, but the Sanfords were always a weak-willed bunch."

"What do you mean?" Church asked.

"Doc's sister committed suicide, now his grandson. Rory's dad was a gambler, married some no-good gal from Memphis who left him the kid to raise. Seems Doc's the only Sanford any good to himself."

"Doc's Judge Callahan's uncle," said Brandy.

Phillips had to think a moment before nodding. "Yeah, but they don't no way act like kin. Not after what Doc's sister did to L. J.'s father."

"Do you know the whole story?" Brandy asked. "Doc told me some, but he was rambling and he only gave me one side."

"Yeah, I know," said Phillips, and proceeded to tell it, with other officers chiming in to add details.

Joseph Lee Callahan, the father of the present judge, married Cynthia Louise Sanford, older sister of Troy Sanford, after her family was hit hard during the Depression. She brought land, but no money, to the marriage, which remained childless for ten years. In those days people blamed the woman for being barren.

Then the rumors started that Cindy Lou was having an affair with Carl Mishinski, a biology professor at Jackson Purchase Normal School. Mishinski was certainly a damyankee, professedly a Darwinist, and possibly a Bolshevik. The community was shocked when the Callahans rented a house to such a scoundrel, so when rumors of the affair began, nobody was surprised.

No one was surprised, either, when Joey Lee burst into that very house to catch his wife and her lover *in flagrante delicto.* He shot Mishinski, and dragged Cindy Lou home by the hair. The shooting was ruled justifiable homicide.

Seven months later Cindy Lou gave birth to a baby boy, a sickly little thing of uncertain parentage whom Joey Lee nonetheless claimed as his own. The boy had only what social life money could buy, for everyone believed him to be Mishinski's child, especially as Cindy Lou doted on little Lee Joseph while cringing from her husband.

That Joey Lee abused his wife was probable. In the 1930's, 40's, and 50's no one in West Kentucky saw much wrong with that when the woman had been caught in adultery. Her husband had had the goodness of heart not to turn her out, and even to claim her bastard child and raise it as his own. To the residents of Callahan County, Joey Lee Callahan was a hero, his wife a slut.

One day when her son was in high school, Cindy Lou Callahan took the same gun that had killed her lover and blew her brains out. A few people had the audacity to suggest that Joey Lee had finally gotten fed up and killed her. But the official ruling was suicide.

Eventually Lee Joseph Callahan was sent east to college. Joey Lee, by this time a state senator, went as part of a legislative team to inspect a coal mine in Appalachia. The mine shaft collapsed, no one escaped, and none of the bodies were recovered. Lee Joseph came home for the memorial service, but then stayed far from Murphy all through college and law school. He returned a changed man.

In four years of college and three of law school he had turned from the sickly, cringing youth they had been so sure was the by-blow of a Bolshevik Darwinist into the image of Joey Lee! Education had given him presence and breeding. Lee Joseph Callahan took over the family property, served on the city council, and eventually became a judge.

Joey Lee, who despite all had recognized the bond of blood with his son, was elevated in local opinion from hero to saint. Lee Joseph, adopting the less cumbersome "L. J." his grandfather had used, became the hero who had overcome a difficult childhood to be the man his daddy would have been so proud of if he'd only lived to see it.

Brandy listened in amazement. What a wonderful novel that story would make, if only William Faulkner were still around to write it! Most people took it, from the Callahan side, as the bond between father and son triumphing over the misery caused by an unfaithful wife. But the Sanford side would take a modern slant, an abused wife practically driven into the arms of another man—or even, as there were no witnesses to her adultery other than her husband, and the child turned out to be his, two innocent people having their lives destroyed by the jealous, possessive husband.

Cindy Lou had never testified, never to the day of her death either denied or admitted her guilt. Had she actually committed suicide? Or did Joey Lee finally get rid of her, intending to replace her with someone better suited to be a politician's wife? For like the present judge, Joey Lee had also had aspirations to become governor of Kentucky, cut short by the mine accident in which he died.

It was a rare thing for a woman to commit suicide by shooting herself. That was a man's way. Women took pills or drowned themselves; they closed themselves in the garage or the kitchen and turned on the car engine or the gas stove; they slit their wrists. They just didn't shoot or hang themselves when there were other methods available.

Brandy considered suggesting to Church that here was the plot for his novel. The recounting of the story took up the rest of their duty shift, and afterward Church drove her home, reminding her that she and Dan were due at his house on Thursday for Thanksgiving. The snow had melted. The tire tracks in Brandy's muddy driveway indicated that Dan had been in and out several times. His car was there now.

When she opened the front door, the smell of roast beef filled Brandy's nostrils. A bouquet of chrysanthemums adorned the dining table set with her best dishes.

Dan emerged from the kitchen to offer her a kiss. "A celebration of our engagement."

"To remind me that you're a better cook than I am!"

"It's an easy meal—what's wrong? I don't think it's my cooking you're upset about."

"Rory Sanford's dead," she replied. "Doc's inconsolable and irrational. He's all alone now, Dan."

He hugged her, and it was good to cling to his solid warmth, knowing he would always be there for her.

She realized she had picked that thought up from Dan. The sun was setting. Touching him, she could feel his love for her, the sense of security she, of all the unlikely people, gave him. And she could feel his sincere sympathy.

"Do you have to work tomorrow?" he asked.

"Yes, but so do you."

"Can we meet for lunch, then shop for an engagement ring?"

She hadn't even thought about a ring. "You are a traditionalist, aren't you?"

"I wish I could give you the whole world, except that I know it wouldn't make you happy."

"You know that, do you?"

"You're no materialist. But I can't let you do all the giving, Brandy."

She laughed at the absurdity of that statement. "You're the one who gives all the time," she said. "I feel so guilty that you're willing to work our time together in around my job."

"Guilty enough to give up the job?"

"No."

"Then I'll live with it. Now come and have a glass of wine and relax until the roast is done."

It wasn't "done" at all, by the standards Brandy had grown up with. Dan had prepared a small standing rib roast, very rare in the middle, but he gave her the brown end cut, just nicely pink on the inside. She now understood his taste for extremely rare meat, and said nothing.

However, she couldn't help mentioning, "We can't afford to eat like this every day."

"This is a special occasion—and you need red meat today, Brandy. Would you rather I had made liver?"

"Ugh!" she replied, wrinkling her nose.

It got the expected chuckle. Under Dan's spell, Brandy enjoyed the luxury of good food and pleasant conversation, followed by a contented cuddle on the couch while they ostensibly watched television but actually Brandy, at least, took a nap. When she woke, it was only 9:00 P.M.. Dan unbraided her hair, combing it with his fingers.

Her love for him came tumbling over her, and she snuggled against his warmth, not wanting to move. But she could sense that he wanted to. "Let's go to bed."

They went upstairs and made love. It was better than last night. Exulting in the afterglow, Brandy wondered how long it could keep getting better.

It was not until the next day, when she met Dan for lunch, that Brandy once more broached the topic of vampires in Callahan County. They drove through Kentucky Fried Chicken, and sat in the car to eat Hot Wings. "Can one vampire control another?" Brandy asked.

"By influence, you mean? I don't know. I've never tried."

"What about vampire families?"

"Families?"

"So the gene is rare—if both parents have to carry it for a child to be a vampire, then there's the chance that other children in that family would also be vampires."

"My brother wasn't. I've never encountered any related vampires. The Andersons were married, not blood-related, and I didn't know about them until they were dead. Did they have any children, Brandy?"

Good question. "Wow. Not in their identities as Chase and Jenny Anderson, but who knows how old they really were? I have to develop a whole different line of thinking. I'll backtrack them and see what I can find. But to get back to families: people used to routinely have ten, twelve children. Where you find one vampire, wouldn't you expect the same parents to produce more? In a subsistence-level society, where few children lived to adulthood, wouldn't the vampires be most likely to survive?"

"I don't *know*," Dan said. She could feel his frustration. "There is a total absence of scientific research." He gave her a sad smile. "When you live even as long as I have, you develop patience. Imagine what a couple of centuries will do. I really do intend to take up biology and genetics the next time I have to change identities—but you want answers *now*."

"Yes—because it affects you, Dan. We know a vampire was able to influence the Andersons so they never reacted when their brains were blown out. Can any vampire do that to another if the victim doesn't have his guard up?"

"That's possible."

"But you don't know it."

"Legends of 'master vampires' who control others may come from such events. The old myth says one vampire creates another, after which he controls the new one, either until the master vampire is destroyed or until the new one learns to control his own powers. Take away the misinformation, and it would make sense that an older, more experienced vampire could take advantage of a younger one. Or a more cunning, cleverer vampire could manipulate a more naive or less intelligent one, no matter which is older."

Brandy nodded. "So, we don't have to assume that the Andersons were overpowered by a larger *number* of vampires. They were never more than petty criminals. I don't think they were very smart. A single vampire more cunning than they were might have controlled them."

"That seems to be a viable hypothesis."

"Thank you, Professor," she teased him. "You were with me when it happened, so you are not the erudite vampire we're looking for. At the same time, we can assume your intelligence gives you some protection from him."

"Or her," Dan added.

"So, does this other vampire know you're one?"

"I don't know. The things I use to keep everyone else from guessing my secret—the mirrored wall, the crucifix, the first date at an Italian restaurant—wouldn't fool another vampire." Then he became very serious. "Brandy, I honestly don't know what's going on, and it worries me."

"It worries me, too. I don't like wondering if some combination of Dracula and Van Helsing is out to get you!"

"Usually knowledge is power, but a little knowledge is a dangerous thing."

"That's 'learning,'" she corrected automatically.

"Do you have an eidetic memory?" he asked.

"No, but a pretty accurate one, and trained for police work. Dan . . . do you know how to use a gun?"

"No, and it wouldn't do much good against another vampire. I'm going to have to rely on my intelligence and hope that what's going on has nothing to do with me."

"Such as what?"

"Such as a crime ring made up of vampires," he replied. "Think about it: strength, invulnerability, hypnotic powers, the ability to see in the dark. The Vampire Mob. I think I'll write a book!"

"And show your fangs on the Tonight Show," Brandy commented. "But seriously, that's a great idea. If you're a crime boss, I mean. Dan, have you ever taken drugs?"

He blinked. "*That* one came out of left field! Yes, I tried pot in the 60's with everyone else, and I did inhale. It had no effect. I've never tried anything stronger."

"There's another advantage to a ring of vampires: you don't have to worry about them getting hooked on drugs. Can a vampire become an alcoholic?"

"I've never been drunk," he said, "though I've pretended to be. Won a few bets in college drinking some of the frat men under the table."

"See? Vampires make almost perfect criminals, and you don't have to worry about losing them to the two major addictions. Suppose there's a crime ring made up of vampires, selling drugs, stealing cars, the whole business? That explains so many in the same locale. The Andersons got carried away — or maybe they simply got careless, and had to be disposed of."

"They must have become dangerous to the ring or they'd just have been broken out of that police car, not murdered."

"You're thinking like a cop now," Brandy approved. "Anyway, if we're right, you're not involved. Stay out of it, Dan. Whoever is running things here has no compunction about killing vampires . . . and knows how to do it."

TWELVE

Thanksgiving

THANKSGIVING MORNING GAVE BRANDY the luxury of not going to work. Dan got up very early on school days. Except immediately after he fed, he needed only three or four hours of sleep. Monday through Wednesday she had risen to coffee already hot, and her fiancé working in his office until he heard her clock radio. The weather had returned to cold rain, so Dan made oatmeal, insisting that Brandy needed to start her day with something warm inside her.

She stifled an off-color suggestion as to what.

But on Thanksgiving morning they could stay in bed and make love. Later, Brandy insisted on exhibiting her culinary skills. She did know how to make an excellent fluffy omelet, and she had croissants to warm, with strawberry jam her mother had put up last summer.

Alone, Brandy had often taken toast, pop-tarts, or corn flakes back to bed with a cup of coffee, a magazine, or the Sunday paper. Now she had someone worth putting on the black lace nightgown and peignoir she had been saving, if just for the pleasure of letting Dan take it off her.

They giggled and sighed the morning away, and too soon it was time to join the Joneses for Thanksgiving dinner. Brandy wore her new red dress.

Church and Coreen welcomed them warmly, and Dan presented the children with computer games while Brandy offered the mince pie she had baked. The crust was Kroger's ready-made, but the filling was her mother's famous green tomato mincemeat. Almost every day Brandy discovered something she missed, not having her mother in town.

Jeff's leg was now in a walking cast, the wheelchair abandoned in favor of crutches. Still, the boy had long therapy ahead, and the doctors would not know for months whether he would have a full recovery. His parents made the best of things, praising their son for his courage and progress.

Brandy showed off the diamond ring Dan had insisted on giving her, even though she could only wear it on special occasions.

Bings, pops, and doodle-oodle-oo's soon sounded from the little room where the computer was installed, accompanied by laughter as Jeff and Tiffany tried the new games with Dan and Church cheering them on.

Coreen basted the turkey and told Brandy, "Let the big and little children play. You and I will have a nice glass of wine, and you can tell me all your plans."

Brandy was pleased to share her happiness. "With two drivers we can make it to Florida in one day. We'll have Christmas Eve and Christmas with Mom and Harry, and a couple of days for playing tourist before I have to be back."

"Just be careful you don't do too much honeymooning before the honeymoon," Coreen warned.

"With our schedules? Not likely. Besides, for all his romantic streak, Dan has a very practical side. He wants to work out a budget." She wrinkled her nose in distaste. "I'm satisfied if my checkbook balances."

"Unglamorous as it sounds, Dan's right," said Coreen. "If all you do is make sure you don't bounce checks, you'll never save up for important things—like kids. Till you have some, you have no idea how much they cost!"

Even though the house was closed up against the cold, rainy day, Brandy could hear raised voices coming from outside. "Speaking of marriage," said Coreen disgustedly. She called, "Church! The Williamses are at it again!"

The computer noises paused.

Church came into the living room, muttering, "Dammit, not on Thanksgiving!" too softly for the children to hear the profanity. "I've been over there three times before," he told Brandy. "Idiot won't press charges—which I guess I can understand."

"Does he have a gun?" asked Brandy.

"No, thank God." But the shouting grew louder, a female voice screaming obscenities.

Dan joined them, asking, "What's going on?"

The phone rang. Coreen studied the ceiling for a moment before answering it. "Yes, Mrs. Gordon, we hear it. Yes, my husband will go over and try to calm them down." She hung up. "Just because Church is a cop—"

"It's all right, Honey," said Church.

He dug in his pocket for his keys, and unlocked the solid doors of an old oak desk in the hallway. There, out of sight of his children, he kept his gun and badge.

"Can I help?" asked Brandy.

Church eyed her. "Maybe."

As they opened the front door, the voices became even louder. A man's voice pleaded, "But Baby, it don't make no difference. It'll be just as good."

"I told you a tom turkey, and you got a goddamn hen!" the female voice raged, and let loose with another string of invective.

Brandy fought down a grin. "A case of husband abuse?" she asked Church.

"A few weeks ago she hit him with a frying pan. I guess he's too embarrassed to go for help. I've tried talking to him, but he insists his wife is just 'feisty.'"

Dan followed the two police officers out of the house, joining several other people who had come out to see the excitement. "Stay back," Brandy warned them all. A crash came from inside the Williams house.

Church banged on the front door. "Police! Open up!"

"Now see what you done!" Mrs. Williams screeched. "Damn you, Bobby Williams, you ain't nothin' but trouble!"

"I said open up in there!" Church reiterated.

"She may not respond to male persuasion," said Brandy, stepping forward. Putting on her most professional attitude, she called, "Mrs. Williams! I'm Police Detective Mather. Open the door, please."

"Well—open the goddamn door!" Mrs. Williams ordered.

"Aw, Leola," her husband whined, but in a moment it opened.

The scene was straight out of a *Naked Gun* movie. Bobby Williams, the husband, was well over six feet tall and must have weighed 250 lbs. His wife was one of those tiny, scrawny women who probably didn't top 100 soaking wet. She wore a housecoat with lace edges of her slip showing, and her stockinged feet were thrust into worn bedroom slippers. Her hair was lacquered into a puff thirty years out of date, and her eyes were heavily made up with blue shadow. Blusher a shade too dark for her complexion hollowed cheeks that were already too thin, and lip liner ringed her mouth, lipstick chewed off in the center.

Obviously she had dressed up for church that morning, but taken off her good dress and shoes to cook dinner. Retaining the girdle that made her move like Frankenstein's monster suggested that she intended to dress again later in the day. Perhaps they expected company.

Leola Williams held a rolling pin in one hand, and something clutched tightly in the other. "I don't need no police," she told them. "I k'n handle this damn fool." She raised the rolling pin to threaten her cringing husband.

"Of course you can, Mrs. Williams," Brandy said calmly. "But you wouldn't want to hurt your husband by accident. Why don't you just put the —"

"You lookin' at her?" Mrs. Williams shouted to her husband. "Her in that devil's red dress? Is she what you want, you two-timer?"

"No, Loley," her husband protested, but it was no use. Leola Williams was determined to hit him, police or no police. Brandy made a grab for the woman's weapon arm while Church dragged her intended victim out of the line of fire.

The frustrated assailant turned her wrath on the interfering police officer. Expecting it, Brandy wrested the rolling pin out of the woman's hand.

"You husband-stealing bitch!" She writhed like a snake, bringing her free hand up to strike at Brandy's face.

In horror, Brandy recognized what was in Leola Williams' left hand: skewers for the turkey. And they were aimed at Brandy's eyes!

"Brandy!" Dan's voice. In his rush he blocked Church's way.

Brandy managed to deflect the woman's blow, but the skewers scraped painfully off her jaw. Church grabbed Leola Williams from behind. She screamed and the skewers went flying. The woman struggled, kicking like a mule.

Dan grasped Brandy, eyes on her wound.

"It's all right," she said, but he was already bending his head to lap up the blood.

The pain eased at once, but she had to push him away, whispering sharply, "Dan! People are watching!"

Fortunately, Leola Williams put on a better show. Brandy had to help Church get the cuffs on her, just as a siren drowned her curses.

Officer Phillips ran up onto the porch, reporting, "Coreen called for backup, Church. Looks like you need it!"

Cuffed and facing a uniformed officer, Leola Williams finally came to her senses. "Loley!" bawled her husband. "Don't hurt her, Officer!"

Church looked at the man in disgust. "You may not be willing to press charges, but Officer Mather and I are. Assault on a police officer." He shoved the woman toward the uniform. "Read her her rights."

He turned to Brandy, tilting her face to expose her injury to the light. He blinked in surprise. "What have you got, Brandy, the opposite of hemophilia? What do you call it when blood clots too fast?"

Dan's fault. "She didn't get me as bad as she wanted."

Church's gaze shifted to Dan, saying, "No thanks to you, Professor!" His anger was very real, very dangerous, held under tenuous control. "If you're going to be involved with a cop, you will learn right now that you *never,* under any circumstances, interfere in a police action."

"I'm sorry," Dan said contritely.

"Sorry doesn't cut it," said Church. "You learn now and you learn good that if you get in my way I go through you, just as Brandy would through Coreen."

"You said it isn't easy," said Dan. "I accept that, Church. Can't you give me a chance to learn what it means?"

Church shook his head. "It's not up to me. It's the criminals, and the idiots like these two, that won't give you a chance. You got lucky this time: you didn't get her killed. Next time you might not be so lucky."

Dan was as pale as Brandy had ever seen him. "I understand."

"You better. I'm sorely tempted to file obstruction of justice charges to drive my point home. I hope I won't regret not doing it."

It took over an hour to finish up the Williams booking, but Coreen had years of experience at holding dinner. Only about forty-five minutes later than planned they sat down to give thanks that they were not Leola and Bobby Williams.

On the way home, Dan said, "Church loves you."

Oh, God. "We're friends. Dan, there's nothing—"

"No, of course there's not, or Coreen wouldn't love you, too. What I mean is, they're your family as much as your mother is. Church especially. I've got to work very hard to get off his shit list."

As a teacher in a conservative community, Dan rarely indulged in foul language. But Brandy couldn't follow her inclination to tell him things were all right, because they weren't. "Church doesn't know the half of it," she said. "Dan, you *cannot* drink my blood in front of witnesses!"

He winced. "It was instinct."

"That excuse didn't work for Falstaff, and it won't for you, either. If Church hadn't been busy subduing the prisoner—"

"I understand," said Dan. "I was caught unprepared. Next time I won't be."

"How can you be prepared for something like that?" Brandy asked. "You're a civilian, Dan. When there is police activity, *stay out of it!*"

"That's what I meant," he explained. "I should have stayed with Coreen, no matter how frightened I was for you." He stopped at a light, hands tight on the steering wheel. "If I keep my promise not to ask you to find another line of work, can you let me be scared when you're in danger?"

"Yes," she replied. "I know you're human. But what if I'm hurt, bleeding? It happens all the time. Even if I weren't a cop, I'm an athlete— and I'm such a klutz at household chores that I always get bruised and cut. You don't normally lunge for any free-flowing blood, do you?"

"Only yours," he replied. "I . . . didn't expect that reaction. Our match is something I've never known before." She could see him pondering it as he added, "Broad daylight, less than a week after the full moon—I didn't expect such an effect. I should have. The night you cut yourself, I gave myself away. You just didn't know what it meant."

"I do now."

"But that was at night, and later in the month. So it didn't prepare me for today's reaction. Now I know I must *always* control myself with you . . . except when we're alone."

"All right," she let him off the hook, a bit annoyed at her satisfaction at how much he needed her.

∾

The time between Thanksgiving and Christmas always flew, even in ordinary years. This year it traveled at warp speed.

Dan had final exams to prepare, give, and grade. Brandy had hours of overtime to make up for the time she had taken off for her mother's wedding, as well as to build up for her trip to Florida.

When she was off duty, Brandy's time was taken up with Christmas activities, and when she was on there was no respite: the holiday season brought an increase in both crimes and accidents. Even the weather ate time: fog and freezing rain added to any drive or walk, and it took longer to dress and undress, clothing, coats, gloves, boots.

There was no more snow; Western Kentucky settled into its usual early winter rain, fog, and sleet. People put up decorations, and lit colored lights against the gloom.

There were no more corpses with mysterious smiles. The polaroids on the "unsolved" bulletin board faded and curled. Neither Church nor Brandy had time to pursue private investigations. Brandy kept her antennae out for hints of other vampires, but in midwinter everyone was pale, and even Dan didn't need sunglasses.

Guilt prodded each time she passed the "unsolved" board—yet how could she approach Chief Benton with speculation about vampires? Then Doc Sanford was forced to retire. His beloved grandson had been innocent, but Brandy had not the first clue to the identity of Carrie Wyman's real killer.

A Christmas card from Carrie's parents sent her into tears.

The first Christmas after her father's death, Brandy had learned why Christmas was only for children. Losses accumulated as the years passed, and the holidays became a time to count the missing. When Dan held her while she wept, she realized that he understood only too well.

Brandy had searched out his past once she had his birth name, and one day dumped before him photocopies of his birth records, schooling, marriage, work, and service record. "You never told me you were in the army."

"Peacetime service in Germany. Nobody paid attention to me; Elvis Presley was there at the same time."

"You knew him?"

"Not really. He said hi to everyone, tried to fit in, but I wasn't one of his buddies."

"Germany," said Brandy. "Does it have something to do with the real story of how you got your contraband Christ?"

He gave her a look compounded of admiration and exasperation. "I'll tell you about that sometime when you have an evening to spare." She knew he would. It was beginning to sink in that, having lived so many years, Dan had much more life experience than she had. He wasn't hiding anything; they just hadn't had enough time since he had told her his secret for most of it to come under discussion.

Living with Dan, Brandy got a taste of what it would be like to be married. It was nice, but not particularly romantic. On the few mornings she could stay in bed, Dan was gone to campus. They had dinner together most evenings, Dan trying to schedule his time in the computer lab on those evenings Brandy had to work. Next semester, he said, he would match her schedule.

Every other Thursday, Dan played poker with several JPSU faculty, and on alternate weeks met with the chess club. In the summer he played on the faculty softball team; there was normally far less call on his time socially than at this season of party-party-party. Brandy went with him as often as she could manage, starting to worry about the responsibilities of a faculty wife.

When they found time to make love it was sweet and tender, but at the end of a long day it put Brandy straight into blissful, relaxed sleep. It bothered her to miss the sharing of afterglow, and it also bothered her that Dan was always the one to initiate their lovemaking. She was usually too tired to think about it.

One morning she woke, as usual, when Dan slipped out of bed at 3:00 A.M.. Her habit was to turn over and go back to sleep. This morning, she listened to him moving about in the bathroom, then going into his office. She heard his computer give its wakeup "boink!" and keys tapping softly as Dan called up the program he wanted to run. Usually he read e-mail and graded student work in the early morning hours.

Before the screech of the modem told her he had logged onto the university mainframe to collect his mail, Brandy shrugged out of the Olympic sweatshirt she slept in on winter nights and slipped into a clingy red gown Dan had given her as an early Christmas present. Then she tiptoed into the office, sneaked up behind him, and kissed the back of his neck.

She couldn't startle him; they were too closely attuned. He settled back into her embrace, and she leaned over and kissed his mouth from her rather awkward position.

Dan let Brandy experiment. He wore nothing but a wool bathrobe and warm slippers, so it was easy for her to expose him without making him get up. The desk chair rolled and tilted; that should have worked to erotic effect, but as Brandy attempted to duplicate scenes she had seen in movies, the chair almost fell over.

Fortunately, her lover had great patience, and even greater strength. When Brandy thought she had found the balance and began rocking, the chair rolled across the room and would have spilled them if Dan hadn't caught the edge of the heavy work table before Brandy's leg banged into it.

They were both laughing helplessly by then, but the humor did nothing to dampen their ardor. Carefully, Dan lifted Brandy and took them down to the floor, where he let her play out her fantasy of aggression. It was fun, but her afterglow was spoiled by the realization that her knees hurt, and that Dan, on the hard floor, was probably less comfortable than she was.

"Well, that wasn't the best idea I've ever had," she apologized, taking her weight off him.

"Oh, I liked the *idea* very much," he assured her. "I think a heavy recliner might work better, though—if it didn't go over backwards."

"The bed is just fine," she told him. "I don't think we're going to make it as stars in erotic films."

"I didn't know that was one of your goals. I'll be happy to help you practice. If you ever *do* master that chair, you could probably manage a hammock, standing up."

"Don't you laugh at me," she warned. "The next thing, you'll be saying my lovemaking is as bad as my cooking."

He wrapped both his warm robe and his arms about her, kissed her tenderly, and asked, "When have I complained about your cooking?"

It was true; he hadn't. He never complained about anything.

Dan kissed Brandy once more, then told her, "I'd love to try it again, but you have to be up in a few hours."

"I don't care."

"I do—I'm part of the civilian populace you're supposed to protect!" He kissed the tip of her nose and added, "Any time you want to experiment, you know where to find me. The only problem is—now I feel so good, I'm afraid I'll give my students all A's!"

Finally Brandy's vacation began. Dan tucked his sunglasses onto the visor of her car, and packed plenty of sunscreen. They set out well before dawn on one of the shortest days of the year.

Brandy dozed while Dan drove, waking up about half-way to Nashville. When they stopped for gas below Chattanooga, they changed drivers. That put Brandy behind the wheel as they sailed through the fourteen-laned center of Atlanta.

Shifting lanes to stay with the most rapid flow of traffic, Brandy didn't realize her companion's silence was not courtesy, but anxiety. After the I-75/I-85 split south of the airport, she put the car back on cruise control and was stretching the kinks out of her right leg when she sensed Dan striving to relax from even greater tension.

"What's wrong?" she asked.

"Nothing," he replied.

"You're lying, Dan. I scared you."

"Yes, you scared me, cutting in and out of traffic at top speed, but I refuse to complain about women drivers."

"Women drivers!" said Brandy. "I'm a *cop*, Dan. I took special training to drive like that. Movies and TV to the contrary, haven't you ever noticed how *few* real-life police chases end in accidents?"

"You weren't chasing criminals through Atlanta, and you were breaking the speed limit."

"So was everyone else," she pointed out. "Do you want to drive it on the way back?"

"Now what is the diplomatic answer to that one?" he asked. "If I say yes, you're insulted, and if I say no, you think it's grudging."

"Just tell me the truth," she replied. "What scared you? We weren't in any danger."

"We were in *constant* danger. One wrong move on that stretch of road, and you've got a thirty car pile-up."

"That's true no matter which of us is driving."

He was silent for a moment. Then he said, "You're right. It's not your driving. I'm likely to survive an accident . . . but it reminds me of your fragility."

"Good," said Brandy.

" . . . good?"

"Dan, you think it's because you're a vampire, but you're dealing with what everybody faces who loves a cop: we live in constant danger. My mother has never accepted it—she still wants me to find other work. So far you've been in denial."

"I haven't—"

"You have. It's normal. Now that you're ready to talk about it, I think we should sign up for the counseling when we get back." She reached over to squeeze his hand for just a moment, before putting her own back on the wheel.

After a time, Dan asked, "Is this why you've refused to set a wedding date? You think I don't really know what I'm facing?"

"Perhaps you know better than I do. But you've been . . . too accommodating. We never fight, because you always back down. Maybe after she died you regretted every fight you had with Megan. Maybe you feel dependent on me for your life. Maybe it's something I don't even know about. Whatever it is, it needs to be worked through before we get into a marriage with only a 25% chance of survival."

He didn't question the statistic; everyone knew law enforcement officers had terrible divorce rates. "What about you?" he asked. "Why are you willing to live together but not to commit to marriage? Is it your perfect record, top cop, Olympic gold medalist? Is it the same reason you won't apply for the sergeant's exam? Are you afraid to fail, Brandy?"

She loosened her grip on the steering wheel before she replied. "I don't have a perfect record, Dan. My little brother died under my care. Nothing will ever change that."

"I'm sorry," he said softly. "I thought you had accepted that a ten-year-old girl should never have had that responsibility."

"I accept it. And when I'm ready, I'll accept the responsibility of marriage—but first I'll make damn sure I'm properly prepared for it!"

THIRTEEN

Christmas

THAT CHRISTMAS BRANDY'S MOTHER was happier than Brandy remembered since her father died, and Harry was obviously in love with her. Feminism be damned, nothing made a woman feel better than knowing that she was loved.

It was just strange to share such a feeling with one's mother! Away from the stress of her job, Brandy relaxed, watching Dan, thinking how attractive he was, how courteous, how intelligent . . . and how good with children.

Harry's son, his wife, and their children were also visiting. While Brandy never knew what to say to small children, Dan had a parade of tricks with coins and napkins and paper clips. Brandy was slightly less frightened of motherhood knowing Dan would make such a good father.

Dan and Brandy left after Christmas to see some of Florida, Disney World and Epcot, then over to the east coast to visit the Space Center. Despite sunscreen, Dan burned that day. "I'm always most sensitive just before the full moon," he explained. "I should have covered up more."

But even in late December it was too warm and humid in Florida for anything but shorts and teeshirts. Dan wore a wide-brimmed hat and his ubiquitous sunglasses, so his arms and legs bore the brunt of his reaction. Brandy hurried them back to their motel room, where they stayed until the sun hung low on the horizon.

"Let's go down to the beach to watch the moon rise," Dan suggested.

Brandy smiled. "You are such a romantic. Most men would rather watch a football game."

They had to drive a few blocks, for as last-minute tourists they could not get a beachfront motel. There were other people watching the sky glow orange and red, go mauve, then turn gold as the moon rose out of the ocean.

As they stood atop the dunes, looking out over the sea, Brandy felt like the heroine of a romance novel. When Dan gave her a gentle squeeze, Brandy turned in his arms and kissed him. He responded avidly, not resisting when she searched out the ridges in his palate. The bond between them grew so strong that Brandy felt Dan's Craving—a bone-deep hunger, a yearning in every cell of his body. "Let's get you home," she said in concern.

"I'm all right," he insisted. "You're here, Brandy. I feel no need to hunt. And I'm used to controlling it."

Brandy looked around. "Do you want to do it here?"

"Yes, when you offer that way. Turn it off, Sweetheart—I want it to be special tonight."

Brandy didn't know what she had turned on, but when she concentrated on the beauty of the night instead of Dan's need, she felt him relax. Nevertheless, she steered them in an unhurried walk toward where they had parked the car.

Theirs had made four cars in the small pulloff when they arrived. Now two were gone, and as they strolled across the sand a family packed kids, coolers, beach chairs, and an umbrella into a station wagon and backed out.

If Brandy's attention hadn't been on Dan, she might have been more alert. As it was, she pulled the car keys from her belt pack as she reluctantly let go of Dan's hand.

Brandy started around to the driver's side while Dan moved toward the passenger door. She heard him draw a sharp breath, and turned in time to see his head come up sharply.

"Dan, what's—?"

His eyes were focused over the roof of the car on something behind her. Before she could turn, she felt the jab of a gun muzzle against her back.

Brandy couldn't tell if it were she or her assailant trembling, but she heard the nervous tension in his voice.

"Gimme the car keys an' yer money, Lady. You, too, Mister—yer money an' no tricks, or she gets it!"

Don't try to be a hero, Dan! Brandy willed as she pulled bills from her belt pack, praying that on this of all nights her influence would hold him.

Dan remained where he was, his eyes fixed on Brandy's assailant. "Son, you don't want to do this," he said in the most reasonable tones. "Just put your gun up on top of the car, and you won't get into trouble."

Dan was trying to use his influence on the young carjacker. He didn't answer—maybe it was working!

But the gun continued to vibrate against Brandy's back.

"Come on, Son," said Dan. "You're tired of this. You're so very tired—you want to rest. Sleep now—"

"Shut *up*, you fuckin' asshole, 'fore I blow the bitch away!" The gun jabbed Brandy's ribs. "Gimme them *keys!*"

Brandy surrendered them, feeling Dan's astonishment and fear. "Let it go, Dan," she said as the thief pushed her aside and opened the door. He couldn't figure out how to hold the gun and find the ignition key at the same time.

It was the moment of greatest danger: was the boy terrified enough to turn car theft into murder?

Brandy tried to back off, willing Dan not to startle the thief. At her movement the gun came up, aimed at her.

"No!" Dan yelled—and plunged through the car window to grab the boy's gun arm.

The startled thief pulled the trigger by reflex. The shot went through the windshield.

Dan's torso was in the car, his legs partly out the window as he wrestled for the gun. A second shot went through the roof before the boy screamed and slumped, the gun falling from his limp hand.

Brandy scrambled for the weapon. Only once it was safely in her possession did she look at Dan.

"Oh, my God," she whispered. His fangs were extended, his eyes red. And he was bleeding.

The shots would surely bring someone.

"I'm all right," Dan tried to reassure her, untangling himself. "I think

I broke his arm." But his own legs, bare from the cuffs of his shorts to the tops of his sneakers, were a mass of cuts.

Red and blue lights flashed. "Dan! Get control of yourself," Brandy said urgently.

For a moment he stared, uncomprehending . . . but then with obvious effort he retracted his fangs. A police car pulled up and two officers approached. Brandy turned her mind to police business. Showing her I.D., she explained what had happened—the truth, but not the whole truth.

Dan held himself under silent control. Brandy could feel not only his Craving, but the stinging pain of the cuts on his legs. It was after sunset. Why didn't they heal?

The officers examined the car, the woman asking, "Did the carjacker break this window?" while her partner examined the unconscious thief.

When the man touched his shoulder, the boy woke with a start. He lifted both hands to fend the policeman off; Brandy was happy to see that his arm wasn't broken. "Lemme 'lone, Man! I dint do nothin'!"

"These people say you pulled a gun on them and tried to steal their car," the officer said mildly.

The boy started to sneer at Brandy, but when his eyes moved to Dan he suddenly panicked. "Keep him 'way from me, Man! He tried t'kill me!"

The police officer turned to look at Dan. "Sir?"

"He had a gun. I was afraid he'd shoot Brandy, so I—" Dan merely lifted one hand.

The boy shrieked. "He's a fuckin' monster!" He reached inside his shirt, causing both officers to reach for their guns—but it wasn't a weapon he was after. It was a gold cross on a thong, which he held out toward Dan, in classic vampire film fashion.

Dan held his ground. The male officer said, "We'll need your statements. Will you press charges?"

"Of course," said Brandy, despite the strong negative she felt from Dan.

"I had to fall in love with a cop," he said glumly. The two officers exchanged a knowing smile.

"We'll make it as fast as possible, Sir," said the male officer. "Can you drive your car?"

Brandy replied, "Sure—it's just a broken window. We'll follow you in."

The thief practically dragged the officers to the police car in his efforts to stay away from Dan. "He's a vampire!" the boy insisted as the cops tried to read him his rights. "He attacked me! Get a mirror—you'll see!"

"You're not getting out of this by talking crazy, Kid," the female officer told him.

"I'm sorry," Brandy told Dan as they brushed the glass off the seat. The shot had gone through the windshield high on the right, not blocking the driver's view. Dan was more comfortable now, but his pain still assailed her.

"You're not responsible for criminals," he said.

"But I am. If we don't press charges, that boy will be out doing the same thing to someone else."

"Brandy, I'm not arguing. Any other night, it never would have crossed my mind not to press charges."

"Your injuries aren't healing."

"As soon as I feed, they will."

"I'll try to expedite things."

Dan was silent for a few minutes. Then he asked, "You . . . don't suppose they'll believe that boy? Would they give him a lie-detector test?"

"Not when he was caught red-handed."

"I almost killed him," Dan said quietly. "My influence didn't work. When he threatened you, I *wanted* to kill him."

"You didn't give him anything more than a bruise, and that was in self-defense."

"I meant to," he said. "I don't have my usual strength tonight, or I would have hurt him badly."

Realizing that Dan's mood was probably a reaction to his Craving, Brandy tried to reassure him. "Stop worrying, Dan. We'll just give our statements. They won't need both of us for his trial. I'll fly down and testify; the prosecutor will want my credibility as a police officer."

"I couldn't influence that boy. I've never met anyone it didn't work on before. His statement that I'm a vampire will be public record."

"You can't think anyone will believe him!"

"*He* believes it. And I can't change his mind."

"Don't worry about it," Brandy insisted. "If he tells his lawyer, he won't be allowed to testify. It sounds too crazy. And even if his accusation did end up in a court transcript, who'd believe it?"

"Anyone who knows as much about vampires as you and I do," Dan replied flatly.

The local police obviously didn't. Officer Wimbledon, the petite blonde female half of the partnership, pointed to Dan's reflection in the one-way mirror in the interrogation room where they made their official statements. "Vampires!" she snorted derisively. "I hope you won't hold this against Florida. We've got some weirdos running around, but so has every other state. You here on vacation?"

"That's right," said Brandy. "We were supposed to start back to Kentucky tomorrow, but I'll have to get that window and the windshield glazed."

Wimbledon gave Brandy the address of a glass shop. "Tell them I sent you. They'll take care of you first thing in the morning. Want to call your insurance agent?"

Brandy did not want something else to delay getting back to their room—but it had to be done. With the police and the insurance agent, and Dan arguing against a trip to the emergency room, it was 1:33am before they were finally free to go.

By that time, Dan was wincing if anyone put so much as a hand between himself and Brandy. Because of the glassless window, they had to lock maps, tour books, the box of tissues, the pillow, and the umbrella into the trunk of the car. The simple task seemed to take forever.

They were hardly in the door before Dan's hands were on Brandy's shoulders. She put both safety locks on the door, then turned to face her vampire lover.

Despite his extended fangs, she kissed him gently with every ounce of reassurance she could muster. He returned the kiss with enthusiasm, and pulled off Brandy's teeshirt. She responded by doing the same to his. Quickly, eagerly, they stripped one another, then Dan picked Brandy up and laid her on one of the double beds.

Safely in control, Dan teased her, tickling her throat with his tongue, tracing a wet path down to one breast, suckling that nipple and moving across to the other. When he grazed the tips of his fangs, feather-light, across sensitized skin, she gasped in double arousal.

Their rapport, already stronger than Brandy had ever felt it, grew as Dan set out to pay her back for the delay. Always delightfully oral, tonight he had her writhing and gasping before he entered her, returned to kiss her mouth, then nipped little kisses down to her throat.

Brandy pressed upward, wanting the circuit completed. She felt his fond amusement as he gave her her desire . . . and his. Sweet satisfaction sang through her veins. Twice pierced, she was giver and receiver, lover and beloved.

The blissful flow ended with a shared burst of ecstasy that left her sated, panting, cradling her love in her arms as their breathing returned to normal. Dan's face was human again, his eyes brimming with love that hovered on the edge of adoration.

Brandy sifted her fingers through his hair, basking in his contentment. Finally, though, she pulled herself together enough to realize how hot and sticky they were.

"Like something out of an Italian movie," Dan completed her thought, and Brandy chuckled. "Let's take a shower."

There was blood on the sheets and on Dan's legs: his cuts had reopened with their burst of activity. But the injuries were gone now, even his earlier sunburn completely faded. "You couldn't heal until now."

"No. The night of the full moon I cannot heal until I've fed. Even the little blood I lost took its toll. But it doesn't matter now, Brandy. I'm fine, thanks to you."

She glanced at herself in the large motel mirror. She was disheveled, but glowing. The marks on her neck had already closed, showing only as small red dots. Otherwise, she looked healthy, happy, satisfied. "I feel as if it's you who give me strength."

"That's as it should be," he told her. "I don't think vampires would be able to feed if it were not a reciprocal relationship."

"You don't think people are naturally selfish?"

"Babies are selfish," Dan agreed, "but isn't learning not to be self-centered a major part of growing up?"

Was that why Dan seemed so . . . alien at times? "I guess I'm not grown up yet," said Brandy.

"Oh, Brandy. You have no idea—at least I hope you haven't—how I have to fight my desire to keep you to myself. I've gotten used to never being sure when you'll be available. That doesn't mean I like it."

"Well, you have me for tonight," she told him.

In the shower, their stomachs rumbled louder than the water. While the clean second bed was an advantage to being in a motel, the lack of a kitchen was not. They had meant to go out for dinner soon after their sharing and its inevitable aftermath. Now it was 3:00 A.M., and the only restaurants open were fast food places by the interstate.

Brandy dug into their picnic supplies, finding half a loaf of bread left,

202 ~ Blood Will Tell

some oranges, pretzels, cheese, peanut butter, cold drinks, and a couple of beers. "Why don't we just eat enough to tide us over," she suggested, "and have a big breakfast while the car's being fixed?"

Dan peeled and sectioned an orange while Brandy made sandwiches. Naked, they sat on the unused bed and fed one another until one kind of hunger was temporarily satisfied and they reached once again to assuage the other.

~

Brandy woke at sunrise, later than she had intended. Dan was still asleep, so she tiptoed around, and woke him only when she was about to call the glass shop.

Waiting for the car to be repaired was not the way they had planned to spend their last morning in Florida. Fortunately, there was a Denny's across the street, so they tucked into steak and eggs while the windshield and side window were replaced.

Brandy called the police, and was told that the young thief, Jerome Courtland by name, had decided to plead guilty to attempted robbery to avoid assault with a deadly weapon charges. "The way they walk in and out of Florida's prisons, he'll probably be out in six weeks!" Brandy told Dan in disgust when she returned to their table.

"But we won't have to testify," said Dan, "and the boy won't have the chance to say anything about me in court."

So his fears of last night were not simply anxiety brought on by his Craving. "Dan . . . do you want to visit Jerome Courtland before we leave?"

"Why?" he asked.

"To make him certain you're not a vampire. He thinks he knows the rules, from Dracula movies. If you visit him in daylight, in the interrogation room where he can see you in the mirror, he'll be sure he's wrong. We can even stop at a Wal-Mart and pick up a cross for you to wear."

Dan put a hand over Brandy's. "Thank you," he said. "If the case were going to court, I'd do it. But since it's not, it's probably best that he simply not see me again. Eventually he'll forget."

"But you won't."

"I don't know why I can't influence him. *That* power is at its strongest during the Craving—a survival characteristic to make prey vulnerable and allow me to escape without their remembering me. I need to know why Jerome Courtland is completely impervious!"

Brandy frowned. "Dan . . . do you think he's a vampire?"

"If he were, he'd have been out to get blood last night, not to steal a car."

"Could he have fed before we encountered him? You said you can't tell—you weren't sure about Land till he died."

Dan puzzled over that. "Do you think this Courtland kid's that good an actor? Why pretend he believes the old Dracula routine? What about the danger in giving the police the idea that there are vampires around?"

"He has fingerprints, so if he is a vampire he's young—maybe he's using reverse psychology. Or . . . could he be older than he looks? Thirty or forty?"

Again she watched Dan mull over her question. Odd how sometimes he seemed so puzzled by questions he ought to know an immediate answer to. Finally he said, "No, he's really the age in his records. What was it—nineteen? A vampire would continue to mature into his thirties, and then stop."

"He could be like you at that age, figuring out the rules. He already knows he doesn't have to kill to live."

"He does?"

"Florida has become famous for murders the past few years, but there's no serial killer leaving a trail of drained corpses. Not even a full moon killer."

"Yes—you'd know, wouldn't you?" Dan thought it over. "He *could* be a young vampire, still experimenting. He might wear that cross for the same reason I have a mirror and a crucifix in my living room. So, what should we do, Brandy? If he's not a vampire, we could make fools of ourselves. But if he is . . . he probably needs my help."

"Wait," said Brandy, "until he asks you for it."

"What?"

"If Jerome Courtland is human, he'll soon convince himself that he imagined what he saw. If he's a vampire, he'll come looking for you—his lawyer can get him your address. Let him come to you if he needs your help."

"Sometimes you're too smart for your own good," said Dan, and they left it there and started back to Kentucky.

But on the way home, Brandy noticed something. The waitress where they stopped for dinner warned them away from the special, and told them which dishes were actually prepared fresh. The attendant where they stopped for gas not only pumped it, but checked the oil and cleaned their windshield. And when they stopped for the night, the desk clerk didn't charge extra for a ground-floor room.

When they were inside, Brandy asked, "What are you doing, Dan?"

"What do you mean?"

"You're testing your influence on everyone we come into contact with."

"Do you blame me?" he asked. "Brandy, I've always been careful to avoid influencing people indiscriminately. As a consequence, I had no idea some people might be immune."

"You've decided Jerome Courtland isn't a vampire?"

"The more I think about it, the more certain I am that his panic was real. Another vampire wouldn't pass out with terror. One with criminal tendencies would try to blackmail me. And he didn't try to use influence on us. That leaves Courtland as a normal human being who is immune to influence. How many such people are there?"

"You've decided to find out?"

"I can't test the whole world, but I need to know what the chances are. I thought I would easily get us out of that situation last night—and instead I made things worse. What if Jeff Jones had been immune?"

Brandy remembered Dan rendering Church's son unconscious with the "Vulcan nerve pinch." "He might have gone into shock and died. But that wouldn't have been your fault, Dan, any more than it would have been mine if you hadn't been there."

"I know. But . . . I've gone to many people to feed my Craving over the years. It never crossed my mind that I couldn't prevent a donor from panicking."

"You just wouldn't have gone through with it."

"My point is, it *never happened*. But then, I've developed a group of regular donors wherever I've settled for any length of time."

Brandy had deliberately not pursued that question. She didn't want to know who in Murphy Dan had fed on. Now, forced to think about it, her police officer's mind insisted that she ask, "Was Carrie one of your regular donors?"

"No. I stayed too late, wanting you . . . and then I took the easy way when I left you and the Craving hit me."

"If you didn't know there were people you couldn't influence, why did you risk having regular donors?"

"Risk?" Dan asked.

"You established a pattern. Someone might have noticed."

"*You* might have noticed. Not everyone thinks like a cop," Dan reminded her. "And . . . I didn't want to hurt anyone."

"I of all people know it does no harm."

"I was afraid of spreading disease, Brandy. I appear to be immune to all human diseases, including AIDS. But that one really made me think. I don't know if I don't get sick because the bugs don't like my taste, or if my immune system kills them."

"You're human. It's probably the latter."

"Perhaps. But people can carry diseases they're immune to. I don't want to be responsible for spreading AIDS or hepatitis. It's not possible to tell without a blood test, but at least I could live where such diseases are less prevalent, and pick donors at least risk."

"You always chose people you knew?"

"Never close friends." He smiled. "Until now."

"Since your wife . . . became too sick," Brandy corrected, and again saw that puzzled look flicker momentarily in his eyes.

"Yes," Dan agreed. "Since Megan got ill."

Brandy didn't attempt to stop Dan from testing his influence; the more information he had, the better off they both were. They returned to Murphy and Brandy's routine.

On New Year's Eve, Brandy had to work. Although Callahan County was dry, plenty of alcohol flowed that night, and the police were kept busy with traffic patrol and "drunk and disorderly" calls.

As midnight approached, though, those cops not out on call gathered in the squad room, ready to drink a toast in coffee at midnight. At 11:30 P.M., the door burst open to admit Dan Martin, Coreen Jones, Melissa Blalock's husband, and the wives of two other officers. They brought a cake and what looked like champagne—but turned out to be sparkling grape juice. Plastic wine glasses were passed around, and everyone prepared for a festive moment.

Then the dispatcher reported, "Silent alarm at the courthouse."

"Damn!" said Brandy, and gave Dan a swift kiss as she grabbed her coat and followed Church out into the cold. Reynolds and Menafee, rookies stuck with New Year's Eve duty, were close on their heels.

The courthouse was just around the corner—they saw nothing out of the ordinary. A few Old Timers gathered outside for a New Year's toast, that was all.

The elderly men who hung about the benches by the courthouse were not homeless. But tonight they had gathered to see in the New Year together. They were passing a couple of bottles wrapped in paper sacks around, but the police ignored that breach of a city ordinance. A dry county had no equivalent of Cheers to provide such people a home from home.

All the men had that "lost old man" look, clothes that had stretched out of shape while their bodies shrank or increased in girth. Their attempts to keep warm included sweaters or suit coats hanging below waist-length jackets, work boots with what had once been dress pants, caps with ear flaps tied down against the cold.

The usual crew were there, the same people Brandy saw on the benches year in and year out. "Hey—what're the police doin' here?" one of them asked as Brandy and Church approached.

"Did anyone go inside?" Brandy asked.

"In the courthouse? It's locked," one of the other men responded.

"Naw, we're all here," said the first man, looking about him to count heads. Then, "Where's Troy?" he asked.

"He was here a minute ago," said a man wearing a day-glo hunting cap. "You think he went inside?"

The west door was firmly locked. When the police went around to the east, however, they found the door open, bent metal and splintered wood indicating forced entry.

Telling the Old Timers to stay outside, Brandy and Church moved into the cold building. There was no one in the ground floor hall, and all the offices were locked and dark. As they turned back toward the east end, however, a soft electronic "beep" sounded from somewhere above.

The second level held the courtroom and judge's chambers, soon to be moved into the modern annex being built a block away. Callahan County's historical courthouse in its traditional square could not be expanded; it would be preserved with the sheriff's and tax assessor's offices on the ground floor, the upstairs converted to other uses.

But just now there was still that atmospheric old courtroom. Church and Brandy carefully climbed the worn marble stairs, finding the door to the courtroom a victim of the same tool used below. The room was dark, but at the other end the door to the judge's chambers stood open, pouring a shaft of light across tables and benches.

As they approached, Brandy heard the soft click of computer keys manipulated by a hunt-and-peck typist. Staying out of the light, Church bent to retrieve a crowbar abandoned beside the door.

From inside the chambers Brandy heard swearing in a familiar voice, then, "Dammit, tell me what I want to know!"

Brandy and Church stopped in the doorway, seeing the old man struggling with the machine. "And just what is it," Church asked, "that you want to know, Dr. Sanford?"

FOURTEEN

Discovery

DOC SANFORD LOOKED EVEN WORSE than last time Brandy had seen him. His good wool coat was open over a shapeless suit, worn too long without cleaning or pressing. The old man's shirt collar was frayed, his wrinkled tie knotted untidily. He wore a snap-brim fedora that had lost its snap; his ears and nose were red with cold. She realized with a shock that he had turned into one of the Old Timers.

He smelled of whiskey.

"Come on, Doc," Brandy said gently. "Let us take you over to the station, and you can tell us what you were trying to do here."

"The proof's in that damn machine!" said Sanford.

"What proof?" asked Church.

"The proof that Judge Callahan killed my boy!"

"Now, Doc," said Church, "you come along with us, and you'll see things clearer in the morning."

"Aren't you gonna arrest him?" asked Menafee, who had followed them in.

"Jurisdiction problem," Church prevaricated. "Courthouse is county property. We'll just take Doc over to the station and hold him for questioning."

"You know him." Menafee finally got it.

"Doc Sanford. He was coroner till a couple of months ago," Brandy explained. She realized that Church was annoyed that Doc Sanford had tried something Church's position as a police officer put off limits to him.

The anger had gone out of the old man, leaving him in the bleak mood in which Brandy had last seen him. It seemed the only thing that could get him moving anymore was his hatred for Judge L. J. Callahan.

Reynolds was carefully bagging the crowbar. That gave Brandy an idea. "Bring the computer, too. It's evidence. We'll get an expert to examine it. Turn it off, then unplug it and bring it over to the station."

Doc Sanford's bloodshot eyes fixed on Brandy, and for one moment she recognized the man she used to know. "You believe me," he said incredulously.

"I just believe in thorough police work," she told him, the two observing rookies very much on her mind.

As they escorted Doc Sanford back to the station, bells began to chime, firecrackers went off, and shouts of "Happy New Year!" filled the air. It wasn't as big a celebration as the one that had heralded in the year 2000, but in the squad room they were met with hugs and kisses.

As they hadn't cuffed Doc Sanford, Coreen didn't realize he was a suspect—so after thoroughly kissing her husband she turned to the old man and gave him a hug, saying, "I'm glad you came to our little party, Doc. Maybe this year will be better than last."

"It couldn't be worse," Sanford replied.

Dan, still holding Brandy after their New Year's kiss, gave her arm a reassuring squeeze when she stiffened in reaction to Doc Sanford's remark. "Does anybody know where Judge Callahan might be?" she asked.

"Probly at either a New Year's party or midnight church service," said Phillips. "Why?"

Brandy and Church explained what they had found at the courthouse. "We have to charge Doc," Church finished, just as Reynolds and Menafee arrived with the computer.

"That bastard Callahan'll press charges," said Sanford. "He'll do anything to get me."

"Doc," Brandy said gently, "you broke the law. And you know the problem with the jail. We're trying to avoid transporting you to another jail because tomorrow—uh, today—is a legal holiday." If they could stall, on a regular work day he could be arraigned and released.

But Doc Sanford was following his own train of thought. "You get your computer expert onto that machine afore Callahan finds out we got it! Callahan's schemes are all in there, under secret codes!"

Dan Martin spoke up. "Doc, if Judge Callahan were doing something illegal, he'd never use this computer."

Brandy asked, "This isn't the one you installed for him?"

"This is an old 486, probably belongs to the county. The judge would use his system at home for personal files."

The news seemed to take away all Sanford's strength. He slumped into a chair and repeated, "At home?"

Dan asked, "Can we plug this in here, or do you have to dust it for fingerprints or something? I can check to see if it was damaged."

"We caught Doc in the act," said Church. "Go ahead and check it out."

It took Dan only minutes to verify, "No harm done."

"Good," said Brandy. "Doc, if you offer to pay for the doors you broke, we may be able to keep this down—"

"Callahan's gonna throw the book at me!" said Doc Sanford. "God damn it, why didn't I break into his house?"

"Doc," said Dan, "what do you know about computers?"

"I used 'em at the hospital and the morgue. You think an old man can't learn modern technology?"

Brandy was glad Dan didn't remind him that he hadn't recognized the age of the computer. Neither had she. Except for those colorful Apple things, they all looked alike, beige box, keyboard, screen.

Dan explained to Sanford, "You know what you need for your work—but you're no hacker. If you broke into Judge Callahan's house, you couldn't access anything he wanted kept secret. I couldn't, and I set up his system."

"Then why couldn't you?" Sanford asked belligerently.

"Because after I set it up the judge chose his own passwords."

"No," said Sanford.

"Dan knows computers," Brandy assured him. "There's no use trying to get at Callahan's home computer," she warned.

"No!" the old man shouted, lunging to unsteady feet. "He killed Cindy Lou! He killed Rory! I'm gonna prove it!"

"Doc," Church said, trying to get the old man to sit down again. "Doc, there's nothing you can do tonight."

"Dr. Sanford," said Dan, "it's late, you're tired—"

"No!" Sanford flung Church's arm off and tried to head for the door. "I'm gonna wring that bastard's neck!"

But the old man ran straight into Reynolds' arms. The young cop easily restrained him.

"Don't hurt him!" said Brandy as the doctor went limp.

"Put him in the interrogation room," said Church. "Reynolds, you keep an eye on him."

"He's passed out," said the young cop.

"He's old and frail," said Brandy. "Look in on him during the night. We'll charge him in the morning."

"Okay, okay," the young cop grumbled.

The party mood was effectively damped. Dan, Coreen, and the other non-police personnel soon left. Some hours later, in the early morning darkness, Brandy went home to find Dan already—still?—up.

It was still. "Brandy," he told her as he made a pot of tea, "I found someone else I can't influence tonight."

"Doc Sanford," she realized.

"Yes. I've tried influencing a couple of dozen people since that kid in Florida. It worked on everyone until tonight. From that small sample, it appears about one in twenty-five is immune."

"Maybe Doc was too drunk to concentrate."

"Did you test his blood alcohol? He didn't act really sloshed—more like he'd had just enough to get up his courage. Anyway, when school starts next week I'll have plenty of opportunity to try influencing students."

"You do that," said Brandy, too weary to think. "I'm going to bed," she said through a yawn. "Happy New Year."

~

Because the Callahan County court system was backlogged with cases, Dr. Sanford made a plea bargain that never would have been permitted in less busy times. The community was awash in car thefts, breaking and entering, and malicious damage. Callahan County citizens eagerly pressed charges.

Even malicious mischief, though, rated a jail term, fines, or both. The sentencing hearing would give Judge Callahan his chance to "throw the book" at his old enemy.

On January 5th, Brandy took a call. "Streetwalkers!" the outraged caller exclaimed. "Soliciting in the parking lot at the shopping center! Murphy has never had such a thing," she huffed.

She was right; except for that prostitution ring at the university a few years ago, Murphy's few ladies of the evening had always remained discreet. "I'll look into it, Ma'am," said Brandy. When she hung up, she turned to Church. "You're not gonna believe this one." But before they could get their coats on there were two more calls, from the managers at Video-Mart and Grand's Hardware.

At first everything at the shopping center looked normal, the lot half full, cars jockeying for parking slots near store entrances.

A woman got out of the passenger side of a pickup truck while a man exited from the driver's side. The man headed for Video-Mart while the woman, wearing a heavy jacket but with legs protected from the cold only by flesh-colored stockings, looked dazedly around the lot. She was young, Brandy saw, pale, and heavily made up compared to the Avon-perfect look of most Murphy women.

"I'll tail that one," said Brandy, slipping out of the car. "You see if there are any more." She walked toward the entrance to Video-Mart until she was out of the young woman's range of vision, then turned to tail her.

A late-model Buick slid into a parking space near Brandy's target. The girl hurried toward the driver. "Lookin' for a date, Sir?"

With the hooker's attention diverted, Brandy moved close enough to see the man's bewilderment turn to shock as he realized what she was offering. His face turned red and he exclaimed, "Get away from me!"

As he tried to avoid her, she demanded, "Then give me some money, Man. I ain't had nothin' t'eat all day."

"Go away before I call the police!" the man threatened angrily, and the girl stepped back and let him leave, after he carefully made sure his car was locked.

Brandy watched, needing more to make an arrest stick. The hooker next approached a man walking up the aisle between rows of cars. He ignored her. "Blow job, Mister? Only ten dollars," the girl offered in desperation.

"Go away!" the man growled.

Brandy flashed her badge as she came up behind the girl. "Excuse me, Sir—I'm arresting this woman for soliciting. You witnessed what she said."

An uptight righteous sort, the man said, "Good work, Officer! I'm glad to see the police so prompt. We've never had this sort of thing in Murphy."

"Hey, I dident do anything!" the girl protested. She was familiar somehow, but Brandy couldn't place her. Her accent was pure West Kentucky, a weird combination of bad grammar with hyperenunciation that caused her to turn "didn't" into two clear syllables.

"You offered sex for money," Brandy told her. "You have the right to remain silent—"

Church was out of the car now, quietly stalking another target. In moments he had made an arrest, too.

"I think I saw a third one actually pick up someone," he said, pointing to a beat-up Chevy. Brandy could see a man in the driver's seat, slack-jawed and wide-eyed.

"I don't think he'll agree to be a witness," said Brandy. The third hooker exited the car. She stopped a moment at the car's side mirror, running a comb through her bleached flyaway hair and replacing smeared lipstick.

As her "client" recovered enough to remember what he had come to the shopping center for, Church called for more police. "We'll bring in the two we caught, but there's at least one more here, and we're still down at Video-Mart! Better send a car up by Grand's, too."

"Shouldn't we pick up the johns?" Brandy asked. "They're breaking the law too."

"I know," Church agreed, backing out of their parking space, "it's not a fair world, Brandy. We'll talk to the chief, but I don't think he'll agree. These women don't seem to be getting that much business." He nodded at the hooker they had left for their colleagues, who was cringing as a white-haired man threatened her with his cane.

The two they had arrested had had little success. One had $35.00, the other $20.00. Under the harsh interrogation lights they were not the hardened floozies of *film noir*, but burnt-out shells of young women.

Melissa Alice Trenton was twenty. Wan and listless, she answered their questions as if she didn't care. She was hooking, she explained, for living expenses. She was adamant that she and the other girls were just friends, not part of a prostitution ring. They had no pimp, no madame.

They got the same story from the girl who had jogged Brandy's memory, Paula Denise Pringle, age eighteen—one of the Pringle twins who had tried to frame Ricky Chu. The reason Brandy hadn't placed her, besides the grotesque makeup, was that she was even paler than Trenton, with deep circles under her eyes. Her hands shook as she chain-smoked, and when she took a deep drag her hollowed cheeks turned her face into a skull. After a cup of coffee, she finally took off her coat. Brandy frowned at her thin, malnourished frame. Anorexia crossed her mind . . . but only because her police experience had taken place in Murphy.

Church, who had moved there from Chicago, immediately recognized the far more probable cause: "Oh, God," he said. "We've got crack cocaine in Murphy."

Suddenly there was an explanation for the rash of crazy crimes. Crack was addictive, cheap, and mind-ruining. The four young women selling themselves at ten dollars a "date" couldn't think clearly anymore. Needing rent and crack money, they had all gone in one car to the same shopping center where they had "hung out" in more carefree days.

They priced themselves cheap to attract as many johns as possible, not reasoning that they could get the same amount from fewer customers at higher prices. They chose the shopping center because it seemed a good place to find lots of clients, never giving a thought to being caught.

Both male and female crack addicts stole for dope money, but their crimes were often senseless. They broke into homes and took whatever cash they found, a television set or a VCR, but also a set of barbells, a *Star Trek* collector's plate, a broken alarm clock, a set of used playing cards, a cookie jar. Whatever took their fancy they stole — "The only kind of thief who forgets in mid-crime what he's stealing!" Church reminded those in the department who had rarely dealt with crack before.

The Pringles were sad but not surprised at Paula's arrest. She and her brother had always been smartass kids, but before Christmas Paula had become impossible. Her grades plummeted. She dropped out of school a semester short of graduation. When they caught her stealing and tried to get her into counseling, she left home.

Paula and the other girls had once been on the pep squad together. Then they had all been introduced to crack, at some party they could no longer remember. One by one they had left home rather than give up their addiction, and now shared an apartment in a complex inhabited by cokeheads, crackheads, winos, cockroaches, and rats.

Their lawyers pled them into rehab programs, so there was a chance they might turn their lives around. They gave up their direct supplier, but he was just another high school kid, this one too smart to take drugs himself, but also too scared to give up the names of anyone higher up. Meanwhile, the search began for the crack house in Murphy.

"If we don't find it," said Church, "we'll know where it was when it blows up." But the traffic led them to it quickly enough—they just didn't yet have the evidence to get a warrant.

In her concern about the deadly drug in her home town, Brandy couldn't take Dan's problems very seriously. However, as police work frustrated her, she found puzzling over the "real" rules for vampires a welcome relief.

At the end of his first week of classes, Dan reported that he could influence everyone on the JPSU campus that he tried his power on. At this time of year, with the sun setting early, he had hundreds of guinea pigs in evening classes and computer labs. "With a larger sampling, it appears that less than one percent of the population is immune," he told Brandy over dinner. "It's not so strange, then, that I never happened on anyone before."

"And then suddenly two in one week," said Brandy. "If they'd both been here in Murphy, I'd suspect a connection."

"But they weren't. One was in Florida, and that kid got his information about vampires from Bela Lugosi movies."

"So? What does Doc Sanford know about vampires? Dan, what would happen if another vampire were to try to influence me?"

"I . . . don't know," he admitted. "I'd expect my influence to be stronger. But you're suggesting that you might be immune to the influence of other vampires?"

Dan rose, and started clearing plates away—his turn to clean up as for once Brandy had done the cooking. "What about Dr. Sanford? He doesn't act as if he's under anyone's influence, with his obsession about Judge Callahan. Unless . . . you think there's a vampire who wants to get rid of the judge, who's given the doctor that obsession?"

"If so," said Brandy, "it's certainly not effective."

"But then the Andersons show that not all vampires are very smart."

"True. But Doc Sanford's family really was hurt by the Callahans. And I've got a hunch that the judge was mixed up in framing Rory Sanford—Church thinks it might have been to protect one of his drug cohorts."

"And Carrie's murder? I still think that was a threat or warning to vampires, Brandy."

"Maybe so—but whoever framed Rory didn't know it."

"What makes you think that?"

"The fork. Your fangs punctured her throat. The murderer used a knife. But whoever framed Rory bought the cannibal theory, and provided a fork of the right size and shape to cause the puncture wounds." She sighed. "It seems I'll never find out who really killed Carrie."

"As long as you know it wasn't me—" Dan began.

"No!" Brandy interrupted. "That's not enough, Dan! My best friend's been murdered, and I have not one single clue!"

The cold, wet weather of January curbed outdoor activities, but Dan had access to the university swimming pool. Brandy loved swimming with Dan, for she rarely found anyone who could keep up with her. She couldn't help wondering whether Dan held back—his perfect health should allow him to win every race, but perhaps his technique wasn't quite as good as hers.

Then one evening Brandy found herself leading Dan by half the length of the pool. She pulled herself out and sat on the edge, waiting for him to reach her. "What's the matter?" she demanded as he grasped the rim to surge up out of the water with his usual grace.

"I guess I was distracted," he said.

"By what?" Brandy asked, for the only other people there were two college boys practicing back flips.

"Something that came in today's e-mail," he replied. "Brandy . . . if this is true, everything I've believed about myself could be completely wrong!"

"What're you talking about?" she asked.

"Let's go home. We can't discuss it here."

At home he took two printouts from his briefcase and handed one to Brandy. "Remember that mystery document from Rett Land's hard disk, the one no one could translate?"

"Yes. You sent it to some specialist in ancient languages."

"She worked on it over the holidays. Here it is."

There was a cover letter:

Dearest Dan:

Your mystery document proved utterly fascinating. It's in a subdialect of Medieval Greek, spoken about a thousand years ago—where in the world did you get it? Do you have the original manuscript, or any idea where this Professor Land of yours found it? You have sent me only a fragment—where is the rest?

My dear, I know ancient texts are not at all in your line. What you have sent me is a chapter out of an alchemical treatise—one of the earliest examples I have ever seen. It is unique to my knowledge in combining the tenets of alchemy with the myth of the vampire, prevalent to this day in the area in which this dialect originated. This document is important to historians, folklorists, and linguists. Dear boy, you must get me the rest of the text!

I eagerly wait to hear from you, or from colleagues of Dr. Land who may know the source of this fragment. I cannot stress enough how significant this document is, or how frustrating not to have the original manuscript! I cannot believe it is a hoax—but without the original I can do nothing beyond the translation you asked for. Please let me hear from you soon!

Sincerely,
Amelia Messanourski

"Well, your friend is certainly excited about it, 'Dear Boy,'" said Brandy.

"Dr. Messanourski was a visiting professor at Florida Central. I helped her with computers. I was pretending to be twenty-five, and she was really around sixty."

"So she's around seventy now. Retired?"

"She'll never retire. She loves teaching." He pushed back a lock of hair brought down by their swim, looking at that moment younger than Brandy. "Dr. M's a bloodhound. I had no idea what was in that file, or I never would have sent it to her."

"Whatever it is has frightened you. Why, Dan, if it's only folklore—alchemy, of all things?"

"A vampire was killed over it," he replied grimly. As Brandy would have protested further, he shook his head. She could feel him controlling his fear. "Read it."

The first part was some formula she could not follow, explaining how someone referred to as "the Numen" should purify himself before—she saw the word "vampyre," and realized that the Numen was being instructed as to how to prepare—Dr. Messanourski had put "program" in brackets in the translation after the word "prepare"—his vampires.

Brandy looked up at Dan. "Does this say what I think? That vampires are controlled by a person called a Numen?"

"That's what it says," he agreed. "That part's just alchemy, though, Brandy—superstitious nonsense."

"Out of that superstitious nonsense came the science of chemistry," Brandy reminded him.

"I didn't want to hear that," Dan said. "I'm trying to believe this has nothing to do with me. If I thought it was true, I'd be scared to death."

"Dan," Brandy read his feelings, "you *do* think it's true, and you *are* scared to death."

His mouth tensed. "I'm not certain," he insisted. "I'm just afraid it might be true. Please—read the rest, and show me where it contradicts reality as we know it."

The document next distinguished between two kinds of vampires. Dr. Messanourski had translated the first as "temporary," putting in brackets [insignificant, expedient, disposable]. For these, the Numen chose weak-willed persons from the lower classes, to be servants or soldiers. Once their purpose was fulfilled, they were destroyed. The Numen was not to expend much effort on disposable vampires.

"This implies . . . that vampires are created by the Numen," Brandy realized.

"Yes."

"But you know that isn't true."

"Do I? Read on," Dan said flatly.

Brandy's stomach tightened as she read about the second, "long-lived" vampire. "Select with utmost care, to obtain a specimen with high intellectual ability. University students with academic rather than spiritual goals make good candidates, but do not choose one too young, as he will not age once he has been turned."

"Well, this part's all wrong," said Brandy in relief. "You've been a vampire all your life, Dan. You told me you started showing the signs at puberty."

"That's what I told you," he agreed. "It's what I remember . . . but—" He broke off. "Read on, Brandy."

The long-lived vampire was to be programmed and set free to live for several centuries, gaining knowledge along with life energy and experience. When the Numen decided he was "ripe," he would "call" that vampire and "harvest" him—absorbing all his knowledge, energy, and experience. Dr. Messanourski had added, [The vampire is like a storage battery, trickle-charged until the Numen needs him. The Numen recharges by drawing the energy all at once.]

Brandy raised her eyes to Dan's. "You think . . . that's what happened to Everett Land? One of these Numens—"

"Numena."

"Never mind the grammar lesson!" she snapped. "You think a Numen drained him to recharge himself?"

"If that hadn't happened to Rett, I could dismiss this document as superstition or misunderstanding, like the rest of alchemy. But it did happen. Read the rest."

Next came instructions for programming the vampires. For the disposable ones, the document provided a variety of options. "If they are to be soldiers, it is not expedient that they fear the light of day, but if they are intended to terrify, confinement to darkness will make them even more fearsome. Vampires intended as soldiers may feed without killing their prey, while those used to strike fear in the Numen's enemies will be all the more fearsome if they bring death at every visit. All vampires must feed at the full moon; those used to terrify may be programmed to prey— and kill—more often, even every night."

There followed a long passage about controlling disposable vampires: if the Numen wanted them to stay within a certain territory, they should be unable to cross running water; if he wanted his assistants to control them, he should cause garlic to weaken them, cold iron to bind them. As Brandy started to turn the page, Dan said, "Look at this part," and pointed to a passage near the bottom.

"The Numen cannot waste effort on temporary vampires. However, it is essential that none ever leads the authorities to the Numen. To this purpose, instill the belief in every disposable vampire that he may not enter holy ground; that any religious object, viz. the cross or a saint's relic, will burn his flesh; and that he will choke attempting to speak the name of God, Christ, or any saint. The purpose of this is that such a vampire, being of a low and superstitious nature, may not upon his first craving for blood rush to the priest to confess his sin, resulting at best in his being put to death as an abomination and at worst in his leading Church authorities to the Numen."

"This is amazing," said Brandy. "It explains why there are so many different rules for vampires, not only in different cultures, but often in the same culture. Every vampire could operate by his own individual set of rules!"

"Except for the Craving at the full moon," Dan agreed, "and common physiological attributes. But go on. You haven't come to the long-lived vampires yet."

The Numen was cautioned to take care what he programmed into vampires intended as his own prey. No fear of religious objects, as in the time and place the manuscript was written, scholarship was controlled by the Church. A scholar-vampire must walk in daylight, and not draw unwanted attention. For the same reason he was not to kill his prey.

"Here's the final straw," said Dan, pointing to a passage he had marked with a line down the margin beside it:

"To prevent the long-lived vampire from crises of religious conscience, it is best to implant the belief that he was born with the need to drink blood, and all the physical characteristics that go with it, viz. superior strength, sensitivity to sunlight, night vision, etc. Let him believe himself a superior form of human, for men of intellect do not take well to another's dominion over them. Suppress their memories of the Numen's role; instruct them to create their own memories, consistent with their life histories, to account for their state. Each man best knows himself; a vampire will create a more accurate and believable personal history than the Numen could invent."

"Oh, God," Brandy whispered, thinking of the times she had watched Dan puzzle out answers to questions about his personal history. "Have you . . . been lying to me?"

"I don't know. If I have, I've been lying to myself at the same time." He shook his head. "After reading this, I doubt my own memories!"

His fear was now palpable. Brandy wanted to reassure him—but how? "Dan, it could all be coincidence. Or Professor Land could have written this."

"What makes you think that?" Hope warred with fear.

"He was a language expert. Maybe this is a hoax."

"He wouldn't have been killed over a hoax."

Dan was right. Vampires were real; Brandy lived with one. Everett Land's mysterious death fit the idea of a Numen "harvesting" a vampire—

one who had discovered the secret of his creation. Obviously, knowing this secret would put any vampire in jeopardy—

"Dan—you said this came by e-mail!"

"I've deleted all reference from my hard disk and from the mainframe. But . . . if someone is monitoring my mail, he could have accessed it before I did."

"Wouldn't he have deleted it?"

Dan's black eyes widened. "He wants me to know."

"Knowledge is power," Brandy said firmly. "Either he didn't see it, or he doesn't know how to delete it. If it's the same person who tried to destroy this document by formatting Dr. Land's hard disk, our suspect is not a computer expert."

"But he is Rett's murderer," said Dan.

"He probably has the rest of this file, and the original manuscript, too. Why do you think Dr. Land had only this one chapter on his computer?"

"Perhaps he never had the complete manuscript. Or, he might have put one chapter at a time on the hard disk. The rest could be on the missing zip disks, or on floppies. Or if he had the hardcopy manuscript, this could be the first chapter he chose to work on—look at the information in it!"

"He was killed for that information," said Brandy.

"Or to keep him from obtaining it, or from acting on it," said Dan. "And now . . . I know it."

"So do I," said Brandy. "Dan, I see nothing here that contradicts reality as we know it. It explains the Andersons: disposable vampires killed not just before they revealed their nature, but before they could reveal the existence and identity of the Numen who created them."

"You're reading my mind. Go on."

"The number of vampires in Callahan County—a Numen lives here, creating vampires, using them, disposing of them when they become dangerous. The university is a source of scholars to become his long-lived vampires. I wonder . . . how long has he been operating here?"

"I don't know how long a Numen lives," said Dan, "but if he creates vampires he intends to harvest centuries later, you might as well call it immortality. I agree with Dr. M: we need the rest of this document."

"We'll find it when we find the Numen," said Brandy. "Dan . . . have you had any blackouts? Lost time, hours you can't account for, since this translation arrived."

"Not that I'm aware of. Why?"

"How long have you had it?"

"Since yesterday. I saw the word `vampire' in it, skimmed it as I made the printouts, and deleted it. It was only in the system a couple of hours, so if the Numen didn't see it then, maybe he won't find out."

"I'm pretty sure he doesn't know," said Brandy.

"What makes you say that?" he asked with eager hope.

"He hasn't made a move against you, although you've had the information almost two days."

Brandy felt most of Dan's tension drain away. "You're right. He'd have made an attempt to get it away from me."

"Dan," Brandy said, "if that document is true, he would have made you destroy it and forget you ever saw it."

He was silent for a moment. Then, "That's what I find hardest to believe. I have no gaps in my memory. If I wasn't born a vampire, when could this have happened to me?"

"The document says you make up the memories to fill in the gaps. Dan . . ." Did she dare? They needed every ounce of truth and trust between them now. "I've seen you do it."

" . . . what?" He stared at her in shock.

"Usually when I ask about your life before we met, you have a ready answer. But sometimes I ask questions no one else has. I've seen you pause—I thought you were searching for the right words, but what if you were creating a memory that would fit your life history?"

He put a hand to his head. "No," he protested softly. "Sometimes I have to think to remember, just as you do."

She looked into his eyes. "Dan . . . the first time it really bothered me was when I asked you about Megan."

"I thought you had accepted that I was married before."

"Not that. When I assumed that you . . . fed from her."

"I did," he said positively. "It was wonderful, but not as wonderful as what you and I have."

"I don't think it ever happened," said Brandy.

"Brandy, the records will be on file—"

"I don't mean your marriage. I just don't think you were a vampire then. How old were you when Megan died?"

"Thirty-two."

"And that's how old you've stayed. Maybe your grief at her death made you vulnerable to the Numen. Intelligent people are not easy to control. In medieval times they were probably drawn in by the chance to learn alchemy, but modern scholars require different lures. You were grieving after Megan died. I remember how distracted I was when Dad died—even though I genuinely liked school, my grades dropped and my freethrows went to hell. I couldn't center, couldn't find the zone. For it to be a wife, not a parent, and a cruel, slow disease instead of a sudden shock—it was far worse for you."

"I remember blowing up on the job," said Dan. "My boss suggested I get out of the east coast pressure cooker. He helped me find a new job as an engineer on a federal highway project, Interstate 24." He paled. "Oh my God. I was here. Only for a week or so, but *I had completely forgotten it!* We stayed in Paducah and drove all over this area to study putting a four-lane highway through this terrain!"

"It's all right," Brandy said gently, disturbed by the terror emanating from this normally fearless man.

"It's *not* all right," he insisted. "Years later, in a new identity, I came to interview at JPSU with no recollection that I had ever been in West Kentucky before."

"But you remember it now."

"Yes," he said in puzzled tones. "Did I just make up that memory? Or is it real, but I had suppressed it?"

"We'll track Eduardo Tomas Donatelli's employment records," Brandy told him. "I suspect it's true."

"If it is," he said, "you realize there's not just *a* Numen in Callahan County. *The* Numen who made me a vampire is here."

"I had already assumed that," said Brandy, "and I have a hunch who it is. I'll research police records and the newspaper morgue. I don't want to be put on insanity leave, if I accuse the wrong person."

Their rapport as strong as ever, Dan did not ask her the identity of her suspect. Instead, he said, "I'll check the news stories, and make copies of anything significant."

"Do you know what to look for?"

"Local officials involved in the I-24 project. It has to be someone I met."

"Murphy's paper is small. Scan *all* the headlines in issues around the time you visited," suggested Brandy. "I'll check murder and accident victims, get the autopsy reports and see how many times onset of rigor mortis is suspiciously absent."

"How far back do you plan to go?"

"It depends on what I find."

Brandy found four cases in the past two years in which people died by means that would kill a vampire, all petty criminals with drug connections. There were other cases in which the heart or the brain was destroyed, but in two the remains were skeletal and in the others rigor set in as expected.

But four cases were significant, as with Rett Land and the Andersons they made seven instances in two years of unexplained absence of rigor, the only sign Brandy knew of that the corpses had been those of vampires.

Then, on a hunch, she searched the musty archives for the autopsy report on Cynthia Louise Sanford Callahan. It was brief, attesting that she died of a gunshot wound to the head. No mention was made of the onset of rigor—but no note, either, on anything unusual about the corpse.

Still, Brandy wondered: why would a woman take a man's way out? Did her husband pull the trigger? Or had he or someone else turned her into a vampire because, like her brother, she was immune to influence? Had she chosen one of the very few ways a vampire could commit suicide?

Brandy told Dan that evening. He had found something equally interesting, a news article from 1898: SCHOOL TEACHER MISSING. MYSTERIOUS BODY FOUND. There were no photos, but the story indicated that the corpse of a woman apparently in her nineties was found when the principal's assistant went looking for Miss Abigail Santee, who had failed to appear to teach her class. Miss Santee was nowhere to be found, but the aged dead woman lay peacefully on the couch in her parlor. The follow-up story the next week (for the local paper was a weekly at that time) indicated that Miss Santee was still missing, the dead woman not identified. The members of a local church provided her with a Christian burial.

"What else did you find?" asked Brandy.

"Similar cases in 1924, 1947, and 1962."

"I'll see if coroner's reports still exist on any of these," said Brandy. "It looks as if Murphy, Kentucky is where old vampires come to die."

"No," said Dan. "It's where they are enticed to be killed. To be . . . harvested."

FIFTEEN

Invitation

BRANDY NOW HAD EVIDENCE that a Numen—a creator and exploiter of vampires—was operating in Callahan County . . . and had been for over a century. Although she had no direct proof, her suspicions fell on the most powerful man in the county: Judge Lee Joseph Callahan.

However, his birth records were on file in the county records. They might have been faked, as a Numen obviously had hypnotic influence, but the Callahan family had moved to Western Kentucky right after the Civil War; the whole community knew their history.

Dan was the only person Brandy could talk with about the Numen, and talk was all they seemed to do. "Maybe the Numen is just *associated* with the Callahans," Dan suggested. "Judge Callahan could be a vampire under his direction."

"I don't think so," said Brandy. "He's a good ol' boy, not the scholarly type. He's a politician, Dan."

"If I were a Numen," said Dan, "I'd follow Machiavelli's advice to change with the times. It would be convenient to control a powerful politician."

"I suppose you're right," Brandy conceded. "I've wondered if that perfect tan is makeup. But he never wears sunglasses, even in the summer."

"I've considered getting contact lenses," said Dan, "but I don't need any correction."

"If Callahan is a vampire," said Brandy, "I wonder how the Numen feels about his plans to run for governor."

"I assume the Numen would be the power behind the throne," Dan suggested.

Brandy shook her head. "We don't know enough. The library will have books on county history."

They found three such books, one from the early 1950's, one put together in the late 1970's, and the most recent from just last year. Spreading them on the coffee table, Brandy began looking for references to the Callahans.

There was a photograph of Joseph Lee Callahan, with the reproduction of an oil painting of his father, Lee Joseph, grandfather of the present-day judge. The man in the painting sported mutton chop whiskers, a mustache, and center-parted hair, but there was no denying his resemblance to his son. And Joseph Lee, except for his dark hair . . . was the spitting image of the judge on the bench today.

The thought, "spitting image," triggered something Doc Sanford had said. "Joey Lee," everyone had called the man in the photograph—the man Sanford said killed his sister.

Brandy studied the three versions of the Callahan story. The earliest book had a photo of the Callahan family in the 1950's: Joey Lee, Cindy Lou, and a skinny, solemn boy identified as Lee Joseph.

"Oh, God," whispered Brandy. "That boy never grew up into the man we know today."

"How can you be sure?" asked Dan.

"Look at this family history. In every generation there is one son, and the father never lives to see him completely grown. See here? Joey Lee's father was killed in World War I, when Joey Lee was fifteen."

"So?"

"After high school, the male heir goes off to college—spending several years away from Murphy. When he returns . . . he's all grown up and the spitting image of his father!"

"Brandy, are you suggesting that . . . ?"

"The real son disappears. The presumed-dead father returns sans aging makeup and takes his place."

"You think all these Lee Josephs and Joseph Lees are the same man . . . a man capable of murdering his own children?"

"Are they his own?" asked Brandy. "It's not in these sanctified histories, but Judge Callahan's father married Doc Sanford's sister. She had an affair. Joey Lee shot the man, but Cindy Lou gave birth to a son."

Dan flipped to the reproduction of a news story in one of the later volumes: STATE SENATOR CALLAHAN KILLED IN MINING ACCIDENT. "The bodies were never recovered."

"And just how did Joseph Lee's *father* die?" Brandy wondered. It was in the 1950's volume: in World War I France, Callahan and several other soldiers took shelter in a deserted farm house. The building was hit by mortar fire. That Lee Joseph Callahan received a posthumous medal for dragging one of his buddies out of the burning building. He died trying to save the rest.

At least the surviving soldier remembered it that way.

But how hard would it have been for the "hero" to exchange dog tags with a man whose body was about to be reduced to ashes?

"Look!" said Dan, searching the volume from the 1970's. TRAGIC SAGA OF CALLAHAN FAMILY read the headline. Joey Lee Callahan had had an older sister, it seemed. Not ten days after he returned from law school, she drowned.

There was only one survivor of each generation of Callahans. Callahan wives died young, often tragically, and since the family set down roots in West Kentucky every Callahan boy had lost his father while he was still in his teens. The article concluded with the death of the current judge's wife, in childbirth. The infant also died.

"So," said Brandy, "the trick didn't work this time."

"How are you reading this?" Dan asked.

"Numen or vampire," said Brandy, "Lee Joseph Callahan has found a unique way of coping with his long life. Instead of moving and changing identities, each generation he fakes his death and returns as his own son!"

"What happens to his real sons?" asked Dan.

"We don't know that he ever had any," Brandy replied. "If the boy the current judge replaced *was* the son of that Darwinist college professor, I doubt Callahan would feel any compunction about killing him."

"Or turning him into a vampire," suggested Dan.

"Possibly. In the war he could wait for an opportunity to fake his death. But he had to arrange that mine collapse—which killed two other state legislators and nine miners! Who knows how many other people he's killed?"

Dan sat very still, one hand on the open book. Very quietly, he asked, "What if we're right?"

"We are right. We have to do something about it."

"Brandy, a man with the history we're theorizing won't hesitate to kill us."

"I know," she replied. "First we have to find out if Callahan is vampire or Numen."

"How do we do that? You can't arrest him."

"If Church is right that Callahan is connected with the drug trade, we might get a warrant to search his house."

"For the Numen manuscript?"

"If he hasn't destroyed it." Brandy closed the book and sat back on the couch.

"I'm so sorry I got you into this," said Dan

"What do you mean?"

"A little knowledge is dangerous. Even worse is false knowledge. I don't know how much of my own memory is true. Now I don't even know—"

When he broke off, Brandy encouraged, "Know what?"

"I don't know if I can give you children, Brandy. When Megan and I were trying to have a baby I was tested. I was fertile then . . . but now I know—or think I know—that I wasn't yet a vampire."

"So?"

"Callahan appears to have no children of his own."

"We don't know about the earlier marriages, or the baby that died with his last wife. There were no rumors concerning her—and believe me, in this town there would have been at the slightest suspicion of adultery!"

"If she knew about it," said Dan. "A Numen's power of influence must be far greater than a vampire's. What if he hypnotized his wife and a man of his choice into having an affair just long enough for her to become pregnant?"

"That's sick," said Brandy.

"Sicker than killing his own sons?"

"We don't know that's true, either," she said. "Our problem is to investigate Judge Callahan without his knowing that we've guessed what he is. I can pick up the —. Oh, my God," she said, her skin tingling in sick realization.

"What?" Dan asked.

"He pulled the same trick on me that he did on his wives!"

"What are you talking about?" She could feel Dan's bewilderment, tinged with anxiety. "Brandy—you're not pregnant? You told me you were on the Pill."

"I'm not pregnant. But . . . much as I love you, you're not the kind of man I was ever attracted to before, Dan. It was a distraction. Church and I must have been getting too close to Callahan's drug connections. He . . . made a pass at me himself, and I wasn't too polite in my refusal."

"That doesn't speak well for his influence."

"It didn't take him long to figure out that you were a better diversion."

She felt Dan's horror at the accusation as a physical pain. "Brandy— I love you!"

Tears burned behind Brandy's eyes as the clues fell into place. "Why kill Dr. Land on campus? Surely a Numen could lure his own vampire to him. Callahan risked 'harvesting' Land in the same building where you have your office. I was on duty. You knew Dr. Land; he knew you'd go to see what had happened. Maybe he influenced you to do so. God, he's efficient—but then, a Numen who lived for centuries would learn to be, wouldn't he?"

Dan sat staring at her. Brandy wanted to take away his horror—but how could she as piece after piece of the puzzle fell into place? "Dr. Land had obtained this knowledge he wasn't supposed to have. Callahan decided to 'harvest' him—according to that manuscript it would give him Land's knowledge. He'd know whether Land knew you were a vampire, and whether he had shared any of this with you."

"He hadn't," said Dan. "I suspected Rett, but I have no idea whether he suspected me. He never said anything."

"Callahan saw a way to kill two—no, three—birds with one stone," Brandy continued. "He harvested Land, brought you and me together, and took whatever Land had on disk—and the manuscript if it was in Land's office."

"But why kill Rett? Why not just take the manuscript and 'program' him to forget he'd ever seen it?"

"Maybe his time was up anyway," Brandy suggested. "Maybe Callahan needed the recharging—it was over twenty years since the last mysterious aged corpse."

"That made the papers," Dan added.

"True. But if the Numen really gains all the knowledge of a vampire he harvests, perhaps he killed Dr. Land to be able to read the manuscript for himself."

"If he didn't already know what was in it," said Dan, "how did he become a Numen?"

"I don't have all the answers," said Brandy. "They're in that manuscript . . . if it still exists."

"So you want to search Callahan's house."

"Yes. I suppose you can expect some kind of new instructions if he notices I'm on his trail."

"Brandy—" Dan began indignantly, but broke off to say flatly. "You really think . . . Callahan programmed me to distract you from your investigation."

"I do. Look what he did to Church."

"To Church?"

"Dan, you were *there* when Jeff was injured. You heard the silent dog whistle. Sandy was lured within the sphere of influence, and directed down that dangerous drop so the children would follow. Someone heaved the boulder that crushed Jeff's leg—Callahan or one of his vampires. The children saw him—remember the Dracula monster?"

"Brandy—it's coincidence," Dan said desperately.

"Coincidence that we were there, maybe, but no coincidence that one of Church's kids was badly injured. He couldn't think about anything else for weeks. Church was distracted, I was distracted—"

"No," Dan protested again. "Judge Callahan can't be responsible for all that."

"Oh, no? He arranged financing so Harry could sell the TV station, freeing one of his most severe critics to leave town. My God, how this all fits together! Harry then proposed to Mom—maybe Callahan even influenced them to get together in the first place. I was tied up for a month with the wedding, and then . . . oh, God."

Brandy squeezed her eyes shut, but tears leaked anyway.

Dan, who had been afraid to touch her for the past few minutes, dared to take her in his arms. "Tell me."

"The day of Mom's wedding, my two main emotional supports were removed: Mom and Carrie."

"Leaving you . . . dependent on me," said Dan. "And ..."

"What?" Brandy demanded at the stab of guilt she felt lance through him.

"I—resisted taking you that night! So Carrie was not only murdered, but in a way that could have exposed me as a vampire if I hadn't obeyed the command at the next full moon." His arms were tight about her, as if he feared she would flee from him. "Oh, Brandy, I'm so sorry, so sorry. How can you trust me? I can't trust myself."

She clung to his solid physical presence, but her mind was in turmoil. "I do trust you," she said. "I love you. But I can't trust the Numen's influence. Still, we know you can resist." She managed a teary smile. "Even if you didn't know you were under compulsion, you resisted the night of Mom's wedding, because it was *wrong* to base our relationship on influence. I trust in that, Dan, in your sense of honor."

"Thank you," he whispered hoarsely.

"Besides," she added, "I just realized that Callahan came on to me *after* you and I met. Maybe . . . he couldn't influence me because I was already half in love with you."

He managed a sad smile as he replied, "I think I fell all the way in love with you the night we met."

"And Callahan started using you once he recognized the attraction. It's probably the same thing as letting a vampire create his own beliefs and memories: it would have been very hard work to make me fall for Callahan against my inclinations, but because I cared for you it was easy to manipulate me through you."

"But . . . what do we do about it?" asked Dan.

"We've got to set you free," said Brandy.

"How?"

"Callahan expects you to keep me under control. Dan—you won't be insulted if I hide my birth control pills?"

"Why?" he asked in honest puzzlement.

"Because the most obvious way to distract me again would be to have you replace them with placebos."

"At least that would tell me I can father children," he said wistfully.

"Would you remember the order, or carrying it out?"

"Perhaps . . . if something caused me to think about it."

"What do you mean?"

"Ever since I remembered coming to West Kentucky after Megan died, more memories have returned. It's slow—I recall as events remind me." He stopped, reluctant.

"What don't you want to tell me?"

"That's what I get for falling in love with a detective," he said, but the familiar joke fell flat. He steeled himself and began, "You said I'm not your type: you're more right than you know. I didn't avoid athletics in school because I was afraid of revealing my powers. I was lousy at sports. I wore thick glasses, and was the fastest kid in my class with a slide rule.

"A lot has come back about Megan. The memories of feeding from her were manufactured. The memories of loving her weren't. It was a sweet, comfortable, unimaginative kind of love." Brandy felt his ineffable sadness. "To tell the truth, you're not my type either, Brandy. Any Brenda I would have gone out with would never be nicknamed Brandy!"

"At least I don't spell it with an 'i.'"

Dan ignored the feeble humor. "You were a cheerleader, a Homecoming Queen. I was the acne-scarred captain of the chess team. I dated the girl with glasses, a big nose, and a National Merit scholarship."

"Does that describe Megan?" Brandy could not help asking.

"She was beautiful to me," Dan replied.

"And it wasn't compulsion," added Brandy, disentangling herself and standing up.

"Brandy . . . if I didn't love you, I'd have used influence. I know I was ordered to. Compelled to. I was supposed to get you off the police force."

"What?!" She turned to face him.

Dan's eyes were unfocused, a frown furrowing his brow. "I was supposed to make you fall in love with me, marry me, and leave the force. I . . . couldn't."

"You hate my job."

"That's me," he said, "not the compulsion." Then his sad resignation lifted. "Brandy, you're right! I can and do fight the influence when it goes against my own beliefs!"

"But the Numen works with your natural inclinations," said Brandy. "You're a romantic. You believe in love at first sight."

"I doubt love can be compelled. The important thing is that I'm capable of resisting. That means there's a chance I can break free altogether."

"We have to get that Numen manuscript," said Brandy.

"Neither of us can read it."

"Your friend Dr. M is eager to translate it."

"Brandy—she'll want to *publish* it!"

"Isn't that exactly what we want?"

"For everybody to know the formula for creating and controlling vampires?" Dan asked in bewilderment.

"First of all," said Brandy, "'everybody' won't read a long and boring scholarly text. Those who do won't believe that the methodology will create vampires, any more than they believe that other alchemy texts really tell how to turn lead into gold."

"Except for . . . scholars who are vampires," Dan realized. "They'll believe it."

"And," added Brandy, "the truth may set them free."

Dan nodded. "We must get that manuscript."

"If Callahan has it, it'll be in his vault."

"A safe deposit box?"

"No—a safe room in the basement of his house. Church looked it up last year when he hoped to get a search warrant. He wanted to be sure it covered everything on the property, so evidence couldn't be denied on a technicality."

"How are you going to get into his vault?" Dan asked.

"There are only two ways: a search warrant or . . . breaking and entering."

Brandy wanted a legal search of Judge Callahan's property with plenty of backup, too many police to influence, sheriff's deputies and state troopers. She wanted Judge Callahan in jail while she and Dan made and dispersed copies of the Numen manuscript. To do that, they had to get incontrovertible proof of Callahan's involvement in some crime . . . such as the car 108 murders.

There was no telling how many vampires there were under Callahan's influence. Brandy was certain that with the evidence of what he was in Dan and Brandy's hands, the judge would not hesitate to order their murder. How fast could he create temporary vampire hitmen?

A little knowledge was a *very* dangerous thing! Seeing Dan almost afraid to touch her, unsure which thoughts were his own, Brandy *had* to break Callahan's influence. If she thought she could get away with it, she was almost tempted to get a shotgun and blow the man's head off.

Almost.

She could never commit cold-blooded murder . . . not even of a man as evil as she suspected L. J. Callahan to be.

She needed proof!

Brandy was in court the day of Doc Sanford's sentencing hearing. She hadn't seen the old man recently, and felt guilty about getting so caught up in her own concerns.

Sanford wore a new suit with white shirt and tie, and someone had taken him to a barber. He sat up straight on the bench as he waited his turn, his attorney at his side. The bloated look of too much beer and not enough food was gone from his features; she saw no signs of a hangover.

But when it was Sanford's turn, and he and his lawyer went forward to learn the old man's sentence, the sun coming in the large old-fashioned windows struck Doc Sanford directly in the face. He winced and squinted, sure sign that he was not in as good condition as he pretended. Nevertheless, he stood straighter than Brandy had ever seen him, facing his fate with military stoicism.

Brandy waited for the axe to fall. Even with the offense plea-bargained down to malicious mischief, the judge could break the old man's spirit with jail time, or his bank account with fines. There was a murmur of amazement throughout the courtroom, then, when Judge Callahan announced, "Thirty days, suspended, and the cost of repairing the damage you did."

Brandy felt her jaw drop, and saw the same thing happen to Sanford's attorney. Everyone who knew of the enmity between these two men was left flat-footed by the light sentence. And Doc Sanford said, "Thank you, Your Honor," as if he were actually sincere.

Brandy would have liked to talk to Sanford, but she was a witness in the next case, and so could not leave the courthouse. If she could have, she should have been out on the streets—for Murphy's crime wave had not yet crested.

The streetwalkers didn't try the shopping center again, but new girls popped up on the court square, at gas stations, convenience stores, and motel lobbies. These were not vampires, but crack addicts, as were the thieves and burglars who had the city complaining about police inefficiency.

Church growled, "The stuff rots their brains. We've got to close that crack house!"

The pushers they caught were school kids, not adult suppliers. One of the children was Charlene Swenson, the girl who had fingered Rory Sanford. Brandy had to tell the girl's mother her daughter was found offering her classmates joints laced with rocks of crack.

Charlene was too smart to use; she was saving money to buy the Nintendo set her parents feared would interfere with her schoolwork. Darla Swenson listened to her daughter calmly explain her intentions, then turned to sob on Brandy's shoulder. "You told me to search my children's rooms, and I didn't do it. I trusted them. I thought they deserved their puh- puh- privacy!"

"Be thankful Charlene's not using," said Brandy. "Talk her into giving up her supplier. Make a deal. She's a juvenile—once she's an adult her record will be sealed."

That perked Dr. Swenson up. "It will?"

"That's right. But Darla, you *must* get your family into counseling or you may lose Charlene long before then."

"I will," the woman vowed. "We've always had a good relationship. I'm sure I can talk Charlene into cooperating with the police. After all, she did before."

But Charlene Swenson was a poor witness. She had been approached, she claimed, by a student whose family was moving to Albuquerque. The routine was established: after school each Thursday Charlene went to the bleachers at the athletic field. A high school kid would sit down next to her, and they would exchange drugs for money. It was a different kid each week, she said, but always with a plaid scarf wrapping his or her lower face against the cold.

"They come from behind me," she added. "They told me not to look at them. One boy had a knife."

But when Charlene returned to the bleachers under police surveillance, no one approached. The crack got distributed anyway. That weekend three teens high on it smashed their car into an overpass on 641 north. The car caught fire and all three died horribly.

Brandy watched the community she had grown up in—the community she was sworn to protect—falling apart around her. If only she could tell Chief Benton what she knew.

But her chief would never believe a tale of vampires controlled by a creature no one had ever heard of. To convince him she would have to expose Dan.

The one person she wanted most desperately to let in on the secret was Church. Dan, though, said, "If he believes you, he'll put it on record. Brandy, the world isn't ready to accept a vampire as a next-door neighbor . . . or a teacher to their children."

Brandy worried that she and Dan could not fight the army of vampires Callahan could raise. They had to make a surprise move, soon, before Callahan found out that Dan had broken his control.

It appeared that Callahan had not yet noticed. The judge had officially declared his candidacy for governor of Kentucky, and was gearing up for the May Primary.

When Brandy got home one evening, there was no smell of cooking, although it was Dan's turn to make dinner. Despite the depression he had been fighting since discovering that he literally didn't know his own mind, he had continued to be the domesticated male most women only dreamed about. Brandy worried that it was programmed into him to add to his attraction, but she didn't want to add to his concerns. And, she admitted to herself, she enjoyed living with a man who had few of the irritating habits women complained about.

But now she wondered if it were over. Dan was stretched out on the couch with his laptop computer, grading student projects. An empty coffee mug stood on the table, along with the day's mail. Sylvester was curled up on the back of the couch.

When Brandy came in, the cat came gracefully to be petted. Dan glanced up and said, "Let me just finish this."

"No problem," Brandy told him, and went to put her gun safely away. Dan was still rattling away on the computer keys, so she picked up the mail. Automatically she put back on the table the three opened envelopes, which would be Dan's, and sorted through the rest. Advertising, a credit card bill, and a reminder of Sylvester's annual shots.

Dan pressed a couple of keys, and the computer made soft thumps and moans as it saved his comments to his student. He popped a floppy disk out and put it in his pocket, setting the computer, still running, on the coffee table. Then he stood and came to take Brandy in his arms.

He was still the most intoxicating kisser she had ever known. When they broke apart she smiled at him. "You seem to be feeling better."

"I shouldn't be," he said.

"Dan, you're not going to lose me because you didn't make dinner. I'm happy that you've broken through another layer of programming, even one that I enjoyed."

"What?" he asked, obviously confused. "Dinner's in the refrigerator. All I have to do is grill the chicken. What do you mean, another layer of programming?"

"Ever since you started sorting out the real you from programming, I've expected you to turn back into a frog."

"A frog?"

"Like most men. Leaving the seat up, not remembering to take the garbage out, never cooking a meal or washing a dish—the usual."

"That's not programming. Maybe if I'd had sisters Mom would have made them help around the house, but as it was, my brother and I had to do it. We complained, but we grew up used to doing our part. Megan was a real estate agent—back before every woman on the block had her license. She sometimes had to work evenings, just as you do. If I didn't cook, I had to run out and get a pizza or a bucket of chicken. We didn't have microwaves, then, or Domino's."

"I'm sorry," said Brandy.

"I should think you'd be glad to know that *something* in my character is real," he said bitterly.

"I don't see any change in your character," Brandy told him. "I don't think it's possible to change that, just as hypnosis can't make someone act against their nature."

"I pray you're right," he said. "It's the one hope I've been clinging to. Brandy, I can't believe what I feel for you is false. I love you with all my heart."

"And I love you," she assured him, relieved of one more fear that he would turn into a stranger when he sorted out the truth.

"Are we going to face Judge Callahan?" he asked, catching her completely off guard.

"What? Dan, you can't want to confront him directly!"

It was his turn to be confused. "No," he said, "I meant the invitation. I thought you looked at the mail."

"My mail, not yours."

"Two of these were for both of us," he explained, handing her two of the opened envelopes. One was from Brandy's mother, with photos from Christmas. The other was a formal invitation to a political fund raiser.

For $150 per couple, they could attend a ball at the estate of Judge L. J. Callahan. "What do you think it means?" asked Dan.

"That we're registered Democrats," Brandy told him. West Kentucky was one of those areas where registering as anything else locked a voter out of the primaries.

"Look at the date," said Dan. "It's the night of the full moon."

"We'll leave before midnight. Or we don't have to go. I've never supported Judge Callahan's fund raising."

"I have," said Dan. "I *thought* I believed in him."

Brandy turned over the envelope. As Dan had said, both their names were on it. "Dan," she asked, "have you changed your address on your voter's registration?"

" . . . no." He picked up the third envelope, a gas card bill, and showed Brandy the yellow change-of-address sticker put on by the post office. Dan had been living here less than two months; almost all his mail still was forwarded from his old address.

"I forgot about voter registration," he said. "I think I'd have remembered to do that when I went to the court house to change the address on my driver's license."

"You haven't done that, either? Dan . . . are you still paying rent on your apartment?"

"I've sublet it—one of the new faculty just moved in. Brandy, I'm not going to run out on you. I just haven't gotten around to some of the formalities. But I think you're missing the point about the invitation."

"No, I'm not," said Brandy. "It wouldn't make any difference if you *had* changed your address: as two separately registered voters, under two different names, we should *each* have received an invitation. This is a message, Dan. Unfortunately, I'm not sure what it says!"

SIXTEEN

Full Moon

JUDGE CALLAHAN WILL EXPECT ME at his fund raiser," said Dan. "If he doesn't know I'm resisting him, there's no reason to make him suspicious."

"Dan . . . are you certain that Callahan is the Numen and not just another vampire?"

"I . . . wish I remembered what he did to me, the way the true memories of my childhood and my marriage have come back. But I'm sure we have the right person."

"Church has been saying that about Callahan's drug connections for the past two years," Brandy said glumly.

Dan suggested, "We can hack into his bank accounts. Drug interests may be supporting his campaign—they'd probably love a governor in their pocket."

"You've never wanted to do anything illegal on the computer," Brandy pointed out.

"Maybe I'm desperate. I want my mind back, Brandy—I don't want to spend my life wondering whether what I do is because I want it or because he does, and whether what I remember really happened."

"Okay. I'll get my files. You call Domino's."

"Domino's?"

"Leave the chicken for tomorrow. Let's break into the bank!"

For this procedure they moved to Dan's office upstairs, where his state-of-the-art desktop was. "The first thing I'm going to do," he said, "is create a false phone I.D. so if I trip a call tracer it'll give the wrong number."

"You can do that?"

"It'll fool one of those electronic devices that records a caller's number. Let's hope we don't have the bad luck to hack in just when someone's tracing calls through the police or the phone company."

Callahan's accounts in Murphy were in good order. But Brandy was reminded of something else. "Can you get into the university's accounts?"

"What for?"

"A hunch. They just announced that a $500 Humanities Scholarship is available for next fall. Most of Rett Land's estate went into that scholarship account. Let's see if it's still there."

It wasn't. In November all but enough to sustain the scholarship had been transferred to the university's general fund. A few days later the same amount was withdrawn.

"Well," said Dan, "that looks suspicious, but I'm afraid we'd have to break into the Accounting Office to find out who that check was made out to."

"Too dangerous," said Brandy. "Let's get back to Callahan's accounts."

When they delved into his campaign account, once again everything appeared to be above board. Brandy yawned. "You won't find anything in that one," she said, getting up to clear away the pizza box and Coke cans. "Campaign finance laws are so stringent you can't get away with *anything.*"

Dan scrolled down the list of deposits and checks.

"All withdrawals from campaign accounts have to have dual signatures," Brandy added, not remembering where she had come across that piece of information.

"Not if they're electronic," said Dan. "All you'd need is both passwords. Until computers can read handwriting or thumbprints, computer theft is easy if you have the passwords. I shudder to think what will happen with electronic signatures."

"I wish you'd stop sounding like an expert criminal!" she told him.

"Brandy, if I'm going to teach how to safeguard against computer crime, I have to know how it's perpetrated."

Brandy carried the trash down to the kitchen. She had just turned the coffeemaker on when Dan called, "Brandy—come here and look at this!"

There was over $120,000 in the campaign account. Almost every day there was a deposit, ranging from a low of thirty-six to some of several thousand dollars. Money went out of the account at about a third the rate it came in—normal enough, if you considered that the majority of campaign expenses came just before elections.

Then suddenly, in November, there was a deposit of $92,000 in one fell swoop. Three days later $44,000 came in. Five days after that, $71,000.

"Fund raisers?" Brandy suggested.

"Not this one," said Dan, pointing to the exact amount withdrawn from the university's scholarship fund, deposited on the same day. "Your hunch pays off."

"What about these other large sums?"

"Isn't that about the time the crime wave began?" asked Dan. "When crack was introduced in Murphy?"

"Callahan couldn't be stupid enough to put drug money in his campaign account!" said Brandy. "Those accounts are strictly audited."

"How often?"

"Uh . . . I have no idea," admitted Brandy. "But if that money doesn't have proper documentation, Callahan's in big trouble *whenever* the audit happens."

"Not if he's dead and gone," said Dan. "Lee Joseph or Joseph Lee Callahan has faked his death at least twice, reappearing as his own son. He may have done something similar before, as Callahans go back into last century. But he doesn't have a son at present. I think he's outstayed his welcome in Western Kentucky. Look at this, Brandy."

Dan scrolled down to a series of transfers. Every few days, $9500 was transferred to another account in the same bank. The I.D. number of that account traced to one Mary Lee Josephs, and had been opened last July.

Brandy grabbed the phone book and quickly confirmed, "No such person in Murphy."

"Unlisted number?" Dan suggested.

"Yeah, sure. Mary *Lee Josephs*? Jeez, he's not even *trying* to hide."

Dan sat in stiff silence, staring at the screen until Brandy asked, "What's wrong?"

"The opening date. That was when I was working for the judge, installing his new computer system. Brandy . . . I think I opened this Mary Lee Josephs account for him."

"What? How?"

"I remember teaching him electronic banking. I wouldn't have *consciously* showed him how to create a fake account, or created one for him . . . but I have a hazy memory about a college account for a goddaughter."

Brandy nodded. "That's how hypnosis works: you get someone to do something he'd never do by making him think it's something else. But what good is a fake account?"

"Callahan isn't stealing; he's transferring his own funds to this other account. No money is missing. A bank audit won't turn up anything. With the ability to influence people, I'm sure Judge Callahan even had a signature card created for Mary Lee Josephs."

"Then what's he doing with that account?"

"Laundering money," said Dan. "There it goes through another wash cycle." The deposits, all under the $10,000 which would automatically be reported to IRS, stayed in the Josephs account only for a day or two and then were transferred to a bank in Miami. From there they went into the corporate investment account of something called Caribbean Enterprises, which kept a balance of billions while amounts in the tens of millions went in and out daily, to and from banks all over the world.

"Looks like Caribbean Enterprises is a regular laundromat," said Brandy.

"Mmm," Dan said, studying the dispersal of funds. "What a way to make an illegal fortune: front for shady businesses, and take a slice off the top of every transaction. Something this big . . . it would practically be a criminal-style Switzerland!"

"What do you mean?"

"Look at this money going to South and Central America, the Middle East, the Cayman Islands, London, Zurich. I'll bet almost every government in the western world would like to shut it down — but with so many big-time crooks involved, who would dare squeal? And think of the pressure they can put on dirty politicians! Whoever runs Caribbean Enterprises is virtually safe from prosecution."

"Dan," Brandy observed, "you are practically shouting, 'Why didn't I think of that?!' Is *this* your own nature coming through?"

He turned to her with the devilish gleam that she hadn't seen since he had read the Numen fragment. "I admire a great scam, Brandy, just as I admire a great computer game. But no, I don't want to go into business laundering money from drugs or slavery or pornography or whatever exploitation has put that money into dirty hands. Okay?"

"Okay." The sun was long since down, and their rapport was at its height. Dan spoke the truth — or at least the truth as he knew it. "I'm sure the FBI and CIA already know about Caribbean Enterprises," Brandy said, "but as soon as I can figure out a way to get that information legally, I'll report it." She sighed, realizing, "This could be a boost to my career, but it's no help with Callahan."

Dan nodded, and cut the connection with the Miami bank. "There's no way to track where the money he sent to Florida went. He probably has a new identity set up, with passport and credit cards waiting for him to fake his death here."

"Where do you think he'll go?" asked Brandy.

"It could be anywhere. If he gets away, all I can do is wait for some kind of offer I can't refuse in Timbuctoo or Fiji!"

"That's assuming—" Brandy stopped as fear lanced through her.

"What?" Feeling her horror, Dan turned his desk chair and took her hands. "Brandy, what is it?"

"I can't see him taking the risk of having you trail after him again," said Brandy. "Oh, God, Dan—Callahan will want to do what you've just done with computers. He has you in Murphy for the same reason he brought Everett Land here: he intends to . . . harvest . . . you."

"Well, he's not going to!" Dan said decisively. Brandy could not hear, see, or feel the least fear in him. "Before he makes his move, we've got to know what we're fighting—and that means getting the entire Numen manuscript."

"What happens when he discovers it's missing?"

"It won't be. We'll photocopy it—on his own copier! We're going to that ball. You get the plans showing where the vault is in his house—and what kind of security system it has. What better time than a party to break into the safe? Isn't that how cat burglars do it?"

"Only in the movies," said Brandy. "Are you *sure* you weren't a criminal before you were a vampire?"

He laughed, that deep, sexy chuckle she now knew was purely himself. "No—but I was a risk-taker. Maybe that's why you appeal to me so much, Brandy: you're like the part of me I've suppressed for years." He snapped off the computer and took Brandy in his arms for a soul-searing kiss. Then he carried her to their bedroom, where they made love for the first time since Dan had learned he was not acting fully under his own motivations.

Tonight he was in control, though—and happy, as if set free of a great burden. Brandy rejoiced as she shared his excitement, his anticipation, his love of a challenge. She thrilled to his pleasure as well as her own, in a unity she had never believed possible.

~

The fundraiser for Judge Callahan was formal, so Brandy had to buy an appropriate dress. It wasn't easy to find the right one: appropriate but unmemorable, and allowing complete freedom of movement. How much easier if she could just rent a tux!

Dan studied the plans of Callahan's security system. This was West Kentucky, not New York or California; there were no walls around the Callahan homestead, no guards or electric gates. There were hunting dogs in a big run, who gave tongue any time someone came near, and a security trained German Shepherd who was the envy of the police department. Fritz was gentle as a kitten unless given the attack command. Having seen Dan's power over Sylvester, Brandy understood why Callahan's dog was perfectly behaved.

The judge's house had been built last century, a beautiful red brick two-story with columns and an entrance hall featuring one of those glorious curved staircases seen on Hollywood sets. As the Callahans grew wealthier, the house had been expanded by the addition of a ballroom.

The house had the traditional safe behind the painting in the library, and a security system that wouldn't do a bit of good when the place was full of invited guests. It was disabled, lest the silent alarm bring the police if someone looking for an unoccupied bathroom or a moment's privacy went beyond the rooms that were opened for the evening.

Rather than give up his reputation for hospitality or insult his guests with security guards, the judge had years ago installed a safe room. Dan had been in the cellar, in Callahan's office. "It never occurred to me to look for a hidden room," he said as he studied the plans.

"Why should it?" Brandy asked. "The safe room was built from an old hiding place for runaway slaves. The house was a stop on the Underground Railroad." It was one of the things she had been taught in the Murphy School System, something the community took pride in.

"How altruistic," Dan said sourly. "I wonder how many people Callahan sheltered found their 'freedom' as his temporary vampires?"

Brandy shuddered. "What's in the office now?" she asked. "Which wall is the fake?"

"Let's see, you come down the stairs here. To the right is the old root cellar, used as a pantry. To the left is Callahan's office, desk in the middle, high ground-level windows behind it. Facing the desk, there are filing cabinets on the left. The desk has computer, telephone, and in and out trays. A small worktable in front of it holds a laser printer, a scanner, and the copier."

"No fax machine?"

"Fax/modem in the computer. The right wall is all shelves, some books, supplies, lots of file boxes. The vault has to be behind that wall."

Brandy studied the diagrams. "The lock is electronic. We might get into the office . . . but not into the safe room. We need one of those gadgets that runs through one combination after another until it hits the right one."

"I can build one," said Dan.

"*What*?!"

"I'm still an engineer. But I have to see a lock like the one Callahan has installed. I assume it's programmable by the owner?"

"Yes. He can change the combination any time."

"Can you get me one of those locks, Brandy?"

"Uh . . . I don't know," she said. The installer in St. Louis would require a police requisition to release the specs on Callahan's lock. Drive to St. Louis and pretend to be a wealthy couple building a safe room? There wasn't time. Ask the installer to come down and install one on her house? She didn't have a room secure enough to warrant such a device.

But she remembered who did. "I could lose my job and we could both go to jail," she warned. "The only other such lock I know of in Murphy is on the hospital pharmacy."

"*Mission Impossible*," said Dan. "I need the brand and model number, so I'll have some idea of what I'm looking for."

"What will the brand and model number tell you?"

"You'd be amazed at how much information on how many different things is available either in the library or on the Internet."

"Okay. Then what?"

"After I build the device, I have to test and calibrate it."

"By breaking into the hospital pharmacy?!"

"It's amazing what official-looking I.D. you can make with a laser printer and a laminator. I'll be from the manufacturer, there to perform routine maintenance."

"Dan—" she protested.

"The sun sets early in January. After sunset, I can influence anyone I encounter to accept me without suspicion . . . and not remember what I look like."

"Are you going in disguise?"

"Maybe just a little. Wouldn't want a fake mustache falling off in the middle of the caper. But some gray in my hair wouldn't be a bad idea, to give me more authority."

"You're enjoying this, aren't you?" asked Brandy.

"Aren't you?" was all he replied.

Brandy had to admit she was. The hardest part was waiting while Dan went off to the hospital a few evenings later. He dressed in a white shirt and tie, neat slacks, and a warm waist-length jacket. He carried the device he had built in his own well-worn briefcase, and looked like a typical computer repairman. Waiting and jittering, Brandy knew how Dan felt when she went into danger. He wouldn't even let her drive him to the hospital. "Suppose someone sees you, or sees me with you. Come on, Detective, you know it's safer if I work alone."

He was home within forty-five minutes, high on success. "Nobody was suspicious," he said. "I only talked to the pharmacist and her assistant, and I left them with the suggestion that they not mention my visit to anyone."

"But did your gadget work?"

"Perfectly. I reset the combination several times, and it opened all of them."

"You did remember to set it back to the original?"

"Of course." He gave her the smile that was no longer rare. "We've got it, Brandy. All we have to do is sneak out of the ballroom when the judge is occupied, go down to the cellar, and find and copy that manuscript!"

Brandy took the afternoon of the ball off. When Church asked her why she was supporting Judge Callahan, she explained, "I have to support Dan. It's important that he not make political enemies until his tenure is confirmed."

"And of course you don't enjoy getting to wear a pretty dress and go to the ball," her friend teased.

"Hey—if Callahan wins the primary he'll have to resign from the bench to run for governor. He won't be able to help his drug-pushing cronies, and we may finally be able to hold some of them and get them to implicate him!"

"Well, haven't you turned devious!" Church laughed.

"I wish you and Coreen were coming tonight," Brandy said sincerely. She'd give anything to have Church running backup. But it was far, far too late for an explanation that would have to begin, "Church, you know the man I'm planning to marry? Well, it seems he's a vampire, and it was Judge Callahan who made him that way."

Oh, no. But soon, she hoped, her fiance would trust her partner with his secret . . . especially as they would need all the help they could get to prevent Callahan from harvesting Dan before escaping to his new life.

That was the one thing that terrified Brandy about tonight's work: if they were caught, wouldn't Callahan kill Dan then and there?

The only thing to do was not get caught.

Before her hair appointment, Brandy went with Church to lunch at Judy's, where they encountered Dr. Troy Sanford. The man had kept the neat appearance she had seen at his hearing, and had begun volunteer work with an anti-drug youth group. It was obviously good for him: Doc looked younger and healthier than he had since his grandson had first gotten into trouble.

He was full of plans. "I've got to stay sober for a year," he said, "to prove myself—but then I'm gonna run for coroner again. You'll support me, won't you?"

"Sure thing, Doc," said Church. "You're one of the best medical examiners I've ever worked with."

Brandy doubted Sanford could get re-elected. However, it would be cruel to discourage him when he was in the process of recovery. He sat straight as he had in the court room, and his eyes were clear and bright.

And, wonder of wonders, he said not a word about Judge L. J. Callahan.

I wonder if he was a secret drinker for years before we knew about it, Brandy thought as she noticed Sanford's eyes. It wasn't merely that they were no longer bloodshot. The grayish edges around the irises were gone, as were the bags beneath, features of Doc's face for all the years Brandy had known him. It was like looking at a different person. Still, she couldn't help wondering how he would react if he knew the secret she and Dan shared.

Brandy had to keep herself from snapping at the hairdresser, who wanted to do her hair in complex curls that would flop in her eyes with any exertion. "No," Brandy insisted, "I want a nice, smooth French twist, an elegant look." What she really wanted was a hairstyle that wouldn't get in her way, no matter what she had to do.

She nearly had a fight with Dan, as she did not want him to go into a sensitive situation without feeding first. "No, for three reasons," he told her. "First, I can't feed until after sunset, you are wearing a low-cut gown, and it takes a couple of hours for the marks to disappear completely. What message would Callahan think we were sending if you arrived with my marks on your throat?"

Not giving her time to protest, he continued, "Second, my influence is at its strongest *before* I feed. While I'm at my weakest at the full moon, I'm not really *weak*; I'm just like anyone else. I'm far more likely to need to prevent someone from noticing what we're doing than to have to fight someone, or break down a door."

"What's the third reason?"

"You're supposed to be under my control. Any other full moon night he'd expect me to plan a spectacular end to a romantic evening, not spoil it by feeding before the party." His best rakish smile. "He'd be right."

Brandy had chosen her silver-gray satin cocktail dress because it draped comfortably, didn't bind, and wouldn't wrinkle. Dan zipped it up for her, stood back, and said, "You look gorgeous."

So did he. Because he didn't have the bulky musculature currently in style, he looked elegant in a tux, like James Bond, Cary Grant, or Fred Astaire. That could be a problem, she realized: he would attract every female eye at the ball!

The Callahan home was decorated beautifully, and staffed tonight with caterers who made everything run smoothly. Dan tendered their invitation, they gave up their coats, and then moved under the magnificent staircase, past the doors to kitchen and pantries, out to the anteroom and the reception line that led into the ballroom.

Brandy gasped in amazement. Standing next to Judge Callahan was Donna Tremaine, his campaign treasurer, and next to her her husband Al. Then came the campaign manager, Vince Hamrick, and his wife. But there was one more person in the receiving line, the last person

Brandy would ever have expected to see there: Dr. Troy Sanford!

They were still back far enough for Brandy to whisper to Dan, "Do you see—?"

"I see him," Dan replied. "What's he doing here—and in Callahan's good graces?"

"What's Callahan doing in *his* good graces?"

Then they were too close to discuss it. Judge Callahan was in good ol' boy mode, engulfing Brandy's hand in both of his. "How beautiful you look tonight, Brandy. And Dan," releasing his right hand to shake Dan's, "I don't see enough of you, Son. Glad you could come. Do you know Donna and Al Tremaine?" The judge introduced them down the line, ending with, "And of course you know Doc Sanford. I'll bet you're surprised to see him here, aren't you?"

"We certainly are," Brandy said firmly. "Doc, what's happened to change your mind?"

"I guess when I quit drinkin', my mind cleared up," said Sanford. "Sanfords and Callahans were always good friends up to my generation. 'Sides, I figger it's wrong to blame the judge here for what his daddy mighta done."

Stunned, Brandy and Dan continued out into the ballroom, where they took the opportunity of a turn about the floor to speak in relative privacy. "Influence!" Brandy hissed into Dan's ear. "It has to be!"

"But Doc's immune to influence," he responded. "At least to mine. Could that be because he was already under Callahan's influence?"

"Why would Callahan let him go on speaking against him for all those years?" Brandy wondered. Then it struck her. "Dan—try to get a really good look at Doc. Two weeks ago he was a wreck. Suddenly he's healthy and fit." She remembered Doc squinting against the sun in the courtroom.

"You think Callahan's turned him into a vampire? It's all I can think of to account for it," Dan agreed. "You don't suppose Doc actually got something on the judge?"

"Maybe. Or maybe breaking into the judge's chambers was just the last straw. Doc is dangerous to us, now."

"I know," Dan agreed. "Right now, though, we'd better look as if we're having a good time. Come on—there's Dr. Randall. Have you ever met him?" Dr. Randall was the university president.

Had Dan and Brandy been inclined to become social butterflies, approaching Dr. Randall and his wife would have been the perfect move.

In the next forty minutes they were introduced to several members of the board of regents, two state legislators, the CEO of the largest company in Murphy, and numerous prominent citizens.

It was too cold for the doors to the garden to be open, but rooms at both ends of the ballroom were available, one a bar, one a buffet, one a smoking room, one just a place to sit and talk. Once they escaped from more introductions, Dan and Brandy looked for Doc Sanford. Making the rounds of the rooms required more polite conversations. Finally Dan looked at his watch. "Doc probably left while we were stuck here," he said. "If we're right, he won't have much control over the Craving yet. He's probably gone to feed."

When he mentioned it, Dan's own Craving increased. Brandy wanted desperately to satisfy it. "Let's get that manuscript, and then get out of here," she said.

They made their way around the edge of the ballroom, and emerged under the great staircase. Brandy could sense Dan using his influence to keep the woman checking coats occupied with a couple who were leaving. When all three had their backs to them, Dan and Brandy slipped quietly into the parlor opposite. A door led through the breakfast room into a hallway lined with doors. One was the door to the cellar.

There was only a token lock; a credit card quickly slid the bolt back, and they were through and down the stairs with no one the wiser. At the bottom they turned left into the office, laid out just as Dan had said. The computer was humming, its monitor turned off, just as Dan left his in his university office. The copy machine stood on the worktable. Brandy was wearing gloves that matched her gown; she turned the copier on to warm up, and took a peek inside to make sure it was loaded with paper.

Dan didn't need gloves to avoid leaving fingerprints. "Look," he said softly. Amidst the clutter on the shelves, there was an empty space the size of a filing box, revealing the combination lock to the safe room.

Brandy's instinct said, *Wrong!*—but as long as they had come this far—

Brandy had made sure there was no separate alarm from this lock to the police department. The safety device inside, in case someone cut the power, was a cellular telephone. Unless Judge Callahan lay in wait for them inside the safe room, no alarm would sound.

Swallowing with difficulty, Brandy said, "Go ahead."

Dan pulled the lockbreaking device from his inside jacket pocket. A trill of beeps sounded . . . and the lights on the lock blinked in rapid succession. There was a click, and a panel of shelves slid inward.

The safe room was dimly lit, and the door opened only about eighteen inches. At first Brandy could see nothing. Dan stepped through, and she followed.

The light was dim because it came from candles, dozens of them, in all shapes and sizes. Fewer than a quarter of the candles were lit, though, so it took a few moments for Brandy's eyes to adjust. She became aware of shapes, not the smooth surfaces and sharp angles of the modern outer office, but ancient warped wood, blobby wax, and round but ragged ends of scrolls—the very stereotype of an alchemist's den.

When Brandy took a step forward she realized Dan had stopped, his night vision giving him immediately the scene that Brandy was only slowly taking in. In the middle of the room loomed something that seemed to change shape as the candle flames flickered in the draft from the open door. She could not make it out at first, some kind of bench or . . . altar . . . and upon it a . . . figure —

Someone lay on the altar, a composition in black and white. A man in a tuxedo. It was Dr. Troy Sanford, lying on his back with his hands crossed on his chest. There was an utterly peaceful smile on his face. He was absolutely serene, indescribably old . . . and undeniably dead.

SEVENTEEN

Secrets
of the Numen

DAN INSTINCTIVELY TRIED TO TURN Brandy away from the gruesome sight. She pushed past him. "I've seen a hell of a lot more corpses than you have. Let me examine him."

There was no use searching for vital signs, but she performed the routine anyway to get her mind functioning again. By the time she was finished, she was able to turn from the desiccated corpse and say, "Harvested."

"Are you sure?" Dan asked hoarsely.

She stared at him in disbelief, but then remembered, "You never saw Dr. Land's body. I did. I'll never forget."

Dan nodded. Attuned, she felt the sickness within him, so strong it obliterated even his Craving.

Sanford had died peacefully, but all the life, all the vigor he had shown only an hour ago was gone. He looked terribly old, but not the way he had on his drunken binge. Then he had been bloated, sloppy. Now his body looked like a mummy's, the skin tight over shrunken flesh beneath. Even his hair seemed whiter and thinner than an hour ago.

"It's a trap," Dan said flatly. "Callahan knew every step we took. The manuscript isn't here."

"Oh, but it is." Just like in the movies, the voice came from behind them. Judge Callahan stood in the doorway, holding a scroll. "Read it if you can," he added, handing the brittle object to Brandy.

She accepted it but set it aside, waiting for Callahan's next move and desperately wishing for her gun.

"A gun would do you no good, my dear," said Callahan.

"It would if I blew your head off," she told him, trying to convince herself that he had seen her aborted reach toward what wasn't there rather than that he had read her mind. If a Numen could read minds—

"I do have limited telepathic ability," he once again answered her thought. "I've been following you, Brandy, through your link with Dan here."

Dan lunged at that, fangs extended, eyes glowing red.

Callahan merely waved his hand. Dan stumbled back, fangs retracting, his face a portrait of disbelief.

"No, my wayward young vampire, you shall not feed until I give you permission!" Callahan told him. "*If* I decide to give you permission."

Brandy forced herself to silence—but she could not control her churning thoughts. With his best political smile the judge said, "Yes, that's right: if he does not feed before sunrise, he will die in the light of the sun."

Dan sat, dazed, on the edge of the altar which bore Doc Sanford's body. Again Brandy refused to respond to Callahan. To contain her thoughts, she clenched her hands until her nails dug into her palms.

"You love him?" asked Callahan. "I will tell you a secret—it's in that document if you could read it. Your lover need not die at dawn, even if he hasn't fed. As long as he remains out of the sunlight, he can remain alive indefinitely, growing weaker while his Craving grows stronger. But if he is released . . . he will kill."

"Dan won't kill me!"

Callahan smiled, and put out his hand. To Brandy's horror, her hand lifted automatically, and he took it, opening her fingers to expose the bloody palm. Dan gasped, but remained frozen.

"Ah, my dear," said Callahan, "I will not allow Dan to kill *you*. I have other plans for you." He lapped the blood from her hand. All pain instantly stopped.

Callahan turned her hand over and kissed the back of it. "We have formed a connection. I must return to my guests. After they have departed, you and I will prepare for our journey. Say your farewells to your erstwhile lover. If you are very good to me, Brandy, I shall allow you to take a keepsake of your lost love."

He turned to Dan. "Hand over that electronic lockpick."

Brandy felt Dan's resistance. Callahan moved majestically to his side, touched Dan's shoulder, and Brandy's fiancé sat paralyzed while the judge removed the instrument from his pocket.

Callahan backed through the narrow doorway and closed the panel. Dan remained in trance. Brandy shook him. "Dan!" He blinked and frowned, but at last his eyes focused on hers. "Do you know where you are, who I am?"

"Brandy," he whispered.

"Thank God. Now, first order is for you to feed, get your strength back. Then we get out of here."

"Can't . . . feed," he told her. "So . . . hungry."

"Of course you are. But I'm here for you."

He panted as if the air were thin, but his fangs did not extend. "Here!" said Brandy, raising her left hand, the one Callahan had not contaminated. Dan licked the drops of blood eagerly. The tiny wounds closed.

Dan moaned. His Craving overwhelmed both of them.

Brandy was carrying an envelope purse into which they had intended to put the photocopies of the Numen manuscript. Therefore it was almost empty. Comb, lipstick, face powder—keys! She tried to cut her hand with the sharpest one.

It hurt far worse than she expected, and Dan gasped with her pain. "Don't," he said.

"I have to. You need strength to fight Callahan."

"It's no good," he said. "Trying to feed only increases the pain."

"I won't let you die!" she told him, but stopped trying to draw blood and turned instead to finding the cellular telephone that was supposed to be in the safe room. She'd call 911—and then Church, just in case a Callahan henchman was in the dispatcher's chair tonight.

Although her eyes had adjusted to the dim light, the corners of the room remained in shadow. The phone ought to be near the door. She picked up a candle and began lighting the ones around the entranceway. It didn't take long to find the empty cradle where the cellular telephone belonged.

"I should've known," she said in disgust. "Come on, Dan—let's figure a way out of here."

"He's too strong for us to fight."

"Nonsense!" said Brandy. "You could break that door down."

"Perhaps, on another night," he conceded.

"Tonight, as soon as you've fed. Ordinary teeth can draw blood, Dan. Bite me, drink my blood, and we're outa here!" She held out her hand, showing the blue veins.

He shook his head. "He consumed your blood. He has put his mark on you, Brandy. You are forbidden to me."

"That's nonsense!" she said, trying to ignore the inner voice that queried why she had thought the word "contamination" in connection with Callahan's touch.

She knew Dan was right.

How did she know Dan was right?

And for that matter, how did *Dan* know the "why" of what was happening?

"Dan!" she gasped. "It works both ways!"

"What are you talking about?"

"Callahan said we had formed a connection. He could read my mind. But you and I can also read his."

"I never could before," Dan denied. "I worked with him all summer and never even knew I'd met him before I came to the university."

"But you're not suppressing that knowledge anymore. You and I have been reading each other's minds since we met. It started before you first fed from me."

"Our perfect match," he said in something like awe. "That's what allowed me to escape his control. Callahan is trying to break it, Brandy."

"He can't. But he's connected to both of us now. Don't you see—that increases our ability to follow what he's doing!"

Dan's dark eyes unfocused, and for a moment Brandy feared that Callahan was influencing him. But no, Dan was trying to read Callahan. "He's telling the caterers to close the bar and the buffet, so people will leave. He's . . . going to disappear after tonight!"

Suddenly Dan was back with her, looking straight at Brandy as he said in astonishment, "I saw his plan! He doesn't care about the next audit. He's been transferring funds since the last one, money he's been stashing for years against this day. This afternoon, before the fund raiser, he moved his personal funds into Caribbean Enterprises, as well as all the money from the tickets to this affair."

"He'll be caught," said Brandy.

"He'll be gone. He'll be . . . dead." Dan jumped up. "The chemicals are here! Ammonium nitrate and fuel oil."

"You're a bomb expert, too?"

"Callahan is. There's a tank of fuel oil on the grounds, and of course a farm has ammonia fertilizer. He plans to blow up the house when he leaves."

Dan was right, Brandy knew—she had studied bombs at the Police Academy. ANFO, ammonium nitrate and fuel oil, was one of the commonest incendiary mixes.

"You think Callahan intends Doc Sanford's body to be identified as his?"

"One of us, anyway. He may make it appear that Doc tried to kill Callahan and got caught in his own bomb."

"He may *intend to*," Brandy corrected. "He won't get away with it. Dan, what are you doing?"

He had picked up a candelabrum to search the nooks and crannies. "If he has the chemicals down here, we might be able to blow the door open."

"Dan . . . we'd smell them in this small space. More likely they're in the storage room."

Nevertheless, she joined the search. There were no modern containers in the place. Jars of oils, spices, herbs, and incense occupied a wicker bookcase. They might start one hell of a fire, but it wouldn't burn that metal door. It *would* sear their lungs and kill Brandy—and even a vampire would die if the fire reduced his body to ashes.

Brandy left Dan to search, glad he was able to act. She picked up the manuscript they had come for. Even its alphabet was unfamiliar. It would do them no good without someone to translate it.

Carefully, she unrolled it, staring at the symbols in the flickering candlelight. She spotted something familiar: a passage on programming vampires. The section they had the translation of!

"Dan, look here," she said. "Can you read this?"

"No, of course I—" He stared. "This is what Rett had. We shouldn't be able to tell that!"

"Callahan can read it," said Brandy. "He got the ability to read this language when he harvested Dr. Land."

"Can you read any more of it?" Dan asked.

Here and there Brandy could make out a word: Numen, vampire, blood. "It won't do much good to translate three or four words per page," she said.

"I wonder—" Dan said, and turned back to the bookshelves. Then, "Yes!" as he pulled out a book, musty with age, and carefully opened it to the title page.

"My God," said Brandy, "this is an illuminated manuscript."

"You don't think such information has ever been allowed to see print, do you? But this is in an archaic form of German, Brandy. I can read German."

"You learned it while you were in Germany with Elvis," she remembered.

"Actually, I got fluent later. Never mind. We can read this."

"Not before Callahan gets back," Brandy pointed out, dismayed by the thickness of the tome.

"We can find out *something*."

Maybe enough to save their lives. She helped him prop the heavy volume on a tall stand, and bring enough candles about to read by.

Dan began leafing through, reading chapter headings. "The Alchemical Art of the Numen"; "How the Alchemist Purifies Himself"; "The Technique of Creating Vampires"; "Varieties of Vampires"—the chapter they had translated; "Controlling and Destroying Vampires"; "The Harvest"; "Dangers to the Soul of the One Who Would Become a Numen"; "That Which Weakens the Numen"—

"There!" said Brandy. "Find out what weakens a Numen!"

"The Numen is physiologically similar to the vampire," Dan read slowly, stumbling over archaic wordings, "but has no Craving. He consumes blood for pleasure or as a link to his vampires, but spiritual attributes are the Numen's sustenance. Harvesting strengthens him, but he must avoid polluting his soul through the Harvest of temporary vampires.

"A Numen weakens himself if he chooses weak-willed individuals as the long-lived vampires whom he will Harvest. No matter how intelligent the chosen one may be, if his will is weak he will endanger the Numen in two ways: first, a weak-willed individual constantly seeks protection; in him the commands to protect the secret of his state will turn to cowardice. He may become a hermit, and not gain the experience the Numen seeks from his Harvesting.

"Second, when the Numen Harvests a vampire he acquires not only the knowledge, experience, and life force of that individual, but also something of his character. It is especially important that the novice Numen, Harvesting his first vampires, not absorb cowardice and weakness of will."

"That's no help," said Brandy. "He's just Harvested Doc Sanford, probably the most stubborn old cuss in Callahan County. Skip over. What does it say about how to destroy a Numen—or at least how to control one?"

"Maybe a Numen *can't* be destroyed."

"If he's physiologically a vampire he can," said Brandy. "I wish I had my gun!"

"Here's something," said Dan. He was growing accustomed to the dialect now. "Grave danger to the Numen is to lose control of a long-lived vampire. Should a vampire of intelligence and strength of will become aware of the Numen, and realize that his life is not his own, he will certainly seek to become a Numen himself."

" . . . what?" whispered Brandy.

"Fight fire with fire," said Dan, searching rapidly over the next couple of pages. "There has to be another way! I want my freedom—but not by enslaving others!" He fell silent, reading to himself.

"What does it say?" Brandy demanded.

"The single greatest danger to the Numen is one of his own vampires . . . Harvesting . . . the Numen."

"That's what you'll have to do, Dan."

"Brandy! How can you say such a thing?"

"Judge Callahan is about to kill us, then disappear, to re-emerge somewhere in the Third World where he can become a dictator with powers of life and death!"

"We don't know—"

"We *do* know he intends to kill you. Will you let him?"

"Not if I can help it. But I won't become like him!"

"Does it say in there that you *have* to use vampires to gain political power?"

"No . . . but it does say the Numen has to Harvest vampires."

"Well," said Brandy, "what choice do we have? Callahan plans to kill you and take me with him. I don't want to be one of his vampires, Dan. What are our choices?"

When Dan didn't answer, Brandy said, "We could set fire to this place." She picked up a stool and smashed it against the metal door, choosing a jaggedly pointed length of wood. "I know where your heart is. Shall I make certain you can't recover from smoke inhalation?"

"Brandy!" he gasped. "How can you even suggest—?"

"I *won't* be L. J. Callahan's puppet!" she insisted. "If you don't Harvest him, he'll Harvest you. Without you, I can't prevent him from turning me into a vampire—unless I'm dead before he gets here."

"No," Dan protested.

"Give me other options."

Dan was silent.

"Do you want a suicide pact?" Brandy asked.

"That won't keep Callahan from moving elsewhere and creating more vampires."

"Then what do we do?" Brandy asked, still holding up her wooden stake.

"Fight him," Dan said grimly. "We fight him on his own terms . . . and God have mercy on our souls."

～

They continued reading the German manuscript, searching for clues to both stopping Callahan without Dan's having to become a monster like him—and accomplishing that very thing. "Turn his weakness against him," Dan read, despair in his voice. "I don't know Callahan's weakness."

"Of course you do," she replied. "It's the same weakness all tyrants have: power madness."

"How do we turn it against him?"

Brandy sighed. "It's called a sting. We've got the bait: you and me. What we don't have is the trap."

The electronic lock emitted a series of beeps. Brandy shoved the book back onto the shelf, then turned to stand beside Dan as the door opened. Callahan was back.

"You're looking pale, Dan," he said. "It's almost midnight. You have not succeeded in feeding."

"Does that make you feel powerful," Brandy sneered, "making someone suffer? Are you in the drug trade because you enjoy making addicts crawl to you, watching them destroy their lives and families?"

Callahan replied calmly, as if they were holding a normal conversation.

"As a matter of fact, I avoid such weak people. I run drugs because that is where the money is. Two centuries ago I ran slaves, and when I saw that trade coming to an end I moved into tobacco. Nicotine is more addictive than cocaine. I see at least another fifty years of world-wide tobacco trade, perhaps even a century, but it is time for me to leave the United States now. It's becoming too difficult to change identities here. Of course," he added as he approached Dan, "once I Harvest you, I will have all your computer knowledge to help me."

"No," said Brandy, stepping between them.

"It is necessary," said Callahan. "I could leave Dan trapped here, to suffer the agonies of deprivation until someone releases him and dies for his efforts, but I'm afraid I need his knowledge and skill for my new life."

"No," Brandy insisted. "I won't let you."

"*We* won't let you," said Dan, standing beside her.

"You would defy me?" asked Callahan.

"You seem surprised," said Dan.

"You have more strength of will than I expected—but that will only make your Harvesting more valuable."

Callahan put a hand on Dan's throat.

Brandy chopped down on Callahan's wrist with the shard of wood she still held. The force of the blow would have broken a normal man's wrist, but Callahan's hand was only knocked away from her lover, who had the presence of mind to aim a punch at the Numen's jaw.

The blow glanced off, of course, as Brandy felt the pain in Dan's hand. And he couldn't heal until he had fed.

In fury, she turned the point of the wooden stake toward Callahan— then, knowing that fighting in anger gave the advantage to her opponent, she deliberately zoned, took careful aim, and with all her weight behind her weapon, launched herself toward the monster's heart.

He was wearing a vest!

The garment designed to stop bullets easily deflected a piece of wood. Callahan smiled and wrestled it out of her hand. "Did you think I would not expect that?"

"Would it have killed you?" Brandy demanded.

"No," replied the Numen—but Brandy knew he was lying. A heart was a heart, human, vampire, or Numen. "It *could* put an instant end to your friend here." Callahan held the stake against Dan's chest. He did not flinch. "Ah—brave, are we?"

"I'd rather die cleanly than contribute life to you!"

"Very good!" Callahan said. "An interesting Harvest—I haven't had a real challenge in centuries." He gestured toward the body on the altar. "I should have turned old Sanford into a vampire years ago. He'd have made a worthy opponent with time to mature—as you have matured, Dan. Only half a century of experience, and you defy me. Everett Land lived for more than three hundred years, and if he had not discovered that manuscript he might never have guessed."

"So vampires can . . . mature," mused Brandy, watching for any sign that Callahan was distracted. "They discover what the Numen has done to them and resist his influence."

"Those intuitive leaps make you an excellent detective, and will make you very useful to me as a vampire, Brandy."

"I won't let you turn me."

"You have no choice," Callahan told her. "The long hours of winter darkness are a good time to create vampires. Even here beneath the ground, sunrise affects the process. But you and I will be ready to leave before dawn."

"I'm not going anywhere with you," said Brandy.

"Where I am going, a successful man must have a beautiful, obedient wife." Callahan smiled. "You thought your silly threats about harassment turned my attentions from you, but it was just simpler to let Dan control you. You will be my wife for twenty or thirty years, and then I will turn you loose to ripen."

"I'm the wrong choice," said Brandy. "You can't change my personality— you have to work *with* it. I'll never be *anybody's* obedient wife."

"Oh, very good!" said Callahan. "It would almost be worth Harvesting you immediately, to gain that intuitive gift! However," he added, "you are wasting the hours of darkness." He jabbed toward Dan with the stake, and this time Brandy's fiance flinched. Callahan smiled, and pulled a pair of handcuffs from his pocket. "I really can't have you interfering when I must concentrate," he said, and cuffed Dan to a pipe running over their heads.

Normally, Dan could have broken the cuffs. But Callahan knew his weaknesses. "There," the judge said. "Now you may feed—if you can!"

The Craving that suddenly overpowered Dan made Brandy reel. His fangs extended and his eyes burned scarlet in the candlelight. She lunged toward him, wanting, needing, to assuage that hunger.

"Oh, no," said Callahan, stopping her with an arm about her throat. He sidestepped the heel she automatically attempted to bring down on his instep. "You are mine, Brandy, not his."

"Let me go!"

"When you are ready to obey me."

His forearm against her throat cut off her air as he dragged her to the altar where Doc Sanford's body lay. Brandy kicked, and dug her nails into the back of Callahan's hand, but could not make him let go. The edges of her vision went dim, and she lost consciousness.

Brandy came to gulping air. She was lying on the altar, Callahan standing over her, shoving the hand she had scratched into her mouth as she gasped for breath. She tried to spit out the metallic taste of his blood.

Callahan smiled. "You are sealed to me in blood, Brandy. You cannot resist my will."

"That's what you think!" she spat, trying to sit up. She couldn't move!

To reinforce her helplessness, Callahan straightened, not touching her. "Go on," he said. "If you have the strength, go to your lover. Feed him. I won't stop you with any physical restraint."

Hypnosis, Brandy told herself. There was no real hold on her. She *could* get up, go to Dan, give him the strength he needed . . . but her limbs would not obey her will.

Dan moaned, his Craving a devouring force, triggering a similar need in Brandy.

What?

"Yes," said Callahan. "Feel the Craving, sweet Brandy. You want blood. You need the power of the vampire. Leave your weakness behind. Feed."

"No," she managed to gasp out. It wasn't her own Craving; it was Dan's, channelled through their bond. "Dan!" she cried, "I Crave to give you my blood, to renew *your* strength! Don't let Callahan use it against us."

She felt Dan somehow suppress his own need and send supporting strength to her. "I love you, Brandy," he whispered hoarsely. "Please, come to me. Together we can stand against anything."

"I'm coming!" she said, commanding her body to obey—but nothing happened. "Dan—help me! Break Callahan's influence with yours. Please!" she begged.

Callahan stood back, smiling that damned politician's smile, demonstrating his strength by doing nothing.

"Brandy," Dan called to her on a wave of overwhelming desire. "Come to me. Nothing can break our perfect match. No power is stronger than the power of love."

Callahan burst into laughter. "You poor, romantic fool! There's no such thing as a perfect match. I made that up and put it into your head when you resisted bringing Brandy into your power . . . and mine."

"No match?" Worse than the hoarse disillusionment in Dan's voice was his wave of palpable agony. Callahan laughed again.

"No match," said the Judge. "Oh, you were in love all right. You could not bring yourself to use her, even when I made you attack Brandy's best friend."

"I didn't kill Carrie!" Dan asserted.

"Of course not. You don't have the nerve to kill anyone. *I* killed her. But you would have been indicted for the crime if that had proved the best way to manipulate you. You showed me a better way. If loving Brandy stopped you from touching her, then the way to get you to bond her to you was some transcendent form of love, such as she could never know with mortal man. How could you deny her that?"

Chills ran through Brandy as she lay helpless on the altar. It couldn't be—she had *felt* the perfect bond between them, had known love beyond anything possible with a mortal. Mere mortals never read each other's minds —

"That is simply a function of vampirism," Callahan answered her thought. "It aids their ability to please a sexual partner, of course—I'm sure Dan is quite a competent lover, but after all, you had no basis for comparison. You were a virgin."

Brandy clamped her teeth over the demand to know how Callahan knew such a thing, but he read the thought. "I know all about you, through Dan. He had no idea what he transmitted to me. What you had with Dan is nothing to what you will have with me, Brandy."

"I don't love you. I *won't* love you."

"You will, when I turn you. Then, bound by your own Craving, you will weaken your former lover even more by assuaging it with his blood, and rejoice as I Harvest him so that we may depart for our new life."

"No," she protested, but it was mere stubbornness. She had no strength, no will left, nothing but disillusion, despair, and the determination to fight to the bitter end.

Callahan set an incense burner to the right of Brandy's head. A bitterly spicy fragrance wafted through the room. The judge began to recite in what might be Latin—prayers, incantations, Brandy couldn't tell.

As a good police officer, she ought to be planning how to get out of here. Nothing held her, no handcuffs, no straps, yet she could not move off that wooden altar.

Callahan chanted something in another language as he drew symbols on Brandy's forehead, cheeks, and hands with scented oil. Then he dotted oil on her eyelids and ears, and pushed aside the decolletage of her gown to draw something over her heart.

Dan struggled. The handcuffs cut into his wrists. Brandy smelled his blood, familiar, not the vile smell of Callahan's. It aroused her Craving—

Her Craving?

Callahan put an oily finger to Brandy's lips. She could not even hold her mouth shut against him! And try as she might, she could not bite the invading hand. He painted a symbol on her tongue, then dipped the finger into the oil again and traced paths on the roof of her mouth.

She knew what those paths meant, had explored them in Dan's mouth to both their pleasure.

This was not biologically possible. Incantations and scented oil could not make fangs grow!

The finger was withdrawn. Brandy was left with the cloying, unpleasant taste and texture of the oil.

Callahan loomed over her, chanting louder. When he stopped, Brandy felt Dan's attention focus at the sudden silence.

The Numen opened his mouth. Fangs unfolded and his eyes dilated just as they did in a vampire. "Now," he said, "I make you mine."

There was intense physical pleasure as fangs slid into her throat and the flow began, ecstatic, transcendent. Her mind fought with her body, not wanting that pleasure from Callahan, only from Dan. She could not move—

Try as she might, Brandy could not scream.

But Dan could.

EIGHTEEN

Harvest

*D*AN HOWLED LIKE A WOUNDED ANIMAL, the perfect expression of Brandy's own frustration and despair. She wanted to join him, scream, cry, and most of all push away the creature draining her blood!

The indescribable pleasure went on and on—the way she always wanted it to do with Dan, and he would never allow. Brandy's will drained with her blood, and she sank first into nameless bliss, then unconsciousness.

~

She woke to overpowering hunger.

It was dark. She sat up, her body leaden, weak. Sliding off the altar, she kicked aside the husk of something empty of the life she needed.

There were two potential sources of satisfaction nearby. A pleasant ache suffused her palate. Instinctively, she opened her mouth, wide as for the widest yawn. Fangs unfolded, fitting perfectly against the backs of her upper teeth, extending over the lower ones, pinching her lower lip if she tried to close her mouth completely.

A single candle flame illuminated the room, yet she could see every corner. The soft thud of heartbeats and the susurrus of breathing pounded in her ears, while a world of scents competed for attention.

But the overpowering sensation was a need for life. She turned toward the stronger of the two sources she could now see, hear, smell—and longed to taste!

He came to her, yet denied her his brighter, stronger flame. She was directed toward the weaker source—a more appealing one once she was near. The scents of fear, anger, and despair stung sharply in her nostrils.

Noise. Two syllables of sound, meaningless.

The bloodscent was familiar, welcoming—hers!

At first he drew back, making sounds she ignored. The scent of life was hot in the back of her throat. Her mouth sought blood running bright and fresh below soft skin. She tasted salty-sweet moisture, savored it on her tongue as his throat moved.

Only the fresh, hot blood and the tang of fear had meaning. She plunged her fangs into his throat and sweetness flowed into her mouth.

No pleasure she had ever known matched the blissful flow of strength and warmth. She gloried in his resistance, wresting strength against his will, feeding on his despair.

It wasn't pain. Her prey's agony was mental, emotional, feeding her mind as his blood fed her body.

The texture changed. The challenge, the denial, disappeared. He gave—gentle welcome flowed on a wave of selfless love.

Brandy.

The empty syllables found meaning. They formed her name.

. . . Dan?

Concern and relief flowed to her with his love. *Take, Sweetheart. Go on—take all I have. Live!*

She drew upon that blessed gift, knowing only the sweetness he gave her so willingly.

Yes, Brandy—drain it all. Take me with you, my love. One day you will remember.

Remember? Remember what?

With a sharp shock, Brandy knew who she was, where she was, what was happening—

Callahan pulled her back. Dan cried out as her fangs ripped his throat.

The Numen held Brandy away from her prey and took a perfunctory swipe at the wound with his tongue. Dan's bleeding stopped.

Brandy doubled over in pain at the interruption of her feeding—but it lasted only a moment. Her fangs retracted. The sensory overload dimmed to a tolerable level, although she could still see clearly. She had actually been more than satisfied, she realized. Dan had wanted her to —

"Yes," said Callahan, "he wanted you to kill him, so I could not Harvest him."

"Dan, no!" Brandy exclaimed.

Callahan stared at her. "You still care for him."

"I love him," she replied. "That's why you want to kill him. But Dan— you would have let me kill you?"

"What's the use? It would be an empty victory. If he needs computer skills, he can find another specialist, turn him into a vampire, and Harvest him."

"That's right," said Callahan. "I didn't get as much from Doc Sanford as I would have after a century or two, but I gained some useful knowledge of forensic medicine."

"You don't have to kill Dan," said Brandy.

"Ah, but I do," was all the Numen said . . . and neither of them had to ask why.

Dan and Brandy knew, without having to articulate it, that Callahan had expected Brandy to be completely in his power. Instead . . . she loved Dan and loathed Callahan more than ever.

Their perfect match might be a myth, but the love between them was not.

Their only chance now was for Dan to Harvest the Numen, and become one himself. Did he know enough? He had read part of the book silently—Brandy didn't know if he had found the technique, or only the idea.

Even if he had the knowledge, did he have the strength?

Brandy doubted Dan would be standing if not handcuffed to the pipe. Her newly-acquired night vision showed that he was pale, even his lips drained, with only unhealthy spots of red in his cheeks. The wounds Brandy had put in his throat remained raw and sore. His eyes were sunk into bruised circles. Despite his extended fangs, he did not look dangerous. He looked helpless.

Oh, Dan, I'm so sorry!

Callahan laughed. "You gave him an easy death, Brandy. They fight the Harvest—how can they help it? I take not just their life force, but their memories, their very souls! But Dan has no strength left to resist. It will be brief."

"Please, don't kill him," said Brandy. "I'll come with you if you don't kill him!"

She couldn't tell whether she hid the thought that she would find a way to come back to Dan, for what Callahan answered was, "Oh, you will come with me, Brandy, and willingly. Once I contain Dan's essence, you will love me as you do him."

"No!" she exclaimed, remembering that she had a vampire's strength. With that and her police training—

Callahan dealt a blow to her left cheek that made her ears ring and knocked her, dazed, toward the door.

Yesterday such a blow would have meant a concussion, a broken cheekbone—maybe even a broken neck. Tonight the pain was as great—perhaps even greater, as she could not escape into unconsciousness—but her recovery was swift.

The misery subsided with the throb of her heartbeat, and she picked herself up from beside the box in front of the door. Box? Her bruised brain took a moment to process the information that books and scrolls, and some of the bottles and jars, had been packed while she was unconscious.

But she had no time to worry about what Callahan planned to take with him.

Callahan and Dan locked eyes. Brandy felt Dan's resistance as the Numen began the Harvest.

It was as if Dan's own ideas were suddenly shut off to him, and although he knew they were there he couldn't follow his own train of thought—the way memories get blocked when you can't remember someone's name, or the answer to an exam question on a topic you know perfectly well.

But instead of a specific piece of information, the mental block walled Dan off from all he knew, from his own name to how to create a web page! Brandy felt him panic as his mind was shut off. That must be what amnesia victims feel.

But if she could feel—

Dan—connect through me!

His mind reached gratefully to hers, to her knowledge of him, of the two of them together—

Callahan loomed between them.

Dan hung from the pipe, Callahan stood before him, and Brandy sat on the floor near the door. No one moved, yet battle raged for control of Dan's mind.

Callahan expanded his influence to hold Brandy off—but when his concentration wavered, Dan was able to integrate himself.

The Numen turned to Brandy, this time physically. He dragged her to her feet and fixed her eyes with his.

Callahan was centuries old and very powerful. Brandy's will gave before his strength—until Dan was there again, in her mind, supporting her ....

Together, he told her. *Use my Craving.*

Although she herself was replete, Dan's bottomless hunger gnawed voraciously. Brandy felt the ache in the roof of her mouth.

She let herself be directed through Dan's knowledge. Her fangs extended—she fastened them in Callahan's throat!

Callahan roared and tried to break the thread connecting him to Brandy, but a brighter, stronger one connected her to Dan. He fed her the power to maintain her hold. In a flash she knew what she had to do—what Dan had tried to get her to do to him.

It hadn't been a suicidal death wish: he had tried to make her Harvest him, hoping that with their combined strength and knowledge she could escape.

Even the aborted attempt had given her the strength to defy the Numen. He couldn't control her because of what she had received from Dan—not his blood, but his essence.

But . . . she didn't want Callahan's craving for power, his ruthless disregard for life.

Search for good in him, Dan instructed, guiding her toward a bright spark of determination, loyalty, righteous stubbornness—

Doc Sanford.

The essence of the old man, so recently Harvested, was as yet unintegrated. Brandy grasped gratefully at the clean strength, somehow sharing with Dan those characteristics, that knowledge—

Medical knowledge!

In massive sensory overload, years of training and experience flooded over and through them . . . and with it despair, frustration, anger, the passions of a lifetime of battling Callahan without ever knowing what he really was.

Death.

One by one, everyone he loved died.

Heartache, grief, despair.

Callahan threw negatives at them, trying to disengage, but together they held on, accepting the aches of old age, the frustration at the lack of accomplishment, and the obsessive belief that somehow Lee Joseph Callahan was at the heart of all his troubles.

Which he was.

Callahan set out to destroy the family who had been his friends. The Sanfords were resistant to his influence; he had to manipulate them in other ways. The carrot had worked for generations; only when he made the mistake of marrying Cindy Lou Sanford did he have to use the stick.

She had married him for love . . . but he had lost that love because he could not return it. When she saw through the facade, he disgraced her before the community, ruined her reputation lest she ruin his.

It was a masterly plan, given that he could not influence her. He could, however, choose a man exotic enough to attract a country girl's attention, and cause *him* to fall in love with *her*. Love begot love, and with carefully calculated emotional abuse he practically forced Cindy Lou into Carl Mishinski's arms. Then the exposure, the "justifiable homicide," the raising of the bastard child as his own, increasing Callahan's moral standing in the community while undermining Cindy Lou's.

Stubborn Cindy Lou. She had actually tried to patch up their marriage, spent endless hours in church, tried to drag him to counseling. In the end he made her a vampire—and when she understood her husband's true evil she fought him in the only way left: she killed herself. Damn stubborn Sanfords!

Eventually he had succeeded in discrediting the whole family. Dr. Troy Sanford was the last and most difficult, but finally he had driven him to drink. Even that hadn't been a permanent solution. So, he had turned the man and Harvested him.

As part of Callahan's getaway plan.

Brandy's police instincts screamed *Ambush!* Barely in time she and Dan braced for Callahan's attack.

He had set them up, allowing them to see what they already knew or had guessed. It was a lure for them to open willingly to the knowledge—

—whereupon Callahan fastened on Dan's mind and began to pull from it his computer knowledge!

Dan resisted.

Brandy interposed, and felt Callahan grab for her deductive techniques. She felt that creepy sense of not knowing something—and not knowing what she had forgotten!

Dan was there, reassuring, shunting her knowledge around the barriers the Numen created. Together they fought Callahan to a draw.

It was not enough. The only way to stop him was to Harvest him. That meant separating his mind from his memory, then from his personality—

Suddenly Brandy understood the peaceful smiles Dr. Land and Doc Sanford had worn in final repose. Not the relaxed smile created by a vampire's influence.

The smile of total imbecility.

Brandy! Don't drop out! I can't fight him alone, Dan pleaded.

She could not allow Callahan to drain Dan's mind.

But—how could she do that to anyone, even someone like Lee Joseph Callahan?

Upon her hesitation, the Numen attacked again. As her mind faded, Dan was there, telling her, *We have to do it together. Neither of us can escape alone.*

In the metaphysical void they inhabited, she leaned on Dan's strength and faced the truth. It was still stalemate unless she was willing to kill.

Kill the bastard!

The voice was so real, she almost turned to see if Doc Sanford's body had risen to join them. Then she realized it was his personality within Dan or herself—a reminder of the casual cruelty Lee Joseph Callahan was capable of. Simple murder was the least of it. Psychological torture, economic destruction, false evidence to convict innocent people of heinous crimes.

This man headed the drug operations in the county named for him. To accumulate fast money for his getaway he introduced the horrors of crack to a community that had hitherto been free of it.

Callahan had traded in slavery, torture, pain, disease, death. He had killed Carrie! He could not be allowed to continue.

He could not be allowed to live.

Brandy and Dan joined forces. Callahan countered with attempts to pull their knowledge, thoughts, memories away from them—but working together they continued the inexorable process of draining his mind . . . his soul.

The deeper they went, the more horrors they exposed. Brandy shuddered at the cold calculation of Callahan's investments, monetary and personal, in the drug trade, the arms trade, and . . . the slave trade. He made money from prostitution in the U.S., Mexico, and South America. He had a stake in an international business that kidnapped young men and women in the Caribbean, drugging and debasing them and shipping them to the Mideast or the Orient as playthings of the wealthy until they died of disease or despair. Each new wave of filth pouring over them only added to their determination to stop Callahan.

The Numen's courage never faltered. He fought by striking, by shielding, by pouring forth the worst that was in him in hopes that they would resist receiving it.

Sick at heart, they accepted.

It was a hard fight for the valuable knowledge: languages, history, economics, psychology, archaeology, poetry, drama, science. The knowledge of the atom bomb was there—not only since diagrams appeared in every encyclopedia and on the Internet, but since the Manhattan Project itself. More recent knowledge of genetic experimentation told of secret projects to cure diseases . . . or create deadly new ones.

Slowly, inexorably, they found personal memories, the vampires Callahan had created, the ones he had Harvested . . . and the ones he had simply murdered, like Chase and Jenny Anderson. He had made thousands of such creatures, hundreds at a time in the superstitious days in which he had originated, fewer and more selectively in more enlightened times and places.

As they uncovered those memories, Callahan began to struggle again. *You have gotten this far two against one,* he told them, *but only one of you can become the Numen. When you fight one another for that crown, that is when I shall win!*

Divide and conquer? answered Brandy. *It won't work.*

We're in this together, Dan agreed, and Brandy felt his warm presence shoring her up for the final battle.

Callahan fought for his life—for his very soul. They drew his memories, his emotions, his personality—

They were no longer witnessing. They were actually absorbing the creature's cold-blooded ruthlessness!

Together! Dan insisted. *Stay with me, Brandy.*

The final barrier was cold beyond belief—no feeling except the passion for power and an obscene glee at the weakness of others. A barrier that should shatter like ice held like tensile steel. They could not penetrate.

Not penetrate—absorb.

Greater fear than Brandy had ever known weakened her limbs. She leaned into Dan's embrace for warmth, for courage to accept that into herself.

Together!

Paralyzing cold cauterized feeling. There was no warmth, no love, no pity, no joy, no hope.

Brandy's heart shattered.

Her being was suffused with terrible, unspeakable knowledge. She could not absorb it, could not contain it —

Yet it poured through her, beyond her, into Dan, and back in a feedback loop—something howling and gibbering, screaming in agony and utter, obscene ecstasy!

It seemed to go on forever—and then all was darkness and silence.

Brandy opened her eyes.

She was back in her body, reality in the form of the cold floor against her legs and Dan's warm body against her back. The broken handcuffs dangling from Dan's wrists told her that when she had sensed his touch it had not been merely in the dream landscape of their mental battle.

"Dan?" she murmured, squeezing his hand as she turned to see his face.

There was only a single candle burning, but she saw clearly. Dan, too, was just waking from their altered state. His dark eyes looked at her in wonder.

She stared at him in the same way. The wound on his throat was gone. His eyes were clear, his skin tone normal. He had always looked like a man in the peak of health; now he practically glowed with well-being.

"We survived," he said.

Still holding his hand, Brandy carefully got up. She wouldn't have had to be careful; she felt wonderful.

Physically.

Mentally, emotionally, she was numb.

What had been Lee Joseph Callahan lay beside the corpse of Dr. Troy Sanford at the foot of the wooden altar. His eyes were closed, and his face wore that serene smile Brandy now knew the source of. She felt nothing as she took in the fact that it appeared to be the corpse of someone very, very old. The flesh had melted away from between skin and bone, leaving a mummylike appearance.

"We have to get out of here," Brandy said. "The moon will set soon."

Dan went to the lockplate and punched in the combination. The metal door slid open.

He twisted off the handcuff dangling from his left wrist. Although she didn't really need to test her strength, Brandy broke the one off his right wrist. She put the broken pieces into her purse. "Don't leave anything we don't want the fire marshall to find."

She put her purse into the box by the door, and picked up the scroll they had originally come to get. She could read it now, as easily as printed English. There was another scroll with the same information in Greek, one in Hebrew, and a book in Chinese. Callahan's own journal was there, several volumes of cramped writing, in Latin. She knew what it was, knew it was valuable, knew now that the translations of the Numen document varied, and that the German translation Dan had read from — was it only hours ago? — was incomplete and flawed. It was left on the shelf, to be incinerated with the rest.

In the outer office, Dan picked up Callahan's notebook computer, its hard drive containing what the Numen had intended to take with him. The hard drive on the desktop had not only been wiped clean and reformatted, but had a complete erasure program run on it.

They had no need to talk to one another as they completed Callahan's plans. The incendiary materials were in the storage room. They moved them into the safe room, so that the fire would reduce everything there to ashes. If enough of the two corpses remained for identification by dental records, it wouldn't be hard to believe that Doc Sanford had gone completely 'round the bend and blown up the judge and himself.

There was no one else in the house. Callahan had wanted no witnesses.

Their car was outside. They put the box in the trunk, then went back inside to set the fire.

By the time Dan and Brandy were outside again, the house was exploding. They drove away by the light of the setting moon, lights off, turning in the opposite direction from the one from which the County Fire and Rescue Squad would come.

Gray dawn was breaking as they pulled into the yard of Brandy's house. Once inside, Dan went straight into his office and plugged the telephone cord into the back of Callahan's laptop.

"What are you doing?" Brandy asked.

"All that money," he replied. "I'm moving it to where only you and I can get at it, before Callahan's financial contacts find out he's dead."

"Good work. Dan, they'll probably routinely question every guest at the fundraiser. You and I left at about 10:00 P.M., and came back here."

Dan nodded. "Ten o'clock. Brandy, what's the number for the account in the Bank of Zurich?"

"1879403," she responded automatically. Then, "You didn't know that?"

"I do now," he replied, still playing with the computer. He smiled wickedly. "Not only will we never have to work again," he said as he studied the screen, "but if we wanted to we could purchase a small country!"

Brandy came to look at the screen. The figure in the Swiss account was one of those "beyond comprehension" amounts that simply didn't seem real. "Travel," said Brandy. "Servants. Political power."

"Ye-es," Dan agreed. "We'll groom you, Brandy—first the legislature, then the governorship."

"Why me?" Brandy asked. "Why not you?"

"You know Kentuckians, Sweetheart. They don't trust anyone with a Ph.D. But the cop on the corner is perfect. We'll go after Callahan's supporters, the people we met at the fundraiser last night. With judicious influence—"

"—we'll have them right in the palm of our hand!"

Brandy and Dan looked triumphantly at one another, their minds meeting and racing with plans for power.

"Mmmmrrrowrrr?"

Sylvester jumped up on Dan's desk, green eyes wary. He looked from Brandy to Dan and back, poised for flight—the way he acted around strangers.

"What's the matter, Silly Cat?" Brandy asked him

Sylvester stared blankly, as if wondering how she knew one of his nicknames. When Brandy reached toward him, he backed off. "What's the matter with you?" she asked in annoyance.

Sylvester jumped off the table and headed for the door.

"Stop," Dan said.

Well, that was certainly useless with a cat . . . but before Brandy could say it, Sylvester stopped, turned, and came back, beginning to purr and wind about both their ankles.

"Influence," Brandy recognized.

"It's even stronger than before," said Dan. "Try it," he added as he picked up Sylvester and handed him to Brandy.

She took the cat, willing him to purr and snuggle, which he did exactly as her thoughts directed. It was weird, it was delightful, it was—

It was completely unnatural!

Golden light crept through the curtains as the sun rose.

Deliberately, Brandy stopped trying to influence Sylvester. Her cat continued to purr in her arms for a moment, but soon, in typical cat fashion, squirmed to be free. As she let him go, Dan opened the curtains and stared out at the bright sunlight. "It doesn't hurt my eyes."

"Nor mine," said Brandy. "But . . . it hurts my conscience."

He turned to her, and she saw that he understood her meaning. "We almost succumbed to power madness."

"How do we know we won't when the sun sets tonight? What are we, Dan? Have we become Numena?"

"I don't know," he said. Then, "I didn't feed on blood last night. My strength returned from . . . what we did to Callahan."

"We Harvested him."

"We killed him," Dan said bluntly.

"In self-defense," Brandy protested. "There was no choice, Dan."

"I know. He intended to kill me, use you—and no jail could have held him if by some miracle we could have restrained him. It wasn't just ourselves we were defending."

Brandy studied the man she loved, trying to sort out her feelings from his, and both of theirs from what they had absorbed from Callahan. "Will we ever be free of him?" she asked.

"We are," Dan insisted. "Any other vampires he created are also free. He didn't think we could work together—for all his knowledge, he thought what we did was impossible. That means—"

"We don't know *what* is possible," Brandy finished the thought. "We don't know what we're capable of doing."

"For good or evil," Dan agreed. He turned to the computer to exit from the banking program. Then he turned the machine off and took Brandy into his arms, a hug of support as he said, "We'll have to watch one another, Brandy. Be each other's conscience."

She nodded, clinging desperately to his familiar physical presence as she wondered how much either of them had been changed by the infusion of Lee Joseph Callahan. How far could she trust Dan now? How far could she trust herself? What had seemed so clear last night was frighteningly complicated in the light of day.

Doc Sanford's words came suddenly back to her: "Blood will tell." He had meant character, upbringing, the values handed down from one generation to the next.

Was her blood strong enough to resist the contamination of Callahan's? Was Dan's? Only time would tell. Only in time would their own blood tell its story, for better or for worse.

THE END

About the Author

JEAN LORRAH is Professor of English at Murray State University in Kentucky. She currently lives with her dog, Kadi Farris ambrov Keon. Dr. Lorrah has published fifteen science fiction and fantasy novels, and two children's books previous to BLOOD WILL TELL, but this is her first contemporary novel.

NESSIE AND THE LIVING STONE by Lois Wickstrom and Jean Lorrah won the Independent E-book award as best children's book of 2000. In March, 2002, BLOOD WILL TELL was awarded the Lord Ruthven Assembly award as the best vampire novel of 2001.

You can always find the latest news about her work at:

www.jeanlorrah.com